THE RAPUNZEL ACT

ABI SILVER

Published in 2021
by Lightning Books Ltd
Imprint of Eye Books Ltd
29A Barrow Street
Much Wenlock
Shropshire
TF13 6EN

www.lightning-books.com

ISBN: 9781785632266

Copyright © Abi Silver 2021

Cover by Nell Wood
Typeset in Minion Pro

The moral right of the author has been asserted. All rights reserved. No part of
this publication may be reproduced, stored in a retrieval system, or transmitted,
in any form or by any means without the prior written permission of the
publisher, nor be otherwise circulated in any form of binding or cover other
than that in which it is published and without a similar condition being imposed
on the subsequent purchaser.

British Library Cataloguing in Publication Data
A catalogue record for this book is available from the British Library.

Printed by CPI Group (UK) Ltd, Croydon CR0 4YY

For Noah, Nathan and Aron

'Meanwhile, sitting in the sky boxes, running the concessions, selling hot dogs to the crowd, are the lawyers, politicians, racism-mongers, white and black, opportunists of every variety. The rest of us watch while the wrestlers sweat and thunder. We watch, thanks to the biggest casher-in of all, the huge, dish-linked, lap-topped, ad-powered, fame-fueled, deadline-tooled media luring us so far into the myths, the dream, the beastliness, the spectacle, that we hardly notice the fact that we've become the spectacle ourselves'

Henry Allen, 'One Nation Under OJ's Spell,'
Washington Post: **26 September 1994**

'The liberated man is not one who is freed in his ideal reality, his inner truth or his transparency; he is the man who changes spaces, who circulates, who changes sex, clothes and habits according to fashion, rather than morality, and who change opinions not as his conscience dictates but in response to opinion polls'

Jean Baudrillard, *America: 1986 and 2010*

PROLOGUE: THE CHASE

THE SUN WAS SINKING behind Shoreditch Park's granite monolith, casting its long shadow across the grass. The air was alive with the sounds of an English summer evening; voices raised in animated conversation, the pounding footsteps of transient joggers, the grinding rattle of skateboards on asphalt, the music blaring out from the nearby pub and the low hum of rush-hour traffic, two streets removed. It had been another glorious June day, the kind that makes tourists, boating on the Serpentine or picnicking on Parliament Hill, declare London the best city in the world and locals proclaim their love for their hometown. The thermometer hovered around 22 degrees Celsius.

Debbie was reaching the penultimate part of her training session. Sometimes, at this stage, she moved the team to penalties, sometimes to set piece corners. Today, she had asked them to push on for the 'golden goal'. It was their first practice since they had taken a break, a month earlier, and they were noticeably tired.

She was occupied trying to watch all the players, making a mental note of what to say to each one in her debrief at the end. Debbie always tried to make her feedback meaningful – *try moving forward earlier, mark more closely, own the ball* – and to give plenty of praise. After all, the team was young and inexperienced, and she would always remember the coaches who had taken time with her.

She checked her watch: 6.48pm. Later on in the season, she would push the girls harder, finish the session with them breathless and cursing. But not today. So, at first, she didn't see the couple striding towards her across the fields. Older man, tight-fitting raincoat, a bulge just below his left armpit; younger woman, hair cut short, razored at the sides, trailing behind. A warning shout and she noticed them crossing the pitch, their expressions grave, their attention fixed on her. The man waited to speak till he was very close. 'We're looking for Debbie Mallard?' he said, clearing his throat.

Debbie's first thought was that they might be scouts from Arsenal Ladies or West Ham. She had lost two of her best players to their under-21 squad last year. Two talented girls, full of energy and determination; a striker and a left back. She had gritted her teeth and wished them the best of. She wouldn't stand in the way of progression for any of the girls, whatever the personal impact. Hackney South was never going to win the FA Cup. But the man's solemn air was more akin to a politician about to deliver bad news, albeit with the usual spin. God knows there had been enough of them on TV over the past few months.

'Yes.' She flung the word out over their heads, simultaneously waving the girls to play on.

The man hesitated and opened the button on his jacket and it gaped tantalisingly. His face was flushed from the walk.

'I'm Chief Inspector Dawson. This is PC Thomas.'

Debbie had not identified the couple as police and it bothered her, too, that neither officer was in uniform. That suggested some need for secrecy, and now the intruders' identities were revealed, Debbie chastised herself for not considering the possibility earlier. At least they weren't journalists.

'If this is about my moped, your men found it,' she said, shaking her head, 'returned it in one piece, and with petrol in the tank.'

'It's not about a moped.' Chief Inspector Dawson dug the toe of his shoe into the grass and ran the tip of his index finger around the inside of his frayed collar.

'Girls, move to penalty shoot-out. Siobhan, you go in goal first and rotate as usual,' Debbie shouted, circling her hands around each other. She took a few steps back, standing just outside the makeshift touch line, and the police officers followed suit. She waited until the first penalty was taken: a barnstorming shot straight into the top left corner. No one, not even Jordan Pickford, would have reached that one. She clapped her hands loudly and the hollow sound bounced off the high wall dividing them from the kids' adventure playground. 'Fantastic penalty, Judy,' she called, the grin spreading across her face. 'Let's see more like that one.'

She turned her head towards the police officers.

'What is it you want?' she said. 'I'm Debbie Mallard.'

Dawson forced a lukewarm smile and his eyebrows raised. PC Thomas coughed into her hand. Debbie folded her arms.

'It's...this is a very public place to talk,' Dawson stammered. And, right on cue, the arm of a giant, eavesdropping crane, overhanging the neighbouring building site, swung towards them with a creak and a groan.

'We don't have an office or a changing room,' Debbie said. 'I'm working on it. The girls shower at home. Welcome to the world of fourth division amateur women's football. Can it wait ten minutes? We're nearly done.'

She glanced from Dawson to PC Thomas and, this time, both remained silent. 'What is it? You're making me nervous,' she said.

'Send the girls home early,' Dawson said, touching Debbie's arm fleetingly. 'They look all done in, anyway.'

'I'll decide when they're "done in". Maybe you should tell me what's going on?' Debbie drew herself up to her full height and flicked at her long blond ponytail. A sudden gust of wind and Dawson's coat blew apart, revealing his holster and gun. 'It's your wife,' he said, fastening his buttons and motioning to PC Thomas to move in closer.

'My wife? You mean Rosie, my ex-wife?'

'Miss Rosie Harper. I'm so sorry to have to bring you such bad news. Miss Harper is dead.'

Debbie's body crumpled sideways without warning and she might have fallen, if Dawson had not grabbed her and guided her, gently, to her knees on the grass.

'I don't understand. I just saw her,' she said. 'How can she be dead? Was she in an accident?'

'You saw Rosie today?'

'A few hours ago. She was fine. Are you sure it's Rosie?'

'I'm afraid so. She was murdered.'

'No!' Debbie wailed.

One of the girls came rushing forward, but PC Thomas waved her and the others away, flashing her badge defensively.

'This afternoon. They found her about an hour ago,' Dawson said.

Debbie lifted her head and stared at Dawson. Then she hugged her chest and began to sway and choking sounds came from the back of her throat.

'Air, I need some air,' she said, struggling to her feet, her arms flailing to capture the elusive air.

She staggered across the pitch and over to the toilet block, tucked underneath the trees. Dawson tried to follow her inside.

'I just need a minute... to wash my face,' Debbie said, spinning around suddenly and filling the doorway with her imposing frame.

Dawson and PC Thomas exchanged glances. Dawson sniffed the air and withdrew with a nod. *How are the mighty fallen* he mused, as he sank down onto the remains of a nearby bench. *Who would've thought it? Danny Mallard, hero of Euro '96, now 'Debbie'.* That much he had read, *but coaching an amateur team of schoolgirls? Danny Mallard!* He allowed the name to circle around his head again. The goal volleyed in from 30 metres in the quarter final, the header, finding the most acute of angles in the semis, the run from the far end of the pitch and the sublime nutmeg of the keeper to score the winner in the final.

And then he'd married Rosie Harper, the BBC's pin-up girl, and they became the "golden couple", gracing the covers of many a glossy magazine. *The perfect match*: that had been the cheesy headline, when they exchanged their marriage vows at a remote Scottish castle, later that year.

Dawson's eyes narrowed, as he tried to superimpose the face of the middle-aged Debbie over the youthful image of Danny he recalled. Not just his consummate skill but his presence

Danny striking the ball with a confidence belying his years, Danny taunting his opponents as he shifted his weight from one foot to the other and Danny's fist-pumping, supercilious strut of celebration, when the ball hit the back of the net, sealing the match and the title.

The girls had packed their stuff up now, one of them scowling at Dawson, before collecting the bag of balls and hauling them into her car.

'Make a note of everything she said,' Dawson snapped, checking his watch. 'That she saw her a few hours ago, that she particularly said "ex-wife".'

PC Thomas nodded. Dawson kicked at the grass again. His stomach grumbled and he tapped at it smartly, as if he was switching off an alarm. He checked his phone. His wife was away this week, which meant no evening meal unless he made it himself. His teenage daughters were unlikely to have considered his needs, even if they were home. No messages.

Who'd have thought it? He said the words aloud this time and PC Thomas frowned.

He worried, suddenly, how she would sell this back at the station. Would she try to imitate him, his mouth hanging open, his face flushing crimson as he tried to pretend this was a normal situation, well as 'normal' as any other day in his turbulent life. She'd laugh, that was certain, as would all the others. But he thought he'd handled it pretty well, given the circumstances. The diversity training the Met had insisted they all undergo had clearly done the trick; a whole series of previously standard, universally understood, derogatory words, now consigned to the dustbin of unacceptability. Of course, it was harder to wash away the underlying sentiments, but you had to start somewhere.

Another two minutes passed and the field was empty, apart from a water bottle slung in the nearest goal, rocking backwards and forwards in the wind. PC Thomas had completed her notes and returned her book to her pocket. Dawson gestured towards the toilet block.

'You want me to go in?' she asked.

'It is the ladies.'

'On my own?'

'I don't think you're in any danger,' Dawson said, 'but I'll be right behind.'

PC Thomas rose, straightened her shirt, prodded tentatively at the toilet door, then went inside. She returned almost immediately.

'She's gone,' she said.

'What?'

'She's gone. Must have slipped out when we were talking.'

'You're joking.'

Dawson slammed the flat of his hand against the door and rushed at the chilly bathroom. The two cubicles and outer washroom were glaringly empty. He rubbed his smarting palm across his forehead. He'd been too slow, too trusting. He should have sent Thomas in with her.

He ran out of the building and around the back and followed the winding path left to the main road. Debbie Mallard was nowhere to be seen. As his stomach erupted for a second time, Dawson shouted at no one in particular, then, seeing PC Thomas approach, he closed his mouth tight, to ensure that none of those now forbidden words he was struggling to restrain came spewing out. Instead, he stamped his foot twice, the second time more forcefully than the first, before heading off towards his car at speed, with PC Thomas close behind.

***

Inspector Dawson knocked at the door of Debbie Mallard's rented ground-floor flat, half a mile away. No reply. He surveyed the narrow street, keen to spot any sign of movement, but all was surprisingly still. A black cat padded its way along the pavement, darting into a garden fifty metres away. Dawson's gaze returned to PC Thomas, who was leaning against the police car with her arms crossed, squinting into the sun.

He bent down and squinted through the letterbox. A shooting pain across his back caused him to grunt, then stiffen and shift his position. He was just straightening up, when he thought he saw something inside the property, less an object and more a change in the light, as if someone or something had cast an abrupt shadow across the hallway.

Dawson rolled back his shoulders, as his absent wife had suggested (he had refused, despite entreaties from her to see either a doctor or a physiotherapist – 'just a twinge' he had told her), pressed a thumb into the aching spot and clenched his teeth, in order to stifle the inevitable moaning the action would normally produce. Now he leaned in close and placed his ear against the door. He heard nothing for a few seconds and then the tiniest click, like the sound of the arms of a mechanical clock shifting forward or a key turning in a lock. All his senses were at attention. He held his breath and dropped to his knees on the cold, concrete step, to peer through the letterbox once more. This time nothing.

He stared over his shoulder again at PC Thomas. Her eyebrows were raised expectantly in his direction. He shifted his weight back and rocked on his heels, preparing to rise in the manner which, he gauged, would cause least discomfort, when he heard the sound of an engine starting up nearby. Craning his neck to the right, he spotted a moped pulling out of the street next to them.

Dawson stumbled to his feet, cursing as another wave of pain radiated across his lower back and, as he reached the gate, he could see the tall, helmeted figure astride the bike, her long blond tresses poking out and flapping behind her.

For a second, both he and PC Thomas were rooted to the spot, then he battered his way through the low metal gate towards his car.

'That was her…wasn't it?'

'Yes guv. Shall we?'

'Follow her?' He stamped his foot in annoyance. 'Damn right we follow her. Did you get the number plate?'

'Yes. Should I…?'

'Get in. I'll drive. You call it in.'

***

Debbie kept her head down at first. Zigzagging around vehicles, even though the traffic was slow-moving, required all her concentration. The bus lanes were the worst. You would cut inside the stationary traffic only to be trailed by a black cab, or worse, a bus barrelling disinterestedly along. True, the cyclists often came up fast, silent apart from a low whistle, as the wind caught their spokes, but they were unlikely to cause as much damage as an 11-tonne vehicle.

Debbie had heard the two police officers arrive outside her flat, the sound of the engine dying, the car door being closed with suspicious care, the surreptitious opening of her garden gate, before she caught the older one, Dawson, invading her hallway with his piercing, pillar-box stare. Well, if they really wanted her, they were going to have to catch her and she was confident that she had the upper hand, in the evening crush.

As she swerved to avoid a broken bottle in the gutter, she tried to calm herself. She needed to be focused and keep her cool. This was no different from situations she had encountered numerous times on the pitch, throughout her career. Granted, most often she'd rehearsed her moves over and over, those set pieces she'd used to devastating effect to win the league three times, but she was also adept at taking her chances, trusting her instinct to take over and guide her on.

A police siren sounded close behind her. Debbie darted into a one-way street and halted in a dank and smelly doorway, her heart thumping inside her chest. She steadied herself with one hand pressed against the brickwork, and then a sudden lurch from her stomach and she vomited into the gutter. The whine of the siren, gradually increasing in volume then joined by a second and a third, their timing slightly out of synch and creating a weird, discordant rhythmic lament, accompanied her retching.

Debbie wiped her mouth, put her moped in gear and shot out of the alleyway onto Hackney Road. She had no game plan, no strategy. Rosie was dead. All was lost.

PART ONE

LONDON, JUNE 2019 (SAME DAY)

1

CONSTANCE LAMB WAS SITTING under the arbour in Haggerston Park, reading through some notes. A newly planted honeysuckle wound its way around the overhead wooden slats, filling the air with its sweet, intoxicating scent. Constance sometimes came here on a summer's afternoon, to sit in the shade on the low benches, as a break from work or, like today, to wind down in the evening, before heading home. An oasis, a little patch of green, amid the grey and brown of the nearby, abundant housing estates.

The park was divided in two by a red brick wall, partly covered by creepers and trailing plants. The lower southern part of the park, with its entrance on Hackney Road and quick access to the shops and stalls of Columbia Road, housed the tennis courts and football pitch and the downtrodden children's farm. This end of the park was less structured, essentially a large playing field, bisected by a walking path, although there were some log piles along its northernmost end – an attempt to encourage wildlife to linger – and the construction of the gazebo where she was now seated, a couple of years back, had added an air of gentility.

In the distance Constance could see the City – the Gherkin, the Shard and the Cheese Grater all rising high into the sky, their occupants seemingly far removed from the people living around the park where she sat.

Two girls played catch with their older brother; their ball had now rolled twice against Constance's feet and the youngest girl had collected it from her, wearing the widest grin. Constance wanted to tell the girl that she had played here too, at around the same age, but the words didn't come. Instead, she read her notes over and looked, periodically, out across the grass.

And then, a troop of brownies appeared through the gap in the wall, led by a woman whose body jerked from side to side, walking slowly along the path in Constance's direction, their bright yellow t-shirts giving them away, even from this distance. Constance should have been a brownie, she thought, but it hadn't featured in her childhood agenda. Schoolwork and self-preservation had taken precedence over formal leisure activities.

The girl at the front held a rounders bat, her friend was tossing the ball from hand to hand, and they were chattering as they snaked along. Constance closed her tablet. There was no point pretending she was working. She might as well take a real break, enjoy the entertainment and resume work later, at home. She extracted a cereal bar from her pocket and snapped it in half.

The tranquil idyll was suddenly shattered. A flock of starlings sped by overhead, calling loudly, the ground beneath Constance's feet began to vibrate and she heard an engine roaring. She squinted out towards the lower part of the park. A moped appeared, driven at considerable speed along the narrow path. Its helmeted driver, head down, blond hair streaming out behind her, was heading straight for the brownie caravan.

'Watch out!' Constance called, but the young ears of the girls had picked up the danger signs even before she had and they were already scattering, with high-pitched squeals of fear and excitement filling the air.

Constance marched forwards. She was unsure what her plan was, but it involved either ensuring the children were removed from the path of the rampaging moped or somehow diverting it instead. She waved her arms above her head. Then she shouted again, but the moped sped on, swerving around the shrieking girls and quickly disappearing behind her.

'Are you all right?' Constance asked two of the girls, who had strayed over in her direction.

They shrugged, as if it was an everyday occurrence to be almost bowled over by a speeding moped, and retreated to join the rounders game. Their leader was already creating makeshift bases, with a collection of discarded jumpers.

Constance ate the second half of her cereal bar. She tucked the wrapper back in her pocket, dropped her tablet into her bag and began to walk home. As she crossed Whiston Road, a police motorcycle exited the park, just behind her, then three police cars came screeching around the corner and streaked past in close succession. Maybe if she caught the local news, she would find out what was causing all the excitement.

2

Judith Burton was at home, selecting which balsamic vinegar to drizzle on her avocado salad, when her phone rang. She had built up quite a collection and, if time permitted, she preferred to match each one to her meal, the way some people might choose a suitable wine. The one with a hint of pomegranate would do the trick, but the pesky bottle was continuing to elude her.

She had spent the morning in a leisurely fashion. First she had walked to the ponds on Hampstead Heath for a quick dip. She had swum regularly for years, but had avoided the well-known, natural swimming location till now, through a mixture of prudery (they said some of the women swam naked) and concern about how clean the water was. Then she had read an article about the number of bacteria sharing the average, man-made, public pool, and its growing resistance to chlorine, and she'd decided to have a go.

She'd found the experience particularly liberating, even wearing a costume. True, the water was chilly, despite the warm weather, but it was also immensely calming to glide along, with the sun overhead and the birds swooping low, dipping the tips of their wings in the water and chirping from the branches overhead. There had been one scary moment when a duck had landed close by, but, after the initial splash and element of surprise, Judith found she liked watching it dabbling and grooming itself, before it paddled away to the reeds at the side of the pond.

She had dried off on the grass, read a book for half an hour and then sauntered home, feeling restored and invigorated, picking up the ripe avocado and fresh leafy ingredients on her way. That was the nice thing about living alone and not having any regular employment. When the fair weather arrived, you could take full advantage.

'Not interrupting your lunch, am I?' Constance asked from the other end of the phone line, checking her watch.

'One second and I'll put you on speaker,' Judith plucked a piece of grass from her hair and continued her perusal of her kitchen cupboard.

'I can call back if you're busy?'

'No, go on. I am listening, just wrestling with a difficult legal problem, that's all. But I always have time for you.' Judith stood on tiptoes and peered into the depths of her food cupboard.

'OK. I'm advising Debbie Mallard,' Constance said.

'No, doesn't ring any immediate bells. Should it?'

'Do you have your laptop there?'

'That question tells me that it's a while since we worked together.' Judith tried a different approach to seek out the most suitable vinegar, shifting a couple of bottles around on the shelf, taking care that they didn't clang together and give her away.

'You did mention a "legal problem". It wasn't too much of a leap to think that you might be online.'

'I lied.'

'What?'

'About the legal problem. I am actually searching for suitable condiments to accompany my lunch.' Judith gave up on her tentative rummaging and banged the cupboard door shut.

'The footballer, was married to Rosie Harper,' Constance said crisply.

'Rosie Harper. The darling of the Beeb! Why didn't you say so? I saw the footage of the chase on the News last night. Someone filmed it on their phone, I think. Enormously exciting and so very incriminating. Fleeing the scene on a moped. Not the best look for a grieving spouse.'

'I'll call another time, when you're not eating.'

'No, now is perfect...really. Has she been arrested?'

'They questioned her and let her go home. She's arranged to see me this afternoon. I...I thought you might be interested in coming along. I know it's short notice. I did try your mobile three times.'

Judith wrestled with her handbag before locating her mobile at the very bottom, tangled up in her swimming goggles. She swiped the screen with a tea towel and Constance's missed calls miraculously appeared.

'What time?' she asked.

'I said 2.30. If it's not...'

'I'll be there,' Judith said.

'Are you sure? I could always fill you in, afterwards.'

'Oh no. I wouldn't miss this for the world.'

Judith exited the kitchen with her plate in her hand and without the vinegar, instead searching 'Rosie Harper murder' on her PC, blowing up the text to 175% and scrolling down to see what was on offer. Top of the list was a video extract from yesterday morning's BBC Breakfast: 'Rosie's last broadcast'. There was a well-groomed, fresh-faced Rosie Harper, seated next to co-presenter Jason Fenwick, interviewing a young girl who was campaigning for CBD oil to be available for her epileptic brother. Rosie was a real beauty, Judith thought, without and within. She appeared solid, serious and totally credible, but with her heart firmly fixed on her sleeve. Judith watched her for some minutes. She could have easily watched for longer.

With a sniff to acknowledge the horror of someone so full of life being struck down so brutally, Judith moved on to the online newspaper sources from earlier in the day.

The *Telegraph* majored on the risk to life posed by the high-speed pursuit, at great expense, in a busy area in the rush hour. *Who would pay to clean up the damage to the park?* a local councillor asked. The *Times* focused on Rosie herself, her background and family and last programme. Judith couldn't resist a quick peak at the *Sun*, when it popped up on her screen. It put Rosie's dog centre-stage, recounting how the five-year-old collie, Belle, had alerted neighbour Lynn Harris by barking loudly. And last was the *Guardian*'s piece about the chase, which she almost ignored; she had watched it on the news, so there seemed little point reading an account of it, but then the photographs drew her in and she found her way to the last paragraph.

Ms Debbie Mallard was eventually apprehended at her mother's house in Bow. She made no comment when she left, accompanied by the Metropolitan Police. Officers had found Debbie on the touchline, in the middle of a coaching session with Hackney South ladies, a fourth-division amateur team. Debbie has been living quietly, out of the public gaze, since her transition from superstar international footballer Danny to Debbie in 2017. A police source refused to comment on whether Debbie was a suspect.

Judith sat down in her armchair and lay her plate down on the armrest. Refused to comment, she murmured. Then she rose and collected her mobile from the kitchen, placing it face up next to her, while she ate her lunch, so that she would be sure to reach it quickly if Constance called again.

3

ANDY CHAMBERS WAS ENJOYING a soak in the bath, having dispatched his daughter, Mia, to the park with a friend and her au pair, when his phone rang. He wasn't often at home during the week, but a trial had run two days short and, for once, he had decided to gift himself a day off. He listened to the ringtone once, twice, three times before he decided to grab it – one of the occupational hazards of being a criminal lawyer was fearing the worst whenever the phone rang – sloshing soapy suds onto the floor and leaving wet patches on the landing carpet, as he hurried to his room.

'Hello?' The call ended just as he picked it up and he cursed himself for his earlier indecision. *He who hesitates*, he declared to his phone and then, as he turned to return to his water therapy, he caught sight of himself in the bedroom mirror. He straightened up, drawing his shoulders back and puffing out his chest. He didn't look bad for thirty-three years old, he thought, probably not much different from his wedding day eight years ago.

Halfway back to the bathroom he paused. All was quiet in the house. Still with his towel clutched around his nether regions, he tiptoed to the door of Mia's room and pushed it open. The room was tidy, the bedclothes neat, some clothes folded on the chair, ready for someone to return them to their rightful place, a pile of colourful picture books stacked from largest to smallest in the centre of the floor. When he saw the room like this, it was hard to believe that his life was anything other than peaceful and harmonious. The truth was that Mia, his whirlwind of a daughter, following close on the heels of her twin brothers, had almost beaten him into total submission. He had often appeared in court short on sleep or ill-prepared, because of his lively offspring. He and Clare, his wife, had hung on in there these last five years and were, finally, poised on the threshold of Mia starting full-time school in September, clinging desperately to the prospect of some modicum of normality returning to their lives.

As he smiled to himself and padded back to enjoy at least another ten minutes of unadulterated pampering in the bathroom, his phone went again. This time he grabbed it on the second ring.

'Andy Chambers,' he announced in a deep baritone, to compensate for the fact he was almost naked and dripping. Instinctively, he grabbed a jumper from the nearby chair and held it up to cover his chest.

'Andy, my name's Phil Ash,' said the caller. 'You don't know me, but I'm assistant to Graham Hendricks. You know who Graham is?'

Andy sat down heavily on the bed. Graham was CEO of Horizon, one of the largest independent broadcasting companies in the world and a personal friend of Nick Major, his head of chambers. Andy had been introduced to Graham only a few days before at a garden party, held to celebrate the retirement of one of their most senior barristers.

'Yes, of course,' he stammered. 'How can I help you?'

'Graham wants to see you about something. Are you free to come over to his office this afternoon?'

'Yes, certainly,' Andy lied. He had arranged to meet a friend for a squash game, yet another neglected hobby of his, but a meeting with Graham Hendricks could not be passed up. 'Can you tell me what it's about?' he asked, partly from curiosity and partly to assist him when he tried to extricate himself, with as little grovelling as possible, from his prior arrangement. 'Is there anything I should read in advance?'

'No. He'll tell you when you arrive. I'll send you the office location. Come at three. Oh and don't tell anyone you're coming.'

4

JUDITH STOOD OUTSIDE Constance's office later that afternoon, knocking and then pushing the door open without waiting for a response. She was dressed in navy, wide-leg trousers, teamed with a cream blouse, her outfit completed by a swirling silk scarf. It was one of her 'throwback' outfits, purchased in her previous life, the one she had retired from seven years ago, before making her comeback with Constance at her side, but if you kept clothes for long enough, she found, they invariably came back into fashion.

It wasn't that Judith was thrifty; quite the reverse. It was more that she felt a connection with one or two items worn for memorable occasions, her mawkish attachment to pieces of fabric not usually extending to the majority of people around her.

'Hello,' Constance glanced up from her work.

'I'm now up to speed with who Rosie Harper is or was,' Judith announced, as she swept into the room, 'the highs and lows of Danny Mallard, including a potted version of his biography – I've ordered the official full version from Amazon – and the already leaky walls of Hackney police station are giving away a few early morsels. I am slightly less au fait with Debbie Mallard, though, our new-born outlaw. What can you tell me about her?'

Constance saved her work but kept her laptop open. Then she shrugged and waved at the empty seat opposite.

'OK. So, 43 years old, white, London-born, only child. Played most of her career, as Danny, for Arsenal, but also played for England, moved to manage West Ham in 2010. On the personal side, as you know, she transitioned from Danny to Debbie in 2017. What else? Divorced around the same time from Rosie, lived separately in a flat not far away. Nothing fancy, so I'm not sure where all her money's gone. They have two children; Laura is 21 and Ben is 16. That's what I have so far.'

'That's a good start. And the day of the murder?'

'She'd been at the house in the afternoon. Claims she left at 2. Rosie was found around 5. She'll be here in five minutes. Like I said, if you stay, you can ask her anything else yourself... Oh... and just in case you think it's important, I saw her.'

'You saw her?'

'I didn't know it was her, Debbie, at the time. I was in my local park, when this moped came speeding through and then all these police cars followed. It's not a problem, is it, that I saw her?'

'I don't see why. She must have passed numerous people on her way to, what was it, her mother's house? Unless you interacted with her?'

'There wasn't really any time for that.'

'How did she seem?'

'What do you mean?'

'Was she angry, frightened?'

'She just drove pretty fast down the path. It was quite a sight.'

'A sight?'

'She's quite tall, and she was travelling pretty fast.'

'OK. It's right you told me, but I can't see any problem. It's not often we have first-hand verification of our client's evidence. I have to say, given everything I have read, I am quite intrigued by the prospect of meeting her.'

***

Debbie arrived at her appointed time. She sat herself down, removed an enormous wide-brimmed hat and smoothed her hair; a few stray strands had stuck to her pink lipstick and she prised them off. She grunted at Judith, pointed at the jug of water and Constance poured her a glass. She downed it in one.

'Is it hot outside?' Constance asked, gesturing at the hat.

'Not really, but I had a new fan club surrounding my flat and I thought it might help. I think one or two of them followed me here. Is there anything I can do to get rid of them?'

'Reporters?' Judith asked.

Debbie nodded. 'With cameras and mikes. Knocking on my door and up and down the street. One of them was there all night, slept in his car underneath my window.'

Constance made a mental note of Debbie's appearance; turquoise three-quarter-length trousers, set off with a pink t-shirt, face evenly coated in a neutral foundation, lashes curled and dark and tiny gold hoops in each ear. But there were purple shadows beneath each eye and grey patches above her top lip, which confirmed her story of an interrupted night's sleep.

'If you don't speak to them, they'll gradually lose interest,' Judith said.

'I hope so. Have the police said anything, about any suspects?' Debbie's hands enveloped her glass.

'Nothing yet,' Constance replied, 'but I'm keeping in close contact. I do need to ask you a few questions, if that's OK, and they're things the police might ask too.'

'Why did you run from the police?' Judith interrupted, before Debbie had a chance to respond.

Debbie's jaw tightened. 'Everyone's interested in me,' she said. 'I want to know what happened to Rosie.'

'That's understandable, but, because you ran, the police suspect you. And you admit that you were there, at Rosie's house, earlier in the day.'

'I thought it was some kind of sick joke, at first,' Debbie said. 'When I was at West Ham, the lads used to do all kinds of stupid things, to wind each other up. *Pranked you* they would say, as if that made it fine to scare the living daylights out of you. Then I saw the guy's gun and the police car parked up.'

'Where did you go?'

'At first I just knew I had to get away. Then I thought I would go to Rosie's, just in case they'd got it wrong – mistaken identity maybe. I got halfway there and then I couldn't go on. I didn't want to see Rosie dead in the house. So I went home.'

'What happened then?'

'I heard sirens coming at me from all directions. I just bolted. I had no idea where I was going. But once I hit Broadway Market, I wasn't too far from my mum's house. I don't know how I got there, really. The bike pretty much took me there on its own. I wanted to stop. I really did. But they were behind me all the way, shouting stuff.'

A tear had slowly bisected Debbie's cheek, leaving a pale streak in its wake.

'You went to your mother's house?' Judith took over again.

'Yes.'

'What did you tell her when you arrived?'

'I'm not sure.' Debbie reached for the water jug, her hands trembling so much she gave up. 'I don't remember,' she said.

'Then the police came?'

'They took me to the police station and then, later on, to see Rosie.'

'I'm sorry. It must have been very difficult for you,' Constance said, as she refilled Debbie's glass.

'It's funny. It didn't really look like Rosie. I'm not religious – never have been. But they say, don't they, that your soul leaves your body when you die. That's what it was like. She was always so full of life. It wasn't Rosie lying there on that table. That's what I told Ben and Laura too.'

'Your children?'

'Yes.'

'You were at the house in the afternoon?'

'Yes.'

'Why?'

'We had things to talk about.'

'Was anyone else home?'

'No.'

'Where did you go next?'

'Home. Then I headed to my training session. I coach a ladies' team. I was there a few minutes early, maybe around 5.45.'

'Did Rosie seem worried about anything when you were together?'

'Nothing unusual. She didn't say.'

'Did she have any enemies?'

'I don't think so, but I wasn't living there any more and we didn't really chat. It was more stuff about the kids – Ben, mostly. She tried to include me in that.'

'You were divorced?'

'Two years ago.'

'Did she have a new partner?'

'If she did, she didn't say,' Debbie said, 'but I wasn't top of her list to tell.'

'What about family?'

'Rosie? Her father died last year. Her mother, Elaine, lives in Essex. She's a witch. And she has one brother, Ellis – a total wanker.'

Debbie's voice had descended at least an octave and her face was a contorted mass of bitterness. Constance waited, a trick she had learned from Judith, and this time Judith remained silent too. Debbie unfolded her legs and then re-crossed them.

'Ellis is a waster, lives here and there. Claims he's got this successful interior-design business, but just sponges off Rosie and Elaine. He's here, already. I got the police to drop me at Laura's flat. And there he was, "Uncle Ellis", feet under the table, drinking tea and pretending to feel sorry for me. He gave me this bear hug. If the kids hadn't been there, I'd have punched his lights out.'

'And you went home last night, eventually, to your own apartment?'

'I needed some time to think straight. Not that anything makes any more sense today.'

'Who were Rosie's friends?'

'You think it was one of them?'

'We want to talk to them.'

'TV people. I was never too interested. You could start with Jason Fenwick.'

'From *Breakfast Time*?'

'Yeah. They go back a long way. If I were you, I'd start with Jason, if you can find a slot in his diary.'

***

'First impressions?' Judith was sitting back, eyes half-closed, delivering her question with her usual aplomb, after Debbie's departure.

'I expected someone more sporty-looking,' Constance said, 'but she seems genuine.'

'Hm. If you look really hard, you can see Danny the footballer, underneath.'

'I didn't mean that.'

'I wasn't being facetious.' Judith leaned forwards onto the table. 'I mean, that was quite an act!'

'You didn't believe her?'

'I haven't decided yet. But the drama, the pathos! We had the wilting rose in the sun hat and "I couldn't go on" regarding the chase and Rosie's spirit leaving her body and the vitriol directed towards her wicked in-laws.'

'She's probably still in shock.'

'Then I would have expected wooden grief, not a BAFTA-winning performance… You know, maybe you're right and I'm being unfair. It's not even twenty-four hours. But, even so, I do find her behaviour strange. No one would list "maternal" as one of my attributes, but if your spouse had been murdered and you had children, wouldn't you go to them first? Instead, what? She runs to her mother and leaves the kids to find out for themselves? And, you heard. She didn't stay with her kids last night either. She went home to her own flat. Wouldn't you have thought they would want to be together, to console each other, after such a terrible thing has happened?'

'She might have needed some time alone, even if it was just to cry, and she didn't want the kids to see her like that.'

'Perhaps. How was it left with the police?'

'If I don't hear from Dawson by tomorrow lunchtime, I'm to contact him, find out what's going on. But I thought I would also go and visit the house – Rosie's house, have a look around the area.'

'Good idea. Take some photos too and send me them.'

'Sure.'

Judith tapped her fingers on the table, squeezed a smile at Constance and then sat back in her chair again, to think some more.

5

ANDY SAT IN THE RECEPTION of Horizon's London headquarters, in Canary Wharf. He knew some people would be impressed, all that sparkling glass and shiny chrome, air conditioning and white noise. But far more, he imagined, would balk at the lack of fresh air and natural light which accompanied any journey out to this hub of finance, nestling in the dog-leg of the River Thames.

The underground had led Andy straight into a subterranean tunnel, flanked by fast food outlets from every corner of the globe, with neat signposting to Horizon's offices, negating any need for him to pop his head above ground or check out Google Maps. Their clinical and well-flagged location had immediately made him homesick for the crumbling brickwork of Monument and the sensation of rain on his face.

'Mr Hendricks will see you now,' the receptionist called out, pointing a perfectly manicured finger along the glossy corridor. 'Number six. Turn left at the end and it's on your right.'

Andy felt himself propelled along by some higher force, past an eclectic collection of artworks; a giant, green, enamel shell on a raised pedestal, a man, hand raised in welcome, made entirely from coloured string, some black and white photographs of trees, or was it the same tree, through the seasons.

'Ah, Andy. How nice to see you. Come in and sit by me. Coffee?'

Graham Hendricks was of medium height and build, with greying hair and a genial manner, but Andy knew that behind the mask of conviviality lurked a will of steel. Graham's reputation as a self-made, rock-hard man of business preceded him. He had set up his first company aged 11, achieved his first CEO position at 21, and had taken Horizon into the big league five years ago.

Andy shook Graham by the hand and accepted the cup he was offered, seating himself to Graham's left. Almost immediately, as he eased himself into the ergonomic chair, replete with moulded back and tilting mechanism, he felt a rush of blood to his head, as the view from the 20th floor assaulted his senses.

'Ha!' Graham noticed his discomfort and, grinning, he leaned over and, with one flick of the finger, dropped the blinds. 'You're not the first one to get a little vertigo up here,' he chortled, 'and I'm sure you won't be the last.'

Andy took a deep breath. Beads of sweat had burst through his skin and he dabbed at his forehead, with a conveniently placed paper napkin.

'You're probably wondering why I've called you up, out of the blue, like this?'

Andy wasn't sure if Graham expected a response, but his professionalism carried him through his temporary, adrenaline-fuelled crisis.

'I was curious, I have to admit,' he managed, taking a slurp of coffee and feeling his pulse leap even higher.

'I have a proposition for you,' Graham continued. 'You're a good-looking man, some experience of life, not too young, not too old.' Graham laughed when he saw Andy's baffled expression. 'Oh your face!' he said. 'It's definitely a business proposition, don't look so worried.'

'I'm relieved to hear that,' Andy said, his body finally starting to adjust to the altitude.

'It's confidential, though, at least for now. If I tell you, it stays with you. You don't share it even with your wife or your clerk or your closest friend. Is that clear?'

'Yes, of course.' Now Andy really was intrigued and more than a little flattered.

'Horizon is going to take a leap into programming in a new area and I'm recruiting people to front it. For reasons which will become clear in a moment, I need someone with a legal background and a reasonable knowledge of the criminal law and process.'

'Sounds like you have come to the right person, then?' Andy had now recovered sufficiently to treat Graham to his broadest smile. Graham's eyes flitted over Andy's face. Andy remembered being told Graham had a photographic memory and he sensed Graham processing and storing each and every detail of his anatomy.

'Do you have experience then, in front of the cameras?' Graham said.

'Well, I…not TV cameras, no. But, I mean, it's just an extension of what I do every day, isn't it? I'm used to being in front of an audience, a live audience in fact, and one which often answers back. TV must be easy in comparison.'

'Not easy, no. But we'll give you some opportunity to

acclimatise. It will mean taking at least three months out of your practice, though, and giving this job your full attention. Is that something you could readily contemplate?'

Andy was certainly not against a change from his daily grind, but he still wasn't sure what was on the table.

'You'll be well remunerated of course, a daily rate plus a bonus if our viewing figures are good enough.'

'You are offering me a position on one of your shows, as a presenter?' he asked.

'That's exactly it. Now, assuming you're OK with the confidentiality aspect, let me tell you a little bit more about what we're proposing. I think you'll like it…a lot.'

6

CONSTANCE WASN'T CERTAIN she would be able to distinguish Rosie's house from the other almost-identical town houses as she walked along East Road, but there was no doubt which it was. Not only was there a policeman standing on the front steps, but there were piles of flowers knee-deep on the pavement outside.

There would have been plenty of opportunities for the assassin to have been seen, she thought, all those windows overlooking the street, a busy thoroughfare linking the station, the nearby public gardens and local shops. She would need to check with Dawson if his officers had gone house to house, asked for sightings, although it never ceased to amaze Constance how unreliable eye witness evidence usually was. Either people saw nothing – Mr Moses, her senior partner, often told a story about how, when he was a boy, an entire troupe of elephants from the local circus were paraded through his town, albeit in the early hours of the morning, and no one noticed – or they totally misremembered what they had seen, substituting a familiar or desirable image for the real one.

She remembered a line from a film – or was it a book? – where a murder had taken place on a busy street like this and everyone was stumped; something about how the killer must have blended in, so he could lurk unnoticed. In the end, in that story, it had been the milkman, or someone dressed up as the milkman; she wasn't sure which.

A better ending might have been the opposite: someone so out of place, so noticeable, that connecting him with the murder was totally absurd – so no one did. In fact, maybe that was the answer to Mr Moses' elephant conundrum; people did see them trumpeting along the pedestrianised precinct, but couldn't quite believe what they saw, so they just blanked it out or thought they'd imagined it.

Over the years, Constance had learned how important photographs were to the investigative side of her work. Not only did they jog your memory, they often highlighted things you had never seen or noticed yourself. So she took out her phone and snapped some photographs, from different angles, in both directions along the street, before slowly approaching the house and crouching down among the floral tributes.

One of the pictures she had seen, from her recent perusal of all things Rosie-related, was of Rosie at an upstairs window of this house, her face pinched and gaunt. It had coincided with breaking news of Debbie's transition. She imagined Rosie mouthing something unintelligible from behind the glass to the unwelcome reporters below and tugging the curtains across. Today, when Constance looked up, the house was quiet and empty.

Lower down, Constance noticed a security camera directly above Rosie's front door, the smart brass door knocker, the wide letter box, the trough overflowing with purple blooms on the front window ledge. The messages accompanying the flowers were simple and heartfelt: 'rest in peace Rosie', 'we miss you' and 'one more angel in heaven'. Several well-wishers had printed off images of Rosie and tucked them into their bouquets.

As Constance reflected on who might have bought the blooms, the faces to match the many names, a man came hurrying down the street, mid thirties, sandy-brown hair, wearing jeans and a navy polo shirt, espadrilles, no socks. He marched straight up to the policeman.

'I'm hoping you can help,' he said, without looking at Constance, who continued her perusal of the flowers. 'I'm Ellis Harper, Rosie's brother. Is there any chance I could come inside?'

Constance was careful not to show any obvious interest in Ellis, but she was keen to take in everything she could from her stooped position. The policeman raised one hand towards Ellis' chest and spread his frame out to block the entrance.

'I'm sorry, sir, no one can come in. Not even family. Can I help you with something?'

'It's for Ben, Rosie's son. He's running out of clothes. I said I'd ask.'

'If you'd like to leave your number, I'll ask Chief Inspector Dawson to call you. He's in charge. He won't be releasing any clothes now, but maybe in a few days.'

'No, that's fine. I'll pick up some things for Ben from the shops then, and I'll come back during the week. Any idea how long you'll be here?'

'I think we're nearly done.'

Ellis stood gazing up at the house's façade before casting a glance in Constance's direction again and striding back the way he had come. Constance rose and stretched out her legs, nodded to the policeman and then hurried off after Ellis, taking care to stay a fair distance behind.

***

Ellis walked purposefully along the street, sidestepping a pile of beer cans lined up in a row, then re-tracing his steps and kicking at them, so that they ricocheted off each other and rolled into the gutter. Then he stopped, drew back into a doorway and checked the messages on his phone before continuing on his way.

Constance wasn't in the habit of undertaking gumshoe surveillance, but Ellis intrigued her – 'waster', 'bear hugger', 'gofer' – and she had the time to spare. Rosie's house wasn't going anywhere fast. She followed him all the way to Upper Street, where he entered one boutique and then another, exiting with purchases each time. Then he treated himself to an espresso and a chocolate twist, in a café, before riding the underground to Old Street and taking the short walk to Hoxton Square. Constance watched him enter a property on the west side and take the stairs to the first floor, where he disappeared from view, only to reappear briefly at a window.

Constance took more photographs; the square, the first-floor apartment, the view towards the east side, and revisited some she had taken earlier of Ellis perusing t-shirts in the shops. She wondered if Ben, the nephew, Rosie's son, would appreciate his uncle's fashion choices. But, maybe, probably, if your mother had just been murdered, you weren't too bothered about what you wore.

7

'HELLO DEBBIE, CONSTANCE. Thank you for coming in so promptly.' Inspector Dawson entered the interview room at Hackney police station, late, at 6.15pm the following day, PC Thomas in tow. Constance noticed his crumpled, short-sleeved shirt, tucked into his trousers on one side only, and his tousled hair completed the picture of a man who had wrestled with sleep. In contrast, Debbie appeared well-groomed. Her hair was drawn back into a taut ponytail with an olive-green cat hair clip, her flowery blouse softened her features and her nails were painted today, in a subtle shade of ivory. Constance thought her dressed for a Saturday magazine 'what to wear' photoshoot feature, rather than an interview with the local constabulary.

'Do you have any leads yet?' Debbie said.

Constance marvelled at Debbie's poise in the circumstances, especially after her theatricality at their last encounter. Instead, today, she seemed composed and solid.

Inspector Dawson took a seat at the table, placing a large,

brown envelope upon it, face down. PC Thomas slid in next to him.

'Certainly,' he said, 'and I can deal with things quite quickly, I believe. There's been a development. Two actually...or it might even be three.'

Debbie's eyes narrowed. 'Tell us, please,' she said, resting her elbows on the table.

'First of all, we've found the murder weapon.'

Constance held her breath.

'And what is it?' Debbie asked.

'I can show you a photo if you like.'

Both Debbie and Constance leaned forward, as Dawson's fingers probed the depths of the envelope and pulled out a pile of photographs. He selected one and thrust it in Debbie's direction.

'But that's...Rosie's,' Debbie said.

'Yes.'

'What is it Inspector, please? I can't see,' Constance asked.

Dawson nudged the photograph in Constance's direction. 'It's a trophy, made of some kind of resin, a bit damaged around one of the edges. It was found in a dustbin a few doors from the house. You're confirming that this award belongs to Rosie Harper?'

'Of course I am. It has her name on it.'

'And where was it kept, do you know?'

'I last remember it on the mantelpiece, right in the centre. Rosie had loads of trophies, but this one was always her favourite.'

'Was anyone seen dumping it?' Constance asked.

'I can't tell you that,' Dawson said.

'But you have a suspect?' Debbie stared hard at Dawson, her mouth hanging open.

Constance removed her jacket and draped it on the back of

her chair. Then she unscrewed the cap of her bottle and sipped at her water. Debbie was asking all the right questions, Constance thought.

Dawson nodded. 'That's my second piece of good news.'

PC Thomas, silent and impassive, handed him a bag, from which he extracted a sealed transparent package. Inside it there was a large, black, padded leather glove.

'Is this yours?' he asked Debbie.

'Can I pick it up?'

'Be my guest,' he said.

Debbie lifted the package, squeezed it and held it close to her face, then turned it over. After a few seconds she said, 'It could be.' She passed it to Constance.

'Is there any way of confirming that it's yours?' Dawson said.

'If I had the left hand and it matched. But it's a very ordinary glove. I have at least two pairs like this.'

'It's a make commonly bought for use on a motorbike...or moped, I understand,' Dawson said.

'A bestseller. That's why I bought it.'

'It was found at the scene, close to your wife's body.'

'You think the suspect left it behind?'

'Oh come on, Debbie, drop the act. It's fairly obvious that it's your glove and it puts you squarely in the frame.'

'Did you find the other one, of the pair?'

'No. But we've tested this one, for DNA. We'll have the results soon.'

'How soon?'

'A few days.'

'Can't you do it any quicker?' Constance chipped in.

'That's how long it takes.' Dawson stared pointedly at Constance and she looked away.

'Is that it, then?' Debbie sat back, and snatched a look at Constance too.

'I haven't got to development number three.' Dawson held out his hand and PC Thomas deposited an iPad in it. Dawson fiddled with it for a few seconds, then laid it down on the table.

'Your wife made a call to the emergency services back in 2017,' he said.

Debbie shook her head.

'You don't remember? She said you'd assaulted her.'

'What?'

'The call is very real, I can assure you. We have a recording. Would you like to hear it?'

'This is crazy. This is why you called me in?'

'I'll take that as a yes then.' Dawson pressed *play* on the iPad and a woman's voice blared out.

'What service do you require caller?'

A quiet and shaky woman's voice responded 'Police'.

'Where are you?'

'At home,' followed by a loud sob and the sound of a door being slammed and a lock being turned. Then more sobbing. Debbie closed her eyes tightly and then she stuffed her hand into her mouth.

'Are you in danger?'

'No, not any more, maybe…'

'Did someone hurt you?'

'Ah. Where to start? My husband…he…I got upset. I need the police to come. I need them to stop him.'

'Is your husband there with you now?'

'I think he's gone. Oh God, I hope he's gone.'

'Tell us your address, then we can come and help you.'

'I...I...no I don't want...please...I'm fine now. I don't need help. I don't know...I shouldn't have called. Just silly really.'

'You said he hurt you?'

'Well...he....'

Then a boy's voice in the background. 'Mum, are you in the bathroom?'

There was more rustling and the line went dead.

Debbie wiped the back of her hand across her eyes.

'Look. I never "assaulted" Rosie. I would never hurt her,' Debbie said.

'So you accept that was Rosie's voice?'

'Even if that was her, on the call, you said it was two years ago. How can it have anything to do with who killed her? This can't be all you have?'

'It's more than enough.' Dawson folded his arms.

'What else are you doing to find the killer?' Debbie asked again, her mouth slackening around the edges, her fingers fluttering lightly against each other.

'An eye witness saw you arrive at the house at around the time your wife was killed. You've confirmed the murder weapon was readily available in the living room and will, I'm sure, be covered in your fingerprints, you have a history of violence towards your wife and *your* glove was lying in the middle of a lake of blood on the floor. It couldn't be clearer if your name was OJ Simpson!'

'You think it was me. Oh God. This is some kind of sick joke.'

'I don't see anyone laughing.'

'No, you're wrong. Is this...is this all because I ran away? I saw it made a lot of trouble for you.' The tremors in Debbie's fingers spread across her hands and up her forearms. Dawson passed the iPad back to PC Thomas. 'Why would I want to kill Rosie?' she said.

'We'll have plenty of time to work that one out between now and the trial.'

Debbie sprang up and her chair crashed to the floor.

'No!' she cried out. 'You're wrong. You're so wrong. And if you lock me up, you'll stop looking for the real killer.'

Constance stepped towards her and reached out to take her arm, but Debbie thrust her away and backed against the wall. Dawson ignored Debbie's outburst and took his time packing up the photograph and the glove. Then he rose deliberately to his feet, jabbed at the same spot on his spine which he had tweaked, when he had bent down to peek through Debbie's letter box three days earlier, and began to intone the all too familiar words.

'Debbie Mallard, I am arresting you for the murder of Miss Rosie Harper. You do not have to say anything, but it may harm your defence if you do not mention, when questioned, something which you later rely on in court.'

'Debbie. It's OK. We'll sort this out,' Constance waved at Dawson to allow her to speak. 'And I'll let your kids know where you are,' she said.

Debbie stared through Constance.

'I told you it wouldn't take long,' Dawson chirped. 'Come with me then. We'll find you somewhere comfortable to spend the rest of the afternoon. There might even be some footie on.'

8

CONSTANCE DAWDLED IN FRONT of the window of Tom Dixon in Coal Drops Yard. She smoothed her skirt, ran a finger under each eye and moistened her lips, peering close to the glass to check on the progress of her impromptu grooming session. Then she became distracted by the display; a cascade of copper torpedoes and spheres, shiny red plastic chairs stacked in piles of four and lots of shimmering glassware; vases, candleholders, ornamental dishes. The kind of shop she would love to browse, if she had the time, because of the sheer audacity of its contents.

Three doors down, she entered the Coal Office restaurant, the scent of garlic and rosemary assaulting her nostrils as she spied Greg Winter seated at the bar, a half-empty high-ball glass in his hand.

'Hi.' Constance nudged him from his reverie. Greg leaped up and pulled back a barstool for her, his mouth lightly brushing her cheek on his body's forward trajectory. He was wearing a navy-blue jumper and his curly hair was cut short.

'Hi to you. It's nice to see you again,' he said, sinking back into his seat. 'I had fully intended to wait to order drinks,' Greg continued, 'but then the cocktail list was just too tempting. There's one here that has gin which changes colour in front of your eyes. I had to try it.'

Constance scrutinised Greg for any sign that he might have known that Judith had delivered a similar message to her once before, expounding the restorative properties of 'hydrangea' gin. Perhaps that was what happened when you spent time with people; you gravitated towards the same products, even without prompting. Although, Judith and Greg had not been together for some months now.

Greg was a wealthy businessman with his fingers in a number of innovative schemes. He had acted as expert witness on the first case Constance and Judith had worked on together. The reliability of some lie-detecting software had been challenged and he'd impressed them both with his honesty, in addition to his technical skills. Shortly afterwards, he and Judith had begun to see each other. Things had ended abruptly but, before that, he had taken Constance's brother, Jermain, on in one of his pioneering garden businesses. This was the first time Constance had seen him since then.

'Sounds interesting,' she said. 'And I am late, so I'm pleased you didn't wait.'. She tucked her chair in close as the waiter wafted past, a basket of knotted bread balanced on the tips of his fingers. 'It was nice of you to invite me.'

'It was nice of you to accept.'

When Greg had first called, Constance had considered declining his offer; she didn't want to be disloyal to Judith in any way. Then, she'd reasoned that, as far as she could tell, Greg had not been at fault when they split: *I'm just letting you know that Greg has gone, moved out, and I don't want to talk about it. And it was my decision, before you say anything.* That was what Judith had offered, when his absence become conspicuous. On top of that, Constance was pleased that Greg should seek her out, after all this time. She had always enjoyed his company. And, finally, the factor which had clinched things for her and forced her to accept, despite those reservations – she was curious to find out what he wanted from her, while hoping it wasn't to tell her that Jermain had done something wrong.

'Where are you living now?' she asked.

'Still based in London, although I'm often travelling. But when I'm here, I'm back in Putney, my old stomping ground. You?'

'Hackney, as always, not sure I'll ever leave.'

'You don't think some Prince Charming will come and carry you off on a white charger then, to somewhere far away, like Windsor or Kew?'

'That's very un-PC. You do know that, don't you?'

'What?'

'Suggesting I need either a "Prince Charming" or to be "carried off". I might just be happy the way I am. Or maybe I'll do the carrying.'

Greg shrugged. 'There we go. We haven't even got past introductions and I've already offended you. You can imagine how "foot-in-mouth" I am on the modern dating scene.'

'And what are you working on in leafy Putney?' she laughed, fortified by the knowledge that she could discount any romantic overtures from Greg. That would have been too awkward for words.

'The garden centre app is doing fantastically well.'

'I heard from Jermain. I am so grateful you gave him the chance to show what he can do.'

'Hey. I'm the one who should be grateful. He's really performing...out-performing. I like him and, more importantly, the team likes him. I'm going to spend the rest of this year consolidating, but then we may go for a big push. There'll be a chance for Jermain and some of the others to invest in the business, but only if they want. He might appreciate your advice then.'

Constance laughed uproariously, as well as with considerable relief. 'Now that tells me you don't know my little brother quite as well as you think you do, or he's been putting on a big act for you. Jermain doesn't accept advice from anyone.'

'He's lucky to have you looking out for him anyway,' he said. 'What about you? You said you were heading into court, when I called.'

'A hospital pass and a nasty one. Assault. And they were convicted.'

'Do you think they did it?'

'I don't know. They said they were innocent, said it was self-defence. One of them cried.'

'I'm sorry.'

'Me too. They were three young men who had never had any breaks. Sometimes it happens like that.'

'You think you could've done more?'

'Sure, with more time and an unlimited budget and a judge who hadn't just had to release a rapist on a technicality, but that's often the way. I mustn't let it get to me, must I?... Can I have what you're drinking, do you think?'

Greg held up his glass to the distant waiter, mouthed 'two' and received a reassuring nod in return.

'So what now? Who's next in line for the Lamb treatment?' he asked.

'I've been instructed by Debbie Mallard, Rosie Harper's ex-husband?'

Greg sat up straight. 'Wow. I saw she'd been arrested. It'll be the trial of the century, won't it? Judith must be excited.'

Constance turned around to see if the waiter was on his way back yet. Even though she loved working with Judith, it bothered her that Greg would assume she needed Judith's help. 'We haven't had much chance to discuss it yet,' she said.

'Oh,' Greg's fingers rapped the marble worktop. 'How is Judith?'

'Same as ever, although she confessed you'd been giving her these podcasts to listen to, to make her more empathetic.'

Greg nearly spat out his last mouthful of gin.

'Is that what she said?' he laughed, and Constance noticed the dimples in his cheeks for the first time. 'I think Judith and your brother can shake hands. As if she ever listened to anything I recommended. I didn't know that she'd said that. How hilarious. You do know that she doesn't really mean half the things she says, that she just pretends to be hopelessly old-fashioned and bigoted. It's an affectation.'

'I know that.'

'Although, I'm sure you're a better tonic for her than any podcast.'

'Me?'

'Oh yes. She told me she'd never worked with anyone like you before. Clever, determined, forward-thinking, totally reliable and always challenging her, never saying "yes" to everything, like the others did.'

'Wow. I think my face must be the colour of that drink, if it ever arrives.' Constance looked pointedly at the waiter, who had collected a tray from the furthest end of the bar and was finally heading in their direction. Now, she was ashamed of herself for her negativity towards Judith.

'But,' Greg was speaking again. 'I invited *you* here this evening, because I wanted to hear all *your* news, so the next person who says the "J" word picks up the tab. And I am thinking of having at least two more cocktails before dinner, so you really won't want it to be you!'

9

Laura Mallard arrived at Constance's office the next day, tall and broad-shouldered, with wispy blond hair, its dark roots flaunting themselves under the brash strip-lighting, dragging the scent of cigarettes and coffee in with her.

'What's happening with Dad?' Laura settled herself down opposite Constance, her enquiring eyes emphasising her question. She threw her bag down onto the table, keeping her jacket firmly on.

'Is that what you call Debbie?' Constance said.

Laura shrugged. 'Just habit. Is it a problem?'

'No.'

'I never called her "Mum". I'm not going to start now, am I? I could maybe do "Debbie", I suppose, if I'm going to be a witness.'

'It's too early to decide any of that. Your dad's been arrested, but I'm hoping that we can persuade the police to keep on looking for someone else.'

'I do get it. She sits there with her earrings and her necklace and her long hair and I keep saying "Dad". It'll look a bit weird, right?'

'It might, but I don't want you to worry about that.' Constance glanced at the notes she had prepared, Laura's preoccupation with the trial temporarily distracting her.

'It's OK. You can ask me the questions now,' Laura continued. 'I can't spend too long anyway. I'm on my lunch hour.'

'You're back at work?'

'It keeps me occupied. And Ben's at my place. If we're together, we just make each other worse. They're very chilled at work. They leave me alone. And if what I do is crap, they're hardly going to complain. I read about it – it's therapy really.'

'I understand,' said Constance, not sure she really did. 'We'll just start with some general stuff, then, to set the scene. Facts that will be helpful if…if things do progress against Debbie, although, like I said, I'll do all I can to prevent that. Were you happy, as a family, growing up?'

'Yeah,' Laura said. 'Well, I never really stopped at any time and thought, "whoopee, my life is fantastic". But, yeah. My friends were busy with the usual stuff, parents divorcing, father out of work or buying a sports car or both, mother getting depression or becoming a gym bunny, eating disorders, fatigue syndrome. We were a bit boring by comparison.'

'Really? Your dad was Danny Mallard and your mum was Rosie Harper?'

'That's what everyone thinks. That we had this dazzling life, full of celebrities and parties. It just meant Dad was always away when I was little, although I did go to some awesome football matches, when Mum let him take me, that is. By the time I can really remember, he was coaching though, and that wasn't so much fun.'

'And your mum?'

'She was boring. Always going to bed early, because she had to get up in the middle of the night. And not around that often, because of other stuff she did. And, like I said, she wasn't keen on Dad taking me to matches and stuff.'

'Were you close to your parents?'

'Gran used to help a lot, my dad's mum. She would come over and make breakfast when Dad was away, and dinner sometimes too. And we had nannies, before that, to get us up in the mornings. But, I mean, that ended a few years ago.'

'Do you know anyone your parents might have fallen out with?'

Laura snorted with laughter.

'What? What is it?' Constance asked.

'Oh nothing. Really, nothing.'

'Did they fall out with the nannies?'

'Mum was really strict with them. The last one, though, I really liked. She wasn't English, from Romania, and she lived in. I think mum took her on as a favour for someone. She had dark hair and pale skin, very dramatic looking. Ben called her "Dracula" and all the delivery men fancied her. She used to let Ben watch as much TV as he liked or go on the PlayStation, and spend hours on her phone, "chatting" with her admirers. Then Mum saw her getting out of one of their vans in the early morning; Tesco it was. She was gone by the end of the week.'

'What did Debbie think about that?'

'I remember Dad teased Mum over dinner about Viviana. Said that if she'd got out of an Ocado van, Mum would have let her stay.'

'And what did your mum say to that?'

'She didn't think it was funny.'

'No. Do you know who they all were, the nannies?'

'I could give you a list of the ones I remember and I might even have a few pictures, but I'm not sure I knew any of their second names. Mum made them sign contracts when they arrived, so if you can get to her emails you can probably find out. Knowing her, she'll have a folder for each of them and comments, marks out of ten, that kind of thing. Do you think it was one of them?'

'I'm trying to build a picture of what's possible. Who had keys to the house?'

'Me and Ben…and the cleaner.'

'What about Debbie?'

'I'm not sure. I mean, probably. I don't think Mum changed the locks or anything, when Dad moved out.'

'Did you have a lot of security at home?'

'Dad warned Mum about it. Mum said gates made her feel claustrophobic, said most crime was online these days, but he said they were targets. In the end they put a front gate in and had some cameras installed, but she always left the gate open, said she "forgot", and you can jump over it pretty easily, even when it's closed. There was a panic button in the kitchen. That worked. Ben pressed it once and three police cars arrived.'

'Any problems your mum had, maybe at work?'

'Ask Jason.'

'Jason?'

'Jason Fenwick, the other half of Mum's double act.'

'Your dad mentioned him.'

'He's known Mum for years. She only got the *Breakfast Time* job because of him. She called him her "second husband". And I know that sometimes people wrote pretty gross stuff to her; there were plenty of people she blocked.'

'And were your parents happy, as a couple, before the divorce?'

'They got divorced, didn't they?... I need to smoke,' Laura said suddenly, her hand already thrust deep into her bag. 'It's my lunch break and I always have a cigarette now; it's my one guilty pleasure. Can I?'

'Not here. We can take a walk outside, if you like.'

***

'I think they were happy before,' Laura confided, as they strolled along the pavement and settled themselves on a bench in the park behind Constance's office. Laura puffed on a Marlboro Light, holding it loosely between two fingers. 'But I'm not sure. What signs should I have looked for? Kissing each other, hugging, touching? They used to do that for the cameras, I've seen the photos, but they weren't like that in private – or not after we came along.

'And they were always juggling so many things. I mean, when Dad was playing, he was away or training long hours and she was always nagging him to watch his weight, drink less, train more. And when he was coaching it was even worse, 'cos he had meetings with the bosses and all those high-pressure times, like transfer windows and cup ties.'

'And your mum took on a lot of charity work?'

'Well...Jason said she should do it, said it went with her "profile". Dad didn't agree, said she had enough on her plate. She was late for one of my birthday parties because she was out delivering meals to homeless people. She was asked onto *Strictly*, too, a year or so back. Thank God she said no. Can you imagine how awful it

61

would have been to see her prancing around in those costumes?'

'You're not a fan then?'

'No, and Mum wasn't either. It would have only been about her image. I'm not sure why she refused, in the end. Jason will probably know.'

'Did your parents argue?'

'Not much. So how was I supposed to know, right? Obviously, there was stuff going on with Dad under the surface. He must have been keeping it quiet for years. I remember once I came home early and found him with Mum's clothes out on the bed. I asked what he was doing and he said that he was finding some old ones to give away. I asked Mum later and she didn't know what I was talking about. That kind of thing. I think he was desperate not to embarrass us. It's hardly acceptable playground banter is it? "Hey, Laura. Hear your dad's now your mum."'

'But Debbie transitioned, what, two years ago? Ben was still young. Why didn't she wait?'

'You'll have to ask Dad…Debbie. I'd left home.'

'And your mother? Do you know what she thought about your dad transitioning?'

Laura flicked her ash onto the ground. 'She asked us, me and Ben, not to talk about it to anyone outside the family.'

'She was embarrassed?'

'Wouldn't you be? I mean she was a big TV star.'

'She was worried about her career?'

'Maybe I heard her say it, maybe she was on the phone, maybe she said it to Dad. Maybe he said it. I don't remember.'

'Is that why they split up?'

'Like I said, you'll have to ask Dad. Better than me getting it all wrong. Mum would've hated that. "Get your facts straight!" That was something she was always saying. Look. I've got to get back. I'll make the list of nannies and anything else I can think of, but go and talk to Jason. He'll be able to give you the answers.'

After Laura had gone, Constance returned to her office and reviewed her notes. She had followed her planned questions but, reading back through Laura's replies, she felt that somehow Laura had been the one in control, that she had suffered a home defeat before Laura had skipped away with the ball, with no promise of a return match. She was certainly a cool customer and keen to be involved in…what had Greg called it? 'The trial of the century'. And why had Laura laughed so hard when Constance had asked if her parents had disagreed with anyone? Now she wished she'd probed that further. Was it that Rosie was argumentative, or Debbie, or both of them? Was it the opposite, that they were both super-sociable? That was the thing about interviews. Everything seemed obvious and clear while you were talking, but, afterwards, things often became more opaque and you wished you'd asked for more.

Greg's face settled in her mind fleetingly. She had enjoyed the evening more than she had anticipated. He was easy company, warm and generous, although, despite his protests, she suspected he had only invited her to hear news of Judith. *How would Judith have conducted the interview with Laura?* she wondered. No doubt, more persistently than Constance had.

On her laptop, she called up the image of Danny Mallard lifting the SPOTY trophy, his face a mass of creased joyfulness. And Rosie applauding and cheering from the audience. They both seemed so happy. When had it all gone wrong? Then she pressed the green button on her phone, hoping that Judith was home, had her phone to hand this time and was keen to talk things through.

10

ANDY WAS LYING IN BED, mulling over his meeting with Graham, two days on. He had been preoccupied, at first, with the dizziness which had overwhelmed him at the beginning of their meeting. It was out of character for Andy; he'd jumped out of an aeroplane only last month – with a parachute, for charity – and had no problem with ski-lifts, although he hadn't made it to the slopes since the children arrived. On his return home, he had marched straight up to the counter at his local pharmacy and tested his blood pressure, which was a little on the high side, but not dangerously so.

Once he had convinced himself that he wasn't ill, he had been able to reflect on Graham's offer. It was the chance of a lifetime, he knew that. And he was delighted to have been chosen out of all the multitudes. Despite his daily, confidence-inspiring ritual, involving chanting and chest-thumping in the early morning, which tended to sustain him through most moderately challenging days, he was not without self-awareness. He did appreciate that

Graham's invitation may not have been earned entirely by virtue of his many talents.

Nick, his head of chambers, had scored a very significant victory on Graham's behalf, relating to Horizon's bid for a rival, a year or so back. And, in addition to a fat fee, which had financed the refurbishment of a couple of meeting rooms, it had been rumoured that a further reward had been promised. However, there were twenty-two of them in chambers, ranging from John, aged seventy-eight and still doing some advocacy, albeit at a rather pedestrian pace, to Andy's pupil, the deferential Caroline, wet behind the ears at twenty-four, but with great potential. And Andy had been chosen from all of them. That meant something.

He thought back to Graham's words. 'Five days a week,' he had said, and 'at least five nights, we haven't decided on Saturdays yet', checking that Andy didn't balk at the hours. Andy wanted to say that it was no more than his family had asked of him for the past seven years, without any payment or appreciation, in fact, probably considerably less, as Graham wasn't asking him to get up in the middle of the night and juggle a baby, a bottle and a blinding migraine. But he satisfied himself with nodding energetically and confirming that *wouldn't be a problem.*

And 'very high profile' and 'if you play your cards right, it could make you a star,' to which Andy had replied that *sounded very nice too* and, if it meant he was recognised undertaking his late-night shop at his local Tesco, then he wouldn't mind one bit.

Graham had asked a few questions too: 'How do you feel about taking orders from a woman?' To which Andy had joked that he already did, except this one was 99cm tall and still slept with her teddies. Then he had asked Andy if he felt it was appropriate to call out other lawyers, publicly, if they were poor at their job or made mistakes. *Absolutely*, Andy had replied, with the most enthusiasm so far. *The public had the right to expect competent legal representation and there were no excuses for errors, when people's liberty was at stake.*

Then, finally, what did he think about 'professionals from other backgrounds' solving crimes? Andy wasn't sure what Graham meant at first – thought he might mean people from state schools or deprived families – and he launched into a well-rehearsed speech about the benefits of diversity in the profession, before Graham put him right. What he had been asking about was additional professional disciplines: psychiatrists, psychologists, true crime researchers, AI specialists, experts in body language. This caught Andy off-guard; it was not something he had ever turned his mind towards, but he was able to reply – convincingly, he thought – that he adopted a 'collaborative approach' and felt that a fresh perspective was always valuable.

Alone now, briefly, while Clare was busying herself with the breakfast routine downstairs, Andy found himself frowning hard at the opposite wall. He did have a slight feeling of unease, as he wondered what was behind Graham's questions, but he would have been stupid to say anything other than what he knew Graham wanted to hear, wouldn't he? He had to give himself the best chance of moving on to the next stage.

And while it had been one of the most difficult secrets to keep in his entire married life, he had not said a word to Clare yet, in the main because he knew it would spark off hundreds of questions, to which he still didn't have the answers. And, there was still the chance he might want to say 'no' if the terms weren't right, and he wanted to be able to make that decision alone, without pressure from Clare.

'Andy!' Clare's call broke through his reverie. 'Can you grab a clean t-shirt for Mia? She's spilt chocolate milk all down this one.'

Andy called out his acknowledgement, then rubbed his hand across his face before sitting up, putting on his slippers and heading for Mia's room, which had been transformed, overnight, by his youngest progeny, from an orderly space into the aftermath of a major environmental disaster. As he ploughed forwards through the debris, to sort through her clothes for a suitable replacement top, he pushed away the nagging thought that, whatever Graham offered, if it meant less time at home for three months, that, in itself, might be no bad thing.

11

JUDITH ARRIVED AT Constance's office with a pile of newspapers in her arms, nudging the door open with her elbow and depositing them noisily in the centre of the table. Then she poured herself a coffee. Constance raised both eyebrows.

'What?' Judith grinned. 'Are you amused that my coffee embargo was so short-lived or outraged at my contribution to the destruction of the rainforest? The press coverage is highly prejudicial, of course.'

'Both,' Constance replied, tapping at her laptop. 'You can access the same and more this way, you know.'

Judith sat down and unfolded the first newspaper. 'It's not the same,' she said. 'I like to touch it for it to really stick.' Then she paused and unwound her scarf. 'I mean,' Judith continued, 'first all the stuff about the dog and the neighbour, then endless moaning about the chase. Poor Dawson, there's been a formal complaint to the Met about him overdoing it. Did you know that?'

Constance shook her head.

'The Commissioner just went along with it, accepting that lives were endangered by the chase through the park. I'm not quite sure what he was supposed to do, if not chase a murderer on the run...'

'Suspected murderer.'

'All right. 'Suspected murderer. By the way, just so we're on the same page, I've read everything you've sent me, I've watched Rosie on iPlayer until I can quote her verbatim and I've even watched some football tournaments – various – well, the highlights; a first for me, that one.'

'Great.'

'Which brings me to the relevant stuff – what real evidence do they have against Debbie?'

'Not much, but Dawson thinks it's enough.'

'Any fingerprints on the murder weapon?'

'No. It was wrapped in a cloth and wiped clean.'

'And the glove?'

'They're running more tests, said it's complicated. It's going to be Debbie's though, like everyone thinks.'

'Doesn't mean she killed her.'

Constance was silent.

'How is Debbie bearing up?'

'Pretty awful. The male prison hasn't helped. She didn't sleep at all the first two nights. Luckily, I found her certificate yesterday, so they're processing it and finding her a women's prison.'

'I don't expect them to hurry.'

'Now I'm preparing the bail application, I'm not sure if it's a good idea. Once people know she's out, there's likely to be another siege of her flat. She might do better to stay inside, especially if she's relocating to the women's prison.'

'What about the children?'

'Ben, he's just 16. He's moved in with Laura for now. And, like Debbie said, their uncle is around – Ellis Harper.'

'Ah yes, the sponger.'

'I saw him.'

'You saw him?'

'At Rosie's house. He came, he said, to get some clothes for Ben. The policeman wouldn't let him in.'

'Quite right too. Did you talk to him?'

'I decided not to. It didn't seem like a good time. He was in a rush and I don't think he even noticed me. I talked to Laura though, yesterday. She's a tough one.'

'Tough?'

'She was back at work already, seems quite detached about it all. Definitely no tears.'

'Grief does funny things to people.'

'True, but she was…almost excited at the prospect of her father being on trial. When I told her we were still trying to find another killer, she seemed disappointed.'

'Does she think Debbie killed her mother?'

'No. Well, I didn't ask outright.'

'You didn't ask her?'

'You always tell me not to ask those kind of questions…when you don't know the answer.'

Judith swallowed a large mouthful of coffee.

'That's when we're in court,' she said. 'It might be useful to know what a potential key witness will say in a trial of her father for killing her mother on the crucial question, don't you think?'

'I'll talk to her again, but she implied that their split was to protect Rosie from embarrassment.'

'That's good, then, I think. Anything else?'

'I don't think she and Rosie really got on.'

'Oh.'

'Just things she said.'

'And Ben?'

'I'm meeting him tomorrow. Debbie doesn't want him to give evidence.'

'Ah. We can consider that more as we prepare. Any other leads?'

'Not yet, but I'll try other family. And I'll also see Jason Fenwick, the other presenter. I thought you'd like to come along?'

'Perfect. Anything else of interest?'

'All sorts of stuff, although most of it is just gossip; that Rosie and Danny were having money problems, some "has been" footballer saying Debbie was hard to work with. Early on, there was some positive stuff, focusing on how they'd been the perfect celebrity couple, everyone wanted to be like them, what a role model Danny was for young men.'

'But that was before the arrest?'

'Yes. Since then most of what I've read has been negative, like I said: quotes from footballers – quite nasty stuff; a "friend" of Rosie's and even their marriage guidance counsellor.'

'I saw that, yes. In *The Sun*, wasn't it? Saying that Debbie went to the sessions, but didn't try hard enough. That must be a total breach of her duty of confidentiality. Let's hope all her clients read it and drop her like a stone.'

'There's one really awful photo of Debbie when she was half-way through transitioning, which at least three papers have used.'

'Awful in what way?'

'I'll find it for you. It's when she was growing her hair, so it's all sticking up and she has lipstick on, but no face makeup. And

I'm sure they've photoshopped it. You'll see what I mean. In one photo it's not too bad. In another, they've sort of made the area around her chin all grey, so she looks sinister. And God knows where they got it from.'

'You know they can do anything these days with photographs.'

'And…well you might already know this, if you've been looking at the historic stuff… Just before the Euro '96 quarter final, Danny got in a bit of trouble.'

'What kind of trouble?'

'He was caught with another player at a bar in Málaga. They were drinking heavily; lying back over the bar, girls pouring spirits into their mouths. The photos were on all the front pages and the headlines, "the Duck is plucked" and other less polite rhymes.'

'The Duck?'

'It's what they called Danny, the fans. They used to quack when he got the ball. You might have heard it, if you watched some of the later matches.'

Judith frowned. 'Not the best nickname for a footballer, is it? What about the lion? Or the cheetah? What happened then?'

'They were almost sent home, but the manager pleaded for them. It was Danny's birthday. Once Danny scored his wonder goal, the next day, it was all forgotten by the public, but it didn't make him popular with the FA.'

'No, I can see that. And you're worried there might be other unsavoury stories waiting to emerge?'

'Aren't you? I mean, a Premier League footballer?'

'I hadn't thought, but you're probably right. We should try to find a friendly football fan then, or a contemporary of Danny's. Someone who can tell us the worst, but who won't talk.'

'I'll do my best. And, this may be nothing, but the *Mail* is hinting that the glove the police found at the scene was planted?'

'How does the press even know about the glove?'

'Same way they knew, early on, about the chase and managed to take photos, I suppose.'

'Poor Charlie, that's all he needs on top of the fuss about pursuing Debbie. That's what I mean. We can't even let the police do their jobs, these days. Maybe it was better when we were all ignorant, you know, back in the early twentieth century, when you just did as you were told and stood in line and respected people cleverer than you.'

'You don't really mean that, do you?' Constance said.

Judith laughed. 'No, not entirely.'

'One other thing. There's loads of stuff on Twitter today too,' Constance changed the subject. 'I think it will make the mainstream news.'

'What are they saying?'

'Someone from a women's group launched a poll. You had to vote if you thought Debbie was guilty or not, but you had the option to list your sexuality and gender when you voted. They tweeted the results and it's all got a bit nasty.'

'Ah!' Judith folded up the paper she had been reading and shoved it towards the centre of the table. 'I'm surprised it's taken so long for the battle lines to be drawn,' she said. 'What does this important poll show, to the extent these things show anything at all?'

'They reported 90% of transgender people thought Debbie was innocent and 65% of everyone else thought she was guilty.'

'65%! Before one shred of evidence.'

'The chase.'

'Circumstantial. Doesn't prove Debbie did it.'

'You said the chase was incriminating. It was the first thing you said when we spoke.'

'Superficially, yes, of course. To ordinary people and… sensationalists.'

Constance bit her lip.

'How has it got nasty?' Judith asked.

'I don't even know where to start. They're saying it's wrong to tell people the voting split, said it engenders transphobic tweets. And they're right. Loads of stuff about how Debbie is "unnatural", including from the religious lobby, pretty much encouraging people to stone her. You get the picture.

'Then there's two of the girls from the team she manages now, saying what a wonderful coach Debbie is and that's led to loads of horrible things about how she's only around young girls because she wants to see them in the showers. Honestly, I could spend all day reading it and not even scratch the surface and some of it is… horrific. I just hope Debbie hasn't seen any of it.'

'This is our wonderful democracy at its best then,' Judith sighed. 'I think we can be fairly confident that Debbie won't be seeking it out. But everyone else will have seen it, including her children and potential jurors. We'll have to be prepared.'

Judith took her blue notebook from her bag and wrote the date at the top of the first page.

'Some things never change, then,' Constance giggled.

'That's unfair,' Judith laughed too. 'I have embraced many aspects of twenty-first-century technology, I even have an electric toothbrush! But the feel of the words is as important as their look and sound; the shapes they make when I write them down.'

'If you say so.'

Judith sat back and placed both hands flat on top of her newspapers. 'What is it?' she said.

'What?'

'Something's bothering you.'

'All right,' Constance stopped typing. 'Given the timing, the case is likely to fall within the new "public transparency" pilot scheme. It's going to be filmed for public viewing.'

'I anticipated that.'

'And you're OK with it?'

'Not really,' Judith shook her head. 'But you're the one who's always telling me to move with the times.'

'I was so worried what you were going to say,' Constance spluttered, then broke out in a broad grin. 'I can see that it could be a really positive thing,' she continued. 'I mean, it's great for us, because we can watch the prosecution witnesses later on, really see their reactions when you ask them questions, rather than relying on memory.'

'And see where we've slipped up – all the questions I should have asked, but forgot...'

'And, it helps our witnesses too. You're often saying how difficult witnesses find it being in court, when it's such an alien atmosphere. This way, they get to see the process over and over in other cases, before they give their evidence.'

'I wish I could share your enthusiasm. I just see it as another nail in the coffin of the professions. First, they devalued teachers, then doctors and now it's our turn. Show enough court cases on TV and then every wannabe Harvey Specter will want to have a go. But if Debbie's case is in the scheme, there's nothing we can do, so no point complaining.'

Constance was silent. Judith's stoic response was considerably better than expected.

'What about motive?' Judith asked.

'That's the thing; there isn't one. Well, there's this whisper of "money trouble", like I said, but it's just gossip and Dawson is trying to say there's a history of violence. I told you about the 999 call.'

'So the prosecution will most likely play it as a domestic incident, the culmination of months or years of abuse. Debbie's admitted she was there, too. All right. I'm going to wade through the papers and make some notes. Shout if anything jumps out at you. Otherwise, let's break in an hour for another brainstorm.'

Judith grabbed the top newspaper and peered in close. Constance watched her for a moment. She was pleased that Judith was here, wasn't she? If she'd instructed someone else, she wouldn't have the same collaborative approach. Most barristers expected her to do all the work and they just picked up the papers at the court door. Judith wasn't like that, partly because she didn't need the work or the money. She just loved solving the puzzle.

'Did you used to do them, when you were younger?' Constance asked.

'What?'

'Jigsaw puzzles.'

Judith finished her coffee.

'Yes. Didn't you? Or was there some new-fangled version you completed, online, in your youth.'

'No. There were jigsaws, but I didn't have any.' Constance thought back to the tiny flat she and Jermain had shared with her mum, not far from where they were now. Maybe she had completed some jigsaws when she was really young, those wooden ones that nursery school kids use. But she couldn't remember owning the more difficult variety, the 500 or 1,000 piece landscapes; a scenic railway, a forest, a cityscape: Rio de Janeiro, Venice, New York.

She watched Judith at work and, feeling the heat of her gaze, Judith looked up and smiled at her. She smiled back and returned to her laptop and Google searches.

12

CONSTANCE WALKED THE HALF a mile to Laura Mallard's flat the next day, where Uncle Ellis opened the door and welcomed her inside. The neighbouring bistro was full of customers tucking into elaborate breakfasts, as the sounds of children's voices rang out from the playground of the nearby school, and Constance was pleased that there was no flicker of recognition from her sighting of Ellis outside Rosie's house.

'It was good of you to come here. I'm not sure Ben would have made it to you,' Ellis said, showing Constance into a small double-aspect living room, with floor-to-ceiling windows, and a kitchen replete with shiny white units and black granite tops. Constance peered into the sink, where a frying pan was soaking. Ellis shrugged.

'I thought I could tempt him. He's hardly eaten for days,' he said.

Constance sat down at the small, wooden table in the centre of the room and switched on her tablet. Ellis knocked on the door facing her.

'Ben, are you up? The solicitor's here, the one defending your dad. Are you OK to talk to her?' He threw her a reassuring glance over his shoulder, as he waited for a response.

Constance looked around the flat. There was a low sofa by the far window, its three cushions perfectly plumped and evenly spaced, no newspapers or clutter anywhere. Laura evidently kept a very tidy pad. The walls were painted white and were empty of adornment, but there was a framed black-and-white photograph by the toaster, featuring Danny Mallard holding the hand of a young, blond female mascot, on a pitch in a large stadium. The photographer had focused on the girl, rather than the football star and her expression was one of absolute cool confidence, as she stared straight into the lens.

'You like it?' Ellis said, following her gaze. He picked up the photo and handed it to Constance for a closer look. 'She's always been like that, Laura has,' he said. 'Nothing phases her. Eighty thousand people watching and she just marches right out there.'

'I suppose she had her dad at her side,' Constance said, now able to see the likeness between the feisty subject of the photo and the young woman who had visited her only yesterday.

'Yeah. Even so, a cool customer. She used to play, you know. She was pretty good.'

'Sounds like you're a proud uncle.'

Ellis reclaimed the photo and replaced it on the kitchen surface. Then the bedroom door opened and Ben walked towards them. Constance thought him younger than his sixteen years, his pale skin smooth and unblemished, his chest narrow. As he moved, his jaw muscles were working furiously to control his face. Ellis hovered beside his nephew, placing a reassuring hand on his shoulder and guiding him to the seat next to Constance.

'Hello Ben. Thank you for letting me come today,' Constance began. 'I'm sure it wasn't easy for you.'

'Will it help Dad?' Ben's voice was reedy and weak. He cleared his throat.

'I don't know till I hear what you have to say, but that's what I'm hoping.'

'I should leave you two to talk,' Ellis said.

'It's not necessary, if Ben wants you to stay.'

'I don't want to interfere. I'll go for a walk for, what, half an hour? See if I can find something nice in the shops for lunch. Ben can call me if you finish early.'

He waved a set of keys at them and departed. When the door closed behind Ellis, Ben stared at Constance.

'It's nice of your uncle to come over. Does he live nearby?' she began.

'Near Amersham, but he's staying in London for now, to help out.' Ben spoke quietly.

'That's kind. Were he and your mum close?'

'He lived abroad for a while, in Hong Kong. I'm not even sure when he came back, but they stayed close, yes.'

Constance waited for Ben to continue.

'Laura said it would help Dad for me to talk to you,' Ben finally said. 'He didn't kill her. He didn't kill Mum. I don't know how they can say he did. If you knew Dad, I mean, he's a good person. He does all sorts of stuff now, with sport, to help people. And they loved each other. They really did. He would never have hurt her. You believe that, don't you?'

'Of course,' Constance tried to keep her voice even. 'I'm pleased that's what you think. I need to ask you a few questions now, if that's OK?'

'Will I have to go to the trial?'

'Tell me what you know and then I can decide if it will help your dad or not. Like I said to Laura, we're still optimistic that the police will find some other leads.'

'Is that what *they* said?' Ben said.

'They have to keep some things to themselves. So, on 17th June, the day your mum was killed, can you tell me anything about that day, what you remember?'

'Nothing special. I got up, went to school. That's it.'

'Did you come straight home after school?'

'I went back to a friend's place. When I got home, there were police everywhere. They wouldn't let me see her.'

'That must have been very upsetting. They wanted to protect you. And it's standard practice. They couldn't risk contaminating the crime scene.' As she said the words, Constance reflected on how empty they must seem to Ben. 'Going back to that morning,' she continued, 'where was your mum? What was she doing?'

'She was up early, I think. That was her usual routine. She got up around 4.30, took Belle out, our dog. Then she headed off for work.'

'Did she wake you up?'

'No. I don't want to wake up that early.'

'Did you speak to each other the night before?'

'No.' There was that tension in Ben's face again, his eyes bulging, his cheeks sucked in.

'Not at all?'

'We'd had an argument in the afternoon. I said I was staying at a friend's and I left.'

Constance nodded. Ben wasn't crying outwardly, but he was

struggling to speak.

'What did you argue about?'

'Just the usual stuff.'

'How do you get on with your father? That's what you call him, still?'

'We get on fine and yes, he's still my dad, my "biological father", is that what they say?'

'Do you see him much?'

'Twice a week. I go back there on Tuesdays after school and make him dinner. And then at the weekend too.'

'You make him dinner?'

'He can't cook. Well, only eggs and toast. And I'm usually back before him. Otherwise we just get a takeaway.'

'How was it when your dad moved out?'

'Pretty bad. I mean, I understood why he had to go, but I just wanted things to be how they were before.'

'Did your parents talk to you about why your dad was leaving?'

'Mum just said something about them "needing space", which was a cop out. Dad talked to me. He tried to explain. Said he still loved us, but he knew, if he stayed, it would make things hard for us, but that wasn't really what he meant. He meant it would make things hard for Mum, but he didn't want to say that.'

'In what way?'

Ben's eyes fixed on the photo of Danny with Laura, before darting away.

'Look. I'll give you an example. Dad always came to my parents' evenings. But once he started, you know, changing his clothes, wearing makeup, then she told him not to bother.'

'She probably thought you would be embarrassed.'

'No. She just thought about herself. It's funny, isn't it? She did all those programmes about people *being accepted for who they are*, those special features, but she didn't like it when it happened to her. And I was the one who *was* embarrassed, because although she was "the big TV star" all the teachers kept asking where Dad was. And do you know what she said?'

'No.'

'That Dad was ill.'

Constance tapped away at her tablet. Ben might be young, but he had a fairly good grasp of some of the less tangible consequences of Debbie's transition.

'Did your father talk to you about becoming a woman?' she asked.

'Laura and I knew. We'd guessed from stuff he'd done before. Stuff he thought we didn't know about. Well, we thought he just liked dressing like a woman, we didn't think he actually wanted to be a woman.'

'How did you feel about it when you found out?'

'I don't know. It's not something I expected. But, I mean, it's like everything that's a surprise. You just need a bit of time to get used to it. He still loved us the same.'

'Did your mum and dad argue?'

'A bit, the usual things.'

'Money?'

'I don't think so.'

'One of the newspapers reported you took a part-time job to help out with money at home?'

Ben almost laughed. 'I got a part-time job 'cos I'm sixteen and I don't want to ask my mum for money every time I want to go out. That's all.'

'Did your parents argue about your dad wanting to become a

woman?'

'I expect they did, but not when I was around. There were times when I would get home and it would look like they were maybe talking about stuff and they'd stop and be all red and embarrassed. Is it right that it's going to be on TV, the trial?' Ben interrupted Constance's flow.

'It's likely, yes.' Constance resumed her note-taking.

'I don't see how that's right,' Ben's lip trembled. 'How can it be right for everyone to see it all – everyone seeing everything. I wasn't allowed to see Mum, but then it's going to be on TV. How can they do that?'

'A court room is still a public place, even without the cameras and there would be a lot of interest in the case, anyway, because of who your mum was.' Again, Constance found herself talking in platitudes.

'It's not the same,' Ben persisted.

'No. You're absolutely right. It's not the same,' she conceded with a sigh. 'We can stop with the questions now, if you like. I only had one or two more.'

'Ask them then.' Ben dried his eyes with his sleeve. 'And I'll come if you need me, if Dad needs me. I don't care who's watching.'

'All right. Nearly done. Did you ever see your dad act violently towards your mum?'

'No. Never. If you knew them, how they were, you'd realise how stupid that is.'

'He could be quite…physical on the pitch.'

'Not at home.'

'I understand. Do you know anyone who might have wanted to hurt your mum?'

'She had a whole life outside the family. She met so many

people – hundreds – two million followers on Twitter, thousands on Instagram. Laura and I think she just pissed off some psycho with something she said one morning. There are some serious weirdos out there. That's far more likely than it being Dad.'

***

Constance was leaving the apartment when Ellis came up the steps, with a brown paper bag in his arms. They stood together, on the landing, dancing a silent dance.

'Did you get all you needed from Ben?' he asked, eventually, barring her exit route. 'Sorry. I think I was longer than I said.'

'Yes, all I need for now, thank you.' Constance edged around him.

'Will Debbie get bail, do you think?'

'It's something we're still discussing. I can't say any more than that.'

Ellis nodded. 'Is there going to be a trial?' he asked.

'Probably.'

'It's just…I can't believe you really need him, Ben…and Laura for the trial. They've both been through so much already.'

Constance was almost at the top step, her bag narrowly missing brushing Ellis' arm.

'I understand. But Ben seems to be bearing up pretty well. He wants to help,' she said.

Ellis finally sidestepped Constance and checked the front door was closed tightly.

'If Ben gives evidence, would any…information come out about him, personal information?' he whispered.

'What is it you're worried about?'

'He had issues at school when he was younger, anxiety issues, saw a doctor, was on pills for a while.'

'Oh.'

'It's not always easy being the kid of famous parents. I've seen him taking pills now too, although I don't know if they're the same ones. I don't think it's a good time for me to ask.'

'I see.'

'So, as his uncle, and I might end up being his guardian, if Debbie goes to jail, I worry about you putting him under pressure, what it might do to him. I wouldn't want it to be public that he had those…mental problems, either. And I can't see Laura has anything relevant to say, seeing as she hasn't lived at home for so long.'

'I understand your concern and I will think very hard about what's best, for Debbie.'

'I wouldn't be keeping my promise to Rosie, if I didn't look after them. They're both such great kids.'

Ellis took the front door key from his pocket, eased it into the lock and went inside. Constance heard his feet padding across the floor and him calling out gently to Ben and she wondered what he had bought to tempt his nephew to eat.

13

JASON FENWICK USHERED Constance and Judith into the lounge of his house and offered them tea. He was smartly dressed, in a casual sort of way; open-necked shirt, chinos, loafers with socks. He had a round face and a youthful expression and his middle-age was only confirmed by the grey colour of his close-cropped hair; rumour had it he had dyed it once, with dire results, and then opted for the natural look instead.

The room was what Judith would describe afterwards as 'opulent', even by her own high standards. There were two large white leather sofas and a pale pink velveteen armchair arranged around an unusual table; an elliptical glass slab, supported by a white marble nude in child's pose. Chains of tiny glass beads, of varying shapes and sizes, poured down into the centre of the room, a marble shelf held an enormous vase brimming with giant, virgin white lilies and a floor-to-ceiling wall unit, opposite, was adorned with a selection of books, interspersed with trophies and awards.

The walls themselves were wood-panelled and covered in rectangular modern art canvases, daubed with brash primary colours. Immediately behind the armchair where Jason had settled was a large portrait of the man himself, sitting in that very same chair, fingers loosely intertwined, legs grounded and jaw tight.

'Thank you for making time for us,' Constance said.

'Anything to help Rosie,' Jason replied, with an empathetic smile.

'Tell us about her,' Judith began. 'I understand you worked together for many years.'

The door opened and a woman entered with a tray of tea and biscuits. She deposited it on the table, smiled at them in turn and quickly departed.

'That was my wife, Rochelle,' Jason said. 'Thank you, darling. That's perfect,' he called after her. 'Rosie was a lovely person,' he continued, handing out the tea. 'I knew her from her twenties. We were introduced by a friend.'

'Were you in television then?'

'I was trying to be. That was my dream, always. I was already doing bits and pieces for Channel 4. Then I got my first break with the BBC, working on *Blue Peter*, but all behind the scenes.'

'When did you start to work together professionally?'

'About three years later. I kept trying to get Rosie interested in TV. If you knew her, especially how she was back then, you'd realise how perfect she was for the small screen. Then a miracle happened – a minor one. A *Blue Peter* presenter had to be away for a few weeks and I suggested they trial Rosie as a stand-in.'

'You got her her first big break?'

'I'm proud to say I did.'

'What was she like?'

'Like no one else. When she smiled, the whole room was alight. She had this way of putting people at their ease – complete strangers. Such a talent. She knew just what to say, how to make people feel good about themselves.'

'How close were you?'

'We worked together Monday to Friday: 6 to 9.30 on screen. We arrived around 5 and we would spend an hour together after the show, having breakfast, talking about what had worked, what hadn't, ideas for features.'

'And out of work?'

'Noooo. That was quite enough time together. We didn't socialise outside work.'

Jason drank his tea and offered the biscuits around, before taking one himself.

'Did you know Danny?' Judith asked.

'A little. I didn't like him much, before you ask. And that was from the beginning, before…you know.'

'Why not?'

'I worried for Rosie. I'd seen the papers, like everyone else, all the scrapes he got himself into. She didn't deserve it. And I worried about what didn't make the cut too, what the papers wanted to say, but didn't dare. Most footballers back then, in the Noughties – maybe it's no different now – they were not faithful to their wives, especially the big names.'

'Did you ever have reason to think Danny was having an affair?'

'No. I'll give him that. He seemed to love her, you know, loads of flowers on her birthday, that kind of thing, and he was never caught with anyone else…'

'Like you say, it wouldn't have been good for the breakfast

show?'

'I just cared about Rosie.'

'Of course. How long did you front the show together?'

'It's coming up to eight years now.'

'But you began without her?'

'After the *Blue Peter* success, I tried to get her out front again. She'd have been pushing on an open door with the producers, but she was worried about the kids, especially with Danny being away so much.'

'What changed?'

'He retired from football in 2010, went into coaching. I suppose the kids were older too. And I negotiated a pretty good deal for her. It was hard for her to refuse.'

'She was well paid?'

'How do you think I afford all this?' He waved his arms around and both Constance and Judith found themselves staring at Jason's portrait. He turned around and grinned.

'Before you say anything, I do know that I am not a reigning monarch. Rochelle had it commissioned for my fortieth. I could hardly consign it to the downstairs toilet.'

Judith and Constance exchanged glances.

'Did Rosie ever tell you that Danny had been violent towards her?' Judith asked.

'I wish she had. I'd have told her to leave him then and there, instead of…well, the divorce was very hard for her.'

'In what way?'

'Oh come on! She was a beautiful, intelligent, desirable woman and her husband betrayed her in that…despicable way. She got through it…but she wasn't the same afterwards. It was like a light had gone out inside. The public never saw it – she was the consummate professional – but, occasionally, when she let her guard down, I could see how shattered she was.'

'Did *you* suggest the divorce?'

'Me?'

'I just wondered, an old friend, her "second husband", that's what Laura called you – you might have advised her on what was best, in one of your post-breakfast show chats.'

'I didn't argue with her when it came up.'

'But you told her to keep Danny's transition…to Debbie…you told her to keep it quiet.'

Jason shifted his weight from one side of his plumped up cushion to the other. 'Look, it was impossible to keep it totally under wraps; that was never going to happen,' he said. 'But I advised her to say nothing and ride it out, no public statements, just business as usual. That suited her too. It was in the papers for a week, maybe two, a few unattractive photographs and that was it. She could move on. And she was lucky that Danny's playing career was over and he wasn't having the best time as a manager, and West Ham, well I mean it's not Chelsea, is it? He wasn't big news any more.'

'Did Rosie and Danny remain on good terms, once he became Debbie?'

'She never said a word against him, but I could tell how hard it was for her.'

'Did he ever visit the studio?'

'Not that I remember.'

'What about her children? Did she talk about them?'

'Of course. She adored those kids.'

'Were they close?'

'Absolutely.' Judith stared at Jason. The confirmation had been rather over the top.

'And her parents?'

'Her father died in the last two years or so. I got the impression she wasn't close to her mother. All the stuff with Danny's transition – I think she was most worried about what her mother would say, and I don't think Elaine disappointed.'

'Did she receive any threats from viewers?' Constance chipped in, remembering Laura's words.

'She had her fair share of people writing nasty stuff. Either they didn't like the features, or they were cross they couldn't get on air with their pet projects. But you must know about Nicki Smith; local girl turned international campaigner?'

'Nicki Smith?'

'She runs campaigns, pressure groups.'

'What kind of pressure groups?'

'All sorts of things. At the moment she's on the climate change bandwagon. She was one of the ringleaders of the protests in Trafalgar Square. It was her face on the front of…I think it was the *Telegraph*. You'll have seen it. She's very striking. Has a prominent scar on her face, though. What a shame. You can't miss it.'

'Did Nicki Smith threaten Rosie?' Constance persisted.

'She wanted to get on the show to talk about the third runway at Heathrow, probably…ooh…two years ago, and she also asked Rosie to help campaign against it. And that was a problem.'

'Why?'

'Our contracts don't allow us to get involved in anything political, although I accept there's sometimes a fine line to be drawn between charitable work and political agendas. Rosie agreed Nicki could come on the show, but she explained she couldn't get involved personally.'

'And what happened?'

'Just before they went on air, our researcher found out that, in Hackney, where Nicki lives, they'll probably be better off with a third runway. With the increased air traffic, the planes will be forced to turn much further away from Heathrow, so the noise around there is likely to be far less than it is now. They decided to pull the slot.'

'That sounds wrong?'

'That's what we were told. It was in the news.'

'And Nicki wasn't happy.'

'She blamed Rosie. She kept writing in. She always stopped short of anything really direct, but the tone was threatening.'

'Do you have an address for her?

'I think she provided it, but I wouldn't advise going there. Once she knows who you are, she won't let you go. She hounded Rosie – endless emails. Then she started with Rosie's personal mobile; texts and WhatsApp – we don't know how she got the number – and then on Twitter too. Rosie blocked her in the end.'

'And you say this started two years ago. Was it still going on?'

'A few weeks back, Rosie told me that Nicki knew where she lived. Nicki was standing on the corner of Rosie's street when Rosie arrived home. When Rosie made it clear she'd seen her, Nicki just walked away.'

'Did she tell the police?'

'They said Nicki hadn't done anything wrong. Maybe it was a coincidence she was on Rosie's street, but to keep a note if she saw her again.'

'Do you think she was involved in Rosie's murder?'

Jason shrugged. 'I just know what I told you, and I told it to the police.'

'The emails, text messages from Nicki, do you have any of them?'

'I think they all went to Rosie.'

'Can you check?'

'You think there might be something there?'

'Who knows?'

'You've been very helpful, thank you, especially when you are so busy. Is there anything else we should know about?' Constance asked.

'I just wondered, did no one see anything? It's a great, big long road, where she lives...lived. I mean, my money's on Danny, but I'm trying to keep an open mind, here. Didn't the neighbours see anything?'

'We're not able to tell you that. I'm sorry.'

'Of course. I understand. What about the dog?'

'The dog?'

'I just meant what's going to happen to the dog, Rosie's dog? She was so fond of it.'

Judith shook her head. 'I don't know. I hadn't thought. I'm sure someone is looking after it. We could find out for you. Were you offering?'

Jason's expression epitomised horror, mixed with shame in equal measure. 'Nn...no,' he stammered. 'I mean, I love dogs, but Rochelle. She's very house-proud. Can you imagine what it would do to our carpets?'

Judith stifled a smile.

'How did you know Rosie was dead?' Constance asked, as they stood up to leave.

'I had a call, from the police. They told me the awful news. I was devastated. I shut myself away in my bedroom, had quite a migraine. Rochelle will tell you. I was inconsolable.'

Constance nodded slowly. 'Yes, it must have been awful for you,' she said.

***

Nicki Smith sat in her darkened flat, overlooking Broadway Market, her eyes closed, elbows tucked in tight to her waist, the tips of her fingers meeting, wigwam fashion. The headphones enveloping her ears were sending soothing noises through. She was testing out a new mindfulness podcast, the calming words slowly seeping into her head, her breathing steady – 'In through the nose, out through the mouth,' – count down from ten, her chest rising and falling.

She always made time, every day, for these relaxation exercises. Before that, she had been prone to angry outbursts and the slightest perceived injustice could set her off. But a chance encounter with an altruistic probation officer had changed her life. She'd listened to the CD he gave her all the way through and been surprised how calm she felt afterwards. She had replayed it from the beginning and listened again. In fact, she had listened to it twelve times that night they took her in for something – she couldn't even remember now what it was, it was so long ago. She had been released early the next morning. That, she did remember. And so the CD, and the slow breathing exercises, became her lucky charm, her rabbit's foot.

Nicki wasn't to know that the probation officer had tried the programme himself and found it irritating, making it an easy giveaway, and that the later charges against her had been dropped because of a technicality. One thing she did know, when she left the custody of HM Prisons at the tender age of 21, was that there was no way she was ever going back inside.

The podcast finished, Nicki exhaled loudly, removed her headphones and stared out across the room. She reached for her mobile phone, scrolling through a series of messages and then making her first call.

'I only switched off for twenty minutes,' she said, in response to some remonstration at the other end of the line.

'It's all arranged, don't worry,' she continued. 'I'll be there and I have a whole team on hand.

'…If you want fifty, you can have fifty, 500 you can have 500.

'…And what kind of people?

'…What do you think I mean? I mean usually it's a mix, but sometimes it looks better to have a few oldies or some people with disabilities. Plus the wheelchairs make more problems for the police.

'…No. It's all down to how we advertise.

'…You want us there by 10?

'…No problem.

'…Anything for a good cause and you know how much I believe in this one.

'…We'll show them this time. We need to keep going to build up traction.

'…See you tomorrow.'

Nicki drew back the curtains and flung open her window, allowing the bustle of the fruit market to overspill her space. Some people found it too loud and invasive. They double-glazed their windows and kept their blinds down. Nicki loved it; life was made for interaction and confrontation. Otherwise, how would you ever know you were alive?

She crossed the room to the hallway and the mirror next to her front door. She stood for a few moments, side on, admiring her reflection; a flawless complexion, wide mouth, high cheekbones, full brows and a head of thick, mahogany, cork-screw curls. Then she turned her left side towards the mirror and the image changed. A long, jagged scar splayed out across her left cheek, extending from just below her eye to her jawline. She ran her finger along its length, first down and then back up. But it remained just as present and distinct after her touch as before. With a slight twitch of her lips she grabbed her phone from her bag and returned to her chair, connecting it to her laptop and entering a series of passwords.

Now she could see, clearly, what she had filmed an hour earlier; two women, one older and white, a walking advertisement for Selfridges, one younger and black, sporting a mixture of what looked, to her trained eye, to be Zara and Mango, entering Jason Fenwick's mansion. 'Interesting,' she muttered. She watched them sit down in his living room and engage in animated conversation. She highlighted each of their faces in turn, and searched them against her database; no matches. Then, following a hunch, she googled 'Rosie Harper' and 'lawyer'; nothing. Tutting at herself, she replaced the search with 'Debbie Mallard' and 'lawyer'. And, there it was, in *The Sun*. 'Debbie Mallard appoints local solicitor Constance Lamb to defend her.'

Nicki wouldn't normally spend her afternoon staking out celebrity's properties, especially those she disliked. But, given Rosie's death and the interview she had granted the police recently – there hadn't been much choice, but they had kept it short and civil – she saw this as a necessary precaution.

'Constance Lamb, let's take a look at you, then.' She opened

Constance's contact page on the Taylor Moses website. 'Ah, there you are.'

It didn't take long for her to track the list of Constance's most high-profile cases, and find Judith too.

'So, I wonder what Jason's been telling you two. I think I can probably guess.'

***

'Why does everyone insist on talking about the dog?' Judith asked Constance, as they marched away from Hanover Terrace, skimming Regents Park, on their way to the underground station.

'He just said Rosie loved her dog.'

'He didn't ask how Debbie was or the children, just the dog.'

'People love their pets. If I died, would you look after my dog?' Constance said.

'You don't have a dog. Do you know that one of the papers, the *Mail* I think, published a letter from a reader asking whether the dog would have been traumatised by seeing Rosie's dead body. Really. The dog!'

'And what was the answer?'

'I don't know. I was so astounded at the question, I didn't read on.'

Constance tutted. 'Animals are sensitive you know. I bet she knew something was wrong.'

'Forget the dog. I think Mr Fenwick hasn't told us quite everything.'

'Really?'

'He was hesitant more than once. That tends to mean some economy with the truth. Not always, and I'm not sure if it's anything important. Either he is being loyal to Rosie and doesn't want to break confidences or he's hiding something.'

'He was happy to take credit for her success, wasn't he? And he said she didn't take the job at first, because of her kids. Laura obviously didn't know that. She just complained about her absent mother.'

'Not that surprising, is it? Children often focus on the deficiencies of their parents, rather than their self-sacrifice...so I'm told. And you saw Ben Mallard. How was he?'

'Desperate, sad, lonely. Angry at his mother for pushing his father away.'

'How angry?'

'Oh no. I don't think *that* angry.'

'Who knows? We have experience of what adolescent boys can do, when they're all fired up.'

Constance knew that Judith was referring to the first case they had worked on together, involving a murder in a boys' school, where they had successfully defended one of the pupils. They had both been surprised by the depth of feeling of some of the boys they encountered there.

'And I met the uncle, Ellis, still only briefly, after spying on him the other day. No chance to ask him very much,' she said.

'Hm. How did you find him?'

'Friendly but a bit...assertive; the kind of man who's confident he's right all the time.'

'I thought they all were.'

'He asked us not to call them as witnesses, both of them, Ben and Laura. Said they'd been through enough, hinted that Ben has a history of mental instability. He asked if we'd have to disclose it.'

'What did you say?'

'That we would consider everything before reaching a decision. And I know Debbie said she doesn't like him, but he seems to be keeping a close eye on Ben, cooking for him, just being around, which I'm sure Ben needs, at the moment.'

'That's good. I might go and see Uncle Ellis myself then. He's already met you and he may well have quizzed Ben on what you were interested in. I could try a new angle. I'll put my thinking cap on. Anyone else in the family we should talk to?'

'The mothers; Rosie's and Debbie's. And I'll see who else might be connected. Do you want me to talk to him again? Jason, that is.'

'Maybe. Why don't you do some digging around first, including a few minutes on this Nicki Smith. Sounds like it will be easy to find her in the news, if she's a serial protester, like Jason says.'

***

'This anti-Heathrow stuff is really complicated.' Constance was skimming through pages on her laptop, once they were safely ensconced in her office. 'I mean, loads of environmental groups are involved. I didn't realise. They say it breaches climate-change agreements, as well as causing noise pollution and traffic congestion. And with the stats about air quality, I don't understand why people don't just travel less. Especially now it's getting warmer. Do we really need to fly halfway across the world to fry on a beach and risk skin cancer? We always complain about the hotel and the weather and the delay. Maybe we should all just stay at home.'

Judith laughed. 'Watch out! You're beginning to sound like me!' she said. 'Although I heard a rumour the younger generation were more switched on to environmental issues. My lot were always too preoccupied with securing equality between humans to think about the planet. What about travel as a means of broadening horizons? If Marco Polo had felt like that, we would never have discovered China, although some people these days might think that preferable.'

'But it's costing £14bn. I never realised. You could fund a lot of hospitals with £14bn.'

'So you think Nicki Smith has a point. Fair enough. Is there anything in there about her?'

'Yes. A lot, all toxic.'

'How "toxic"?' Judith asked.

'She's leader of this group called Dead Earth. They're supposed to be environmentalists, but they're more extreme than most. Greenpeace has distanced itself from them. Same message, but they use graphic images and threats. I can see them tweeting at politicians. And Jason was right that she's been involved in lots of other pressure groups – too many to count – but the common theme is anti-government policy. I could spend a couple of hours and then give you a summary.'

'Ask Dawson first. You need to follow up the DNA evidence with him anyway, don't you? The glove, the murder weapon. And has Jason found any of those messages she sent to Rosie?'

'Not yet...'

'Dawson ought to have them anyway, if they were sent to Rosie's laptop. That will be quite enough to do, so I can't spare you to sit trawling the internet all day. Given what Jason said, Dawson should, at least, have interviewed Nicki to see if she has an alibi. If he hasn't, he isn't the police officer I thought he was.'

14

'I SEE THE ROSIE HARPER CASE has been keeping you busy.' Greg lifted his first piece of sashimi expertly up to his mouth, while Constance sipped her miso soup from a bamboo spoon. A rendez-vous in Itsu, close to her office, was all Constance would accept when Greg asked her to meet for lunch. This time he was wearing shorts and, although it was a hot day and she was the one who was clearly overdressed, Constance couldn't decide if he looked good in them or not. It must be difficult when you got older, she thought, deciding how to dress. That conflict between desperately hanging onto your youth and ageing gracefully. Greg must be at least forty-five, she supposed. Would she still wear shorts at forty-five? And would he have worn shorts to meet Judith?

'How do you know that?' she said.

'It was in the papers. There was a photo of you…going into Hackney police station.'

Greg offered her some fish, but she shook her head.

'How's the case going?' he asked.

'The case isn't the problem. The media interest is a nightmare; newspapers and social media and maybe even TV now.'

'It has all the ingredients.'

'And the press seems to know stuff before we do. But we don't want to complain that it's prejudicial, because some of it might help Debbie in the long run, except we don't know that yet and we don't want to draw attention to the stuff which won't. There's a leak from somewhere though. Judith said she spoke to Charlie – Inspector Dawson – about it and he said he would make sure it hadn't come from his team.'

'I'm sure that's what he said. I know Judith rated his father, not sure what she thinks of the son. You mentioned TV?'

'Yes.'

'I don't want to interfere, but I know the man who's funding the new TV channel, "Court TV". He also backed my Trixter app.'

'Oh!'

'You know they're not just doing a live screening, don't you?'

'What else are they planning?'

'All sorts of things. He was full of it, when I saw him yesterday. The hearing will be live during the day and, in the evenings, there'll be a two- or three-hour session, with experts coming in to talk about the case. And, in between, lots of advertisements; that's mainly how they make their money, but he said it's going to be "interactive" with the public. He didn't elaborate, but I can guess what that means.'

This information was not music to Constance's ears. It suggested lots of discussion of the case, with the obvious possibility of people having opinions on what they had seen, which was always dangerous to allow while the case was in progress.

'Judith thinks we should ignore it and carry on,' she said, which was not an entirely truthful precis of Judith's position.

Greg finished his mouthful and laid his chopsticks down on his tray. 'They're predicting at least one million viewers for the opening,' he said. 'And a big campaign is starting tomorrow, posters on the underground, ads on local radio and in all the major newspapers. I'm telling you, the man is slick, he knows what he's doing and he's putting together a huge research team. He doesn't do anything by halves. He wants a noisy, booming, record-breaking debut. You can't ignore it. Judith is wrong on this one.'

Constance pushed her lunch away. Now she wished she hadn't chosen Itsu. Greg had squeezed himself in, wedged between the window and the low, round table, their knees were almost touching and she would have to push past him to leave. 'Eat beautiful' it said on her napkin. She liked the strapline. Judith would hate it, would point out that it wasn't grammatically correct, would think, and might even say, that it was a shame no one had advised the Japanese owners of their mistake, before they daubed it liberally through their marketing material and wrote it above every outlet. Constance would think, but not say, that the 'beautiful' was deliberately addressed to the customer. That it was sublime marketing. 'Eat this and you become beautiful.' That's what it said to her. She dabbed at her mouth.

'You need to plan for this; the impact on you, Judith, Debbie Mallard, the witnesses and maybe even the jury of having all these people watching – and not just watching: analysing, commenting, criticising, sharing.'

'They won't be allowed to do all that; there are still rules.' Constance clung to her previously held positive views of the scheme, despite Greg's revelations.

'This guy will sail close to the wind and worry about the repercussions later, I'm telling you. You need to be prepared.'

Constance eased the plastic lid onto her pot of soup, even though it was still half-full. Then she reached past Greg and dropped it into the bin. 'What should we do?' she said. 'We have a preliminary hearing next week, but we weren't planning to say much about the TV angle.'

Greg shrugged. 'That's your territory,' he said. 'I wouldn't dream of advising you. But my experience, for what it's worth, is that people behave differently when they think the whole world is watching them…and judging them. And I don't just mean the little people.'

Greg finished his food and he smiled at Constance.

'I'm sorry,' he said. 'I'm keeping you from great piles of work.'

'That's OK. I probably haven't been very good company. It was nice to get out though.'

'Should I walk with you, back to the office? It's the same direction as the Tube.'

'No. I need a few things from the shops,' Constance said. 'Thanks for lunch. I'll call you.'

Constance waited until Greg had left, before heading straight back to her office. She needed to think up how to drop into her next conversation with Judith, all the things Greg had just told her about the new TV channel. But without conceding that Judith might have been right after all and without giving away their source. She sensed this wasn't a good time to reveal a lunch date with Greg, however informal.

15

ANDY WAS ON HIS WAY to court when the call came through. It was Phil, Graham's assistant, who delivered the good news. 'Calling on Graham's behalf', 'pleased to offer you the job', 'got the green light for all our plans', 'get you in for some rehearsals'. Andy processed the key messages swiftly, in accordance with his years of legal training.

Despite wanting to jump six feet in the air and whoop and shout, he settled for a more modest 'that's wonderful news' before remembering himself sufficiently to ask what terms he was being offered.

'I'll send something across to look at,' Phil said, 'but I don't think you're going to be disappointed. Put it that way.'

'I'll look forward to it, then. Hm, if you've "got the green light" does that mean it isn't secret any more?'

'Wait, just a minute.' Andy was put on hold and stepped back into a shop doorway. 'Listen,' Phil resumed their conversation, 'Graham says you can tell your wife and anyone at work who needs to approve your three-month absence, on the basis that they keep it confidential too. After we announce the line-up, in the next couple of days, then you can go public. How's that sound?'

'Very clear. All fine, thank you.'

Andy continued his journey, his limbs carrying him forwards, his mind occupied elsewhere. Try as he might to remain focused on the job in hand - a rather nasty assault and battery charge he was prosecuting – the life-changing possibilities of what had just happened to him, were getting in the way. He should call Clare, he knew that, and tell her everything, from the first meeting with Graham to the negotiations with Phil. But the hours were likely to be a sore point. Clare wanted him around more at the moment, and this opportunity would keep him away. The only way to sell it would be as something short-term; short-term pain for long-term gain. That might work.

And then the email from Phil pinged into his inbox and he had to open it. Skipping through the preamble, he sought out the remuneration clause and his heart missed a beat. Wow! More than he had ever imagined; a year's pay in three months. And that bonus provision was there too; a sliding scale; the more viewers he pulled in, the more he was going to get paid. They could have the family holiday that never happened last year, they could think about moving to a place with a garden, they could even contemplate some more help at home, to ease the pain of his absence. He might never have to mop up spilt Coco Pops or clean the toilet ever again.

But it wasn't just the remuneration he would receive from Horizon, it was the doors it would open for him afterwards and for ever more. There may easily be spin-off shows or features on other programmes. He may never have to hang around police stations at night ever again.

He had a rare moment of panic. If things were going public soon, he'd have to tart up his profile on the chambers' website. He'd been meaning to improve things for a while – a newer photograph, updating his key areas of expertise. And what about social media? Clare had persuaded him to adopt that awful photograph as his Facebook backdrop because she said he looked 'wistful'. He'd have to delete it, and some of the ones from his most recent night out with his old school friends, and replace them with a host of wholesome family snaps.

Forcing himself to focus and relax, he scrolled back through to the top of the job-offer terms again and stared at the job title with pride and expectation. 'Chief legal adviser and presenter - Court TV'. What a coup. What an achievement. He was heading for the big time.'

16

JUDITH AND CONSTANCE sat opposite Debbie in a room with pale green walls at Denmow prison. Constance's primary school had green walls. She had asked her form teacher, Miss Singh, why everything was green and she'd shrugged and said, 'Better than purple, isn't it, Constance?' Since then, she'd read that green was considered soothing; Dulux advised that 'celadon, eau de nil and mint green' created 'a peaceful ambiance and relieved tension'. No doubt the prison service had considered how appropriate that would be as a backdrop for prisoners' consultations or perhaps, given the current trend for feature walls and bold colours, this was just what was left behind in the paint shop.

Debbie sat very still, her back straight, her chest hardly rising and falling, although her fingers crept up to her neck once or twice, retreating disappointed; her valuables had been packed away before her incarceration and there was no necklace this time to occupy them.

'I hate the way she looks at us every time we arrive,' Constance had confessed to Judith on their journey over, 'like she thinks we're going to tell her it was all a big mistake, and then we don't.'

'A mistake? What? That Rosie's sitting at home with an intact cranium?'

Constance closed her lips tight.

'I hadn't noticed,' Judith continued. 'You're better at that sort of thing than I am. It must be preferable that she still has hope, though? Otherwise, we'd have even more of a mountain to climb.'

Judith had been careful to watch Debbie as she entered the room today. And it was true that Debbie scrutinised each of them in turn, her eyes roving over their faces, exploring and probing. And that, by the time they were seated, that sharpness had gone.

'Hi, Debbie. We have a court hearing tomorrow, where we are going to ask for a few things, mostly procedural. But we have some questions for you, things it would be good to clarify now, just in case. In particular, to try and work out who might be good witnesses for you and who the prosecution might want to testify against you. Is that OK?'

'I'm not going anywhere, am I?'

Debbie hardly moved as she spoke.

'Can we talk about the day of Rosie's murder again?' Judith leaned back in her chair, hoping her own movement might elicit something reciprocal from Debbie. No one liked to interview a statue.

'But we've been over it so many times before,' Debbie said.

'You left Rosie at, what, 2pm, 2.10?' Judith said.

'Around then, maybe 2.15.'

'And your training session started at 6?'

'Yes.'

'And it's, what, twenty minutes on your moped from one place to the other?'

'Depends on traffic and on where I can park the bike, but roughly that, yes.'

'Where did you go in between?'

'I went home. I told you before.'

'Which is, what, fifteen minutes away?'

'I wanted to grab some lunch, change, pick up my stuff: cones and flags. One of the girls brings the balls. It's not easy to bring them on my bike.'

'Didn't Rosie offer you lunch?'

'No.'

'You usually start at 5pm, don't you?'

'I sometimes do an earlier session for kids who want to get into the team. I cancelled it that day.'

'Why?'

'When I arranged things with Rosie, I thought we might need to talk for longer, that I might hang around to see Ben, after school.'

'Why was that?'

'We were talking about what he was going to do, next year, in sixth form.'

'So you anticipated that your session with Rosie might go on and then you would have to go straight into your 6pm training?'

'Yes.'

'Did you have your *stuff* with you then, the cones and flags you just mentioned? I imagine you wouldn't leave them on your moped.'

Debbie's face coloured. 'No,' she said hotly. 'I must have forgotten them.'

'What clothes were you wearing when you went to visit Rosie?'

'Nothing special, a blue tracksuit.'

'Which you were wearing later on for training?'

'Yes.' Debbie huffed.

'You didn't change your clothes, then, when you arrived home, after all?'

'No, I...I just didn't. I can't remember why now.'

Judith and Constance exchanged looks.

'Isn't that good enough? The police checked my clothes. They said there was nothing on them. You don't have to be a rocket scientist to know that if I had battered my wife to death there might have been just a tiny bit of her blood on my clothing. Oh God!' Debbie lay her head in her hands.

'We only have your word that is what you were wearing earlier in the day,' Judith said. 'Constance, we should look at ways of corroborating that – other people who might have seen Debbie. Street cameras – that kind of thing – would be useful.'

'But the other stuff isn't, is it?' Debbie looked up. 'About leaving the kit at home.'

'Not terrible, but it's an anomaly and juries hate anomalies. At best it makes you look disorganised.' Judith's words hung in the air.

'Oh,' Constance said, remembering her visit to East Road. 'Isn't there a camera outside the front of Rosie's house? That will help.'

'It doesn't work.'

'It doesn't work?'

'It's just an empty box. It did work for a few months, then Rosie got fed up with having it monitored. I don't know why, but I could never get her to take security seriously. She thought she was... invincible, I suppose.'

'That's a shame then, about the camera. But there must be other ways to check. Where is your moped?' Judith asked.

'The police took it.'

'Does it have any kind of tracker? That could help with times as well, couldn't it?'

'It's eight years old. But you can check.'

'And your phone is with the police too, is it?'

'Yes.'

'And that's also old?'

'It's the latest iPhone. Ben insisted, when I was having problems with my ancient model. He took me to the Apple shop. I don't use half the features. They got a very good deal out of me.'

'Connie. You need to talk to Dawson and get access to Debbie's phone. I can't believe we haven't had it already, now I think about it. If they give you any rubbish about there being nothing relevant on it, tell them we will apply immediately to court.'

'Why is it so important, suddenly?' The spark was lit momentarily in Debbie's eyes.

'Even I know that these new phones track your whereabouts and whether you are stationary or moving. It won't solve the crime, but it will go a long way to corroborate what you say about the time you arrived and left and going home in the middle.'

Debbie smiled weakly. 'Good. That sounds good.'

'Can we take a minute to talk about your public image?' Judith asked. 'You were often on the front pages and not always for playing football?'

'So what?'

'It may be used against you, to…show that you're not such an upstanding citizen.'

'Do I really have to worry about any of that, when it was nothing…and years ago.'

'It's part of your public image.'

'Look, I was a kid from the East End and all these doors opened for me. I wasn't going to stand outside and watch the others go in, was I? But it was all harmless stuff.'

'All of it?'

'All of it.' Debbie shifted her weight forward for the first time and sniffed loudly.

'All right. What about on the pitch? You had a few nasty moments.'

'I only ever had two red cards. Sure, I would take other players on, that's how I played, but I was never reckless.'

'What about the tackle on Craig Mosby, in the FA Cup semi-final?' Judith looked on with astonishment, as Constance asked her question. 'His leg was broken in two places. It almost ended his career.'

'All right, maybe that one time. But I slipped. It wasn't deliberate. Anyone could see that on the replay. Craig knew that too. We had a photo together, in the hospital. And it was years ago.'

'Tell us about George Scopos?' Judith continued.

'He's the West Ham owner.' Debbie frowned before replying. 'We…disagreed over the new hires,' she said, 'and he asked me to leave.'

'So the prosecution will bring someone from the world of football, maybe him, most probably the person who liked you least. Have a think who that might be and who we could put forward to say nice things about you. We have the girls you coach now, which is great.'

'I don't want you bringing them into this. They're all kids and they don't need it.'

'Your sentiments are very noble, but this is a murder trial. If I were you, I would accept help where it's offered. Can we go back to Rosie's parents now?' Judith asked.

Debbie scowled at Judith. 'How is any of this relevant?' she said.

'It's relevant to motive. Would you rather discuss this with us now or, for the first time, in front of the jury?'

'Her father is dead. Her mother, Elaine, and me, no, we really don't get on. I've already told you that too.'

'Yes, you called her a *witch* as I remember. Why didn't you get on?'

'They thought Rosie should have married better. She had met Prince Harry when he set up those Games, her programme covered it. That was more what Elaine wanted for her precious daughter.'

'Did they tell you that?'

'Rosie told me, laughed it off. When I didn't laugh, she tried to dress it up with fancy words; her parents worried we were *not compatible*, we had to give them time, as I was *different from other men she'd dated*. But they never liked me. Her father wasn't even going to walk her down the aisle. Point blank refused.'

'What happened?'

'Rosie could be very persuasive. She worked on him till he agreed.'

'How did that make you feel?'

'Is that what they're going to say? That I was full of hatred and resentment since my wedding day and it all boiled over. I wasn't that bothered, really. I was only upset because it hurt Rosie.'

'Elaine will be a witness. What will she say?'

'That I ruined her daughter's life. That her husband's heart attack was because of me, the shock of hearing about me.'

'And what do you say to that?'

'That I was a good husband, always, in every respect.'

'Supportive?'

'Yes.'

'Loving?'

'Yes.'

'Interested in Rosie's wellbeing?'

'Yes.'

'Faithful?'

Debbie was silent. Constance caught her breath. She would never have asked that question.

'Were you faithful to your wife?' Judith asked again and the room shrank in size. Did Constance imagine it or did Judith's lips twitch at the word 'faithful'?

Debbie stood up and crossed to the tiny window. She lay her hand against the pane, noticed her fingernail was broken and rubbed it against its neighbouring finger. 'Not in the way you mean,' she said.

'There's only one way to be unfaithful in my book.'

'It was right at the end and we were already getting the divorce. We were together for twenty years and I never strayed, even though there was lots of temptation. I was…experimenting, enjoying some freedom again.'

'And will the other willing participant in this *celebration of liberty* have anything to say publicly, do you think?'

'No, definitely not.'

'I hope not, for your sake.'

Debbie reached up and plucked at her hair, curling a strand around her index finger.

'Why did you marry Rosie?' Constance asked.

'I loved her,' Debbie said. 'I loved her more than anyone else I had ever met. And I still do.'

Judith closed her note book. 'Can you see that your declaration of love for Rosie, may be...difficult for people to accept, given your divorce and your transition?' she asked.

'I see that,' Debbie said, 'but it's still the truth.'

'All right. One thing we need to decide is whether or not you give evidence in your own defence, which is particularly pertinent, as you keep vetoing my recommended defence witnesses. How do you feel about that?'

'I want to, I think. I want to be able to tell people, to tell the jury, what I just told you. If you believe me, I hope they will too.'

Debbie returned to her seat.

'After tomorrow's hearing, we'll consider everything and talk to you again, though we won't decide finally until nearer the trial. But, if you do give evidence, you have to stay calm, like you are today. Do you understand? No shouting, no swearing, no nasty comments, no sarcasm, no theatricals. Just calm and understated.'

'I'm not stupid.'

'I can see you're not. I am advising you that it's not easy to keep your cool, when you are in the spotlight and questions are being fired at you from all directions. Connie will update you on what happens tomorrow, and any questions, just let us know. Have you thought again about bail?'

'I'm going to stay here,' Debbie said, although she stared for a moment too long through the window. 'It's quiet and everyone leaves me alone. I read and the kids visit. Not much of a summer for them really, is it? Ben was hoping to go away with his friends.'

'I'm sure he'll have plenty of time to do that, once this is all over. You make sure you look after yourself, then.'

***

As Debbie was led out and along the corridor back to her cell, Constance whispered to Judith, 'Did you see what I meant, about how she looked at us?'

'She's scared and trying not to show it and I'm not surprised.'

'Scared of being found guilty?'

'That, yes, but I think she's also scared of being judged by us, on all the choices she's made about how to live her life. And, sadly, we're likely to be more generous in our appreciation of some of those issues than the general public will be.'

'Will you put her on the stand?'

'I don't know. We don't have to. We can make a defence around the lack of evidence and pick apart the circumstantial stuff they have. That might be enough. At least she was calmer today, like I said, more measured, until you caught her out about that tackle. She didn't like that one bit.'

'She didn't like me hinting she'd been irresponsible.'

'We'll have to remember the things which might set her off and make sure we avoid mentioning them in court. But we can't stop the prosecution.'

Constance sat back down and replaced her laptop deliberately on the table. This was her opportunity to bring up the things Greg had told her.

'I thought you were going to tell her about the new pilot scheme,' she said.

'You tell her. You don't need me for that.'

'You know, I've heard there won't just be a live feed,' Constance said. 'There's going to be a new channel, Court TV, in the day, showing the trial live, and a special current affairs programme in the evenings, commenting on the day in court with experts. It's much more…informal than I expected. What do you think?'

'I think they could have been a bit more imaginative with the name…'

'I didn't mean that.'

Judith puffed out her cheeks. 'OK. I can see why they want our case for their little experiment. Shame on them.'

'Debbie wasn't specially selected. They'd chosen a date for it to start. And they're not calling it an experiment.'

'You don't really believe that, do you? It's an experiment. A "scheme", and we – well, Debbie – is the guinea pig. And they want the scheme to be successful, because you can't even begin to imagine how many hoops they had to jump through, just to get to today. Someone important really wanted this. You think they're going to allow it to kick off with some spotty youth, up on a shoplifting charge?'

'You're always so suspicious…'

'And I'm usually right.'

'But does it change how we prepare the case?'

'God, no. Why should it? We can't allow it to. It will be just the same, except people can tune in and watch us, if they want.'

'Do we need to make any special applications at tomorrow's hearing, maybe?'

Judith walked towards the door and rang the bell to be released.

'One or two things, I suppose, nothing major. I have it all in hand.'

'I didn't think you'd be so…calm about it all.'

Judith squeezed a smile.

'Perhaps that's what comes from years of dealing with the unexpected.'

17

JUDITH COULD HEAR THE spectators long before she saw them. Not just their voices, raised in anticipation, high-pitched with enthusiasm and curiosity, but the sounds of their feet on the stairs, the patter of their expectancy, radiating out to engulf her two floors above.

She dived into the nearest ladies' toilet and checked her appearance in the mirror before adjusting her horsehair wig with a grimace. She knew of the school of thought that the more discoloured her ancient head covering appeared, the greater sense of authority it imbued. But she genuinely couldn't remember when she last had it cleaned and that really couldn't be a good thing.

Even though this was only a short hearing, most likely a couple of hours, Judith's pulse was racing. People assumed it got easier, that she took it in her stride, that she could just pick up the papers on her way to court and deliver a perfect performance. And while there were benefits to being older – not least that judges tended to take what you said more seriously than when you were new, and that you developed a sense for what they were really after when they posed an impenetrable or rambling question – she did find, these days, that her memory was not as good as in the past. Names, dates, places, she needed to have them written down, just as a reminder, as a failsafe.

She peered closer into the mirror and traced her crow's feet, with her index finger. She had a pair of reading glasses at home, recommended after her last eye test, and had discovered, when she caught sight of her reflection while wearing them, that the frames covered up all the lines around her eyes and the bridge of her nose. That had softened the blow a little, but there was no way she was wearing them in public; not yet.

Judith pictured Debbie's face beside her own, etched with insecurity and fear; fear of being convicted, not for the crime of which she was accused, but for choosing to be Debbie.

She thought about plastic surgery patients, not the frivolous kind, but the ones who have their faces reconstructed after accidents or burns. Did they recognise themselves in the mirror or were they constantly shocked at the change in their appearance? Was that what it was like for Debbie? How was it when she had first walked down the street as Debbie and spied herself reflected in shop windows and car wing mirrors and men's sunglasses? Did she see a stranger or did she see the person she had always wanted to be, inside her head?

Judith had heard that the first 'face transplant' patient had required extensive counselling to help the process along. What help had Debbie had with her transition? She hadn't only taken on a new face – she had a new gender, a new life, a new persona. And Rosie had not been supportive. Had that left her frustrated, bitter, angry, violent?

Judith applied a light coat of neutral lipstick. Today was not the day to make a big splash with crimson or plum. Today she needed to be focused and composed and to make her points with quiet determination and little controversy. She didn't want to find her words splashed across tomorrow's papers.

***

Jeremy Laidlaw, Counsel for the prosecution, was already in court when Judith arrived and he was standing over the judge's seat, fiddling with some papers and surveying the courtroom from the heady heights of the judge's elevated platform.

'Wishful thinking,' Judith muttered to herself, as she shook hands with Leo Nimble, appearing today on behalf of the press. Judge Nolan entered at precisely 2pm, dishevelled and red in the face, frowning as she took her seat. At fifty-two years old, she was young for a judge; some said she had been promoted too soon, a beneficiary of the push to have more women in the judiciary, but Judith had found her to be bright and fair in the past, if a bit prickly.

'Now what is all this about, precisely?' the judge asked, turning first to Judith, her eyes scanning the large crowd crammed into the tiny, airless room, many of them leaning against the back wall, due to lack of sufficient seating.

Judith resisted the strong temptation to respond that if Judge Nolan had read the papers in advance she would know 'precisely' what applications Judith was proposing. Instead, she took a moment to gather her thoughts and watch Jeremy Laidlaw exchanging a wink and a nod with Leo Nimble. When he didn't volunteer any response, she rose to her feet.

'Your honour, I appear for the defence,' she began. 'I have a series of short applications, some of which are supported by Mr Laidlaw, who appears for the prosecution. They are each designed to ensure that next month's trial runs smoothly, without external interference, either real or perceived. Mr Nimble is here today, jointly instructed on behalf of a number of our national newspapers and I think it is fair to say that he opposes each of my requests, with varying degrees of ferocity.'

'Thank you, Ms Burton. I will be the judge of who is doing what and how they are doing it. Is everyone here part of one or more of the legal teams?'

'Your honour, no. There are members of the press present.'

'Well that's not acceptable, is it Mr Nimble? I suggest you ask them to leave – politely of course. Then, when we have just the lawyers present, I shall be happy to begin.'

There was a rumble of disapproval in the court room as the observers, despite their discomfort, voiced their objection in low undertones. The ones who had arrived early and secured the few available seats were particularly vociferous. Judge Nolan stared blankly at Leo Nimble and waited.

'But your honour, this is an open hearing and the press are my clients.' Mr Nimble rose onto his toes, and Judith stifled a giggle.

'Not any more it isn't,' she said.

'How will I take instructions if my clients are outside?'

Judge Nolan leaned forward and raised her eyebrows, until they were straining to take off from her face. The journalists were silent now, awaiting their fate, a couple of them with pens poised over pocket books. Judge Nolan stared at them with withering ferocity.

'God will provide, Mr Nimble,' she said. 'God will provide.'

***

In the hiatus, while members of the press shuffled out, some complaining bitterly under their breath, Judith took a moment to reassess her tactics. She had been planning to begin with a slow introduction, recounting a little of the background, leading the judge painstakingly through the facts, so that Judge Nolan would be one step ahead, when Judith reached the meat of her applications. But she sensed Judge Nolan's considerable impatience, not just from the commands barked out so far, but also from the way she was flicking through her papers and scrolling, at speed, through her computer screen, the ball on her mouse revolving like a cleanly-struck billiard ball.

And she noted Jeremy Laidlaw's familiar glances exchanged with Leo Nimble as he preened himself next to her. He may well not be as 'on side' as she had hoped. Progressing slowly might allow either of her adversaries the opportunity to take the floor, before she had really warmed up. Once things were quiet again, she decided to dive right in.

'Today's applications all relate to the same core issue. My client cannot possibly hope to have a fair hearing if steps are not taken to control media coverage and its potential impact,' she began.

'Your honour, there are adequate rules in place already to limit the press. These applications are spurious and a complete waste of the court's time.' Mr Nimble was already on his feet. Judith ignored him and ploughed on.

'Your honour, if it is of assistance, I can take you to the very many newspaper articles spawned by this case over the past two weeks, many of which have overstepped the line of responsible journalism into speculation, hyperbole and even voyeurism. As is evident from the number of people who were filling this room a moment ago, there is no doubt as to the level of interest in this trial. I am not seeking today to impugn the integrity of particular journalists or newspapers, but I worry how difficult it will be, in reality, for the press to keep quiet in the face of such a clamouring for information.'

'But the cameras are going to be in here, Ms Burton,' Judge Nolan replied, 'recording our every move. Haven't you lost your applications even before you begin?'

Judith stifled her impatience. The judge was going to need some educating after all.

'Your honour, there will be cameras in here, yes, but there are still steps which could easily and should properly be taken, important steps, in my submission, to ensure that the dignity of the trial process is maintained, as was envisaged, no doubt, by those who made the decision to film these venerable proceedings in the first place. I can take you through each of my points fairly swiftly.'

Judge Nolan checked her watch and then sat forward. 'Go on then,' she said. 'I'm on the edge of my seat.'

'Thank you. The first points concern the jury. Of course, the court has always been a public place, but there is a world of difference between sitting in a courtroom where perhaps twenty people might see your face and absolutely no one is able to take photographs, and what the cameras could potentially deliver.

'As you know the cameras are to be linked up to a TV station, Court TV, providing a live daily feed. My first application, therefore, concerns a prudent, and I say necessary, element of privacy for the jury. My request is that the cameras be positioned so that they do not film the jury at any time and...'

Judith stopped. Judge Nolan had held up her hand.

'Yes. I have the point,' she said. 'What's next?' Judith was uncertain whether Judge Nolan was totally in agreement or bored with her argument, but decided that to disobey her was probably the least best option.

'Still on the jury, this time, on how they conduct themselves,' Judith continued, noticing, out of the corner of her eye, that Jeremy Laidlaw was smirking, as she bore the brunt of Judge Nolan's abrasiveness. 'I also request that the jurors be forbidden from searching for media coverage, not...'

'Your honour, this is tedious.' Laidlaw spoke through his nose, as he allowed his fingers to rest on his bottom lip. 'We already have well-established rules for jurors.'

'Not in the usual terms. I was saying, before I was interrupted, that this time we require something more drastic and with some kind of teeth. Recent research confirmed that most jurors were unaware that they were forbidden from accessing reports about their case, and that even those who appreciated the prohibition, frequently searched online for information, driven by natural curiosity. Coupled with separate figures suggesting that the average person in the UK checks the internet, usually via a handheld device, fourteen times a day, and given the intense public interest in this case, it will be impossible to rely on jurors' good intentions alone.'

'So, what are you suggesting?'

'That jurors hand in all mobile devices registered to them – phones, iPads, laptops – and they sign a paper acknowledging that they will be in contempt of court if found to have accessed the internet before the end of the case.'

'Mr Laidlaw. What do you say about that?'

'It's totally unnecessary and unworkable and I see no basis for departing from the norm. Some of the jurors, no doubt, have important information on their phones, including the contact details of their families.'

'Give them a day's notice. Tell them to write the numbers on a piece of paper. Allow them to use a court phone to make any calls they need, for the duration of the trial. We all managed to stay alive before we had mobile phones. And they won't have any appointments apart from this one.'

'Your honour, if it gets out that that is what *you* ordered in *your* courtroom, we will never get anyone to sit on a jury. Taking away phones from the jury for, what, two weeks or more. It's a huge restriction of their civil liberties. You wouldn't want to be the one to set such a dangerous precedent.'

'It's very good of you to think of *me*, Mr Laidlaw, when you should, instead, be thinking of your overriding duty to our justice system. Mr Nimble?'

'It goes without saying that the jury are capable adults and, if they are to be trusted to sit on a jury in a murder case, then they must be trusted to abide by its rules, without threats or unreasonable restrictions. And I am not sure what Ms Burton is worried they might see, in any event. Contrary to her opening pejorative comments, which I did not interrupt out of courtesy alone, my clients are all responsible newspaper reporters. They know the limits of what they are allowed to report in ongoing proceedings.'

'Anything else for me to consider, Ms Burton?'

'I accept that there is a balance to be struck here, as in many cases which combine elements of privacy, freedom of expression and the need to protect due process of law. In my respectful submission, there is little hardship suffered by jurors in being parted from their electronic devices for a short period; in fact, some doctors and mental health campaigners would laud the separation.'

'We can't treat the jury like naughty children,' Jeremy Laidlaw chipped in. 'And I can envisage a plethora of claims from jurors after the event; lost devices, hard drives wiped, important events missed. We'll spend more time dealing with their complaints and compensation requests than on the case itself.'

'When I said *anything else*, I meant to move to your next point please,' Judge Nolan said. 'I have your arguments, all of you, on the mobile devices.'

Judith took another breath.

'There will be images of the deceased, Rosie Harper, at the scene, which will be shown in the courtroom. Out of respect for the victim and her family, they should not be reproduced in the press or via the TV channel.'

'This strikes at the heart of the new arrangement,' Leo Nimble complained. 'If the public are to be educated, they need to see what the jury sees, warts and all. If there is any concern about the content being upsetting, they know this is a murder trial and, frankly, it will be no less distressing than an episode of CSI.'

'Thank you, all. Ms Burton, your first application is successful. I am happy to make arrangements not to film the jury, so long as it can be managed appropriately and does not cause any technical problems. I can't see the point in exposing them to any more notoriety or pressure than is necessary. And, clearly, no images of the deceased, from the crime scene, should be published or reproduced in any shape or form by your clients, Mr Nimble.'

'I'm grateful...'

'But I am not willing to confiscate the jury's mobile devices for so many reasons, including a lack of resources on the Court's part to keep them safe for the duration. I doubt my clerk, or anyone else's for that matter, is going to be willing to do anything other than provide the usual locker facility.'

Judge Nolan poured herself some water and looked out at the legal teams gathered before her. 'Anything else?'

'The defendant's children may give evidence. I'd like them to be screened from the public. It's a common enough measure...'

'I know when screening is used, thank you, Ms Burton. How old are they?'

'Laura is 21 and Ben is 16.'

'Are there any reasons, other than their age, why you are making this request?'

Judith snatched a glance over her shoulder at Constance.

'Well, just the obvious ones. This is likely to be an extremely traumatic process for them...'

'Your honour, the children's identities are well known. There were never attempts by either of their parents to keep them out of the public eye and, since the murder, many images of them have been reproduced in the press.'

'I'm not sure that's your best point, Mr Laidlaw.'

'Your honour,' now Leo Nimble tried. 'The children are key witnesses. If the public can't see the key witnesses give their evidence, then what's the point of this scheme; where's the transparency? I know my colleague, Mr Laidlaw, will treat them with courtesy, so there is no reason for them to do anything other than give their evidence in the usual way.'

Judge Nolan thought for a moment. 'I agree. Ms Burton, you can rest assured I won't allow any aggressive questioning, but they can't be screened. Mr Laidlaw. Anything from you?'

Jeremy Laidlaw rocked backwards and forwards, like a jumping bean, before he found his equilibrium.

'Yes, your honour, just one application from me.'

'Let's keep it brief and to the point, shall we?'

'The prosecution wants to bring evidence from an expert in the process of transitioning.'

'Transitioning?'

'Yes. The defendant is a transgender woman, who recently underwent gender reassignment surgery. We want to bring in an expert to explain to your honour and the court how that treatment may have affected her.'

'Is Debbie Mallard legally a woman now?'

'Yes, but the expert would address medical issues that are not well understood, which it is appropriate for the jury to hear and evaluate.'

'Is the expert Debbie Mallard's own doctor?'

'No, your honour. But Dr Alves is an expert in the field, who has worked with many transgender individuals.'

'This all sounds incredibly remote and, well, totally irrelevant, quite apart from being inadmissible. Ms Burton?'

'Your honour, I'm with you completely.'

'Thank you. No, Mr Laidlaw, no "expert" on transitioning. Anything else?'

Laidlaw conferred with his solicitor before shaking his head. His face was flushed and Judith had caught a few words of remonstration exchanged between the two. She glanced at Constance.

'No? Then I have a request for you, Mr Nimble.'

Leo Nimble stood up, less sprightly this time around than

before.

'Despite your protestations that your clients are up to speed on the intricacies of what they can and cannot report, I have read some of their work myself over the last few days and I expect you to deliver a refresher course. As you were so keen to communicate with your clients and, as we are on target to finish early, I suggest you take the rest of the morning to do just that. And I don't expect to see you or any of your clients back before this court for the duration. That's all. Thank you so much. See you back here six weeks today.'

***

'What do you think?'

Constance and Judith were seated in a taxi on their way back to Constance's office. It was a rare luxury, but the quickest way to escape from the crowd which had enveloped them as they left the court. They had intended to drive only a couple of blocks and decamp onto the underground, but then it had started to rain and they had stayed put.

'Of who?'

'Jeremy Laidlaw, for a start.'

'I thought he was slippery.'

'Did you? That's interesting. He can be very smooth; I thought he was relatively well-behaved today. But then, asking for an expert in transitioning. I've never heard anything more ridiculous in my life! At least Bridget gave him short shrift.'

'He winked at me.'

'Ah. That's why you disliked him. I thought it wasn't like you to be so uncharitable. How do you mean *winked*?'

'When you were speaking, he sort of leaned back, puffed out his chest and stared me out. Then his eye kind of squeezed closed very quickly.'

'Sounds like he winked at you. You could do worse than Jeremy Laidlaw. Comes from a wealthy family.'

'Oh stop.'

'And he is very clever, although they say he's a bit lazy. And he doesn't get on well with his solicitor; quite an unnecessary public display of disagreement, I thought. But he knew just which buttons to push today, telling the judge that it would lead to a proliferation of claims from disgruntled jurors if they had to give up their devices. That's what nailed it. She didn't care about limiting their freedom.'

'He was also giving these little sideways looks to the other barrister, all sort of "boys together".'

'You were observing him quite closely, then. He and Leo are at the same chambers, so they will have wanted to help each other out. You know – *you scratch my back*. He wasn't always quite so smug though. Clearly, being crowned king of the hotties has gone to his head.'

'Hotties?'

'Yes, I know. It's hardly my choice of words, just in case you were wondering. He topped a league, voted the most attractive male barrister, some years back. He's had a swagger ever since.'

'Yuck.'

'And rumours are that he spent a year in Hollywood before bar school and only came back here when his father threatened to stop his allowance. The TV stuff will be a gift for him.'

'And Nimble?'

'A bit parochial but he did his job. No, after today I'm more worried about our delectable lady judge.'

'She was a bit fierce, wasn't she? Why did they choose her, do you think?'

'She has enough experience. And she was prepared to do it. I heard a number of judges are taking a sabbatical to coincide with the pilot and only coming back once the dust has settled. She must be attracted by the prospect of her name in lights. It's a shame about the screening for Ben and Laura. I couldn't say anything...about Ben's issues – not without permission. And if I had, I worried whether Leo would keep them to himself.'

'Agreed.'

'At least she wanted to keep the press in check.'

'Yes, and it was good about the jury, so at least the public doesn't get to identify them.'

'Hm. If we'd lost that one, I would have been very concerned for the future of British justice.'

18

ELLIS HARPER WAS SITTING outside the Birdcage pub, a whisky glass perched on the table. It was a good people-watching spot, positioned on the corner of Columbia Road and Gosset Street and opposite a small park. Dog walkers, cyclists, joggers, all headed past in a variety of colourful gear. Judith had smiled at him from a distance of a few metres and held out her hand as she approached.

'Is that Lagavulin?' she asked, as she clambered onto the bench next to him, slipping on her sunglasses and pointing at his drink.

'It is. You know your whisky then?' Ellis picked up his glass and held it up, so the sun's rays emphasised its amber tones.

'A little. You can't really mistake the odour of peat bog. I'm Judith Burton, in case you thought I was just some random woman with an unhealthy knowledge of whisky. Thank you for agreeing to meet.'

Ellis smiled. 'Anything I can do to help,' he said.

'You don't look like her,' Judith said.

'What?'

'Rosie. You don't look much like her.' Judith shifted her glasses to the top of her head and squinted at him. 'I suppose that's not so surprising. I don't resemble my sister, or at least I can't see it.'

'There you are then. Rosie got the brains. I got the looks.'

Judith laughed gently, her tinkling laugh, reserved for first encounters. 'Although other people say they can see it, the resemblance.' Judith looked around her. 'What a fabulous pub,' she said. 'Your local?'

'No. This is the closest to Ben…and Laura. That's why I chose it.'

'It's very good of you to come and spend this time with your niece and nephew, provide them with support,' Judith said.

'My sister's been killed. I couldn't stay away.'

'And Constance said you set up a meeting for her, with Ben. We're very grateful.'

'He wants to do his bit, to help his dad. I'm hoping you're agreed that he doesn't need to be a witness.'

'We're still not sure. I understand you have some concerns.'

'He's so young. They both are. And this is hard enough on them, without having to talk about things in public.'

'Is that why you've stayed so long? Can your employer spare you all this time?'

'I'm self-employed,' Ellis replied, 'which means I can stay around, to help Laura and Ben, as long as they need me.'

'What do you do for work?'

'Interior design. After the initial visit and measuring up, I do most of my work remotely. And I'm less than an hour away from most of my customers in Bucks anyway, if they really require the personal touch.'

'But you're staying here in London?'

'At the house. At Rosie's. Someone has to, now the police have finished with it. Otherwise who knows what might happen? Could get leaks or squatters even. And I suppose they'll need help to sell it...eventually.'

'Yes. I hadn't thought of that. Were you and Rosie close?'

'Is this an interview?'

Judith laughed, more full-throated this time. 'Of course not. But every little bit of information helps.'

'It doesn't help Rosie.'

Judith waved to a young man collecting glasses and ordered two more whiskies, for herself and Ellis.

'No, it doesn't. So were you?'

Ellis shrugged. 'My work took me overseas when I was younger and we lost touch.'

'Overseas?'

'Hong Kong.'

'That must have been interesting.'

'Sure, for a while. But it was good to come home too.'

'Why did you go?'

'I needed a change of scene. I've used things I learned out there too.'

'I see. You know I've been thinking of sprucing up my apartment for a while and I love Oriental design. Maybe you could send me a few examples of your work. It will give me some ideas, if nothing else.'

'Sure, no problem. I'll choose a couple of the best.'

'That's very kind.' Judith fished in her purse and handed Ellis a business card. He tucked it in the pocket of his jeans.

'And when you returned from overseas, you saw more of Rosie?'

'We were much closer, recently, as I was just up the road. And I love the kids; Ben and Laura. Rosie was so proud of them.'

'Can I ask about your parents?'

'Elaine is still local, living in Essex. She's taking this so badly, but then how else would she? That's also why I'm here. I go to visit her most days and it's nearer. Dad passed away two years ago.'

'I'm sorry.'

'Unfortunately, the news about "Debbie" was out before he died. She didn't even have enough respect to spare him that.' Ellis sighed.

'You don't like Debbie much then?' Judith said.

'I should like the man who murdered my sister, caved her head in and then, what, coolly went off to run some football training?'

'Before. You didn't like her much before?'

'Her, him. No. I didn't like either of them very much. Rosie said that all people have two sides to their personality; their masculine and feminine sides – kind of yin and yang – and that Danny had spent forty years embracing one and now he wanted to devote time to the other.'

'And what do you think about that?'

'Total bollocks, that's what I think. Look. He humiliated my sister, total and utter humiliation. Can you even begin to imagine what people were whispering behind their hands, and how embarrassing it was for her? He didn't care. He wanted to flaunt himself around in stupid, skimpy clothes. But Rosie withstood all that. She shrugged it off and she was striding out on her own. But he couldn't have that, could he? Total narcissist that he is. He couldn't leave her alone. He had to come back and finish her off completely.'

'You seem very certain.'

'You don't know him.'

'The children don't think that – Laura and Ben – and they know him.'

'That's because he's brainwashed them.'

'Is it right that they never liked Danny, your parents?'

'Is that what he said?' Ellis finished his whisky. 'I don't know what they really thought, but they always welcomed Danny, even though he was a bit of a lad, maybe not your first choice for your daughter, if you know what I mean. But Rosie had Dad wrapped around her little finger, so if she'd wanted to marry Hitler, he'd have probably given his blessing. It was only when he…when he dumped Rosie and went off with all this disgusting stuff…that's when they told him what they thought. And I don't blame them.'

'No. You've made that very clear.'

'Look, I didn't say this to the other lawyer. I didn't think it was right, when Ben was there. But Danny's crying, saying how sorry he is that Rosie's gone, how much he loved her. I've known him a few years, OK. So take it from me. Those tears you see. They're all fake. He married her for the fame. It wasn't enough for him to be a footballer. He used his celebrity status to find himself a really special wife. He never loved her. And he knew footballers' careers were short and that he had to think to the next stage. It was all about what she could do for him.

'And the photos they used to print of them gazing into each other's eyes. Also fake. You watch him take a penalty, back in '96 or before. Even when he was in the youth team; he kept his cool. Most kids of that age are…what? Hot-headed, risk takers? Not him. And he's the same now. He is…cold, emotionless, detached. Anything else is false, what he thinks the public wants to see, expects to see. That's why he was rubbish as a coach. Sure, he was a skilful player, one of the best in the world, but he has no heart.'

19

AN HOUR LATER, and only fifty metres down the street, Constance pushed her way through the crowds on Columbia Road, flocking, like the thirstiest of bees, to the striking array of flowers. She came here most Sundays, even if only for a few minutes, and she usually returned home with something to brighten up her flat. Today, the fuchsia gerberas had caught her eye, fifteen for £5, neatly boxed, their blackened centres dark as soot.

'What about a few hydrangeas too?' the stall owner asked. 'They're the best you'll see in here.'

Constance contemplated the enormous lacy-headed blooms and shook her head.

'This is good for today, thanks,' she said, before stepping out of the melee into a cobbled side street and on, into the nearby courtyard. If she lingered, she knew she'd be tempted to buy more and flowers were a luxury, even at only £5 a box. She also didn't want to be late for her appointment at her favourite café. Seated outside Lily Vanilli was Judith, coffee in hand, nestling up to a striking watercolour, which had overflowed the gallery next door.

'Uncle Ellis is an interesting chap,' Judith began.

'You met him, then.'

'We share a passion for whisky, so he says, although I wonder if he really knows his Lagavulin from his Laphroaig.'

'You went drinking together?'

Judith threw her head back and laughed. 'I suppose we did. And I'm still feeling the after-effects. Hence the caffeine fix.'

'What did he tell you?'

'Oh, nothing much, but he insists Debbie is a fraud. Called her a narcissist. I thought that was an interesting choice of word.'

'It just means vain, doesn't it?'

'It's often more than that, and that's what Ellis meant, I think. One of the three dark, triadic personality traits, along with Machiavellian and psychopathic.'

'OK?'

'Callous and manipulative.'

'Manipulating who?'

'All of us. Ellis thinks it's an act – that Debbie has everyone taken in. That she's icy cold underneath and switches emotions on and off. Who knows? Some lions in public are little mice in private, and look at comedians; the profession's awash with manic depressives.'

'Ben says Debbie was more gentle at home than on the pitch, ut that's not that surprising. Although…'

'What? Go on, tell me what you think.'

'onstance took a deep breath and then lowered her voice, gh they were alone in the courtyard and the noise from he bustling café would have hidden most conversations.

't know if it's because of the transgender stuff or not,' she said. 'Maybe it'd be the same if she was still Danny. I'm trying really hard to push all that out of the way, but I just feel awkward in Debbie's company, more than with most clients. Thing is, I don't know how to read her. I mean, I know we all get things wrong, those signs you look out for, to show if your client's telling the truth, but you kind of get used to how a man might react to things and then what a woman might do. That's all messed up with Debbie.'

'All the things you're talking about will be magnified tenfold if she ends up in front of a jury. They'll be confused too,' Judith said.

'Her kids are so positive though. That must help.'

Judith smiled. 'Ever the optimist. Although you're right. The kids are a real asset. We need them, I think, if only to convince the jury that Debbie's a good person.'

'Some people would think what Debbie did was selfish though, wouldn't they? Inflicting pain on the family, unnecessarily.'

'Maybe it wasn't so difficult. Maybe Rosie wasn't as nice as everyone says. What about her public persona versus private? You got a hint of that from Laura, didn't you? We should sound Debbie out on what Rosie was really like. And why should Danny lose his kids, just because he wants to change his gender?'

'Ellis doesn't see it that way, though.'

'Ellis says it's much worse than that. That Debbie never loved Rosie, even when she was Danny. That she's just pretending.'

'It had crossed my mind.'

'Yes. Well, one of them is lying...or mistaken. Doesn't mean she killed Rosie though.'

'You keep saying that.'

'And it's important to remember. All this noise, what Danny was like, what Debbie was like, even what Rosie was like; it's just noise. It's not evidence.'

'The glove, the eye witness who saw Debbie arrive, the 999 call, the trophy, their divorce, the chase. They all point to Debbie.'

'What about Nicki Smith?'

'I talked to Dawson. He interviewed her. She has an alibi.'

'Alibis come and go.'

'All right. I'll talk to her myself. I wanted to anyway, but you put me off. I'll see what she has to say.'

As the queue inside the café dispersed, Constance went off to the counter to order a drink. Then her mobile rang. She ignored the first ring, but picked it up on the second. And then she saw the name of the caller: Ben Mallard.

'Hello?' she said.

'It's Ben. Ben Mallard.' Ben's voice trembled down the line.

'Hello Ben.'

She retraced her steps and sat down again with Judith. Constance switched the phone to speaker mode and they both leaned in close to hear him.

'I've been thinking about giving evidence for Dad. You remember we talked about it,' Ben said.

'Yes.' Constance said, trying to sound encouraging.

'I'm not sure it's such a good idea, now. Uncle Ellis says that if I do, lots of personal stuff will be in all the newspapers. That once I'm a witness, they can ask me anything – about Mum, Dad, me and Laura. I'm not saying I won't do it, just…I wanted to know if that's right, what he said.'

'Your uncle isn't wrong,' Constance said, 'but we can take steps to limit what you're asked. Look, we might not need you. We have lots of other material we can use to help your dad. Is there something, in particular that you're worried about?'

'I wanted to tell you before,' he said. 'I know sometimes it's better to just get stuff out, so it's not a secret any more, not that this really ever was…a secret, that is. I just didn't want to make things worse for Dad.'

Constance counted the seconds, visualising the introverted Ben sitting in his room in Laura's flat, skinny and wan, his phone lying before him on the bed, struggling with his conflicting loyalties. Ben remained silent.

'What is it you want to share with me?' Constance said.

'It was my fault,' Ben said, after a further hiatus, his words tripping over each other, in their rush to escape.

'What?' Judith's question came out louder than she had intended and she clasped her hand over her mouth. But if Ben had noticed the change in tone or volume, he didn't say.

'I asked Dad to go and talk to Mum that day,' he said.

'Oh.' Constance took control again.

'I told you we had an argument, me and Mum. It was stupid. I wanted to leave school and go to acting classes, like Mum did.'

'And your mum didn't agree.'

'She hit the roof. I thought Dad could help. He always supported my acting. Mum was usually too busy to come. And now it's too late.' He began to sob uncontrollably down the phone.

'Listen to me, Ben,' Constance said gently. 'This wasn't your fault, OK? And I don't want you to ever think it was. I'll discuss what you said with Judith, but I don't want you to worry any more.'

'OK.'

'And you did the right thing telling me. Is there anything else you wanted to share?'

'No. That's all. Nothing else.'

'Anything you think of, you give me a call. But remember what

I said.'

Constance ended the call and waited for Judith to comment. Judith pursed her lips and then turned away, muttering 'another one bites the dust'. Constance headed back inside, to buy something tasty to lift her spirits.

20

CLARE CHAMBERS WAS PLACING a tray of chips in the oven when Andy arrived home and wound his arms around her waist. She sighed, spun around and kissed him on the cheek before uncoupling his hands.

'What?' he said.

'Nothing.'

'Tell me?'

'I just had a hard day, that's all. Nothing unusual.'

'Would you like me to make it better?'

'Not now,' she clucked, going over to the fridge and searching around for the rest of dinner.

Andy threw his head back and laughed. 'Not that. I have something to tell you.'

'Oh.' Clare pulled out a packet of fish goujons, grabbed some scissors and snipped the corner.

'I have been offered this fantastic job opportunity,' Andy said. 'Out of hundreds, thousands of possibles, they chose me, your talented husband.'

He forced Clare to sit down and outlined the job offer, while she listened carefully, the TV in the next room providing a fitting backdrop to Andy's words.

'Why you?' she said, when he had finished.

Andy frowned. 'I told you, I...'

'You don't have any TV experience, you're not a QC?'

'OK, but...'

'Not that you're not adorable and we all love you...and you know your stuff, but you're hardly Jeremy Paxman.'

'Thanks for the vote of confidence.'

'You know what I mean.'

'They want someone young and unknown – a fresh face, they said. And I'm not the main presenter, just the "chief legal adviser". Look, as long as I hold my own, it doesn't matter, does it? They're giving me the chance. They're giving us plenty of rehearsal time. Then, it's up to me to show them what I can do.'

'There must be a catch.'

'No catch. Well, it's going to be hard work, I know that, but it's only for three months. Maybe your mum can help a bit more, if it's only three months.'

Clare scowled. She hated asking for help from anyone, including family.

'Can I see the contract?' she said.

'Yes, but...'

'You haven't signed it yet?'

'No...I...'

'Because I want to read it through and we need an employment lawyer to read it over.'

'I'm a lawyer too.'

'You're too…star-struck to read it carefully.'

Andy thought about remonstrating with Clare over yet another dig at his apparent deficiencies, but decided that if this was the only condition Clare imposed he should consider himself extremely fortunate.

'No problem,' he said. 'I'll send you a copy and I'll get an employment lawyer to look it over before I sign. Aren't you pleased?'

Andy was crouching down before her and Clare took his face in both hands and kissed him, this time on the lips.

'Yes,' she said, 'very pleased. My husband on TV. The kids will think it's hilarious. Have you thought about what you're going to wear?'

***

Nicki was sitting in Hoxton Square, watching the doorway of Laura's flat. She had been there for more than an hour, with a newspaper across her knees, which she could lift to cover her face if required, except no one she even vaguely recognised had come anywhere near the property. Her back was beginning to stiffen; they didn't build wooden benches for comfort, she thought. Not even this one with its *love never fades* message, which she had deliberately covered with her bag when she first sat down. Who wanted to be reminded of empty platitudes while eating their lunch?

When she had almost decided to leave – 'five more minutes and I'm off' – she saw a figure cross the upstairs window and then Ellis, Laura and Ben all exited the property simultaneously.

Nicki leaped up and hid behind a portly oak tree, peering out to monitor their activities. Laura was saying her goodbyes, before marching off towards the main road. Ellis took Ben's arm and propelled him along as far as the corner of the square. Then Ben spoke to Ellis and continued on his own. Ellis stood for a few moments, contemplating the ground, before beginning the slow walk back the way he had come.

Nicki grabbed her chance and pressed the screen of her phone. In front of her, she saw Ellis reach into his back pocket, remove his phone, check it, stare up at the sky, and then reject the call. As she watched, he took two more steps, stopped again, looked at his phone a second time, shook his head and then headed back inside.

'Bastard,' Nicki whispered, smiling weakly at an old man who was passing by. He smiled in return and she wondered if he had not heard her curse and was merely being polite, or if he was indicating his agreement with her sentiments.

21

'WE WANTED TO UPDATE YOU on the preparation for your trial,' Constance announced to Debbie, as Judith flicked through her papers. It was a warm day and a shaft of sunlight bisected the shabby room, one of the few with natural light at Denmow. To Constance's relief, this room was painted white.

'And I thought you had come to tell me the police have solved the case and I'm free to go.'

Judith looked up and smiled. Constance remained serious. She wasn't in the mood for jokes today. She thought Debbie appeared both thinner and paler than on their last meeting and had even darker circles under each eye. Even so, her hair was neatly styled and she was wearing pale pink lipstick.

'How are things here? Have you managed to get out in the yard?' she asked.

Debbie shrugged. 'A little. It's fine. Everyone leaves me alone, which suits me. Food's not bad; I'm not the best cook anyway. And Laura and Ben visit loads. Otherwise, it's very quiet. I read, I listen to the radio. Music, plays, even *Woman's Hour.*'

'And you're allowed to wear your own clothes?'

'Yes. Overalls would be awful, clash with my nails.' She gave a brittle laugh. 'And I can grow them for the first time in years. That's one advantage of not scrabbling around in the mud, on the pitch. Just like an extended holiday really.'

'There's been a lot of press interest in your case. You might have seen?'

'I know.'

'It's something we'll have to deal with more as the trial approaches and, as I think you already know, the trial is going to be filmed.'

'Ben said. So I need to look my best, turn my best side towards the cameras.'

Constance was relieved that she hadn't had to break the news to Debbie and that Debbie seemed unperturbed. Maybe when you had lived much of your life in the public eye, the prospect of having your trial filmed was simply a home from home.

'We can discuss preparation nearer the time,' Judith interrupted. 'Look, can we talk for a moment about Rosie? We've all seen the BBC eulogy and we've read the many messages of support. But, clearly you two disagreed over some things, particularly at the end of your marriage. And we've watched some of Rosie's interviews. She was obviously not a pushover.'

Debbie's smile waned. 'We're trying to build up a picture of what Rosie was like,' Constance added. 'I know it's difficult for you to talk about, but it will help us with our case theory.'

Debbie sighed deeply. 'You're right that she wasn't just a pretty face. And if something interested her, she wanted to get involved. She always wanted more control over the content of her programme and the producers didn't like it.'

'She clashed with them?'

'I didn't want to say anything before. I didn't want to make trouble. But there was something going on with her contract and with Jason. He's so spineless, he was happy to just feed the public whatever he was told, as long as they kept paying his salary.'

'Obviously with the recording of the 999 call, some people will jump to the conclusion that you were abusive or bullying towards Rosie, maybe even violent, and we will have to deal with that,' Judith took control again. 'But with the picture you are painting of Rosie, a formidable woman…might anyone say that it was the other way around? That she ordered you about?'

Debbie's face began to change colour, from its pale beige hue to pink, to red and almost to purple. 'You want me to rubbish the memory of my dead wife?'

'I'm not sure I…'

'You do. You want some ammunition to fight back. *Case theory*, you said. You want me to say that Rosie was a bitch, that she didn't understand me or that she…what? – threw me out of the house, at a time when I needed her most? That's almost as disgusting as her murder… At least everyone has their memories of Rosie to hold on to. You want me to destroy those too.'

'Why did you leave her if you were so happy together?' Judith remained calm, but sat back a few inches from Debbie's ire.

'I didn't leave her. I would have stayed.' Debbie sat forward.

'She asked you to leave?'

Debbie's hands went up to her neck again, found a lock of hair and curled it around her fingers.

'It wasn't as simple as that,' she said. 'We reached an agreement that I should go, that it was best for everyone,' she said.

'But, if you had your choice, you would have stayed?'

'Being selfish, yes.'

'What do you mean, "being selfish"?'

'I wanted her to stay my wife but…' The anger was gone from Debbie's voice now.

'You wanted to continue to see your lover.' Judith completed Debbie's sentence.

'I would have been discreet,' Debbie said. 'But Rosie couldn't accept that, and I understood. And she was entitled to want to meet someone else, herself.'

'You were fine with that?'

'I made my bed,' Debbie said.

'Did Rosie find someone else?' Constance asked.

'I've already said that I don't know,' Debbie said. 'I didn't ask. Look, there is something else you should know.'

Judith and Constance exchanged glances. 'Go on.'

'You know how you asked me if I was certain that the person I recently became close to would stay quiet?'

'Yes.'

'I was wrong.' Debbie chewed at her bottom lip. 'I had a letter, asking for money.'

'Threatening to go public?'

'It didn't say that. Just said that he was in between jobs, would appreciate some financial assistance to "tide him over".'

'What did you do?'

'I threw it away.'

'When was this?'

'About a week ago.'

'And you've heard nothing since?'

'No, but it isn't exactly easy getting post in here.'

'All right. No point dwelling on it,' Judith said. 'If you hear anything else from him, you let us know.'

✳✳✳

'You were relaxed about Debbie's lover reappearing?' Constance decided it best to broach the subject, only when they were alone together, heading back to London in her car.

'I was, wasn't I? Give me an Oscar. Sadly, this one's totally out of our control,' Judith answered. 'I've learned to let go of those kinds of things.'

'Should we have a plan B?'

'You mean if Mr Lover Boy pops up somewhere and spills the beans, or Dawson finds him? Definitely. I'm toying with *give up and move to a desert island*, but I'll work on something more constructive.'

'I thought Debbie looked pale.'

'She's clearly under a lot of pressure, although she did manage the odd joke and the lipstick, keeping up appearances and all that.'

'How do you think she learned?'

'What?'

'To put it on...the makeup. I mean, who do you think she asked? She could hardly ask Rosie.'

'Her mother? Laura? A sympathetic friend.'

'It's important to her. I've noticed.'

'I suppose it helps her feel more feminine. It's understandable. The anger seemed genuine this time, though.'

'You criticised Rosie and she didn't like it.'

'We got close to the truth. She's defending Rosie. Either because she doesn't want to speak ill of the dead – very laudable but useless for our purposes – or she doesn't want people to know Rosie pushed her around: pride, maybe even masculine pride, finding its way through. Or it's the guilt thing again.'

'What guilt thing?'

'That she blames herself for making Rosie angry, for all Rosie's bad behaviour, because she feels she put her through the ringer. Ah. What does it matter? Just another area of questioning to avoid in court then, and we're no further forward either.'

'Listen, I know you don't want to ask Ben to give evidence now...' Constance continued.

'That's what I've said.' Judith answered quickly.

'But, I told you *he* was critical of Rosie, and he'll say they loved each other.'

Judith fiddled with her seat belt.

'I know,' she said. 'But the more I think about it, the more I believe Laidlaw will twist it. And he'll milk the sympathy angle. You know: "poor motherless boy", "needs closure" – that kind of thing.'

'Ben wants to help. You heard.'

'Since when were we therapists, on top of everything else? Although I suspect Laidlaw will want him for the prosecution, for all the reasons I've just expounded, so he may get his moment in court anyway.'

'What about Laura?'

'You say she's cold?'

'Yes.'

'Didn't get on with Rosie?'

'I don't think they were close, no.'

'Then we'll have Laura. We need someone to redress the balance and Rosie's own daughter is a good choice... What?'

'Nothing.'

'Tell me.'

'It's just that you're, somehow, so protective of Ben but you don't seem to feel the same about Laura.'

'She's older. She'll cope better. And Laidlaw won't be able to use the same angle.'

'If you say so.'

'Look. It's not entirely logical. I accept that. Just my feeling about what's best. Anything else?'

'No.' Constance set her lips firmly together and concentrated on the road. Half a mile along the way, she turned the radio on.

22

NICKI MET CONSTANCE in the front room of a derelict property which Dead Earth had commandeered as its HQ. The stone floor and ceiling rosette hinted at an illustrious past, but the building had clearly been neglected for some years. It was devoid of any real furniture – instead, a few everyday items were dotted around to fulfil the basic needs of its users – and the paint was peeling from the walls in strips. Nicki was dressed in jeans and a loose-fitting white t-shirt, emblazoned with a picture of Darth Vader's head and the slogan 'Choose the Green side'.

Constance had felt, instinctively, that Nicki might prove a prickly adversary. That was certainly the impression she gave from anything and everything she posted online; fervent, strident, discordant. Those were the words which came to mind if you read her outpourings or watched her in action. So Constance had decided she would need to match Nicki in forcefulness, if she was to take anything useful away from their encounter. She had worn a black leather jacket and her chunkiest shoes.

But Nicki was on home territory and had seized the advantage from the start. Choosing this makeshift office forced Constance literally off-balance, as the inhospitable room offered only upturned packing crates for seats, meaning Constance had to balance her laptop on her knee.

As Constance adjusted her position, Nicki gazed out of the window, exposing her long, jagged, infamous scar to scrutiny. And it was fascinating to look at, beginning just under her left eye and crossing her cheek diagonally towards her ear, before changing direction and arcing down to end just above her chin, where it split into two short branches which gradually faded to nothing.

Before they had met, Constance had imagined something superficial, like a scratch from an over-enthusiastic bout of gardening, or those lines you sometimes have on your face in the morning, if you've slept awkwardly; something you might be able to erase if you rubbed lightly but persistently. This scar was deep, slicing through the epidermis to the connective tissue below, the result of some considerable trauma.

'You said you wanted to talk about Rosie Harper? I'm not sure I have much to tell,' Nicki said, her accent local, but with the rough edges filed away.

'You wrote to her. I have your emails,' Constance began.

'Then you'll know that I was once hoping to go on her show.'

'What happened?'

'I'm not sure. First, it was going to happen, then it wasn't.'

'That's a shame.'

'It can sometimes make all the difference, if a high-profile person gives their support.'

'Difference to what? I understand you're interested in changing government policy on green issues.'

'I wouldn't say that.'

'What would you say?'

'I'd say I'm fighting a war.'

'Which war? Climate change? Animal welfare? Human rights? Privacy? Whistleblowing? Whaling?'

'I thought you came to talk about Rosie.'

'I'm just interested. And now I'm here, this is your chance to impress me.' Constance heard herself speaking the words, coolly, brusquely, but she cringed inside. Anyone who knew her would laugh and tell her to *behave*. But Nicki didn't know her and seemed happy to spar, for now at least.

'They're all battles in the same war.' Nicki's voice remained light, but Constance detected a harder edge. 'We've been under Conservative rule in this country for the last nine years,' she said. 'They haven't tackled environmental issues and they insist on old-fashioned values that fitted better at the turn of the twentieth century. They have a horrendous record on all the other things you listed.'

'Isn't there a risk that by championing so many causes, you won't have any real impact?'

'I have experience in organising action, in lobbying for support, and if I can share that around, for the benefit of different interest groups, then that's good for everyone.'

'Are you a leader? You're listed online as the leader of Dead Earth.'

'I'm a facilitator. I take the lead for a short time, train up a team and then move on. It's more effective than sitting tight and giving orders.'

'You do literally take the lead though, don't you? The papers had you at the front of May's big march.'

'I don't have a problem getting my hands dirty.'

Constance paused. Although Nicki's words were tough, the calm manner she was exhibiting now was a far cry from the shrieking, stamping shrew who had marched along the Strand only three months ago, then clambered up one of the lions in Trafalgar Square to pose, draped around the majestic beast, and address the writhing crowd below. As she spoke, Nicki opened and closed her hands and Constance noticed they were small and neat, hardly big enough to hold a megaphone.

'What does it feel like to be striding out with hundreds of people behind you, following you? And the chanting and the singing. It must be…don't you feel powerful?'

Nicki gave a short laugh. 'You think I do this for the status, that I get off on being a leader?'

'I'm just…'

'You want to know how I felt marching over Waterloo Bridge, me calling all the shots, deciding who goes where, who sings what, when to sit down, when to stand up?'

Constance said nothing. Nicki's eyes shone brightly.

'I felt a sense of responsibility. That's what. To keep the focus on the campaign and not on individuals. The Establishment wants it to be about me. Then they can rubbish me, criticise me, wait for me to make a wrong move. The key is not to let that happen.'

'Who chose the name Dead Earth? It's pretty stark.'

'Isn't it better to tell things how they are? The next generation won't thank us for protecting them from understanding what's really going on.'

'Do you believe violence is necessary to achieve your aims?'

'I believe in force, in forceful, direct action, but not violence, no.'

'What's the difference?'

'Violence is sudden, impetuous behaviour reserved for thugs, resulting in pain, injury, death. The word has the same origin as violation, so it's not surprising I'm not a supporter. Force is different. It's about applying strength, sometimes in combination with others or over a prolonged period, but when you apply force, something shifts.'

'So what motivates you. Why are you doing any of this?'

'All life experiences shape you,' Nicki said, 'but it's all about questioning what we're told, not accepting what we're fed by politicians and their followers and wanting to facilitate change.'

Constance thought that she should ask Nicki about her scar. If there was a time to do it, this was it. But Nicki's large eyes were now scanning Constance's face and she couldn't find the right words.

'What's the biggest challenge facing the planet now, in your view?' she said, instead.

'Greed,' Nicki said.

'Greed?'

'No one is thinking about the common good. If they were, then we would all live a much simpler life.'

'Are you a Communist then?'

'Communism cowed too many honest people into submission for too long. I am not against private ownership or wealth or individualism, but people's values have to change. That's the shift we're trying to achieve.'

'You're a local girl, aren't you?'

'Like you.'

'I heard you lived abroad for a while. Where did you go?'

Nicki's fingers moved down to her improvised seat and she shifted position. 'Somewhere better than here,' she said.

'If things were so bad here, why d'you come back?'

'I missed home.' Nicki's eyes travelled to the window again and her voice softened. Outside, the street market was beginning to pack up. A trader, shouting out his last bargains, lifted his boxes into the back of a lorry.

'Do you get paid for your work? Your *facilitating*?'

Nicki stared at Constance and she suddenly felt cold fingers probe at her heart, despite the ambient temperature in the room.

'Sometimes,' she said, after a short hiatus.

'And, what? It's a standard fee or depends on how much time you spend? Is it results driven?'

'It depends on the work. I'm always conscious of the ability of the organisation to pay, when I consider whether to charge. But I do have to live.'

For the first time, Constance thought she had pierced through Nicki's shell, that her question had exposed her and she was uncomfortable. Now was the time to press home the advantage.

'Do you think Rosie, personally, pulled the plug on your interview?'

'I don't know.'

'What do you think about her murder?'

'I think it's sad they weren't in love any more; Rosie and Danny.'

'You're a romantic, then?' Constance attempted a smile.

Nicki's face flushed red and she checked her watch. 'I have somewhere else to be,' she said. 'Are you nearly finished?'

'I'm sorry. I do appreciate you fitting me in…'

'I have an alibi…for when Rosie was killed. You haven't asked me about that, but the police have probably told you.'

'Yes.'

'She wasn't a very nice person, Rosie Harper, not in real life. Did you know that?'

'Oh. No.'

'Maybe I'm only seeing things from one side. I was there, you see. I knew they'd been up and down about whether to do the Heathrow piece for a week or so. But they called me in, brought me into the studio. They'd even stuck me in makeup. The poor girl didn't know what to do about my scar. She just sat there staring at it, with her hand raised towards my face, wanting to ask if she should cover it or not. I was cruel. I let her sit there for ages before I told her not to bother. Jason came over to say hello, but she didn't. Then, when they got the message to put something else in, at the last minute, the programmer was apologetic; Jason, too. Rosie just kind of smiled and carried on with what she was doing.'

'So you wrote to her, to make her notice you?'

'I was cross with her. She liked people to think that she cared about these issues…and they're pretty big issues.'

'Did she reply to your emails?'

'She did, actually. Twice. Fairly bland stuff, but she did reply. Then she stopped. To be fair, that's twice more than some people. But an email or two, it's nothing; no real effort.'

'Is it right that you went to see her, two weeks or so before she died?'

'Everyone keeps going on about this. No. I was just there, on the corner of East Road, when she drove past. I had been visiting a friend. Now, if you'll forgive me, like I said, I have somewhere else to be, five minutes ago.'

Nicki rose now and, without waiting for any thank you or goodbye, she left the room. By the time Constance had packed away her laptop, Nicki had gone. Constance ran to the door and then to the entrance to the building and looked left and right, but there was no sign of her.

Constance took some photos of the room and the limited furniture, from a few angles. 'Thank you, Nicki. It was a pleasure to meet you,' she said to the shadows, as she shouldered her bag and headed off down the road.

23

ANDY WAS FIRST TO ARRIVE at the TV studio, a modern set of rooms on the fifth floor of a 1960s, boxy construction, just off Gray's Inn Road. He wasn't often early, but he had been for each morning last week, when he had attended rehearsals here. It was not that he was disorganised or lazy; just that he usually had so many things to fit into the hours of the day. In any twenty-four hour period, he was frequently each and all of: lawyer, counsellor, truancy coach, husband, father, son, brother, friend, shopper, cook, accountant and tax adviser. Not surprising, then, that he could ill-afford the luxury of being ahead of schedule, of kicking his heels waiting for others to join him.

But today was different. Today was the day Court TV was finally to air, the beginning of a new life, where all Andy's worries, his conflicting loyalties, his over-spilling diary difficulties would be resolved, in an instant, when he took his place in front of the cameras.

He was asked to wait, seated on a spongy corner sofa, while

the assistant who had opened up went scurrying around. Next to arrive was Katrina Sadiq, the lead presenter, friendly, in a quietly confident way. Her reputation as a canny political correspondent, keen to get to the bottom of every issue she addressed, had preceded her and she hadn't disappointed him so far, with her eloquence and quick tongue. Then Phil Ash breezed in, together with Chris Richards, the second anchor for the show and a collection of other production-related staff. Last to arrive was Graham, carrying a large tray of croissants, which he deposited at the front desk, before shaking hands energetically with each of them.

Andy still felt the studio was small. Once you were seated inside and the lights were switched on, it felt even smaller than when you viewed it through its glass walls. But the team was very attentive and they were each able to practise some short speeches and receive final tips and feedback on their performance. Andy chose to recite Portia's 'quality of mercy' speech from *The Merchant of Venice*, which he thought might amuse, but no one appeared to notice or appreciate his selection. Maybe they were all too nervous, with it being the dress rehearsal.

Then, in the coffee break, when the croissants were handed around, Graham, who had been constantly on his phone since his arrival – at times waving his arms around, at other times running his fingers through his hair – came to address them all.

'Thank you all for coming today,' he said, beaming widely. 'It's great for you all to be here for our first day of broadcasting, even though it's mostly pre-recorded. Phil tells me you have all worked really hard and made yourselves comfortable, which is just as well, as it's going to be your second home for the best part of the next three months.'

Andy thought it much more peaceful, at this moment, than his real home.

'I am conscious that we have gathered, here, a talented bunch of professionals, and that you are unlikely to need too much direction, given your own skills and background. Having said that, you are going to have an extra producer in addition to the usual team, at the end of a microphone to give you direction, live, during the show, and to keep things moving. After tonight, I am going to be away from London for a short while – unavoidable, I am afraid, given my year-end targets – but I leave you in very capable hands.

'Now, tonight is our opening and, clearly, we will be focusing on the background to Court TV's launch, so it won't be as dynamic a show as usual. It will be much more scripted. Even so, we will be highlighting the motto of the pilot scheme – "Equality, Accessibility, Transparency" – and I want that to guide you in all you do. That is why we are here, not to feed our own egos, although I should like to think that you will all, quickly, if not already – at this point he gave a nod in Katrina's direction – become household names. More than that, I want you to become *trusted friends* of the public. You are here to educate and illuminate them and not, I repeat *not*, to just blandly accept things you hear in court.'

'I don't think I've ever been called bland,' Katrina said.

'I do want you to challenge things the judge or lawyers say,' Graham kept going, with a nod to recognise Katrina's comment. 'Andy, you'll remember we talked about this early on and you were so supportive of this principle that poor practice must be stamped out.'

Andy heard Graham's words and smiled, as everyone looked at him with admiration for his high moral compass, but inside he was squirming. Did Graham really expect him to criticise his own colleagues?

'And to be innovative, too. We are going to be bringing along an array of other professionals, each experts in their field, each bringing a different perspective. By the end of the pilot, I want people, high-up important people, to be questioning whether the way things are done now – with wigs and gowns, in dusty buildings, behind closed doors, with rigid rules of evidence and traditional experts – whether that is truly the best way to test a person's guilt.'

Andy coughed into his hand. Everyone looked at him again. He smiled and nodded his continuing approval for Graham's wise words.

'Now. On to our first case!'

Graham walked over to the window, staring out of it before continuing: 'As you all know, it's the one everyone's talking about; the case against Debbie Mallard for killing the beautiful Rosie Harper. What a privilege to be commentating on such a case. Andy, Phil sent you the list of all the lawyers involved, together with the background our researchers had put together, didn't he?'

Andy nodded, his mouth suddenly a desert. He hadn't needed to read through a list to know whose name would be right at the top; it was one he had immediately recognised when it had been revealed by a colleague some weeks back: Judith Burton.

24

'THE KEY FEATURE of a modern, agile, twenty-first-century justice system is accessibility,' David Benson began, reading fluidly from the autocue, his heart swelling as he spoke. 'And the best means of achieving that is to provide transparency for users. And so, I am delighted to have been invited to kick off this new initiative from the Ministry of Justice, our transparency pilot scheme, with a few words. I have no doubt that allowing members of the public to actually see justice being done, from their homes, or even from the palm of their hands while on the move, will enhance the rule of law.

'Not only will filming our courts illuminate what might otherwise be a confusing and opaque process, it will familiarise users of the justice system with all aspects of our criminal trials. No longer will witnesses, jurors or defendants have to fear the unknown. The secrets of the courtroom will be revealed and understood by all and we will create a level playing field. And cases will then be judged most properly on the evidence, as they should be. The criminal justice system of England and Wales will be a shining beacon for the rest of the world.

'No longer will dilatory judges be able to pass the buck for over-running schedules, or prosecuting lawyers be able to blame their failures on faceless behind-the-scenes issues. And where, as is occasionally the case, the prosecution neglects to offer up relevant material to the defence, its failings will be crystal clear and there will be no place to hide. So, I repeat. What we will achieve through this important programme is equality, accessibility and transparency.'

'Stirring words there to begin our show, recorded earlier on today, by the Director of Public Prosecutions, especially for us. Those are the all-important buzz words; *Equality, Accessibility, Transparency.* Thank you, Mr David Benson.'

Two speakers were revealed, sitting on a black leather sofa, the new Court TV logo – stylised scales of justice inside a television-like box – emblazoned on the wall behind their heads.

'I'm Katrina Sadiq,' said the well-groomed first presenter, as the camera panned in close.

'And I'm Chris Richards…' said the second presenter.

'And we're the hosts of Court TV: Behind the Scenes.'

The Court TV logo briefly flashed across the screen, with the letters 'BTS' in italics below, as Katrina inched her skirt down over her knees and Chris adjusted his collar.

'We really will be going BTS – that's *behind the scenes* – to bring you, every night from tomorrow, the low-down on the day in court, from the viewpoint of a whole series of experts,' Katrina continued.

'But tonight,' Chris added, 'we're delighted to be joined by a series of people who have helped to get this new channel up and running. First up, is Angela Langton from victims' group, Innocensate, who campaign tirelessly for compensation on behalf of wrongfully convicted individuals. She'll be telling us how vital and overdue this development is and how she believes that none of the individuals she represents would ever have been behind bars in the first place if they'd had access to what Court TV is going to provide. And, if that's not enough, we'll be screening a short documentary about the journey to today, involving David Benson again and all the other major players.

***

'Oh God. I hate it already,' Judith yawned and turned down the volume on Constance's TV.

'Go home then,' Constance replied, turning it back up.

'You'd think, given how much Court TV must be paying for this privilege, they could have come up with a more impressive set.'

'I don't think...'

'And talk about disingenuous! And from our illustrious DPP. Although I suppose that it is all about "accessibility", if the money goes to fixing your courtroom's leaky roof or covering your legal aid costs.'

'Shh! We have to see this.'

'I don't see why.'

'You do! You're just being stubborn. We need to see their line-up, how they're planning to present things; live footage, commentary. Maybe they'll even bring other lawyers in to explain things, especially at the beginning.'

'But it will all be after the event. Any analysis of our case will be after the event, after the horse has bolted. Why should that interest us?'

'They might be critical of the judge, of you.'

'It wouldn't be the first time.'

'I don't believe it's happened to you before in front of a million people.'

'One million people?'

'That's what they're predicting for the opening audience.'

Judith's mouth was open. 'All right,' she said. 'I'm amazed that many people are interested. I'll sit tight and watch quietly, but only for an hour. Then I am heading home and you'll have to fill me in on the rest tomorrow.'

***

'...In my excitement at tonight's line up, I nearly forgot all of you at home,' Chris Richards was speaking again. 'Many of you will be aware that the case we are reporting on from tomorrow, the Crown versus Debbie Mallard, is the first to be televised. As always, your feedback is really crucial. So, given that this new scheme is intended primarily to educate the public, we're going to ask you, the public, at various stages, to share your views of how you think it's doing.'

***

'Here we go,' Constance muttered.

'It's just feedback,' Judith crossed her legs and folded her arms.

***

'If there are things you don't understand during the trial, you can send your questions in to our experts. We will have lawyers and other experts on hand throughout the day to provide you with live responses. And we'll be delighted to receive your comments too. But please be aware that anything you send in may be made public, either set out in our live feed on our website or on Twitter or on our evening *BTS* show.'

'So don't write in, if you are not prepared to have your views read out on air.'

***

Constance's mobile rang and she turned it face up, glancing at it casually, before grabbing it and running into the bedroom.

'Hi. Are you watching you know what?' the caller asked glibly.

'Greg. I didn't expect you to call,' Constance whispered, shutting the door behind her and holding the phone close to her mouth.

'I know you're probably up to your eyes in paper, well, virtual paper. I just wanted to wish you good luck for tomorrow,' he said.

'That's kind.' Constance could hear the TV loud and clear, which meant it was unlikely Judith could eavesdrop their conversation. 'Yes, we're pretty busy,' she said. 'And I *was* watching. You were right. It is going to be interactive.'

'This is only the beginning. If you need any help, I mean, I'm going to be watching every night, I think. I could let you know if there's anything particularly tricky – save you and Judith having to spend time glued to the screen.'

'We were wondering how to manage it all. Well, not Judith.

She still thinks it's an irrelevance or she's genuinely worried, but refusing to show it. I can't decide which. But, yeah. Thanks. I… need to get on now.'

'Maybe afterwards, we could go out? Whether to celebrate or commiserate. You could introduce me to one of *your* favourite places?'

'Sure. Yes. I'd like that. But let's say "celebrate"; think positive. Good night.'

Constance opened up her wardrobe and leafed through her clothes, pausing, first, at a purple flimsy blouse and then at some black skinny jeans. Then she stared at her phone and ran her fingers over the screen. Finally, with a sigh, she eased the wardrobe shut and returned next door.

***

'Who was that?' Judith was biting the side of her finger as Angela Langton was introduced.

'Oh, just my brother.'

'The elusive Jermain. You didn't have to leave the room. I'm only half-listening to this vacuous programme.'

'I never quite know what he's going to come out with. It's safer not to let anyone overhear.'

Judith laughed heartily, eliciting in Constance a momentary pang at her deception. 'I remember. What did you tell me once before? He called you from a basement in…where was it now?'

'Chile.'

'He does get around.'

'Judith?' Constance paused the TV. 'Do you think there's any chance that the glove was planted by the police?'

'Ooh. Did that come from your brother? Is that the word on the street? Planted?'

'Dawson never mentioned it when Debbie was first questioned and I've looked hard at some of the photographs and you can't see it.'

'You mean it was added later on to make the case against Debbie stronger?'

'Yes.'

'And where would the police have found the glove?'

'Maybe Debbie did leave a pair at the house by mistake, or they found it when they searched her flat, after the chase.'

'So where's the other glove? Their evidence would be far more persuasive, if the second one was found at Debbie's.'

'It might have all been done in a hurry. And Dawson seems to be taking this case personally.'

'Because of the chase?'

'The papers said it was mismanaged. He's very touchy about it.'

'I saw the Commissioner didn't support him, but I'd be surprised if he's planted evidence. Look, Connie, anything's possible, but there's no way on earth I'm going there, not publicly anyway.'

'Couldn't you suggest something, even hint at it, when you have Dawson in the box?'

'You've changed your tune. Last time around you ostracised me when I suggested to Dawson that there might have been some sleight of hand with the black box from James Salisbury's car.'

'That's a bit of an exaggeration.'

'Now you want me to go on UK TV and accuse a senior police officer of being corrupt.'

'I have the feeling the press might get there soon, anyway.'

Judith crossed and re-crossed her legs. She stared hard at

Constance. 'Let them dig themselves a hole,' she finally said, 'and have Judge Nolan to deal with. Rather them than me.'

Constance switched the TV back on. Judith took the remote from her and paused it again.

'Listen, maybe I can do *something* with it,' she said. 'Select the best photographs for me and I'll take a look, OK?'

'OK,' Constance nodded. 'What about motive again? There isn't anything coming out of the prosecution statements yet, or have I missed it?'

'Not that I've seen. I suspect our friend Mr Laidlaw will deal with it on the hoof. He'll probably just go with Debbie losing her temper over this issue about Ben's future – which Ben confessed to. I agree it's not very convincing. I hope he doesn't ask Debbie about her fidelity, though. That could shake things up a bit. Juries don't like unfaithful spouses or ex-spouses, however consensual the arrangements might have been.'

'What if Mr X turns up?'

'Yes. It's possible, isn't it? I wish Debbie'd kept that letter, although we couldn't have done anything with it, except, perhaps, handed it to the police.'

'In which case, we might have seen it across the front page of the newspapers the next morning. What do you think he'll do?'

'Who knows? Either it was a try-on and he'll leave it now. He didn't want publicity and he won't reappear. It has been a few weeks already. Or he'll write again. Or he'll go straight to the press. They're likely to pay far more than Debbie ever could. Like I said before, it's totally out of our hands. Did you get anywhere with speaking to Nicki Smith?'

'I…found her quite interesting, not what I expected.'

'Oh?'

'She was very passionate about her causes, and not at all aggressive, like she is on TV.'

'What did she say about Rosie?'

'That she had an alibi for the murder, which Dawson checked out, and that she had been visiting a friend the day Rosie saw her, two weeks before she died. She also said Rosie was unfriendly when they did meet, just before her interview was pulled.'

'There's a surprise. And her emails to Rosie?'

'They weren't particularly threatening, quite long and rambling, in fact, but I'll look at them more closely when I get a chance. Is it worth trying Jason again? The things Debbie was saying about Rosie arguing with the BBC about her contract?'

'What? She wasn't getting paid the same as Jason, she threatened to sue and the BBC organised the hit?'

Constance's hand hovered over the remote. 'Do you always have to be so confrontational?' she said, striding off to the kitchen to refill her cup with hot water.

Judith followed her and offered her own mug. 'It was supposed to be a joke,' she said, 'but in bad taste, you're right. What do you think they'll write on my headstone? "Here lies Judith Burton. Hostile to the very end!"'

Constance found a packet of chocolate digestives in the cupboard and laid them on the worktop. Judith took one, broke it in half and offered the remainder to Constance.

'You'd like that, wouldn't you? Causing offence even after you're dead.' Constance took the biscuit from her.

'No one wants to be flavourless, insipid or tame,' Judith replied. 'It's just some people can't be honest about it and the rest don't realise that's how they really feel.'

***

Andy sat in silence, watching Katrina and Chris perform through the glass wall of the studio. Graham and Phil sat next to him, together with a series of assistants, with three cameras constantly moving around them. Every few seconds, Graham would point or nod or shake his head and the cameras would obey. Less frequently, he would give instructions regarding camera angles or notice of how many seconds the presenters had left before the next item. Phil, who had undertaken this role in the practice sessions all week, sat quietly, allowing Graham to be the boss.

But while the video featuring David Benson was playing, during which time the presenters took a welcome slurp of water and stretched their legs, followed by a quick touch-up of their makeup, a call came in which Graham seemed keen to take. Slowly and without drawing too much attention to himself, Andy scratched at his right ear and, in doing so, dislodged one side of his headphones, to allow him to eavesdrop on Graham's conversation.

'Yes, yes,' Graham was saying, and 'I value your advice above everyone else, you know that. That's why I've brought you in…

'…You think she'd be good for tomorrow night, then I think she'd be perfect!

'…Very left field, but that's why it's so fantastic.

'…Let's touch base at the end of tonight, but I'm leaving it all to you till I'm back – carte blanche. Phil knows that. OK?'

Graham turned towards Andy, who immediately lowered his hand, so that his headphones snapped back into place.

As the evening continued, Andy's thoughts turned to the lawyers who would be on their feet in court tomorrow and, in particular, to Judith Burton. They had appeared against each other, two years back, in a case where a Syrian refugee, Ahmad Qabbani, had been accused of the murder of an elderly artist. Andy had only known Judith in passing before then, and had been keen to impress her when they finally crossed swords.

In fact, he had been so eager to show her that he was a man of substance that he had probably behaved more antagonistically than was customary. And in the aftermath of her victory, he had felt almost ashamed for some of the side swipes and childish sniggers which he had directed at Judith during her cross-examination. Perhaps, given that he would be in front of the camera and Judith would have no right of reply of her own, now was his opportunity to redeem himself.

After an hour, Andy returned to the reception area to grab some iced water and a packet of mints, and then decided to wander around, just to stretch his legs. When he had been rehearsing from the studio itself, he had noticed a darkened window to one side of where the production team sat. He had wondered, then, what it was for. Now, as he strolled past the door which would lead him to Graham and Phil, he saw another door he hadn't previously noticed, with a small, makeshift 'No Entry' sign, stuck on with Sellotape. It was very slightly ajar and he could hear someone talking from inside the room.

'There you are!' Graham's hand slapped down hard on his shoulder and Andy spun around to see his boss beaming widely at him. 'We're just going into a commercial break so it would be great to get your feedback, with the others, on how we're doing so far.'

Andy had little option but to comply as Graham steered him onwards and he was left wondering, right through the break and afterwards, who might have been behind that door and why he wasn't allowed to find out for himself.

PART TWO

LONDON, SEPTEMBER 2019

25

CONSTANCE WAS SITTING on a bench in Greyfriars' gardens, her back to the traffic. If she blocked her ears and just allowed her eyes to feast on the pink climbing roses and saucer-shaped clematis, she might be in a country garden, albeit one enhanced by the remains of a crumbling, ancient church. To her right, the sun reflected from the shiny panels of One New Change. Then Judith emerged from the crowds of besuited City workers, striding purposefully in her direction. She rose and they walked together towards the Old Bailey.

A sizeable crowd had gathered outside the court, separated by the police into three distinct groups. On one side, there were banners championing diversity and inclusion, rainbow flags, signs with messages: 'Trans Rights are Human Rights', 'Identity not Disorder', 'The Future isn't Binary', 'Trans Lives Matter'. On the other, a larger group railing against domestic violence with equally large flags and boards: 'Justice for Rosie', 'Domestic

Violence Kills', 'Abuse is a Crime Not an Excuse', 'Silence Hides Violence'. Further away from the entrance there was a group of football supporters wearing Arsenal football shirts, one of them carrying a sign reading 'Danny Mallard, Walks on Water', but they were dwarfed by the other two groups.

They were all chanting loudly, their messages of support and condemnation hopelessly mixed, so that it was impossible to make out more than the odd word.

'Oh God!' Judith said, reading the signs to her left. 'Does that mean we're champions of inclusion? I'm not sure I've ever been one of those before.'

'And enemies of women. I haven't been one of those either.' Constance had glanced to her right. 'I wonder what it's like inside the building.'

'Come on. Let's just walk through. They don't know who we are...yet.'

Judith strode on ahead, but Constance hesitated. She had spied the back of a woman's head, a diminutive woman with thick, brown, curly hair, standing unusually erect and bold amid the drifting masses; she had wondered if it was Nicki. Then the crowd surged towards her, she was jostled and lost her balance, and when she recovered the woman was nowhere to be seen.

***

Debbie sat demurely in the dock, her hair neatly braided, a paisley shirt visible beneath her pale blue jacket. She nodded to Constance and then resumed her blank expression. Laura sat on the front row of the public gallery, together with Debbie's mother and, to her other side, sat Ben and Ellis.

Around them, a bizarre ritual was playing out. At least ten people had arrived together, each with a number printed on a piece of paper. They were shuffling around the available chairs, talking animatedly to one another, pointing at otherwise occupied seats, muttering under their breath and generally diffusing around the room.

One of them, a man of around 40, in jumper and jeans, eventually sat down, only to be faced with a chorus of disapproval: shaking of heads, wagging of fingers, facial expressions bordering on aggressive and wild gesticulation. He resolutely ignored them all and began writing notes in a tiny book, with a short pencil. Finally, another man moved over to the door to direct the stragglers, leaving the last two standing at the back.

'It's like musical chairs,' Judith quipped. 'Who are they all?'

'Journalists. Maybe we should have asked for a bigger room,' Constance said, unbuttoning her jacket. 'It's pretty warm in here already.'

'I don't understand why they all want to be here when they could be multi-tasking somewhere else,' Judith said.

'They're all desperate to be where the action is. They've got this system of allocating places. It changes each day, to give each reporter a different seat…that's what I heard, anyway,' Constance said.

'Clearly their infallible system had a minor hiccup this morning. Good job the judge wasn't here to see it. She would have sent them all packing.'

Right on cue, Judge Nolan swept in, her eyes alighting on the two reporters without a seat, for just a moment, before scanning the public and the cameras.

Then the jury entered and were sworn in slowly and laboriously;

seven women and five men. Laidlaw conferred with his team, Constance noticing a chunky silver ring in the shape of a skull on his little finger as he raised his hand to cover his mouth from scrutiny.

'Is he wearing makeup?' Judith whispered to Constance. His face had an artificially smooth texture and beige tint and his lips were more pastel pink than she remembered.

'And the judge, too,' Constance replied. It was clear that Judge Nolan had visited the hairdresser, perhaps even that morning; her brown hair was streaked with purples and golds and was neatly trimmed to feather her face, stripping at least ten years from her age.

'Good morning,' Judge Nolan began. 'As we are now all assembled, I am going to instruct the usher to switch on the cameras. They will be switched off at the end of each session and switched on again when we reconvene. Three of the four cameras are operated automatically, situated above us, one focused on me, the lawyers and the witnesses. You shouldn't notice them at all. This one here in the centre, as you can see, is manually operated and can be used to pick up any other useful images.' Judge Nolan nodded to a man standing in the middle wearing noise-cancelling headphones, very obviously working a large camera, supported by an equally large tripod.

'Members of the jury, I wanted to reassure you that you will not be filmed at any time during the proceedings. Members of the press and public, this is a reminder to those present that any attempts to identify jurors is a contempt of court, punishable with a fine or imprisonment. Usher, cameras please. Mr Laidlaw, I am ready to hear from you.'

Jeremy Laidlaw gave a half bow to left and right as he rose to his feet. He waited until the cameraman's thumb was waved aloft and then launched into his opening speech, setting out the details of the murder and Debbie and Rosie's background, together with a somewhat lengthy exposition of Rosie's charitable acts.

'The prosecution will show that Debbie Mallard killed her former wife,' Laidlaw continued. 'She did this callously and cruelly and for no good reason. Debbie, it's true, was a celebrity in her own right, as she became a highly successful footballer back in the 1990s and early Noughties, but you must put that out of your minds when you judge the facts.

'Everyone is equal in the eyes of the law. This was an act of brutal domestic violence by a cruel and controlling person.' Laidlaw stopped and stared straight at the camera before continuing. 'Sadly, the spouses had fallen out. We will hear from a close friend of Miss Harper, one Caroline Fleming, that this was, in part, but not exclusively, because of the defendant's decision to transition to become a woman.

'Danny Mallard began living as a woman, known as "Debbie", in 2017. And gradually, over the next year, she became "Debbie" in her professional life too, and took steps towards changing her gender legally. She had hormone treatment and gender reassignment surgery at the end of 2017. Unsurprisingly, the transition from Danny to Debbie was a difficult and sensitive issue and caused Miss Harper considerable pain.'

Judith was on her feet in a flash, the manually operated camera nudging in her direction to zoom in and capture not only her words but her facial expressions. 'Your honour. As everyone will appreciate, Miss Harper is not here today to testify as to her response to her husband's transition and the evidence of the other witnesses on this aspect of her relationship with Debbie is decidedly limited.'

'Thank you, Ms Burton. Mr Laidlaw. Don't put words into other people's mouths – especially not dead people.'

'No, of course not, your honour. Shortly after the defendant's decision to transition, she moved out of the marital home and the couple were formally divorced on 28 June 2018. Debbie continued to visit and had regular contact with their son, Ben. Their daughter, Laura, was already living away from home.

'The defence will say that the defendant is not a violent person, that the marriage was happy and their split amicable. This is not reflected by the evidence. We have and will play to the court a recording of a 999 call made by a terrified Rosie Harper in 2017, in which she locks herself in the bathroom and implores police for help. The prosecution will show, therefore, that the day Rosie died was not the first time the couple had fought or the first time Debbie had hurt Rosie.

'Then we have the other real, tangible evidence we can show you; Debbie's blood-soaked black motorbike glove found at the scene. And the murder weapon itself, a "Best Newcomer in TV" award, is important too. It was found dumped in a dustbin a few doors away.

'The defence will talk about motive, no doubt. They will try to confuse you by saying that there was no conflict, Debbie had moved out, transitioned, was living her new life and all was fine. But we will show there were numerous items which caused conflict. First, the children. They disagreed over whether their son, Ben, should continue at school. Also, Rosie was, despite her generous salary from the BBC, short of money. Much of the couple's equity was stored up in their family home and two other houses they owned, in Florida and Spain. In recent years, Rosie had paid the mortgages, while the defendant paid the remaining day-to-day living expenses. The defendant had stopped making those payments when she moved out, and Rosie wanted her to re-start.

'We know that the defendant visited the house on the afternoon Rosie died and the bottom line is that it's very unlikely that another person, well-known to Rosie, visited immediately afterwards. This is what the defence wants you to believe, but there was no forced entry to the property. Whoever killed Rosie – and we say, without a shadow of a doubt, it was Debbie Mallard – was welcomed in, only to abuse Rosie's trust in the worst way possible, by taking her life in this vicious manner.'

***

'Debbie Mallard did not murder Rosie Harper.' Judith paused, stared at the jury, then up at the nearest TV camera and then at Debbie. 'Debbie Mallard visited Rosie, by appointment, promptly at 1pm on 17th June. The appointment was in her Outlook diary. "Go see Rosie", it reads; hardly the actions of a murderer.

'She had been invited over to talk about family issues and she will accept that, when she left an hour later, they had not been resolved. But Rosie was alive when Debbie left; her activity on her laptop shows a hiatus in her work from 1.02pm until 2.15pm, coinciding precisely with the time of Debbie's visit. She then resumed work until 3.02pm, the last time she is recorded as using the laptop. As the evidence will show, she most likely died around that time and was discovered some two hours later, at 5pm.

'The defence has to accept that Debbie Mallard's DNA was all over the room in which Rosie was found; fingerprints and DNA evidence, including hair strands. But that is hardly surprising. She accepts she had visited that day, she was a fairly regular visitor and she had previously lived in the property for twelve years. Importantly, no fresh fingerprints of any kind were retrieved from the murder weapon. And the clothes Debbie was wearing were examined by police, and no traces of Rosie's DNA were found on them. The suggestion that Debbie somehow removed and disposed of her clothing during the afternoon is not accepted, and even if that had occurred, it would not explain there being no traces whatsoever of Rosie's blood on Debbie's person when she was arrested.

'As for motive, Mr Laidlaw would have us believe that this was a simple domestic quarrel which escalated and went wrong; that it is somehow commonplace for people who have been friends, lovers and soul-mates for twenty-two years, sharing life experiences – the good and the bad – to snap one day, leading one to suddenly murder the other. If that were the case, if that were a likely scenario – one which you have no reasonable doubt happened that day – then none of us who has a partner or spouse would sleep soundly in our beds tonight.

'Yes, I accept that most murders are perpetrated by a person known to the victim, but very few by a spouse or partner with no history of violence. Debbie will explain the 999 call, which, it is acknowledged, was a sad cry for help from a woman struggling to come to terms with the prospect of a divorce from her childhood sweetheart, and the loss of the life she had known since the age of nineteen. She will also explain the presence of the black glove at the scene, to the extent she is able, when she comes to give her evidence. No one knows for sure to whom it belongs or how it found its way to the murder scene. It is certainly not a key piece of evidence, as Mr Laidlaw would have you believe, as there is absolutely no proof it played any part in Rosie's murder.

'Now both Debbie's children will give evidence in this trial; unfortunately, it is a quirk of the process that one will appear on behalf of the prosecution and the other the defence. That should not concern you; there are purely procedural reasons why that will occur. What is crucial is that each of them, Laura and Ben, will tell you that they never saw their father act violently towards their mother. Never, in twenty-two years of living together. And neither of them believes Debbie capable of violence. They are the two people who lived with Debbie and Rosie and know them the best of anyone.

'Relevant, too, is Debbie's profession and the way the couple worked together, collaboratively, at family life. When the children were young and Debbie was away a lot, as young, aspiring footballers have to be, especially those who play for their country, Rosie spent more time at home. Danny Mallard played for Premier League side Arsenal from 1995 to 2005. During that time, he captained the team, scored 167 goals and was patron of a charity which helped disadvantaged children overcome trauma through sport. He was called up to the England squad when he was only nineteen.

'When Debbie retired as a player in 2010 and moved into management, the roles reversed. Debbie particularly chose a local club so as to be able to fulfil her parental duties, and you will hear of the close bond she has with her children.

'Yes, Rosie was popular and she worked hard too, exceptionally hard. But she did have enemies. Rosie was sufficiently concerned by threats received in the months leading up to her death to talk to the police, and additional security measures had been put in place at her home as a result.

'I cannot offer you definitive proof of another culprit. What I can do is to prove to you, I hope, that Debbie Mallard should not be sitting here today in this courtroom. She should be at home with her children, helping them to grieve and to rebuild their lives. Debbie Mallard did not murder Rosie Harper.'

As Judith finished her speech, she leaned very slightly towards Laidlaw.

'You've missed a bit,' she whispered, pointing to a spot on her own cheek and nodding her head towards his. Laidlaw's hand flew up to his face before he scowled and allowed it to drop to his side.

***

'What do you think?' Constance asked Judith, as they snatched a quick breath of air, via a slightly ajar window in the toilet, after opening speeches. The heat in the courtroom had been sweltering, exacerbated as it was by the crowds and the extra lighting installed to help the TV cameras obtain the best images.

'I think everyone has gone totally mad,' Judith guffawed. 'Laidlaw is wearing face makeup, has almost certainly had his teeth whitened and I wouldn't be surprised if he hadn't tried Botox too, his brow appeared particularly devoid of furrows. And he was wearing jewellery. Judge Nolan, who I would never have imagined even possessed a mirror or a hairbrush, appears to have spent at least five hours at the hair salon to emerge with lowlights and a cut which would not look out of place in a line-up of The Spice Girls. The usher…'

'I meant about our prospects.'

'Prospects? I haven't a clue. Seven women on the jury? Let's just examine that for a moment. In usual circumstances I would say that was really, really good, facing a charge of murder of a woman by a former husband, but with a defendant who was born a man and who has embraced womanhood and deserted his wife as she approached middle age – they may see it that way however we try to portray it – they may be far more judgemental.'

'I can't believe you just said that. You think women jurors are more likely to convict a woman than a man?

'Why do you ask what I think, if you don't want to hear my opinion?'

'If you were on the jury, you'd be the one sane, well-balanced woman fighting against the crowd?'

'I'm reporting on my personal and extensive experience of trial verdicts and on the statistics for convictions in trials involving murder of spouses and domestic abuse. You know the stats.'

'You are joking?'

'No. And women are more likely to change their minds during a trial. Men tend to plonk themselves down on one side or the other at the outset, beer in hand – metaphorically of course – and stay put.'

Constance stood with her mouth open. 'I wish I hadn't asked,' she managed.

'What does it matter what I think of the jury? Let's move on… Is Judge Nolan good for us, after all? I mean, she is "no nonsense", although I wonder if that will continue now she thinks she's in the movies. It might not be the persona she wants to cultivate publicly. And Laidlaw? How two-faced can you be? Although I predicted it, saying our victim was a model for every modern woman and we all have to embrace that; it's as if Debbie's on trial for murdering Mother Teresa, when Debbie did plenty of voluntary work too. And that, of course, must be ignored. I didn't spy anyone there who was obviously from the Beeb. Did you?'

'No one I recognised. And Jason Fenwick didn't come. You didn't go back on the chase?'

'Better to keep our powder dry on that for now, and it will be more powerful coming from Debbie first-hand, I think. I hope. I had to say something about the 999 call, but I'll let Debbie talk around that too.'

'You want Debbie to give evidence?'

'I'm not sure we have any choice, but I still worry it could be an unmitigated disaster. Better for her to think she will, so she prepares herself, and then pull the plug later on if we need to, than the other way around.'

'And you did give a hint on the glove?'

'Yes, just a tiny one. No one will be able to complain that I started hares running. But it was a genesis, a sprouting of sorts, if anyone was listening very carefully. Is it still packed by the door?'

'I haven't dared look.'

'Oh come on. That's the problem with leaving the court room. You have to get back in. If we keep moving and don't make eye contact with anyone, we should be fine.'

26

CHARLIE DAWSON WAS THE prosecution's first witness. Judith thought it refreshing to see that he had not been prompted by the cameras to undergo any kind of superficial metamorphosis, appearing as his usual, unkempt self. Only his shoes had been polished, although this had done little to restore their former glory after many a soaking in a variety of fluids.

'Chief Inspector Dawson. You were called to the scene of Rosie Harper's murder on 17th June. Can you describe what you saw when you arrived, please.' Laidlaw swung his arms exaggeratedly across his body, the pinky ring making another laboured appearance.

'I received a call at around 5.20pm. I entered the property and found Miss Harper's body, lying half in the house and half in the back garden. There were blood stains trailing from the centre of the living room and various other items on the floor.'

'Who was at the scene when you arrived?'

'Two of my junior officers were there. They had forcibly entered the property when there was no reply. I arrived around fifteen minutes after them. We then called in forensics, and myself and PC Thomas went to talk to the defendant.'

'And the front door of the property was intact when your officers arrived?'

'Yes, there were no signs of any forced entry.'

'Thank you. I want to focus for a moment on what happened when you went to tell the defendant, Debbie Mallard, that her ex-wife was dead.'

'I attended Shoreditch Park at around 6.45pm, together with PC Thomas. The defendant was conducting a football training session for a women's team she manages. We approached her and told her that Rosie was dead.'

'And what did she say?'

'At first she said it wasn't true. That she had seen Rosie earlier that day and that we must be wrong.'

'Then what happened?'

'I told her that Rosie had been murdered. She seemed very upset. She sort of staggered and fell down. Then she entered the public toilets. When PC Thomas went in after her, she had run away.'

'And when did you next see the defendant?'

'I drove with PC Thomas to the defendant's flat, arriving at 7.32pm. I then witnessed the defendant, on her moped, running away for a second time. Eventually, we caught up with her at her mother's address shortly after 8.25pm, where she surrendered to police.'

'Was there any possibility that the defendant did not know that you wanted her to stop?'

'No possibility. She deliberately drove off when she saw us

arrive.'

'Did she give an explanation for why she had run away?'

'She said that she wanted some time on her own.'

'I see. But, just to be clear, the defendant was not a suspect then, so she would have been free to go at any time. There would have been no need for a pursuit across London at great public expense, not forgetting the considerable risk to life associated with any high-speed chase, if she had simply stated in the words of the inimitable Greta Garbo, "I want to be alone".'

Dawson stared at Laidlaw, who had been waving his hands flamboyantly as he spoke, like an old-fashioned marionette. 'The pursuit of the defendant was conducted with the care and high standards of driving I expect from all of my officers. At no stage was any member of the public at risk,' he said.

'Thank you, Inspector, I am grateful for that reassurance. But my point was that none of that would have been necessary, had the defendant simply told you that she needed some time to grieve, some *head space*.'

'That's right.'

'So the only conclusion you could draw when she ran away, not once but twice, was that she had something to hide?'

'Yes.'

'Now, when you asked the defendant about her relationship with her ex-wife, what did she tell you?'

'That they remained on good terms, despite their divorce.'

'Do you believe that to be true?'

'I don't, no.'

'Why not?'

'Because the police were called to the house two years ago by Miss Harper, complaining of an apparent assault by her husband.'

'An *assault*?' Laidlaw's eyes widened and he wallowed in the sibilance of the word.

'Yes.'

'And there's a recording of the call she made to the police that evening, isn't there?'

'Yes.'

'Your honour. I will now play the call to the court. Members of the jury, do please listen carefully. Do you know who is speaking on that call?'

'It's Rosie Harper.'

'And the voice near the end, in the background?'

'I believe it's her son, Ben.'

The court was silent. Laidlaw asked for the lights to be dimmed, which resulted in an eye roll from Judith, picked up by the cameraman. There was a distinctive crackle of a telephone line emanating from various speakers as the 999 call was played in full.

Laidlaw paused while the lights came up, and allowed time for one juror to wipe her eyes. Laura was biting her lip. Debbie's mother gripped her hand.

'Did Rosie Harper make any other 999 calls?'

'Not as far as I know.'

'Did she press charges against the defendant for the violence she suffered that night?'

'No, she didn't.'

'Was Danny Mallard interviewed by police, in relation to his conduct? He was still Danny then?'

'He was, yes. Police attended, but Miss Harper told them that she didn't want to take further action and the matter was left there.'

'I see. Miss Harper wanted to "keep things quiet"?'

Judge Nolan interrupted before Judith could even open her mouth.

'Mr Laidlaw. You're doing it again. Even if Chief Inspector Dawson had interviewed Miss Harper himself – and you haven't clarified whether he did – he would not be qualified to tell us what Miss Harper wanted to do back in February 2017, or at any time, now would he?'

'No, your honour. We will hear a little more about the call later,' Laidlaw said. 'Tell us about the glove found at the scene. It's exhibit two, your honour.'

The black, rubbery glove was handed around the jury and on to the judge, in its sealed transparent package.

'This glove was found lying in the middle of the living room floor, at the place where we believe Rosie fell. It was soaked with Rosie's blood,' Dawson announced dramatically, allowing himself a glance at Debbie as he spoke.

'Who does the glove belong to?'

'The defendant accepts that she owns black motorbike gloves of the same make, but she maintains she wasn't wearing them that day, that they are a well-known brand and that there is nothing to say for certain whether this is her glove or not.'

'And what did DNA testing show?'

'You should ask the expert for more information, but I understand the glove contains traces of Debbie Mallard's DNA, from her skin, confirming she had worn it.'

'And what size is the glove?'

'It's a Large, which is the defendant's size.'

'Does any other family member wear gloves like these?'

'Not as far as we are aware, and we can rule them out as

belonging to Rosie herself. We compared them with gloves found at the property. They're far too big.'

'Thank you, Chief Inspector Dawson.'

***

'Chief Inspector Dawson, I have only a few questions for you, you'll be pleased to hear.' Judith smiled broadly, ensuring she included the jury in the warmth of her gaze.

'Whatever you need,' Dawson replied, clearing his throat as he spoke, keen to flush away the debris of the earlier conversation with Laidlaw.

'I want to begin, if I may, with your *pursuit* of Debbie Mallard on the night of Rosie Harper's murder.'

Judith was still smiling, Dawson frowned and he nodded stiffly.

'You were driving one of the police cars, is that correct?'

'Yes.'

'And how many other cars did you summon to assist you?'

'A call went out to all cars in the vicinity.'

'So, how many joined in? One? Two? Perhaps three?'

Dawson gulped. 'I believe there were seven cars involved by the end,' he said.

'Seven police cars were pursuing Debbie across London, on her 50cc moped. That seems a lot to me. At the time, as Mr Laidlaw has helpfully pointed out, Debbie was not a suspect. Is that correct?'

'That's correct.'

'And you had no reason to believe that she had committed any criminal act?'

'When someone is murdered, we do always think of close

family first.'

'Ah. That's not quite what I asked, Inspector. Did you have any reason, other than proximity to the victim, to believe that she had committed any criminal act at that time?'

'No, except for her running away. That made me suspicious.'

'And, over your long and illustrious career, have you often been in the unfortunate position of having to tell people that close family members have been injured or killed?'

'Yes, I have.'

'You described Debbie Mallard's response earlier. You said she "seemed very upset. She sort of staggered and fell down. Then she entered the public toilets". Do you remember saying that?'

'Yes.'

'And that response, *staggering, collapsing, visible distress*, in your experience as a police officer, is that usual for a spouse or partner who is in shock or disbelief? In fact, I think you also told us that Debbie's first response was to say to you, "This can't be true", or words to that effect?'

'Yes, that is a response we often encounter.'

'Was there anything in Debbie's response to you and PC Thomas which suggested anything other than total shock and disbelief at what you were saying?'

'No.'

'So why on earth did you harness half the fire power of London to hunt Debbie – when she was clearly in a state of considerable distress, her wife had been murdered – to hunt Debbie down in such a barbaric way?'

'When she ran off, as I said, we concluded that she was trying to escape. And if she was so innocent, why didn't she just stop running?'

'Inspector Dawson, I put it to you that the whole chase was a terrifying experience, particularly for someone who has just been told that their spouse has been murdered, who is clearly in shock, and it's not a surprise that Debbie was frightened.'

'I don't agree.'

'All right. Let's examine this a little more. When Debbie ran away, did she choose a high-speed mode of transport?'

'I've said; she was on her moped.'

'And did she run to a railway station, a harbour, an airport – somewhere that would enable her to escape from you?'

'No. I've already said. She went to her mother's house.'

'And you had that address?'

'We found it easily, yes.'

'When you located Debbie at her mother's house, what happened?'

'I knocked at the door and Mrs Mallard, Debbie's mother, invited me in. Debbie was already there.'

'Did she try to run away then or barricade herself in?'

'No, she came willingly with us.'

'And did you arrest her then and there?'

'No.'

'Why not?'

'We didn't have any evidence, then, that she'd done anything wrong.'

'But you had enough evidence to hound her across the capital in this petrifying manner! And you have said already that she had told you that she wanted to be on her own for a while, to process the awful news you had given her an hour or so earlier?'

'Yes.'

'Let's talk now about the 999 call which Mr Laidlaw played to the court. Did Miss Harper, in fact, identify herself at any time on the call?'

'No.'

'But officers attended at her house on the night of 1 February 2017?'

'Yes.'

'How did they know where to go?'

'They traced the call.'

'And you were not one of the officers who attended?'

'That's right.'

'Did the officers who attended file any kind of report?'

'No.'

'How do you know what happened when the officers attended?'

'As part of this investigation, I spoke to PC Jenkins, who called in that night. He remembered it all, with her being a TV star. He told me that Miss Harper said that she hadn't meant to call the police. She said she was fine. They checked she appeared fine and they left.'

'No physical injuries then?'

'I believe not.'

'And Rosie said, "I made a mistake, please forget the fact I called you."'

'Something like that.'

'There is no evidence of any kind, then, of Debbie Mallard actually being violent towards her wife on the night of 1 February 2017, is there?'

'Well, there is the call itself?'

'All right. Let's examine that call. I won't play it again. I have a transcript here, so we can see what Rosie Harper actually says, can't we? So here goes. The emergency operator says, "What service do you require, caller?" Rosie says, "Police". The operator says, "Where are you?" She says, "At home." Then… Inspector, I will read the operator's lines; could you read out Rosie's words please?'

Dawson's eyebrows disappeared into his hairline, but, all credit to him, he cleared his throat, held the paper he had been handed at arm's length and joined in, where appropriate, if a little stilted.

'"Are you in danger?"' Judith said, beginning their play reading.

'"No, not any more, maybe…"'

'"Did someone hurt you?"'

'"Ah. Where to start? My husband…he…I got upset. I need the police to come. I need them to stop him."'

'Let's just pause there for a moment. Rosie Harper is asked a direct question, isn't she? "Did someone hurt you?" Does she answer yes?'

'No, she doesn't.'

'Let's continue then. The operator says, "Is your husband there with you now?"'

'"I think he's gone. Oh God, I hope he's gone."'

'"Tell us your address, then we can come and help you."'

'"I…I…no I don't want…please…I'm fine now. I don't need help. I don't know…I shouldn't have called. Just silly really."'

'"You said he hurt you?"'

'"Well…he…"'

'So, in the second part of the call, again, the operator asks, as I did, "You said he hurt you". Does Rosie Harper answer *yes*?' Judith pressed.

'No, she doesn't.' Beads of sweat glistened on Dawson's upper lip.

'Thank you. That's the end of Rosie's conversation. Then, as you explained, we hear a voice in the background, believed to be that of Ben Mallard, saying, "Mum, are you in the bathroom?" Then the call ends.'

'In summary, if you listen carefully to what Debbie said, instead of indulging in hyperbole or embellishment, while I accept Rosie sounds upset on the recording, she does not actually say at any time that she is hurt or injured, does she?'

'She doesn't say it herself, but when the operator asks if Debbie hurt Rosie, she kind of agrees.'

'Well the operator asks what we would call a leading question. "Did someone hurt you?" She anticipates, understandably, that Rosie *might* be hurt. But even then, Rosie doesn't say yes, does she?'

'No.'

'If that is the evidence of prior violence on the part of Debbie Mallard to which Mr Laidlaw referred in his opening, then we can see that, in reality, it isn't anything of the kind, although even if Rosie had said yes, you are confirming that the police officers who attended found no evidence of Rosie being physically injured in any way. Is that right?'

'Yes.'

'So, I will ask again, you summarised the significance of this call as evidence of an *apparent assault* by Debbie Mallard. Do you now accept that Rosie Harper never says, in that call, that Debbie has hurt her physically or even threatened to hurt her?'

'Sometimes you have to look behind the words.'

'But that would be your opinion of what Rosie Harper meant, which, as Her Honour keeps reminding us, is not evidence in this case. Now what about the glove?' Judith hesitated and Constance looked up. 'There are three major brands of motorbike glove readily available in the UK,' Judith continued. 'The one you found at the scene, a Booster, sells one thousand pairs per month in the UK alone. Did you search the rest of the house for the second glove?'

'Yes. And we searched Debbie Mallard's flat and her mother's house. We didn't find it.'

'Don't you think it a little unusual, if Debbie had killed her wife, for her to have left such an obvious clue lying at the scene?'

'Your honour, Inspector Dawson cannot answer that question,' Laidlaw interrupted and Judge Nolan agreed with an enthusiastic nod.

'Yes, of course. I had just one more question regarding the glove for you, Inspector, as I will save the rest for our forensic expert. It does involve looking, once more, at the photograph of the crime scene we saw earlier. My instructing solicitor will hand up this clicker. Can you see? It enables you to point to things on the screen. Can you take it and can you point for us, to show where, on the photograph, the glove is lying?'

Inspector Dawson took the clicker from Constance and then peered at the photograph. 'It doesn't seem to be visible in this photograph. Is there another one I could see?' he said.

'This photograph is a slightly wider angle. Is the glove there?' Judith allowed a hint of impatience to feed into her delivery.

'I think it's...in the dark area right at the bottom of the screen.'

'Really? You must have better eyesight than me. Here's another photograph of Rosie Harper's living room. Can you point to the glove here?'

'Perhaps rather than making Inspector Dawson run through all 272 photographs,' Laidlaw was on his feet, with one eye over his shoulder, on the rest of his team, 'it would be helpful if my solicitor were able to locate a photograph, showing the positioning of the glove and put it in evidence after the next break?'

'Your honour, that would be perfectly acceptable to me, thank you. I have no desire to waste time or make things difficult for Inspector Dawson.'

Dawson swallowed noisily and his eyes met Judith's. She looked away. 'Moving on then, during the course of your investigation, you and your team have interviewed many potential witnesses, including people working every day with Debbie. Has any of those witnesses told you that Debbie has been violent towards them?'

'No.'

'Has any witness told you that they saw Debbie being violent towards Rosie Harper?'

'No. But in my experience, domestic abuse often stays in the home.'

'Thank you for expressing your opinion, but you are here today to answer questions on the facts.'

'Which couldn't be clearer,' Laidlaw muttered loudly enough for the microphones to broadcast and the audience to smile in collusion.

'Finally, your entry to the property. Your officers broke down the door to gain entry, is that correct?'

'Yes.'

'The door became damaged then, as did the lock?'

'I suppose so.'

'How could it be possible, then, to say, as you did, that this was not a forced entry to the property. Surely any evidence of a prior tampering with the lock, would have been totally obliterated by your men forcing their way in?'

'What I know is that when my officers attended at the property, the door was closed and locked and appeared to be intact.'

'What steps did they ascertain to ensure that the door was intact?'

Dawson took a deep breath.

'No specific tests. They would have looked at the door and the lock.'

'And no doubt, given the dog howling and the panicked call from Mrs Harris over the road, they would have, understandably, been keen to get inside. They probably didn't spend too long in that examination.'

'I think that's probably right.'

'Thank you. No further questions.'

'Your honour, I have just one area to cover in re-examination,' Mr Laidlaw said. 'Inspector Dawson, you told Ms Burton that the officers who attended Rosie Harper, in February 2017, could not see any evidence of her being injured?'

'That's what I was told.'

'And you were forced by Ms Burton here to accept that Rosie Harper herself did not expressly refer to any injury or violence on the call?'

'I think *forced* is a little strong, your honour,' Judith countered. 'It suggests a degree of coercion.'

'I will rephrase the question. You accepted, when questioned by Ms Burton, that Rosie Harper did not expressly refer to an injury on the call?'

'Yes.'

'In your experience, why do members of the public call the police, but then, later on, say they are "fine"?'

Dawson stared hard at Judith before replying.

'Sometimes, especially if they are frightened of their partner or spouse, they play things down. They realise that the only way forward is to accuse the other person of an assault, and they worry what the consequences might be for themselves…and their children. Or they don't want the publicity of a court hearing. Or the partner is the breadwinner and they worry how they will manage financially if they press charges.'

'So, it is possible that Rosie Harper had suffered an assault, which had led to the call, but she then reflected and preferred to sweep things under the carpet?'

'Mr Laidlaw. I'm surprised that Ms Burton has not been leaping out of her seat, especially as she took offence a moment ago at your far less offensive choice of words,' Judge Nolan intervened laconically. 'Members of the jury, Inspector Dawson's thoughts on what is possible, even though he is no doubt an experienced and highly respected professional, is not evidence. I will remind you of this at the end of the case, when I sum things up for you. Do you have any other questions for this witness?'

'No, your honour. Just one comment – correction really – a matter of which Inspector Dawson was clearly unaware. The lock on the front door was subjected to testing by forensic and this confirmed no evidence of tampering. This can be addressed by Dr Marcus, our forensic expert, when he gives his evidence.'

'Thank you. I suggest we start again at 9.30am tomorrow and that will give you ample opportunity, Mr Laidlaw, to find those photographs you wanted.'

27

'So, a fascinating first day in the Debbie Mallard murder trial. We have an action-packed evening for you.' Monday night's episode of *Court TV BTS* kicked off with Katrina back on the sofa. 'First of all, I want to introduce Andy Chambers. Hello Andy.'

'Hello Katrina.'

'Andy is chief legal adviser to Court TV, he's a practising criminal barrister and he's here to answer *all* your questions from today's action – and we've had plenty. Then, later on, we'll be hearing from body-language expert, Katy Moover, who'll analyse what people were really saying, even when they weren't speaking.'

***

Constance poured herself a second mug of coffee and called Judith.

'You need to watch,' she said.

'I have to prepare my cross-examination for tomorrow.'

'They've got a body-language expert and Andy Chambers.'

'Andy Chambers? You mean the Andy Chambers we know?'

'The same.'

'What's he doing on there?'

'He's "chief legal adviser" and he's going to answer the public's questions.'

'Is he really? How enterprising of him. And who's the body-language expert?'

'Someone called Katy Moover. Oh! Katy Moover?'

'What is it?'

'She contacted me a few weeks back. Asked if we wanted any help with the case.'

'I hope you told her that lawyers defended criminal cases –not some jumped-up acting coach.'

'I politely declined, yes.'

'Listen, I really do need to get on. I can't believe Andy Chambers is going to say anything earth-shattering. He's a decent barrister, as you know, but fairly pedestrian.'

Constance noticed that Judith did not tell her, directly, to switch off, to spend her time more profitably. She was leaving it up to Constance to decide her priorities.

She looked across at her open laptop, containing the day's transcript. Ordinarily, she would comb through it, eager to find the tiniest inconsistencies, the leads Judith could pick up and develop tomorrow or the day after. And the things Judith had asked her to cover? If she carried on watching, they would all have to wait. And when would she sleep? While she remembered Greg's kind offer to watch the TV coverage and report back, there really was no way to take this material in vicariously. It had to be consumed first-hand, to savour all the flavours.

***

Andy began with some nondescript background, explaining who everyone was in court and their role, with Katrina prompting him, where appropriate. He also summarised, very broadly, the content of the witness evidence from the day in court. Then, suddenly, in his ear, he heard a low voice talking. *This is great, Andy, but move on to something a bit more challenging now.* The voice distracted him, momentarily, from Katrina, but he tuned back in to hear her saying: '...the tactics employed by Judith Burton. She's the lawyer defending Debbie Mallard. You've worked with Judith before, haven't you?'

Andy hesitated. He hadn't expected the opportunity to discuss Judith's performance quite so soon, to promote his own agenda. Then he remembered that he was supposed to be helping the public understand what was going on, not getting personal. And what did the voice in his ear mean by 'challenging' and how could he reconcile all these different objectives? Perhaps he could allow himself to be a little provocative, after all.

'Yes,' he said, feeling his pulse begin to quicken, the anticipation of undertaking something really naughty kickstarting his sympathetic nervous system into action.

'And when was that?'

'A year or so back, I was prosecuting a case against a Syrian refugee and Judith was defending.'

'And she won, if I'm not mistaken?' Katrina was smiling gently. When Phil had talked about research in rehearsals, Andy hadn't appreciated Katrina might be researching him.

'The defendant was acquitted, which was clearly the right decision in that case,' he said. There, he'd been totally fair and avoided pointing fingers.

'No hard feelings then?'

'No.' Andy hadn't felt bad about Ahmad Qabbani's release at the time, so why was it causing him so much embarrassment now?

'I understand that, where cross-examination is concerned, Judith is a true veteran,' Katrina was saying. 'Can you explain, for our audience, what methods she's employing with Chief Inspector Dawson and why she's so successful?'

Andy paused again. Now was his opportunity to be magnanimous, to laud Judith's skills. But, something held him back. Should he do this? Give away the secrets of great cross-examination technique, honed to perfection by years of practice? However much praise he directed towards her, it might lay Judith's systems bare and vulnerable to future attack. And was this even what the public wanted? Katrina was waiting for his answer. When it didn't come, she went further.

'For example, one of the main pieces of evidence against Debbie Harper was an emergency call she made back in 2017.'

'Yes,' Andy said.

'Can you analyse, for the benefit of our viewers, how Judith dealt with that?'

Andy was boxed in. There was really no way out. Katrina knew her brief. He had to answer – and with more than a monosyllable.

'Yes,' he repeated. 'This really was a masterful piece of cross-examination by Judith.' If he stuck to saying positive things, he couldn't be criticised, could he? 'As we discussed, she begins with a call which, to any casual listener, sounds like a woman reporting violence by her husband against her, and that's how the prosecution presents it. Then Judith breaks it down into its constituent parts, to show the jury that the call is not what it seems. That's her aim in any event. To say, forget your overall impression of the call, examine it really closely and you'll see that Rosie Harper never says she's hurt, or that anyone hurt her.'

'Is this one of Judith's tactics, then?'

'I wouldn't call it a tactic; that sounds rather underhand.' Andy swallowed hard as the camera closed in on him, 'It's her job to analyse the evidence carefully. It's the right thing for a defence lawyer to do.'

'Why did she make the police officer, Chief Inspector Dawson, read out Rosie Harper's words?'

In his ear, the voice intervened once more. *Come on, Andy, I want something controversial here*, it said.

'Again, to make the jury really focus on what was said, not jump to conclusions,' Andy's voice quivered as he hovered on the brink, then decided to dive right in. 'But, you're right,' he said, 'making Inspector Dawson read out Rosie's words was brilliant, because it made the whole incident sound less hostile, having a man – and a physically strong man – read out those words, no one felt for a second that Rosie was really being threatened.'

'I understand.' Katrina smiled again, enveloping the public at home with her warmth and radiance. 'That's a wonderful insight into how defence barristers unpick the prosecution evidence. By the end of that exchange, we're persuaded, or at least some of us were – we were debating the issue before we came on air this evening and we were fairly evenly matched in our views – that Rosie had wasted police time with that call.'

'There are twelve people on the jury; they may be equally divided.' Andy grinned. He was on safer ground, now. But Katrina remained one step ahead.

'I was going to add, though, that, while we've been talking, we've had a number of calls to the show, all of them condemning Judith Burton for her cross-examination, saying it belittles the whole issue of domestic violence, particularly against women. What do you think about that?'

'Oh, I...I am sure that was never Judith's intention.' Andy refused, still, to call Judith out.

'Perhaps not, but if that's the effect, does that matter?' Katrina said.

'The key point to remember,' Andy was trying to remain in control, reminding himself he was chief legal adviser, not the person sitting opposite him, 'is that Debbie Mallard is entitled to have the evidence against her tested, and tested thoroughly. I would suggest those viewers who are calling in challenging Judith's cross-examination ask themselves the question whether, if that call was being held up as evidence against them, they would want their lawyer to question it or just to give up. And, you've also got to remember that the person giving evidence is a police officer. He's not personally involved in the case, and he's used to giving evidence, so he's a pretty robust witness, which barristers always consider before they ask their questions.'

'Thank you, Andy. We'll be hearing more from Andy later on, after more questions have come through. But now, we're turning to Katy Moover, psychologist, voice coach and body-language expert. Hello Katy.'

Andy shifted to the right on the sofa to allow the expert in. *Well done!* the voice in his ear said warmly. And Andy thought he probably had done fairly well, for his first outing.

***

In her flat, Constance fidgeted and stared at her phone, half expecting Judith to call any moment, to express indignation at Andy's deconstruction of her performance. But all was quiet. Judith must be occupied elsewhere.

***

Katy Moover began with some background, explaining some of the usual ways she would judge if a person was being truthful, simply from the way they moved their faces and bodies. After a few minutes of scrutiny of both Laidlaw and Judith in full flow, Katrina directed Katy to the footage of Dawson talking about the motorbike glove.

She paused the recording at the point at which Dawson took the clicker from Constance.

'If you watch the Chief Inspector here,' Katy said, when he says the glove "doesn't seem to be visible" he crosses his legs, see, and folds his free arm around his body.'

'What does that show?'

'It's very defensive.'

'Do you mean he's lying?'

'No, not necessarily. Rather, he feels sensitive about this question; he knows it's an area of weakness. And then,' she shifted on a few frames to the second, wider-angled photo, 'now when he identifies the shadow at the bottom of the screen as being the glove, look how he sticks out his chin.'

'And what does that mean?'

'It's a sign of obstinacy. He's saying, with his body, "I'm sure that's the glove and I'm not budging".'

***

Constance awoke with a jolt. She was lying on the sofa and the end credits of *Court TV BTS* were flashing across the screen. She knew that she ought to rewind and find out what Andy had said in his second session, what questions the viewers had posed, but, instead, she stretched out her aching limbs and shuffled off to bed.

28

Judith leaned against the wall of the toilet cubicle, breathing heavily, trying hard to relax. Five minutes earlier, when she had picked up a garbled message from Constance that she was going to be late, she had forced her way, alone, through an agitated crowd, demonstrating outside the court building. Jeremy Laidlaw, just ahead, had been cheered. A woman carrying a banner reading 'Laid-ies Champion' had handed him a bunch of carnations as he passed by, kissing him on the cheek. In contrast, a man had called out to Judith.

'Hi there, Judith? How's it going, do you think? Judith? Judith, over here!'

Judith had nodded non-committally and kept moving, alarmed to be plucked from anonymity so abruptly.

'Are you a role model for young women?' was his follow up. But this was met with some raucous laughter, which quickly morphed into a chorus of booing and hissing, growing in volume as she headed towards the thickest part of the crowd. Then someone shouted 'shame on you' and, within seconds, the call was taken up, the chanting of 'shame on you', 'shame on you', assaulting her ears, as she dived through the doors.

It must be something associated with whatever Andy Chambers had said about her last night, Judith concluded. Constance had given her a précis, but perhaps she had sanitised it or not provided all the angles. Judith wished now she had watched the programme herself. It was so much easier to respond, to fight back, if you understood who the enemy was and why they were all fired up in the first place.

She checked her watch. 'It's nearly time,' she whispered. Taking another deep breath, she headed out towards the court.

***

'Mrs Harris. You were Rosie Harper's neighbour?' Jeremy Laidlaw began with his second witness. Lynn Harris was one week short of her seventieth birthday. A diminutive but wiry woman, she had been one of the first waiting outside the court this morning.

Lynn had lived in the East End all her life and she was proud of it. She had witnessed the slow gentrification of the neighbourhood, so that her home, which she'd purchased under Margaret Thatcher's right-to-buy scheme, was now worth many times more than she would have dreamed, when she'd moved in as a newly-wed in 1972. But that didn't bother her. It made her feel upwardly mobile, without having to move anywhere. And in no way had that been more proven than by her friendship with Rosie Harper, the TV star who lived over the road. Judith saw all of that in Lynn Harris' peroxide hair, red enamel earrings, leopard-print jacket and pixie boots.

'Yes. And a nice quiet place it was till all this 'appened,' she replied. 'Now it's impossible to go out without being jumped on by someone with a furry microphone on a stick. You may as well forget trying to have any visitors or any parcels delivered.'

'I can see it must be inconvenient for you. Can you describe where your property is and how close it is to that of Rosie Harper?'

'Certainly I can. I live in the middle of the terrace, number 23. On the other side, there are some big 'ouses, like Rosie's, but mine was always big enough for me and Frank, my late 'usband. We never had no kids. I suppose celebrities need more space, for all their trophies and things...and she had to wear so many different outfits for TV. It's on lots of floors, five I think, with a basement too.'

'Your home is directly opposite Rosie's?' Laidlaw was not responding well to Lynn's embroidery.

'Yes. Sometimes, if she was in her front room and I was up in my bedroom, we could wave to each other.'

Laidlaw gave a half smile, but Judith sensed it was more because Lynn had laughed her husky laugh and it seemed churlish not to respond than because he found her at all amusing.

'You knew each other well?'

'Ooh yes. I remember when they moved in. I babysat the children a few times to help them out, when Ben was little.'

'Can you tell me what you were doing on the 17th of June, around lunchtime?'

'I went to do some shopping in the morning and I was returning home around 1 o'clock. As I got out of my car, I saw Debbie parking his – sorry...*her* – moped outside. Then she went into the house, Rosie's house.'

'And what did you do?'

'I unpacked my shopping and made myself lunch.'

'And how can you be sure about the time?'

'When the police came around asking questions, after they found Rosie, I went to my car and I had a sticker from the local shops. I had parked at 12.02, so it must have been close to one when I came back. And I remembered watching *Homes Under the Hammer*, I told the police constable, while I was eating my lunch. That begins at 1.30.'

Judith glanced at Constance's empty place behind her. She had wanted the reassurance that came from sharing a nod or a glance or a gesture, something to indicate to her that Constance viewed Mrs Harris as she did – brash, self-important and ultimately shallow – and that gave her permission to strike, at the appropriate time.

'Are you sure it was the defendant you saw?'

'Your honour, the defence accepts that Debbie visited Rosie, arriving by moped at around 1pm.' Judith smiled at Lynn, as she half-rose to deliver her lines. She wanted Lynn to feel confident, comfortable, even relaxed. Then her attack, when it came, would be all the more devastating.

'Thank you. That's helpful. Move on please Mr Laidlaw.'

'Did you see Debbie Mallard leave the house?'

'No.'

'And what about the moped?'

'I looked out once and it was still there. And the next time I looked, it was gone.'

'And do you know when that was?'

'I told the policeman that I wasn't sure, but it must have been much later on. I don't spend all day standing around looking out of the window.'

The last line was delivered with the emphasis associated with healthy repetition. Judith laughed to herself.

'Did you see anything unusual or hear anything out of the ordinary that day?'

'Much later, it was. Around five o'clock.' For the first time, Lynn's face grew serious and she stole a glance at Debbie. Her bottom lip trembled.

'What happened around five o'clock?'

'It was their dog. It's a big collie; all fur. Rosie was always washing it, especially in the bad weather. It was barking and barking and then, sort of 'owling, like it was in pain. I ignored it at first, but then it went on and on. So, I looked out and I could see the dog; well, really just this great big, bushy tail, moving around and around, faster and faster. There's a gate, you see, at the side of the 'ouse, into the garden. I could see Belle, the dog, through the gate.'

'Did you go outside?'

'First I tried calling her, Rosie, in the 'ouse and it went to messages. Then I tried her mobile and I got the same.'

'What did you do then?'

'I crossed the road, but I couldn't see anything. So I went up the front steps and looked through the window. And then I saw...' Mrs Harris let out a sob and stuffed her fist in her mouth. She stared at Debbie, then out at the crowds of journalists, then back at Laidlaw.

'Take your time, Mrs Harris. Is that when you saw Rosie's body?'

'Mm,' she mumbled, stifling a sob.

'Then what happened?'

'I called the police and they came pretty smartish.'

'Did you see or hear anything else unusual earlier that day? Anyone unfamiliar in the street? Any other visitors to Rosie's house?'

Lynn swallowed and leaned heavily on the witness stand. 'No. Just Debbie Mallard.'

'And can you cast your mind back to February 2017, when Debbie was still living with Rosie? In fact, she was still living as a man, then, as Danny. There was an incident, when the police were called to Rosie's house. Do you know anything about that?'

'I heard them come. I don't remember exactly what time it was, probably around one or two o'clock in the morning. Since my Frank passed on, I'm a very light sleeper,' she added.

'Do you know why they came to the house?'

She lowered her voice and leaned towards Laidlaw. 'I heard a rumour that he 'it her; the defendant did. That's why they came.'

'Mrs Harris, I do need to ask you to clarify your answer,' Judge Nolan intervened. 'Do you have any personal knowledge that Debbie Mallard struck Rosie, back in 2017?'

'Well I didn't see it 'appen.'

'Did you see any evidence of an injury?'

'Elaine, Rosie's mum, she told me that he 'urt her.'

'Mr Laidlaw, is Mrs Harper going to be giving evidence?'

'She is.'

'We'll wait to ask her directly, then. Thank you.' Judge Nolan made some notes and nodded to Laidlaw to continue.

'Thank you, Mrs Harris. No more questions.'

Judith snatched another expectant glance behind her, but Constance was still not there. Then she stared up at the camera above her head. Her pulse was suddenly racing and she clasped and unclasped her fists twice in quick succession. *What, precisely,* had Andy Chambers said on TV last night that had made this morning's crowd so hostile? What could he possibly have criticised in yesterday's performance? She always conducted herself properly, and acted with integrity. People must have misunderstood whatever it was that he had said.

Lynn Harris took advantage of the hiatus to glug down her water and ask for a refill. *Shame on you, shame on you.* Judith stood up tall and, in her head, she turned the words addressed to her that morning, on the garrulous widow. *How had Lynn Harris been taken into Rosie Harper's confidence? she asked herself. Had she knocked at the door one day and invited herself in, and Rosie, conscious of her public image, had felt compelled to oblige? Or perhaps she had sidled over on that memorable moving-in day and offered advice on local haunts.* Either way, Judith found it hard to believe that their relationship had been anything other than superficial.

'Mrs Harris. When you saw Debbie Mallard climbing off her moped, at about 1 o'clock on 17th June, did you speak to her?' Judith began more briskly than she had originally intended.

'No.' Lynn spat out her reply and her trademark laugh was banished.

'Are you certain of that? You see Debbie believes otherwise.'

'She spoke to me. But that's not what you asked,' she said.

'Quite right. It's important that your answers are accurate.' Judith took a deep breath. 'Debbie spoke to you?' she asked.

'Yes.'

'And what did she say?'

'She said '*ello* and asked if I needed an 'and with my shopping.'

'And what did you say?'

'Well, like I said. I didn't say anything.'

'You ignored her?'

'I was busy with the shopping and I didn't need help.'

'I understand. But you didn't say "no thank you" or something similar?'

'No.'

'Or return her greeting?'

'I've already said I didn't talk to her.'

'And why was that?'

'I didn't want 'er to 'elp me.'

'Did you have a lot of shopping?'

'Quite a bit.'

'How many times did you return to your car?'

'Two or three.'

'So, some help might have been nice?'

'I didn't want her 'elp.'

'I see. You don't like Debbie?'

'I just… Look, it's not for me to judge. People can do what they want. It's a free country and all that. But I just didn't agree with what she did to that lovely family. Tore it apart, she did. So, no, I didn't want to be friendly.'

'And that's why you ignored her?'

'If you put it that way, yes.'

'Did Debbie speak to you a second time?'

'When I didn't accept her 'elp, she walked to the door of the house and went inside.'

'Did you see what Debbie was wearing that day?'

Mrs Harris thought hard. 'She had a coat on, maybe black, maybe that khaki colour that's all in fashion this year. Otherwise I can't remember.'

'A helmet?'

'She took it off, had it in her 'and.'

'Gloves?'

'I don't remember.'

'And you had Rosie's telephone numbers, you said.'

'And a key.' Lynn threw back her shoulders and puffed out her chest.

'You have a key to Rosie's house?'

'Not all the time. But when they went away on 'oliday, they would leave a key with me and ask me to keep an eye on things for them.' Judge Nolan looked up and her eyes flitted over Lynn Harris' pocket-sized frame. Judith could visualise Lynn secretly letting herself into the house, or making up some excuse to investigate, a light mistakenly left on, a suspected leak. Either way, she'd be lounging on Rosie's sofa or running her fingers over those 'different outfits' she had mentioned. Why had no one discovered until this moment that the neighbour had a key?

'So, you were on good neighbourly terms?' Judith continued.

'Absolutely.'

'Did you ever hear Debbie and Rosie arguing with each other?'

'No. But lots of things can happen inside the four walls of an 'ouse, can't they?'

'Did you ever hear Debbie raise her voice, perhaps with the children?'

'I wasn't over there that often.'

'Mrs Harris. As Judge Nolan tried to explain earlier, we are only asking you to tell us about things you saw or heard. No one expects you to look through walls or provide an explanation for things you know nothing about. It's far better, in fact, for you to say that you don't know or don't remember, as you did with my question about the gloves, than to manufacture an answer. Did you know that Debbie had moved out of the house?'

'It was ages ago, more than a year.'

'Was it usual for her to visit?'

'She came in the evenings.'

'And did Debbie still have a key to the house?'

Mrs Harris' eyes narrowed as she fixed them on Debbie. 'I don't know,' she eventually said.

'When Debbie arrived, that day, did she knock or ring the bell?'

Mrs Harris paused again before answering. 'I think she had a key, but I'm not certain.'

'Thank you. Now I'm wondering if we can pinpoint, with any more accuracy, the duration of Debbie's visit. What did you do once you were in your house?'

'I unpacked the shopping. Then I ate my lunch.'

'And what did you eat for your lunch?'

'I always treat myself to a Cornish pastie on a Monday, to remind me of me 'olidays. I warmed it up in the microwave and, like I said, I was just in time to watch *Homes Under the Hammer*.'

'Which begins at 1.30, you said and ends when?'

'I think 2.30.'

'And did you watch any more after that?'

'I can't spend all day watching television, can I? I switched off and went to clean upstairs. I clean the upstairs on a Monday and the downstairs on a Thursday.'

'Where is your television?'

'In the living room next to the window.'

'And does that window look out over the street?'

'It does.'

'You told Mr Laidlaw that you looked out twice through the window, the first time you saw Debbie's moped was there and the second it had gone. Do you remember that?'

'Yes.'

'And the dog, moving around, was also easily visible from your window?'

'As soon as I looked out, there she was, marching up and down. You couldn't miss her.'

'And where was Debbie's moped parked?'

'A few car lengths to the left. There was no room right outside the house.'

'When you looked out of the window, you would be looking first straight ahead at the house opposite and then, if you turned your head to the left, you would be able to see Debbie's moped?'

'Yes.'

'When you looked out for the second time, and you saw that the moped had gone, that Debbie had left, could you see the dog then?'

'It was much later, when I heard the dog making all that noise, that I looked out.'

'So you would agree with me that Debbie Mallard left the house some time before the dog began to run around outside and bark?'

Lynn shrank down in the box. 'I'm not sure now.'

'Really? A moment ago, you said that the moped had gone, before Belle, the fluffy collie, was howling and waving her tail around. Are you now saying you were mistaken?'

Lynn bit her thumbnail and turned towards the judge.

'I am trying to remember,' she said.

Judith tipped her head to one side and wallowed, for a moment, in the convenient freeze frame that would produce, for anyone who cared to look.

'I think the bike had gone and then I saw the dog, but I'm just not sure.'

'Are you more or less sure about that than you are about whether Debbie opened the door with a key?'

'I'm not sure.'

'Or what colour coat Debbie was wearing.'

Lynn Harris opened her mouth, closed it and then stared at the judge.

'I'm just trying to remember what I saw.'

'Thank you. I have finished now, Mr Laidlaw.' Judith was quietly triumphant, remembering, in time, the presence of the cameras, and stifling anything but the softest of smiles.

'Mrs Harris, just one more thing to clarify, if you can,' Laidlaw said. 'What was the weather like that day? Is that something you can recall?'

Lynn Harris visibly brightened.

'It was warm, sunny,' she said. 'I had some washing out in the back to dry and it was ready to bring in, when I got home.'

'Thank you. That's all.'

Lynn smiled at Laidlaw, then bowed towards Judge Nolan. As she scurried across the floor of the court, she scowled at Judith.

'Mr Laidlaw, we are still awaiting the photographic evidence regarding the position of the leather glove at the murder scene. Is that correct?' Judge Nolan was propping her head up on her hand.

'Yes, my apologies, your honour. We are working to get you the best image.'

'I understand. But this isn't Wildlife Photographer of the Year. A simple, clear image will suffice. Let's take a short break. Back at 2pm prompt.'

Judith watched Laidlaw carefully during the exchange. Oh,

he was careful to keep his voice even and his body movements fluid, but his hands, those oh so extravagant hands, juddered as he spoke. Judith glanced at his instructing solicitor, a young man in his twenties, who was watching the judge intently, deliberately ignoring anyone else.

'Perhaps,' she murmured to herself. 'Perhaps.'

***

Judith spent the break in a tiny room she had reserved for the duration of the trial. It was nice to have somewhere to sit quietly, without the combined scrutiny of the live, omnipresent audience and the hidden multitudes behind the camera lens. There was a tap at the door and then Constance was inside.

'I hope you've got a note from your parents?' Judith said.

Constance was grinning broadly, despite Judith's admonishment. 'I'm only a bit late and it was worth it,' she said.

'All right. What have you discovered?'

'I finally got Dawson to release Debbie's phone back to us. He had said there was nothing relevant on there, if you remember. But I kept pressing and, in the end, he handed it over. I think he just wanted to get rid of me. I've got two trainees back at the office trawling through it now.'

'Trainees? Do they know what they're looking for?'

'I've briefed them, don't worry. Anything remotely interesting, they'll leave for me.'

'So why are you looking so smug?'

'You remember we talked about how it was a really new phone and you said you could track them?'

'Vaguely.'

'So that's what I've been doing. Then I had to work out how to present the results, that's what took the time. I'll show you now, but, well, I think it's a big help.'

'Fantastic.'

'How was the neighbour?'

Judith shrugged. 'You can watch it back in glorious Technicolor, with a glass of wine, this evening.'

Constance sat down. 'I am sorry I wasn't there,' she said. 'It's not like I had a lie-in, or anything.'

'I know. I know that. I just… I almost went too far with her and I'm not sure why. There's a scene in…God, I can't remember the name of the film. It's one where someone's pretending to be a lawyer and he goes really over the top explaining stuff, until the judge stops him and tells him it's only a preliminary hearing.'

'I'm sure you didn't…'

'I didn't, but I wanted to. I really wanted to. In the end, it was OK, I think. I stopped myself. She didn't have anything that important to say anyway, except she found the body, end of story. And why shouldn't she want to overplay her connection with Rosie? I would probably do the same, in her place. But I looked up at that camera, which, naturally, she was playing to with her smiles and her polished nails and I felt this…desire, this impulse to destroy her, to ensure that everyone could see what a flimsy excuse for a human being Lynn Harris was.'

'Well, the important thing is that you didn't.' Constance coughed and checked her watch. It wasn't like Judith to have these moments of self-doubt.

'No. That's right. Although she had a key to the house.'

'What?'

'When they went on holiday, Rosie gave her a key.'

'You think she's a suspect?'

'What better way to cover up a murder than to discover it?'

'Wow! She really got to you, didn't she?'

Judith laughed. 'I'm fine. You're right. She's just a lonely old soul, making the most of her moment of fame. I need to pace myself, not peak too early. Laidlaw asked her what the weather was like, at the end though, and when she said it was hot, he looked triumphant.'

'And you don't know why?'

'No. Maybe it's because she also said Debbie was wearing a coat, to make her look suspicious. I don't know. Shall we head back to the action?'

Constance picked up her bag, but hovered by the door.

'There is one thing Dawson let slip this morning…but I'll tell you after court? It doesn't impact the phone evidence.'

'I think I should know now. Never hold back bad news.'

'OK.' Constance leaned back against the door. 'All right. Dawson also said something about Rosie's laptop. They weren't going to do any more data analysis, but when I asked for the phone, they reconsidered…'

'*Reconsidered*? Did he really say that? I think he means *forgot* or couldn't spare the resources or didn't have someone with the right expertise, 'cos they've all been sacked as a result of cutbacks. I shouldn't be surprised, should I?'

'Well now they've put it under the spotlight and they think they've found something, after all.'

'What kind of *something*?'

'Dawson wouldn't say, but he says it's definitely relevant to the case. And he said to send you his best wishes, so it must be something bad.'

Judith fingered the curls on her wig.

'And when will we see it? We're already on day two.'

'He's talking to the lawyers and he knows it's very late. Apparently, it was password-protected and it's taken them a while to access it.'

Judith sighed. 'Well there's no point worrying till we know what it is. Come. Show me what magic you've weaved this morning with Debbie's mobile phone.'

Relief flooded over Constance. Judith was concentrating on the evidence again and, as long as Constance could keep her focused and not allow any political sideshow to derail things, everything would be just fine.

29

DR THEO MARCUS WAS SMARTLY dressed in jacket, shirt and orange tie. Judith wasn't a fan of orange clothing. On the rare occasions she had been forced to wear it as a child, it had sucked the colour from her complexion and the energy from her body. Hunters wore orange; in some US states it was compulsory. And the Dutch. And Hindu priests, although they liked to call the colour 'saffron', associating it with austerity and detachment from everyday life. A good reason not to choose orange if ever there was one.

Judith had seen Dr Marcus outside the court room, fussing with his few remaining strands of hair, smoothing his beard and re-tying his tie. If she hadn't been a lawyer, she sometimes thought that forensic pathology would have been a reasonable alternative option. True, she wasn't particularly attracted by blood or guts, but she wasn't repelled either; both professions sought answers and the disciplines were not so different. She used words skilfully to peel back the layers of truth, where the pathologist wielded his scalpel.

'That's Dr Marcus,' Constance had said, as they passed close by.

'Hm. His report's as thin as his hair,' Judith had replied, and when they were further away, 'Do you think he's the kind of man who reads bedtime stories to his children?' she had asked.

'What?'

'No imagination, that's all I mean.'

'Does he need imagination? He's a pathologist.'

Judith had stopped walking and her eyes had widened. 'Logic will get you from A to Z. Imagination will get you everywhere!'

'Did you just make that up?'

'I might have, but it was actually Albert Einstein.'

'You think he told good bedtime stories then?'

'I think he probably did.'

***

'Dr Marcus. You are appearing today as our expert forensic pathologist. Can you explain your role in determining what happened to Rosie Harper, just in general terms?' Was Judith mistaken or did Laidlaw appear a tad less exuberant this afternoon, a little more circumspect. And the ring was missing from his finger.

'I attended the crime scene, examined Miss Harper, directed the collection of evidence, conducted the post mortem and reported on my conclusions. I also supervised the testing of items connected to the crime scene, like samples of hair, the leather glove and the trophy murder weapon.'

'Thank you. And what did you find when you arrived at Miss Harper's home on the evening of Monday 17th June? We have already seen a photograph of her body lying in the garden, when Inspector Dawson gave his evidence.'

'I arrived at 5.40pm. I was very early on the scene, because I happened to be only a few minutes away, when I received the call. The front door is up a few steps from the road. It opens onto a hallway and, to the right is the living room. And in the living room there were signs of a struggle.'

'What signs?'

'The living room is a large room with a seating area at the front of the house and then a desk area in the back corner. And there is a door leading outside, into the back garden. The office chair had been knocked over, Miss Harper's laptop lay on the floor.'

'Was it broken?'

'It was intact. Some papers were also spread across the floor and there were blood stains on the rug.'

'Thank you. We are going to take a look at a shot of the living room now. What else did you see?'

'At the far side of the living room, I could see a woman's body on the ground, head and shoulders furthest away, protruding out into the garden. The first part of the garden is paved and that was where she was lying. Inspector Dawson identified the body as that of Miss Rosie Harper. Miss Harper was lying on her stomach, with her face turned to one side.'

'Thank you, that's the second photograph.'

As the camera homed in on the one visible side of Rosie's face, there were gasps and sobs from all around the courtroom. Debbie looked across at the screen, her eyes narrowed and she looked away.

'Can you describe Rosie's injuries please?'

'You can see there is blood on her face, her hair covers some of the wound, but she had clearly been struck on the back of the head, with a heavy object.'

'Did she have any other injuries?'

'Two of the fingers of her right hand were broken.'

'How do you think those injuries were sustained?'

'My view, and it is only a view, I must emphasise, is that Miss Harper was, first of all, struck from behind and the impact was not, on its own, sufficient to kill her or even render her unconscious, so she turned and put her hands up and was struck again, breaking her fingers. And then she was struck a third time across the temple. It's difficult to be certain regarding the order in which these blows were sustained, but there is a rule that fractures don't cross existing fracture lines, and that bears out the sequence I have just set out.'

'And the third time?'

'The third blow was a massive one. She was left to die.'

'Can you explain more what you mean by that?'

'The blood stains and the marks on the rug were consistent with Rosie dragging herself across the floor to the back door and I can only assume that was after her assailant had left.'

'And the back door was open?'

'When we arrived. But she had opened it, I believe, Rosie had. There was blood on the door handle. I think once she had crawled to the door, she reached up and opened it and hauled herself outside.'

'Do you have any idea how long Miss Harper might have lived after the blow to the head?'

'It's very hard to say. With subdural bleeding, you can live for minutes or hours.'

'Subdural bleeding?'

'Bleeding in the space between the surface of the brain and the skull. Given that Miss Harper appears to have dragged herself a distance of around five metres, it is likely to have been at least ten minutes, but I can't say anything more than that.'

'And the time of her death?'

'On the basis of the medical evidence, it's impossible to say when she died, other than it was in the six hours before she was found. However, I understand the laptop had been used up until 3.16pm and that is why, assuming it was Miss Harper using the laptop, I say death was after 3.16pm.'

'And tell us about her dog.'

'When I arrived, the dog had been removed by a police officer and placed in a police van, but Inspector Dawson told me the dog had been barking loudly and that had alerted the neighbours. And there were prints from the dog through the stream of blood, as if it had run in and out of the living room. Again, this is a guess. Perhaps the dog was in the garden when she was attacked and Miss Harper tried to open the door, because she wanted the dog to sound the alarm which, of course, it did. Or she might have thought she could reach the side gate herself and call out to someone?'

'Where was Rosie's phone?'

'It was charging in the kitchen, in the basement.'

'What about the murder weapon?'

'We didn't find it at the scene. The police carried out house-to-house enquiries and checked all the gardens locally and the weapon was found a few doors down in a dustbin, wrapped in a tea towel.'

'Can you tell us what the weapon was? It's exhibit three your honour.'

The usher brought through another transparent plastic bag and passed it around the jury.

'It's a trophy awarded to Rosie Harper in 2011. "Best Newcomer". It's a TV award. I was told it was usually kept on show, above the fireplace.'

'Are you certain this was the murder weapon?'

'Yes. It had been wiped with a soft cloth, but it still bore traces of Miss Harper's blood. And it is certainly of sufficient weight to have caused her injuries.'

'The post-mortem you conducted confirmed the cause of death?'

'Death occurred as a result of the two blows to the head.'

'You took lots of samples from the room. Can you tell us what you found?'

'We found some of Debbie Mallard's DNA, mostly hair but also skin cells.'

'Anything else of note at the crime scene?'

'No.'

'Perhaps I can jog your memory a little. Was there an item of clothing found at the scene?'

'Oh, yes. There was a motorbike glove. You can just see it, if you flick on a few photographs, it's in photo number 103, ...lying close to Rosie's laptop. There it is. That contained signs of the defendant's DNA on the inside of the glove.'

'What does that establish?'

'That Debbie Mallard had worn it.' Debbie looked at Judith. Judith looked away.

'Is it possible to say when she had worn it?'

'There are some new theories about how to date DNA, I mean, how to determine how long ago it left the body of the individual it belongs to, but it's still in the early stages. What we can say with confidence is that it had been worn by Debbie Mallard and so I can only assume it also belongs to Debbie Mallard.'

Now Debbie stared at Dr Marcus, her lips parted, her eyes boring deep.

'Thank you. Please wait for Ms Burton to ask you a few questions.'

Judith flicked her gown out behind her and, as she rose, she fixed Dr Marcus with a thoughtful look. He shifted in his chair and scratched the top of his head.

'Dr Marcus. Let's start where you just finished with Mr Laidlaw and the glove. You are suggesting, what? That Debbie was wearing the glove when she hit Rosie over the head with the trophy, then she removed the glove from her hand, dropped it and ran off. Is that the case theory?'

'I just report on what I find.'

'Of course. But what you find is supposed to help this court determine what happened. That's the value of your evidence.'

Dr Marcus mumbled his agreement.

'Thank you. You accept, then, that the prosecution is alleging and your evidence appears to confirm, that the glove, which was paraded around the court when Inspector Dawson gave his evidence, belongs to my client?'

'Yes.'

'And so, assuming for a moment that my client is not deliberately leaving clues to her own guilt, the case theory must be that this incriminating glove was left behind, after the murder, by mistake?'

'I suppose so, yes.'

'As a pathologist, it's often important, isn't it, that you can assess when things occurred. You're always being asked about timing, time of death being the most obvious – and we'll come onto that.'

'Yes.'

'This glove found at the scene, using all your modern techniques, do you have any idea when it arrived there?'

'No.' Dr Marcus frowned.

'Might the glove have been lying on the floor *before* Rosie Harper was murdered?'

'That's possible. But it was soaked in Rosie Harper's blood.'

'Imagine this scenario, for a moment…if you can. You enter your house, wearing your gloves. You then remove them and tuck them into your pocket. As you cross your living room, one of them nudges its way out and drops to the floor, but you don't notice. It's been a long day, so you decide to pour yourself a large glass of red wine. As you re-cross the room, the glass slips from your fingers and crashes to the floor, producing a puddle of red liquid, which not only stains the rug you purchased on a recent trip to Turkey, but also soaks your errant glove.'

'Are you asking me a question?'

'I'd like you to consider and, if correct, acknowledge, that the presence of blood on this glove does not constitute any kind of proof that it was used by the murderer in the murder itself?'

Dr Marcus moistened his lips and looked at Debbie. 'That's correct.'

'There were no…forgive me for probing, but this is an important point…pieces of Rosie Harper's skull embedded in the glove or splinters from the murder weapon – anything to suggest it was being worn by the assailant *when Rosie was struck*?'

'No.'

'What about the alternative interpretation – that the glove fell to the ground *after* the murder? It was sitting on the edge of the table, for example, and it was disturbed when the police broke down the door and burst into the room.'

'That's also possible. I can only comment on what I see myself, and I arrived after the police.'

'And that photograph, number 103, can we go back to it for a moment? Thank you. It is, as you say, of the floor area near the back door. We can see a shadow which does appear to be the glove – I accept that – and Rosie's laptop is visible, but Rosie's body isn't there, is it?'

'That's right. This photo was taken after her body had been removed.'

'Do you know when it was taken?'

'It's written on the image at the bottom: 18th June at 19.27.'

'I see. Did you see the black glove on the floor of the living room when you arrived at 5.40pm on Monday 17th June?'

Dr Marcus' lips twitched twice. 'I was keen to get to the body, to see what I could determine. I don't specifically remember seeing the glove, no, but I also don't remember seeing the laptop either, or the phone in the kitchen. It's a high-pressure time and I rely on my team to work together to cover all bases.'

'Thank you. I don't want you to give away any confidences, but Mr Laidlaw had agreed yesterday to search out photographs showing the glove on the living room floor. He discussed this with you?'

'He did.'

'Is this the only photograph you have, which shows the glove on the living room floor?'

'No, there are a number, but this is the clearest image.'

'Moving on then, you have told us about the murder weapon, or what you say is the murder weapon, this trophy.'

'Yes.'

'Were there any fingerprints on the trophy?'

'No. The tea towel had been used to wipe it quite thoroughly.'

'You can test for that, can you?'

'I can tell that it had been wiped clean of fingerprints. I suppose an over-exuberant cleaning lady might have done that, but, again, I am giving an opinion on the most likely scenario, which is that it was cleaned carefully and thoroughly, with the cloth wrapped around it, after the murder. The prints were removed, but not all traces of blood. That's far harder to make disappear.'

'Ah. Now that is interesting. If Debbie had been wearing those gloves, would she have left fingerprints on the trophy?'

'She wouldn't, unless she had picked it up earlier, before putting on any gloves.'

'So, if the murderer took steps to wipe fingerprints from the trophy, then he or she is unlikely to have been wearing gloves during the murder. The presence of the glove is a total irrelevance?'

'You are assuming that the murderer knows about these things. Most killers try to get rid of their fingerprints and if you weren't sure, you would probably give the murder weapon a wipe.'

'Was there any of my client, Debbie Mallard's, DNA of any kind whatsoever on the trophy or the tea towel?'

'No.'

'Then, the forensic evidence linking my client to the crime scene is what?'

'The glove…'

'Which we've already discounted. What else?'

'Numerous fingerprints in the house, including hair on the rug close to where the body fell.'

'Now I'm going to ask you about that all-important timing

again. Any idea how long those hairs had been there?'

'It's not possible to date hair.'

'You are aware that my client lived in the house for thirteen years?'

'I've been told that.'

'And that she was at the house between 1pm and 2pm that very afternoon?'

'Yes.'

'Do you accept that the hairs you found could have fallen from Debbie's head at any time in the preceding thirteen years?'

'No.'

'No? why not?'

'They were long and blond.'

'They were blond?'

'I understand that since Debbie Mallard became a woman, she has dyed her hair. Before that, her hair was brown. So, these were samples of her hair, but since it had been dyed.'

'Any time in the last two years then?'

'If that is when she dyed her hair.'

'And we've heard, from Mrs Harris, that Debbie was a frequent visitor to the house in any event. But if, as Debbie accepts, she was at the house between 1 and 2pm that very day, chatting to Rosie in the living room as she will describe, you would have expected fingerprints and these hairs.'

'Yes.'

'How many fingerprints belonging to Debbie did you find?'

'Many.'

'Give us an idea. One, five, seven? I could go on.'

'Eighteen separate prints in the living room, on the back of a chair, on the base of the chair, on the stairs going down to the kitchen, kitchen worktop, on a mug…'

'A mug?'

'There were two mugs by the kitchen sink, each containing the remains of a cup of tea. Actually, Rosie's prints were on both mugs'

'Rosie made Debbie a cup of tea?'

'It seems that way.'

'And then, what? Rosie tidied the mugs into the kitchen, left them by the sink, the kind of thing you might do after a visitor has left?'

'I'm not a psychiatrist but, of course, it's possible that things happened as you suggest. But many other things are possible too, including Debbie and Rosie drinking their tea in the kitchen and then progressing up to the living room, where a struggle ensued. The positioning of the mugs is really of no value to the case theory.'

'But Debbie had taken no steps to hide her mug or to wipe away her fingerprints?'

'I wouldn't know what steps she took. I can only say what we found.'

'Of course. But leaving eighteen sets of fingerprints. It doesn't sound like the work of a murderer, keen to cover up his or her tracks, does it?'

'Ms Burton. You know you can't ask that question.' Judge Nolan was already looking back at Dr Marcus.

'I'll rephrase the question. In how many cases have you given evidence, relating to what you found at the scene of a murder?'

'At least fifty.'

'That's a lot of cases. In your experience, is it usual to find so many prints of the main suspect at the scene of the crime?'

'It's not usual, no.'

'Can you explain why that is?'

'Again, I can't say for certain, but my experience shows, as you would expect, that most people accused of murder try to clean up after themselves. But not all.'

'Because some people panic, they may be found out, they need to run, so they don't take the time to hide the evidence?'

'All of those things.'

'Your honour, this is pure conjecture, and misleading for the jury.' Mr Laidlaw was screwing up his face.

'Ms Burton. The doctor cannot possibly say why *some people* might wipe their prints from a murder scene and others might not. Even if that were his area of expertise, it would be speculation. Move on.' Judge Nolan scowled at Judith.

'Accepting that Debbie Mallard was at the house between 1 and 2pm that day, there is no real evidence linking my client to the murder, is there?' Judith continued. 'No prints on the murder weapon, no – for example – samples of Debbie's skin under Rosie Harper's fingernails, even fibres from her clothing on Miss Harper's person?'

'None of those things.'

'And the person who used the trophy to hit Rosie over the head, was careful to wipe the murder weapon clean?'

'It appears so.'

'But if the prosecution is right, then that same person, Debbie, while being meticulous in cleaning the murder weapon, was happy to leave a DNA roadmap to herself all over the house. She might as well have walked out of the property with a sign on her head saying, "I am a murderer".'

'Is that a question?'

'Based on the evidence to which I have just referred; namely, a murder weapon carefully wiped clean and then wrapped up and secreted in a dustbin, contrasted with a house full of my client's DNA, what conclusion can you draw about the identity of the murderer?'

'You want me to say the murderer is not the same person who left their prints and DNA around the house. I'm not sure I can go that far.'

'Really? It seems fairly obvious to me, although I am only an expert in common sense, not in forensic science.'

'Ms Burton, watch your tone,' Judge Nolan was glaring at Judith, her head perched atop newly manicured nails.

'If one person hits another over the head, they must be standing fairly close together?' Judith continued.

'Yes.'

'How close?'

'Less than one metre, more likely around 50 centimetres.'

'When a person is hit with force, in the way you describe happened to Miss Harper, would you expect blood to be sprayed out?'

'Not on the first strike. You only get spatter when an implement hits wet blood. So, if the first blow caused bleeding, then the second blow could have led to blood spraying out.'

'How far would that blood spatter travel?'

'A surprisingly long way, certainly as far as someone standing one or two metres away.'

'So it is reasonable to suggest that the person who struck Rosie Harper would have had some blood on their skin and clothing?'

'Yes. But it may not have been large amounts or visible to the naked eye.'

'But detectable when tested?'

'Yes.'

'And Debbie Mallard gave the police the clothes she had been wearing that day. A blue tracksuit. You examined those, didn't you?'

'Yes.'

'And did you find anything linking them to the murder?'

'No. But the clothes were provided the following day and we only have your client's word that she was wearing them when she visited.'

'The police searched Debbie Mallard's home...'

'If you say so.'

'You were also instructed to examine *all* the clothes found in Debbie Mallard's home, weren't you?'

'Yes.'

'Did you find anything linking them to the murder?'

'No.'

'And was there evidence of any other people having been at the crime scene?'

'Rosie's children and one or two of their friends and other people, all of whom the police have eliminated from their enquiries. And the dog, like I said.'

'Ah yes. The dog. Thank you for reminding me. Normally, when there's been a murder, you all wear protective clothing, don't you? Overalls, you cover your hair, even placing protective wrappers over your shoes? We've all seen CSI.'

'Yes.'

'Can you tell us why that is?'

'So as not to contaminate the crime scene.' Dr Marcus shrugged his irritation.

'What kind of things might contaminate the site?'

'You bring things in from the outside, you disturb evidence.

Conversely, you carry vital clues away on your clothing, sticking to your clothes, the soles of your shoes.'

'So, it's crucial isn't it, if you are going to rely on forensic evidence, like DNA evidence, which you have mentioned many times, and fingerprints and the clear absence of evidence linking anyone else to the crime, it's crucial, then, that things have not been disturbed, that important clues haven't been trampled over or inadvertently removed?'

'Yes.'

'But you have just told us that Miss Harper's dog was running all over the scene when the police arrived.'

Dr Marcus swallowed loudly and stared at Mr Laidlaw. 'That was unfortunate,' he said.

'Unfortunate?'

'It wasn't ideal for a crime scene.'

'Do you accept then, that another person might have entered the property after Debbie left and that clues to the identity of that person – the defence says the *real killer* – could have been disturbed?'

Dr Marcus dabbed at his top lip.

'Yes,' he said. 'It is possible, but not very likely.'

'But you accept it's possible. The dog trampling around, a collie, picking things up on its long, thick coat or feet, that bushy tail wagging from side to side, running in and out, masking a crucial clue.'

'I said it's possible. That's why my evidence is based on what I believe happened, supported by what I found. I don't just come up with a story out of my imagination.'

Judith stifled a smile. 'Your best guess then?'

'*Guess* makes it sound very imprecise and unfocused. I draw conclusions from what I find, based on the latest scientific and medical evidence and my own long experience as a doctor and forensic pathologist.'

'Of course that's what you do.' Judith paused and Constance held her breath. 'Where was the trophy found?' Judith continued.

'Inside the dustbin at number 26.'

'If you exit Miss Harper's house through the front door, do you turn right or left to reach number 26?'

'It's left.'

'And how far away is number 26?'

'Five houses....

'Your honour. I have some evidence to admit late. It comes from my client's mobile phone, which was only released to my solicitor by the police in the early hours of this morning. The prosecution, as you know, has had access to my client's phone since 17th June.'

'What is this evidence?'

'My client's phone is a very up-to-the-minute iPhone and that means that the phone's movement is tracked automatically, unless that function is disabled. I noted from Dr Marcus' résumé that mobile phones and tracking is one of his areas of expertise, so, with your permission, I should like to take this witness through this evidence.'

'Your honour. This is outrageous. We haven't even seen the evidence.' Laidlaw's mouth was wide and his eyes were bulging. Judge Nolan took a moment to reply, her eyes flirting languidly with the camera.

'Mr Laidlaw, do you accept that the prosecution has had Debbie Mallard's phone since 17th June and has examined it and has not found anything of interest?'

'That is my understanding. So this evidence is another of Ms

Burton's famous red herrings, no doubt.'

Judith was silent. Judge Nolan bristled. 'Turn off the cameras,' she shouted suddenly, waving her arms around.

'What?' Laidlaw was unable to cover his confusion.

'Off I said. All of them.'

Everyone sat in silence, while the ushers switched off the cameras and the cameraman operating the central apparatus obliged, removing his headphones, resting his hands lightly on the tripod. The judge called the two barristers out to the front, where she addressed them in a half-whisper, delivered with considerable vigour.

'Mr Laidlaw, Ms Burton. It is not appropriate for either of you to make personal comments about each other in my court room or to whisper asides that you suspect may be picked up by the recording equipment, to point-score against each other in this childish way. This is a court of law, not some open-mike event. Do I make myself clear?'

'Yes, your honour.'

'If this happens again, and I sincerely hope it won't, I will switch the cameras off for the remainder of the session. I don't want you bringing the legal profession into disrepute with your petty squabbling.'

Laidlaw and Judith returned to their seats, suitably chastised, and Judge Nolan nodded to the usher and the cameraman to switch them back on. But in the confusion, and departure from the prepared routine, the cameraman swung his camera too far across the court room and focused, for a split second on the jury.

'Shit!' he muttered under his breath, his curse magnified tenfold by his microphone.

Judge Nolan did not appreciate, immediately what had

happened, as she had dropped her gaze to her laptop, but her clerk did, as did most of those gathered, including some members of the jury itself. As Judge Nolan looked up again, she was met with stony silence and solemnity all round.

'What is it?' she asked, her face a mass of confusion.

Her clerk came around the desk, ascended the two steps, which divided her seating from the rest of the court, and whispered in her ear. As her words sank in, the judge's face turned very pale.

'We need to take a short break,' she said. 'First we will turn off the cameras, thank you, and then the jury will leave to their room and I will come and address them.'

As the jury scuttled out, the cameraman removed his headphones, covered his face with his hands and slunk down into his seat. A low chatter began to spread through the public gallery.

'Oh blimey,' Judith said.

'What will she do?' Constance asked.

'What can she do? She'll make sure it's removed from any recording, but that was live. So much for promises of anonymity for the jury.'

'Will we have to start again?'

'Who knows? What a mess.'

It was an hour before court reconvened and this time it looked a little different. The two women who had sat at the far right of the jury were gone, replaced by two unfamiliar men. The cameraman had also morphed into a different person.

'I'm sorry for the delay,' Judge Nolan said, straight into the newly fired-up camera. 'As some of you may have noticed, there was an unfortunate incident with the camera. As a result, we have substituted two of our jurors....'

'And garrotted our cameraman,' Judith whispered to Constance, who placed a hand over her mouth to stifle her giggles.

'Ms Burton. I interrupted your cross-examination of Dr Marcus. Let's continue now, shall we?'

'Thank you, your honour. I was almost finished. Dr Marcus, I am handing you a print-out, showing where Debbie's phone travelled on 17th June,' Judith said. 'I will also project it up on the screen. Can you see it?'

'Yes.'

'The tracker is incredibly accurate. We can see, just after 1pm, that the phone is stationary for one hour and eleven minutes in Rosie Harper's house. You can see that?'

'Yes.'

'And when the phone leaves the house, can you see in what direction it travels?'

'Along East Road and out onto Summer Avenue.'

'Thank you. And to travel towards Summer Avenue, do you turn right or left out of Rosie Harper's house?'

'Right. You have to turn right.'

'Then Debbie Mallard's phone didn't travel five houses to the left on leaving Rosie Harper's house, did it?'

'You're right that the trackers on these phones are accurate, but I couldn't say if a distance of, say, 50 metres would be recorded. It's a relatively small distance.'

'But you are happy, other than that, that this is an accurate picture of the journey of this phone.'

'I would have to examine the phone, check it hadn't been tampered with in any way, but subject to that, yes.'

'Good. So I'd like you, then, to take a look at this path, which my client's phone took *this morning*. Again, I'm projecting it onto the screen. Can you see that?'

'Yes.'

'Can you describe to the court how it differs from the earlier path?'

'Yes. On this occasion, which is a journey timed at 08.01 this morning, the phone begins at Miss Harper's house, then there is a short trip east, which is left out of the house, then it doubles back on itself, passing by Rosie Harper's house and exits onto Summer Avenue.'

'Thank you. This morning, my instructing solicitor took my client's phone, in her pocket, to Rosie Harper's house. Then she walked to number 26, where the trophy was found in the dustbin and then she walked back past Rosie's house, to where we believe Debbie's moped was parked, as confirmed by Mrs Harris, and then continued towards the main road. Would you like to qualify your earlier response regarding the sensitivity of this phone?'

'If your solicitor did as you suggest, and, again, I would wish to verify this myself, then it appears that on 17th June, wherever Debbie may have travelled, her phone does not appear to have passed by number 26.'

'Thank you. No further questions.'

Judith sat down and smiled reassuringly at Constance over her shoulder. Constance returned the smile. Apart from having upset the judge, and that was more Laidlaw than Judith, things seemed to be back on course, after all.

30

'WHAT HAVE WE GOT ON the show this evening, then?' Katrina Sadiq was back, this time cloaked in a vibrant red trouser suit. Chris was more soberly dressed in a blue shirt and dark chinos.

'Well, we will have a summary of the day's events in the Rosie Harper murder trial. Andy Chambers is back to give us the benefit of his legal analysis. And then we also have a reconstruction, based on the evidence provided today by Dr Theo Marcus, the forensic pathologist, but first of all, to open the show, we have our own resident psychiatrist, Dr Leslie Le Mesurier, with some psychological profiling.

Andy was backstage for now, to give the two guests space. It meant he could watch the camera crew at work again, together with all the other staff who kept the show on the road. He couldn't help but feel enthusiastic about the whole enterprise. There was such a buzz with live TV, everything happening in real time, the excitement of creating entertainment on the hoof. He had been a little worried about his slow start yesterday, particularly given the growling voice in his ear, early on. Then, Graham had called him personally, after they'd wrapped it up, from Argentina, no less, told him they'd peaked at 1.2 million viewers during his slot and commended him on his performance. 'Keep it edgy,' he had said to Andy. 'Legal but edgy.'

Phil was there again, with headphones and a mike. But it wasn't Phil's voice he had heard when he was on air; it must have been the stand-in producer Graham mentioned. Still, with all the background noise, and his efforts to multi-task, he couldn't be sure. There were times when he wondered if there really had been a voice at all – another person speaking to him – or whether it had just been his inner self addressing him, reminding him that his ultimate pay was linked to viewers, and viewers wanted discord.

He wondered what Katrina would focus on today. He had seen the backlash against Judith from the domestic violence lobby, for which he had felt more than a pang of guilt. He had tried to reason that he had only praised Judith and it was not his fault if others twisted what he said. But he had known his words could be turned against her.

That made it so much more important, this evening, to put forward his own suggestions, and he had given Katrina a list; explaining why witnesses should stick to the facts and not give opinions, discussing the value of eye-witness evidence, and the vagaries of forensic medicine and why it was not the panacea everyone thought it was. The DNA stuff was topical and he could throw in plenty of anecdotes too, kind of 'after dinner' style. Katrina had reviewed all of these in the blink of an eye and smiled at him politely. He didn't know, yet, whether that meant she liked or intended to run with any of them.

Andy was interested to hear Dr Le Mesurier, in any event.

There had been a debate for years about the value of psychological profiling in tracking down perpetrators, particularly murderers, with at least one high-profile case in the past decade where the police maintained that the help they received in that area was invaluable; sadly, countless more when it had led them up the garden path.

Andy had sounded Katrina out on this one, also.

'I'm interested in who decides on our expert guests,' he had said, peering around the screen as the makeup girl was buffing up Katrina's cheeks.

'I'm sure it's still Graham, from wherever in the world he might be, but we can all provide input. If you've got any ideas, just throw them into the mix.'

'Who is the mystery producer, do you know?'

'Some old friend of Graham's, knows a lot about TV and advertising and what people like to see. I don't know his name. But tonight's experts are genius, I think, whoever suggested them,' Katrina had said. 'Profiling, that would be my dream job, after this of course.'

'Do you think?'

'Oh yes. Absolutely fascinating. Using the clues to find the type of person who would commit the crime.'

'I've never thought much of this idea of "types",' Andy had replied. 'I've seen a lot of criminals in my time and I'd find it very hard to put them into categories.'

Katrina had frowned and pushed away the makeup girl's arm, with a gentle 'that's enough, thanks' nod. She hadn't replied. Now she was up there, in front of the cameras, with Dr Le Mesurier next to her, her admiration for her expert guest clear for all to see.

***

'Dr Le Mesurier, you're a psychiatrist, specialising in crime and you've been watching this trial closely, just as viewers have. Let's get straight down to business. The murder scene – what does it tell us about the murderer, in your expert opinion?'

'Thank you, Chris and Katrina. I'm delighted to be here.'

Andy decided to watch the special guest very carefully, using the skills yesterday's body-language expert had expounded.

'As you know, we saw photographs of the crime scene in court today, so I was able to see, close-up, images of the room in which Miss Harper was killed. There were clearly a number of other heavy objects which could have been used, but the murderer chose this particular trophy.'

An image appeared behind Dr Le Mesurier's head of Rosie being presented with the award and the cameraman then zoomed in to show its features; her name in curly letters, the BBC logo stamped neatly on the side.

'And there it is, we can see Rosie's delight at receiving it.'

'Yes and she never imagined then, of course, that it would be the instrument of her demise.'

A laugh caught at the back of Andy's throat. He couldn't believe this woman. Who was she trying to kid? Then he looked around him at the earnest expressions on everyone's faces and swallowed his laugh.

'You think the selection of this award, as the murder weapon, is important?' Katrina was saying.

'I do. This is only my view, like I say, but it's based on long experience treating psychopaths, sociopaths – including murderers, and people convicted of violent offences. When people use trophies or awards, there is a significance behind it.'

'It was used because it's heavy,' Andy found himself wanting to shout, but he restrained himself.

'That's so interesting. Tell us more,' Katrina said.

'Absolutely. It might be more obvious with items of sentimental value, although, from a psychological viewpoint, it's all part of the same emotional response. For example, I once treated a man accused of killing his wife by making her eat her engagement ring. That one was fairly clear, but there are plenty of others which are less so.

'Photographs are often used as weapons, because of the memories they evoke. But, yes, when an assailant uses a trophy, as was the case here, a trophy awarded to Rosie for tremendous achievement, they are not only trying to hurt the person – their target, if you like – but they are, at the same time, making a statement regarding their own sense of inadequacy.'

'Are you saying, then, that the very fact that Rosie Harper was killed with this trophy, rather than another available object, is evidence that Debbie Mallard killed her?'

'Debbie, or someone else who knew that Rosie had performed well to achieve this award, or who resented her for it.'

'Someone very close to her, then? How likely, knowing the choice of murder weapon, is it, in your view then, that a totally random person, like an intruder, killed Rosie Harper?'

'Given the other available implements, it's not very likely. Look, there was a large glass vase on the table much closer to Rosie's desk which was untouched, there were a couple of pieces of pottery, there were knives in the kitchen. I should add that when murders occur at home, a knife is the most common murder weapon. Yet the killer chose to cross the room – apparently the trophy usually stood over the fireplace – so, to cross the room and pick that up and use it to thump Rosie Harper over the head. And, of course, we also know from the police evidence that it wasn't a forced entry to the home.'

'But the killer left Rosie alive, according to Dr Marcus?'

'Yes. She crawled across the room, horribly injured, and out into the garden.'

'Is that important, do you think, in terms of the sketch of the killer?'

'It might be. It's always possible the killer was scared and had to leave in a hurry, or she thought Rosie was really dead. But it's also possible that she was so appalled that when the red mist cleared, she ran off, because she couldn't bear to see what she had done.'

'What do you mean by *red mist*? Are you suggesting that the person who did this was not sane, when they killed Rosie Harper?'

'I wouldn't say *not sane* no, but to have murdered her so brutally, at least for a short period of time, the killer was not behaving rationally. That's not quite the same.'

'So the kind of person who killed Rosie, is…what? Someone who can detach themselves from reality for periods of time?'

'Possibly.'

'Or maybe just someone who can really hold their nerve under pressure, perhaps when the eyes of the world are watching?'

'That's not something I feel I could rightly comment on, but equally it's not often empathetic people who carry out these kinds of callous crimes.'

***

Constance sighed deeply. She was sitting at home, with her bowl of macaroni cheese untouched before her on the floor.

Are you watching it?

Judith had texted her. She picked up her phone and turned it face-down. It vibrated again, seconds later, with another message. Constance ignored it for as long as it took for the on-screen camera to pan out from Dr Le Mesurier and then focus in again, then sneaked a look.

Are you watching it? Judith had repeated her earlier text.

Constance snorted, stretched out her legs and hit Judith's number.

'Hi Judith. Yes, I am,' she said.

'Am I mistaken or did the psychiatrist just say that Debbie must have killed Rosie because she was jealous of her for winning a television award in 2011?'

'That's pretty much what she said.'

'I told you this was total rubbish. Do we think this is allowed, even under our new, more generous transparency rules?'

'It must be right on the line. But I suppose they'll say it's just commentary and helping people understand the evidence. You have to admit it's interesting stuff.'

'I don't have to and I don't. It's so…banal. The very reason we can make a living, the very reason the criminal justice system exists, is because people are unpredictable. We can't just shove the human race into boxes, then stick our fingers in the phone book and find the culprit for every crime.'

'It makes entertaining television.'

'If you say so. I'm switching off now. I have better things to do with my time. I suggest you do the same.'

Constance embedded her fork in her insipid meal.

'We can't. We…one of us needs to see what they're saying. It's important. How do we counter it, if we don't see it?'

'I've told you, I am planning on ignoring it. That's the best way.'

'We really can't ignore it. It might impact the trial.'

'I hardly think so. It's complete garbage, and even if it's permitted for public consumption, I don't see the judge allowing anyone to reference it at trial.'

'You were the one going on about what the jury might see outside the trial; well, it's this!'

'Ah! Do I detect a sense of disillusionment creeping in? Those potential benefits they promised us trusting, altruistic optimists. What was it? "Equality, accessibility, transparency", trampled by the stampede of the wannabes, wielding their publicity-seeking opinions.'

'All right. I admit I didn't expect quite so much…commentary,' Constance stared back at her screen.

'You watch, if you think it's important,' Judith said, but I don't plan on changing my behaviour, or how I defend Debbie, because of a few people who think they know more than the real experts… even though it probably means I'll get another delightful reception tomorrow morning.'

'What happened this morning?'

'It was nothing. Just stupid.'

'Tell me.'

'All right. Laidlaw got flowers. I got heckled, like I was a criminal. It wasn't pleasant.'

'I'm sorry. I didn't know.'

'The subliminal message, if I read it correctly, was that I was knowingly in cahoots with a murderer and wife-beater. Oh look. Ignore all that. My skin is thick enough to bear it. Anyway, if the worst Court TV can come up with is some crackpot psycho-babble, then I'm not too worried.'

'They're doing a reconstruction next.'

'What?'

'A reconstruction from a neighbour's house, made to look like Rosie's.'

'I might tune in for that,' Judith said. 'Do you think they'll have a six-foot transgender woman with long blond braids shouting "I've always despised you since you won that award" before hitting a Rosie lookalike over the head, and then clambering onto a moped and riding off into the sunset?'

'They might,' Constance said.

'Seriously, we must have better things to spend our time on than this.'

***

Andy was counted down by Phil, as he took his seat in the studio to begin his analysis session. *I've got this*, he told himself. *Nice and easy. I'm in control*, he repeated over and over.

'Andy, hi,' Katrina was well into her stride. 'Let's start with the revelation that two members of the jury have been replaced. Can you explain what happened there?' The hairs on the back of Andy's neck stood to attention. Why did Katrina insist on ignoring his very solid topics of choice and going, instead, to this flimsy one?

'We don't have the full story,' he said.

'You must have some ideas?'

'Well, as you know, the cameras were switched off, and they were filmed, by mistake, when they were switched back on. I don't know for certain, but my best guess would be that those jurors were concerned their identities had been revealed and they wanted to be excused.'

'Would it just be the jurors who were worried?'

'No, I suppose there is always a risk in any criminal trial that pressure might be placed on jury members to vote one way or the other, so the judge may also have been concerned, once their identities were potentially made public.'

'That's Judge Nolan. She turned off the camera, because she got angry with the lawyers. Isn't that right?'

'Well...'

'Come on, Andy. Don't be shy. We can go to the footage.'

'Nooo. You're right. She clearly wanted to speak to the lawyers in private, which is quite usual.'

'Then, when she turned it back on, the mistake, as you described it, happened. Wasn't it her fault then, in reality?'

Andy's mouth opened, as he tried to think of a neat way of sidestepping Katrina's question.

Andy, come on. You know the right answer. There it was, again, the voice in his ear.

'That's a bit like to trying to blame VW every time one of its cars has an accident.' As soon as the words had left his mouth, Andy knew it was a blunder; it was too erudite, too cryptic. He might have pulled it off as witty banter, in a room full of his colleagues, but it wasn't suitable for public consumption. And why had he used VW as an example, the car manufacturer equivalent of public enemy number one, because of the emissions scandal?

'Are you saying the cameraman was at fault, then?'

The Court TV camera drew closer and closer to Andy, so that it was only inches from his face. Andy tried hard not to look at the man behind the lens.

'I think that all of the things which have happened today are very valuable reminders that we are all human and that humans are fallible.' Andy's stomach was cramping, but he was beginning to find some words to drag himself out of the hole into which he had been pushed. 'Sometimes, we think of police, lawyers, the whole system as cold and sterile,' he said, 'shadowy, even. What we've seen today, through the medium of Court TV, is the living, breathing face of our justice system. And yes, there was a hitch, but that can happen anywhere and the system overcame it.'

Bravo! The voice rasped.

'Thank you,' Andy said aloud, before Katrina moved on to her next question.

***

Nicki had changed out of her court clothes – nothing too formal, but she'd wanted to blend in and her navy suit had done the trick. She'd watched the action on her phone from a café opposite the trial in the morning, until she'd noticed someone leaving the public gallery. Then she'd slipped in and taken the empty seat in the back row.

A couple of people had recognised her, despite her disguise, but that didn't bother her. There were myriad reasons for her to attend this high-profile trial, including the real reason why she couldn't stay away.

As she switched her TV to mute and put in her earphones, she sat back and checked her phone. There were four messages since she'd got home, eighteen since the morning, and two missed calls, but none of them from the person from whom she most wanted to hear.

31

'How are you bearing up?' Constance sat next to Debbie in a basement holding cell early the next morning. It was a beautiful day outside, bright and warm, with a touch of a breeze. Down here, it was pleasantly cool. Debbie was wearing a turquoise suit with a pink scarf tied around her neck. She appeared pale and drawn.

'They hid my foundation and lipstick before we left. Said I was beautiful enough without it.'

Constance gulped. Why would anyone do that? She wanted to reach out and pat Debbie's hand or tap her on the shoulder, something to make Debbie appreciate that she was sympathetic. But she held back.

'One of the prison officers took pity on me when I was waiting for the transport. She let me have five minutes in the bathroom and she gave me what she had in her bag. How do I look?'

'You look great.'

'The lipstick's a good colour for me, I thought. I still get shadow around my chin and I don't want to start shaving it there in the bathroom with everyone…I need the foundation to hide it.'

'I understand. You did a good job. Do you want me to say something, about the prison?'

'The same officer said she'd sort me out tomorrow as well, would bring some more stuff. She said we have the same skin colour.'

With a shaky hand, Debbie took a bottle from her back pocket and swallowed two tablets.

'What are those?' Constance asked.

'Just paracetamol, for my head. I thought Judith did well yesterday. She showed Lynn Harris up for what she was. Rosie didn't like her, either. She asked her to babysit once, only once, when we were desperate. Never again. She left Ben in a stinking nappy, because she'd already changed him. Rosie was livid.'

'She gave the impression she was a close friend?'

'Rosie put up with her. Said she was a lonely old woman. I thought she was a nosey old bag, keen to get what she could from Rosie.'

'She said she had a key to your house?'

'It's possible, but Rosie didn't tell me. She knew I didn't like Lynn. And now we know she really didn't like me either.'

'It's a shame she didn't see you leave at 2 o'clock.'

'But my mobile phone did! Who'd have thought it would be so useful when Ben suggested it?'

'I need to ask you about some payments out of the joint bank account you and Rosie shared. It's something the prosecution lawyer is interested in.'

'OK.'

'In 2017 there was a large payment out of £25K and, in 2018, another payment of £15K. Do you have any idea what those might have been for?'

'Can't the police see where the money went?'

'No.'

Debbie opened her hands wide, exposing her fleshy palms.

'I can't think of any big expenses we had then. We had a new kitchen, but that was four or five years ago. And the house in Florida, we've had for much longer. Look, Rosie used to pay all the bills and control the expenses, so I really have no idea. Is it important?'

'It might be. Laidlaw has flagged the payments and he'll ask you about them. What about your money?'

'What do you mean?'

'Well, most people would imagine you living a very luxurious lifestyle.'

'Like I said, we have properties overseas, for holidays, but we never used them much. We both like…liked it here. And I don't have much money left from my footballing days. I had some bad advice about investment. I wasn't the only one.'

'If you remember anything that might be connected to those payments, let me know, won't you?'

'Sure. One thing I do have at the moment is time.'

'Next up this morning is Rosie's friend, Caroline, and then Rosie's mum.'

'I can't wait.'

Constance gathered up her things and then put them down again.

'When I asked you where you went, when you left Rosie's house, you told me that you went home to change and then on to your training. Do you remember that?'

'Yes.'

'The tracker on your phone says something different.'

'Oh.'

'It says you went to an address in Angel and that you were there from 3.15 to 4.45 and then you went to your training. Where did you go?'

'I don't remember.' Debbie closed her mouth and turned her head away.

'I can get the exact address with a little digging around, but I have so many things to do, it would be much better if you just told me.'

'It's nothing to do with any of this, with Rosie, anything.'

'So why can't you tell me?'

'If I say where I went…please leave it alone. Trust me. It's not important.'

Debbie's eyes were suddenly filled with tears.

'It might help your defence.'

'No, it won't.'

'It might provide another person testifying to what you were wearing that day or confirming what time you arrived.'

'The police have already said I might have hidden the clothes somewhere and they don't know what time Rosie died.'

'Lynn Harris says you were wearing a coat. If someone else would say you had your tracksuit on, there wouldn't have been time for you to clean it, not with the football and the police arriving. It would be a big plus point. Would the person you visited remember what you wore that day?'

Debbie swallowed and wiped her face.

'Is it someone you weren't supposed to be seeing?'

'Just because I'm on trial, doesn't give you or anyone else the right to dig into every aspect of my private life. I am telling you that I don't want you to try and find out where I went and you should respect my wishes. God knows, no one else is.'

'All right. I'll leave it alone for now. But I can't guarantee someone else won't find out. Everyone is looking for a new way to make the headlines.'

***

The crowd outside court had swelled from the few early birds, keen to grab a pitch, to a large troop. The "Trans Rights are Human Rights' contingent numbered at least fifty, possibly more, and today they had a new banner; 'Trans-parent not Trans-phobic'. The 'Silence Hides Violence' group was at a similar level, but was increasing at a faster rate. The football supporters were nowhere to be seen today. Two or three journalists were taking photographs and stopping to talk to the crowd, nodding animatedly.

Constance looked out at the sea of faces, their anger simmering just below the surface. She called Judith on her mobile, her hands shaking. It wasn't like Judith to cut things so fine; she was usually here well ahead of the start. Of course, it was always possible that Judith had gone ahead, while she was talking to Debbie downstairs. When she received no response, Constance messaged Judith *make sure you come in the back way today* before heading off for court.

***

Judith did a double-take when Judge Nolan faced her that morning; something unusual had happened to the judge's eyebrows overnight. They appeared at least twice as thick as the day before and stood out, almost to the exclusion of everything else on her face. Judith's hands went up to her own eyebrows, tracing a line with her finger along their length. Then she looked out into the public gallery, searching its rows systematically. Finally, when Constance tucked herself in, she gave her only a cursory nod, before turning back towards the judge.

'I need to let you all know that, in addition to the two changes to our jury which occurred yesterday, one of our jurors,' at this point Judge Nolan paused and stared at Laidlaw and Judith in turn, 'has been taken ill and has been excused. We are going to continue the trial with eleven jurors. Let's start, shall we?'

Caroline Fleming entered the court room noisily, her heels tapping their way across the floor, her pencil skirt restricting her stride, so that she had to haul herself up into the witness box. Her blond hair was cut short and her pale blue t-shirt emphasised her tiny waist.

'Miss Fleming, you were a close friend of Rosie's.' Laidlaw was back, bouncing around energetically at the start of the third day of the trial. Judith noticed the ring was still absent, but he had pulled his gown up short over his arms, to expose his cuff links and a brash, gold timepiece.

'We've known each other since college. I sat next to Rosie on the first day. She was wearing red shoes and I liked her straightaway.' Caroline tucked a stray hair behind her ear.

'What college was that?'

'London School for Performing Arts. Rosie was good; she couldn't dance much, but she could sing and act.'

'And do you know her…do you know the defendant?'

'Rosie met Danny – he was Danny then – near the end of our

first year. We went out a bit together, although it was hard because he was already quite famous.'

'Did you get on with Danny?'

'I didn't talk to him that much. He was really into Rosie, that was clear. He used to send her huge boxes of flowers, that kind of thing.'

'How close were you and Rosie over the last, say, five years?'

'Well, it's funny. We had lost touch a bit, we were both so busy. But when she and Debbie separated, she called me and we met up and then we became much more close.'

'What did Rosie tell you about Debbie?'

Caroline Fleming looked down at her hands. Then she stared at the camera and then the judge.

'Do I have to answer that question?' she asked.

'You do. If we stray too far from relevant matters, I will intervene,' Judge Nolan confirmed.

'I just think it's not fair to ask me. I didn't like Debbie much, when she was Danny. I think that's maybe part of why we didn't stay in touch. Rosie knew I wasn't keen.'

'Was there anything in particular that made you dislike Debbie?'

'It was stupid. We were just kids, I suppose. But that kind of thing you don't forget easily.'

'What kind of thing?'

'We were out once in the local park, a whole load of us. And there was this cat, pretty thing, black with one white paw, it was. We were all stroking it, making a fuss. Then these two dogs came running over, no owner in sight. They cornered the cat.' Caroline grimaced and bit her fulsome bottom lip.

'And what happened?'

'They killed it, tore it to pieces. It was horrible.'

'And what did the defendant do?'

'Danny just laughed. That's the thing. He thought it was funny. Then he saw how horrified we all were, Rosie was almost hysterical, so he pretended he was upset too and hugged her and took her away. But I'd seen what he was really like and I never forgot.'

Laidlaw shook his head sympathetically. Constance glanced at Debbie.

'And when you caught up a couple of years ago?' Laidlaw continued.

'Rosie confided in me, said Danny had left her. She said she didn't know what to do.'

'She said Danny had left her?'

'She said she'd been understanding about the…surgery and everything. That she had stayed with him even though they didn't…they didn't share a bed any longer. But it wasn't enough. He wanted a new life.'

'And how did that make her feel?'

'Used, thrown away, worthless. She felt that all those years of working at a relationship, those shared experiences…she said she couldn't even enjoy her memories anymore.'

'And she mentioned money?'

'She said her money was all tied up in the houses they had bought, that Danny hadn't paid for things, kept saying he would, but then she'd get the reminders and then final notices. She was really stressed about it.'

'Did Rosie ever say that Danny had been violent towards her?'

'She said that they had huge rows about what to do, that when she told him about the bills, he said she earned enough herself to pay them. And she was scared of him.'

'She told you that?'

'She didn't have to. She would shake when she mentioned his name. She told me he'd changed a lot since he began his treatment...'

'When you say treatment, what do you mean?'

'His gender reassignment treatment, to become a woman. She said it changed him.'

There was a burst of laughter from the public gallery, which Judge Nolan silenced with a stern glare.

'His personality, I mean. She said he used to be so chilled. Now he was always on the edge. She didn't know who he was any more.'

***

Judith flicked through her notes, before finding her place and rising to her feet.

'Miss Fleming. I wanted to clarify a few things you just told the court. Is that all right?' Judith asked.

'Of course.'

'What did you do after college?'

'I did some modelling work. Now I'm in PR.'

'Did you want to be a performer?'

'I decided it wasn't for me, after all. I didn't finish the course.'

'Rosie stayed and you dropped out?' Judith's voice descended at least an octave, in sympathy with Caroline Fleming.

'Yes, but I don't see what this has to do with anything?'

'Neither do I, Ms Burton, please move on.' Judge Nolan's newly-pencilled eyebrows reinforced her displeasure.

'I'm interested, next, in the extent of your friendship with

Rosie. You shared a flat together for a short time, before you dropped out, is that right?'

Caroline paused before answering. Clearly the term 'dropped out' offended her.

'Yes,' she replied crisply.

'But you moved out, even before you left college?'

'I got a better offer from some other friends, that's all.'

'It wasn't because you and Rosie had fallen out?'

'No.' Caroline's eyes wandered the court room.

'Miss Fleming. You seem a little uncertain. You have told us already that your friendship had lapsed. Do you want to qualify your last answer at all?'

'I'm fine,' she said curtly.

'Isn't it true – and I can bring in some of your contemporaries if you dispute this, so I ask you to think hard about this question before you reply. Isn't it true that *you* liked Danny? In fact, he approached you first, before Rosie, and that you resented the fact that they had become close? And that once their relationship blossomed, you were jealous?'

'It wasn't like that,' Caroline's voice was calm, but her eyes were wide. 'I didn't want to be in a house with people gazing into each other's eyes all the time and closed bedroom doors. I preferred to live with friends. That's all.'

'And you say that you recently rekindled your friendship and that Rosie confided in you many personal things. Did she tell you that Debbie had been violent towards her?'

'Not in words but, like I said, she couldn't even mention Debbie's name without shaking. And she said they had huge rows.'

'Yes, you've said. You've interpreted *huge rows* to mean violence towards her. Is that right?'

'Yes.'

'I suggest that huge rows can mean different things to different people. My instructing solicitor and I are inclined to have *huge rows* from time to time, about professional matters, but we've certainly never laid a finger on each other. All we really mean by that terminology, is that we've had a robust exchange of views. And, in Rosie Harper's case, she was a fiercely intelligent woman, managing a challenging workload and bringing up two children.

'Likewise, Debbie Mallard is known to be a plain speaker. It would not surprise me to know that, if they disagreed about something – these two strong personalities, with competing priorities – then they might have had a mental tussle, a "war of words", a vigorous altercation. That doesn't mean that either of them bullied the other or threatened the other or raised a hand to the other, though, does it?'

'From what Rosie said and how she said it, I believed he hit her.'

'I see. You told Mr Laidlaw that, in your regenerated friendship, Rosie confided in you about her lack of intimacy with her former husband. That doesn't sound like the notoriously private Rosie Harper I've heard about through other witnesses. I'm wondering how well you really did know her?'

'We became close. She didn't have anyone else to talk to.' Caroline's words were candid, but now her eyes narrowed into two slits.

'What are Rosie's children called?' Judith stood back from her lectern.

Caroline stared at Judith and then darted a quick glance out to the public gallery.

'Her daughter is…Laura,' Caroline stammered.

'And…'

Silence. Judith moved to her right to block Caroline's field of vision and, when that didn't work, she waved her arm to grab Caroline's attention.

'Did you forget her son, Ben?'

'Yes, just nerves, Ben. That's it.'

'And can you describe the kitchen at Rosie's house?'

'The kitchen, no. Well, we always met out somewhere, for a meal or a drink. I didn't go to the house.'

'You went out for meals together. Was that often?'

'Fairly.'

'Can you tell us anything Rosie liked to eat? Did she have a favourite kind of food?'

'She liked Italian food.'

'Italian! Osso bucco, tagliatelle. Did she have a favourite dish?'

'Spaghetti Bolognese…she liked spaghetti Bolognese.'

Judith paused before inclining her body just slightly towards the jury. 'Rosie had been vegetarian for the last seven years of her life,' she said. 'I put it to you that you and Rosie were not at all close.'

'We were.'

'That you have manufactured this…re-kindling so that you can come here today and tell a load of untruths.'

'No.'

'This story about the cat, that Mr Laidlaw had to drag from you. It's straight from a storybook.'

'Your honour, Ms Burton keeps telling her own stories rather than asking questions.' Laidlaw was crouching to deliver his remonstration, which was noticeably less forceful than his previous interventions.

'I apologise your honour. I was carried away for a moment,

with the creative elements of Miss Fleming's narrative. I put it to you, Miss Fleming, that your story about a nineteen-year old Danny Mallard, wallowing in the dismembering of a domestic cat is a total fabrication, dredged up to make the jury believe Debbie is capable of cruelty and violence, when there isn't any real evidence of this.'

'No. It's true.' Caroline's shoulders were thrown back and she was, again, searching the court room for reassurance.

'Who is she looking for?' Constance scribbled Judith a hasty note. Judith read it and dropped it into her pocket. She had a fair idea who it might be, but she was now poised, herself, to go in for the kill and she drew herself up to her full height in preparation.

'But there is a reason why you came up with this story, this fiction about a cat, designed to show the defendant in an unsavoury light, isn't there?' Judith continued, 'Together with the rest of your storyline. You haven't just made it up on the spot this morning.'

Caroline closed her mouth tight and the corners drooped. Jeremy Laidlaw half-stood again and gestured to Judge Nolan with a shake of his head. Judge Nolan leaned forwards in Judith's direction and cupped a hand over her ear. Judith tried to focus, but she could already foresee a whole series of memes which would follow from the freeze frame. She opened her briefcase and took out a newspaper.

'Your honour, I have here an advance copy of this week's *Sunday Mirror* magazine. On page four there is an interview with Miss Fleming, which sets out her views on all the matters she has put forward in evidence this morning, and more. If I could approach the bench, I could share it with you.'

Judge Nolan nodded and Judith hurried forwards, with Laidlaw in hot pursuit. The judge grabbed the magazine, read through the article and her face turned purple.

'Turn the cameras off,' she shouted at no one in particular.

One usher came scuttling towards her. 'All of them?' he asked.

'Yes, all of them! And clear my courtroom. Everybody out... except Counsel. You stay put.'

Caroline hovered halfway down from the witness box, swaying backwards and forwards, unsure whether she was included in the blanket command to leave or the more limited instruction to remain.

'Miss Fleming, you should wait outside too, please, as we will resume once I have spoken to Counsel,' Judge Nolan continued. 'You remain under oath and must not discuss your evidence with any person, or you will be in contempt of court. Is that clear?'

***

'Did you know about this?' Judge Nolan asked Laidlaw, when the public had left, brandishing the magazine like a victor's flag and breathing heavily through flared nostrils.

'Absolutely not,' he replied.

'And how did you get an advance copy?' She turned her attention to Judith.

'I was handed an envelope containing the magazine as I arrived at court this morning. I don't know who sent it, presumably someone who works for the newspaper, and I only had time to open it, shortly before we began.'

'Are you saying this means Miss Fleming has perjured herself?'

'I can't say that for certain, your honour, although I think she has tacitly accepted, already, that some of her earlier testimony was overstated, but that may be the full extent of it. Clearly, we can give her the opportunity to explain when she returns. But it must cast considerable doubt on her overall credibility.'

'Was she paid for this story?'

'Undoubtedly.'

'Mr Laidlaw. Did you not explain to your witnesses, to all prosecution witnesses, that they must not speak to the press for the duration of the trial?'

'Of course, your honour. And I had no reason to doubt the veracity of this witness, or any other, for that matter. I expect the pressures of this particular case might have proved too tempting, on this rare occasion. It is still not, as Ms Burton accepts, evidence of lying under oath.'

Judge Nolan sat back.

'How did you find her, this Caroline Fleming?'

'Your honour, you know I can't divulge...'

'You choose this moment to remember the extent of your professional duties.' She banged her hand down on the desk. 'The world is watching this trial, you know that?' Her eyelids flickered.

'Yes, your honour,' both Counsel nodded.

'Everything we say or do. We were chosen as one of the first cases, to showcase the best of our justice system. Both of you, I expect you to be very careful with anyone you bring into my courtroom. I don't want liars giving evidence or people who just want to be famous. I want witnesses who can help us get at the truth. For God's sake, we have a dead woman here, a good woman. We owe her more than this!'

'Yes, your honour.'

'Mr Laidlaw, Mr Nimble is a barrister in your chambers, isn't he?'

'Yes, your honour.'

'Well, I should like to see him here tomorrow morning bright and early, say 8.30am, to discuss the press coverage of this trial. Can you tell him that, please?'

'Yes, your honour.'

'Now, when we reconvene, we have the opportunity to make it clear to the jury that Miss Fleming's evidence is unreliable. And from now on, if there is anything that you know, or of which you become aware, during the course of this trial, which you feel puts its fairness in doubt, which compromises our justice system in any way, then I expect to be the first person to know about it, in advance, in private. Not in the media and not in my court room! Is that understood?'

***

After a thirty-minute hiatus, the public and press shuffled back into court. Caroline Fleming was restored to the witness box, but she was pale and downcast. Constance used the cover of the noise to snatch a few words with Judith.

'What did Judge Nolan say?' Constance asked.

'That we have to vet our witnesses and make sure they're all telling the truth. Other than employing a mind reader, I'm not sure how we're supposed to do that,' Judith replied.

'And are you going to make Caroline retract her evidence?'

'I'm thinking about it.'

'You must, mustn't you?'

'I have a better plan,' Judith said. 'Oh, don't look so worried.'

***

'Yes. Please continue Ms Burton.' Judge Nolan reconvened the proceedings with a regal wave, as if her outburst had never occurred.

Judith looked at Caroline, then at Debbie and then at Judge Nolan.

'I have no further questions for this witness,' she said.

Judge Nolan raised her embellished eyebrows. 'You have no further questions for this witness?' she repeated.

'No, thank you, your honour.' Judith shook her head, just to make her point crystal-clear.

'Miss Fleming, you are free...'

'I have a question.' Judge Nolan's booming voice cut through Laidlaw's release of his witness. Laidlaw looked at Judith. Judith ignored him. Constance shifted in her seat.

'Miss Fleming. Did you give an interview to the *Sunday Mirror*, to be published this coming Sunday, in which you described matters on which you have been giving evidence today in court?' Judge Nolan said.

'Yes.' Caroline's face was now pale yellow.

'Were you remunerated in any way for the interview?'

'I was.'

'How much were you paid?'

Caroline fidgeted with a tiny, diamante earring.

'Sixteen thousand pounds,' she said.

There was a low muttering in the court, which was silenced when the judge waved her hand over them all.

'And when you were interviewed, were you asked, in particular, if you could "remember" and I use the word in the loosest possible sense, any salacious stories about the defendant, Debbie Mallard?'

'I...that doesn't make what I said untrue,' Caroline pouted

miserably.

'But it makes you an unreliable witness in my court room and I will direct the jury accordingly,' Judge Nolan replied. 'And I urge the police to look carefully at what you have said here today and to draw the appropriate conclusions. I will not have people lying in my court room! Mr Laidlaw, you may now release your witness.'

***

'That was a bit risky, wasn't it?' Constance asked Judith, once they were in the sanctuary of their breakout room.

Judith sat down and eased off her shoes, one by one. 'I needed to show it was all made up, the money trouble, the violence, the cat.'

'It would have been safer just to ask her.'

'There was no reason for *me* to cross-examine Caroline further. I was at a high point. She said she never liked Danny, I'd dropped the hint she fancied him herself, she accepted that Rosie never said Debbie hurt her and I'd made my point, which was that she made the whole *mutilated cat* story up to manufacture an exclusive for the press.

'Then the judge threw a tantrum, which reinforced for the jury that Caroline had done something pretty bad. Why would I give Caroline any opportunity to explain or come back with further negative things about Debbie? And, if I may say so, it worked even better than I planned because, first of all, Laidlaw was so shocked he forgot to re-examine, or maybe he realised what a liability his witness was and that he needed to get rid of her before she did more damage, and then the judge herself called Caroline out as an unreliable witness. I thought it was text-book, better than text-book, a masterclass.'

'How did you know Judge Nolan would come down on her so heavily?'

'I knew Judge Nolan was all fired up, wanted to show everyone that she was in control, especially given all the criticism from yesterday.'

'I didn't see that.'

'Is that because you were too busy watching TV? I read it in the *Mail Online*, I think. They called her the "Red Queen" like in *Alice in Wonderland*. You know, *off with her head!* because she switched off the cameras. They were really scathing. Then the *Guardian* got David Benson to comment that he expected co-operation from *all parts of the justice system*. Poor Bridget. Not sure she deserved that disparagement. But, knowing that she was likely to be more sensitive than usual as a result, I used my judgement, as I always do. God knows what they'll say now she did it a second time.'

'Whatever you say. You're the boss.'

Judith paused with a shoe still in her hand. Constance didn't usually challenge her methods so directly and especially not when things were going well.

'You know that's not how I see us, Connie,' she said. 'We are a team. And we have Rosie's mother this afternoon. I need you onside.'

'It doesn't matter what I say, you just do what you want.'

'That's not true. I listened to you about the glove. I ran with it despite my reservations, and I'm still not certain it was the right thing to do. But I can't go back now and ask Caroline any more questions, even if I wanted to, so let's move on. What exactly do you want me to do next? Go on. I am listening.'

Constance pulled a can of lychee water from her bag, opened

it and took a gulp.

'All right. Here's what I think,' she said. 'Go easy on Mrs Harper. She's lost her daughter. It was acceptable with Caroline to push her around, especially once you knew about the *Mirror* interview, but the public will hate you if you interrogate Mrs Harper the same way.'

'This shouldn't be about what the public thinks of me. I've told you. I'm not changing my ways.'

'Well it is now. You've seen that. You and Laidlaw, with Andy Chambers' commentary. They analyse your every move – how you ask your questions, if you're trying to trip up the witnesses, if you're bullying them!'

Judith sighed, then she began to massage her foot. 'I agree with everything you just said about Elaine Harper, but I can't promise to go soft on her. It all depends what she says in the box. If she's bland, I'll follow suit. But if she's poisonous, you can't expect me to let it go. I'll have to challenge her hard.'

'I understand.'

'Is there something else that's bothering you?' Judith asked.

Constance pouted. How could she tell Judith that she was cross that the Caroline Fleming article had been handed directly to Judith, bypassing her? Judith was the face of the defence, to the outside world, so it wasn't surprising. Even so, it made her feel inconsequential.

'Do you know why we've lost another juror?' she asked, changing the subject, to give herself time to stifle her disappointment.

'You mean on top of the two women who Bridget worried might get nobbled?'

'Yes. I don't even remember who it was.'

'Young guy, blue shirt, second left. It seems that he had been checking the internet in all the breaks and one of the other jurors told on him. That's why he's gone and "now there are only eleven". He wasn't ill, just in big trouble. Apparently, Bridget then read the rest of them the riot act about contempt of court. I heard it from her clerk.'

'Poor Judge Nolan. She must wish she'd taken a sabbatical too.'

'I warned her about them keeping their devices, not that it did me any good. I suspect she'll think I'm smug about all this and come down on us even harder.'

'Not that you are...smug or anything.'

'I don't like the word *smug*. I prefer to say that I predicted, with accuracy, what was likely to occur.'

'Can we move on from this to talk about the money trouble motive?'

'I'm not one to gloat.'

'It just doesn't add up.'

'What did Debbie say?'

'She says she doesn't know anything about the payments out of Rosie's account, claimed Rosie looked after their finances, that she doesn't have much money of her own, which is probably not very helpful to know.'

'Maybe, go and see Jason Fenwick, again. See if you can find out what Rosie was paid and if he knows what those payments might have been. I'm sure he's dying to help, in any way he can.'

Constance opened her laptop and began tapping away. They didn't speak for some minutes.

32

ELAINE HARPER WAS DRESSED entirely in black, with black earrings and black nail polish to complement her outfit. Although she was in her late sixties, she remained a strikingly attractive woman. She had refused to speak to Constance some weeks earlier, but an advance copy of her statement had provided a steer of what her evidence would be, and it wasn't helpful.

'Mrs Harper, I know this must be most distressing for you, so please let me know if you require any breaks at any time.' Laidlaw began at his oily best and was rewarded by a sob from the witness. 'Mrs Harper, when did you last see your daughter, Rosie?'

'I saw her two weeks before her death, on the 31st of May, but we spoke the night before.' Elaine Harper's mouth hinged open on one side only when she spoke, giving her delivery a staccato quality. The physical resemblance between Elaine and her now dead daughter was evident, but where Rosie had been gentle and supportive, at least on camera, Elaine seemed brittle, every syllable delivered like an accusation.

'And when you saw Rosie, what were the circumstances?'

'It was my birthday. I invited her and the children over. We had some Prosecco and a light supper.'

'And did she tell you that anything was bothering her?'

'No. But the children, my grandchildren, were there.' She looked out into the gallery, spied Laura and Ben, gave them a half smile, then returned her gaze to Laidlaw.

'I see. Did you get the impression from anything Rosie said or did that something might have been bothering her?'

'I thought she seemed a bit quiet, thoughtful. And she'd lost weight.'

'She'd lost weight?'

'She was never big but, well, her clothes were hanging off her. And she picked at her food, left most of it.'

'When you spoke to her on the telephone, the night before she died, was she more forthright?'

'She said that Debbie was coming over the next day to talk about Ben, my grandson, and she wasn't looking forward to it.'

'Did she explain what she meant by that?' Laidlaw leaned forward and gave the camera his best shot at empathy.

'She didn't have to. I knew what she meant.'

'And what was that?' Laidlaw was speaking softly, cajoling the witness.

'Danny… Debbie… can I say Danny, is that all right?'

'Yes, that's perfectly all right. We know that you are referring to the defendant.'

Judith rose slowly.

'Your honour. I have no desire to make things more difficult for Mrs Harper than they already are,' she said. 'But my client's name is Debbie now. And she has the right to be addressed in that way, if at all possible, by everyone in this court room. Of course, if Mrs Harper forgets or makes a slip, that is totally understandable. But this court should do what it can to uphold the defendant's right to be called by her name.'

Constance frowned. Judge Nolan frowned and made a bridge with her hands. Debbie stared at Judith. Someone muttered 'hear hear' before a ripple of laughter rose and fell. Mrs Harper opened her mouth to speak, but then the judge cut in.

'Thank you, Ms Burton. You are, of course, correct. And right to point out the other considerations. Mrs Harper, do try to call the defendant *Debbie* or *the defendant* if you can. If you are referring back to events when she was known as Danny, then, I assume, it would be acceptable to call her by that name, if you wish.' She turned towards Debbie and Debbie gave a shallow nod of appreciation.

'I'll do my best, my lady,' Mrs Harper swallowed and glared at Debbie, accusing her, even in that moment, of making life even more intolerable.

'Before the interruption, you were telling us that Rosie was not looking forward to a conversation with Debbie the following day.'

'That's right. Ben wanted to leave school, said he wanted to become an actor. And Debbie was encouraging him. Rosie knew they were going to row about it.'

Judith looked at Ben, who was sitting close to his other grandmother, his face pale and pinched.

'And Rosie wanted Ben to stay on at school?'

'Of course she did. She said he should finish school and then, if he wanted to become an actor after that, it was fine. At least he would have his A levels to fall back on.'

'Perhaps Debbie was trying to be supportive to their son?'

'This was nothing about being supportive. This was all about him...her. She knew that Rosie wanted Ben to stay on and that's precisely why she encouraged him to leave, filling his head with nonsense that he was going somewhere. Going straight to an early death, more like. That's what happens to all these actors.'

Laidlaw smiled, before turning the page of his notes affectedly. Perhaps, his own parents had said something similar to him, Judith mused.

'Did Rosie and Debbie have a happy marriage?' he asked.

'I think they were happy at the beginning. Rosie was. The wedding was very over the top of course, but he was a footballer.'

'Was there a point when Rosie became unhappy?'

'I didn't see it straightaway. I had a feeling, but I didn't want to pry. But after the 999 call, I asked her and she told me. She had to, really.'

'Ah. You've mentioned the 999 call. We heard the call on Monday, when Inspector Dawson was giving his evidence. But it might be useful to hear it again...'

We all remember the call,' Judith objected. 'I don't see how it would be of use to play what would clearly be a distressing call for this witness. We've heard it once and been through the transcript.'

'I want the witness to identify the caller.'

'The defence accepts the caller is Rosie Harper.'

'Your honour, it's clear why the defence doesn't want the call played again, but it's central to this witness's evidence.'

Judge Nolan pressed the end of her pen a number of times in quick succession. Judith weighed up her chances and predicted they were slim. The judge's reprimand of Caroline Fleming would have been perceived by some as siding with the defence. And she'd just upheld Judith's plea to call her client 'Debbie', despite, no doubt, viewing it as petty and pandering to the left.

And while Judge Nolan was not usually one to care an iota for appearances – she was very much a 'judge of the moment' – no doubt she was learning, as was Judith, that in this scenario, with every inch of the screen open to scrutiny, appearances were paramount and 'moments' could be made to last hours. She needed to appear even-handed to have any chance of surviving this case.

'All right. Mrs Harper. You may find this call upsetting,' Judge Nolan said, her eyes lingering longer than necessary on the overhead camera, 'but Mr Laidlaw assures me it's important for you to hear it in this court room, in order to give your evidence.'

Judith smiled to herself. So, she hadn't yet lost her touch.

The 999 call was played for a second time, with the court in sombre silence. It took a few moments after it ended, to appreciate that the sobs they were all hearing were not emanating from the caller, but from Mrs Harper herself.

'Mrs Harper. Do take a few moments to compose yourself.'

Elaine Harper wiped her eyes and nose, gestured for a glass of water and drank it down. Then, as she had almost recovered her equilibrium, the usher mistakenly pressed play on the recording again and Rosie's voice rang out another time. She burst into tears anew. One juror joined her, then one of the reporters on the front row, which set Ben off. When silence was restored and Mrs Harper had used up at least four tissues, Laidlaw continued.

'Can you confirm whose voice was on that recording?' he asked.

'It was Rosie, Rosie's voice.'

'And the voice in the background at the end?'

'Ben, my grandson.'

'How did you get to know about the call?'

'I didn't know about the call when it happened. The first time I heard it was when you played it to me. But I knew the police had been around to the house, because Lynn told me.'

'Lynn is Mrs Harris, Rosie's neighbour.'

'She was worried when the police arrived in the night and she called me.'

'And you raised this with Rosie?'

'I called her straightaway and asked what was going on. She played it down, said it was "a mistake". But she was just covering up.'

'What was she covering up?'

'All the things happening. About a week after the police came, she told me.'

'Told you what?'

'That he, Danny, that was his name then, wanted to be a woman. She said she'd had an idea for a while that things weren't quite right. But he had told her and they'd had a huge argument. And that's why she called the police. And she said she'd fallen on her wrist at work, slipped on some ice, but I know he pushed her. When we next met, he couldn't look me in the eye. He'd hurt my daughter and he was ashamed of himself, as he should have been. And there, that call proves it.'

'Your daughter had hurt her wrist?'

'All bandaged up it was.'

'And that was the day after the police were called?'

'Or thereabouts.'

'Who do you think murdered your daughter?'

'I think he murdered her. Debbie.'

'Why?'

'You'll have to ask him that. I think they had a big argument and all of it came out, all the stuff from when the police were called and the things with Ben. She probably told him how it was and he didn't like it. She wanted to stop him seeing Ben.'

Debbie kept her eyes on the ground, but she fiddled with the cuff of her jacket.

'Rosie told you that she was going to prevent Debbie from seeing Ben?' Laidlaw's lips were desperate to proclaim 'victory is mine' but he managed to rein them in.

'That's what she said,' Elaine Harper confirmed. 'Said it was the only way to stop him influencing Ben, to stop his stupid ideas.'

'Did Debbie love the children?'

Elaine faltered. 'Yes,' she said, the word dragged from her mouth by her conscience. 'For all his faults, I always believed he loved those kids. He spent time with them whenever he could.'

'So the prospect of being separated from Ben would have been very provocative?'

Judge Nolan grunted and wagged her index finger from side to side like a pendulum, until Laidlaw, finally, nodded in her direction.

'I withdraw that last question,' he muttered. 'Thank you, Mrs Harper. Please wait for Ms Burton.'

***

Judith rose to her feet, with Constance's warning, delivered in the break, still in her ears. But she was also acutely aware that conflict over the children, or more specifically, Ben, could be a convincing catalyst for violence. It could just provide the elusive motive. Everything else, Danny's transition to Debbie, money issues, was old news. This was new and current and potentially explosive. She felt the hairs stand up on the back of her neck. She had to find a way of neutralising Mrs Harper's testimony.

'Mrs Harper. You told the court that you last saw your daughter to celebrate your birthday, two weeks before her death.'

'That's right.'

'Before your birthday, when was the last time you saw Rosie?'

'Oh gosh. I'm not entirely sure.'

'I don't need the exact date, but around when, do you think?'

'It had been a while, a month or two?'

'So, you'd last seen Rosie in late March?'

'I'm not sure.'

'And before that?'

'Probably Christmas time.'

'Is it correct that you and Rosie had fallen out in recent years, and that your birthday lunch had been an attempt to smooth things over, after a long period of not seeing each other?'

'I wouldn't put it exactly that way, but we were not as close as we had been, yes.'

'Why did you fall out?'

'That was because of Debbie too.'

'Can you explain that?'

'When she told me that Debbie was…wanted to become a woman, she was cross with what I said.'

'And that was the week after the 999 call, so in February 2017?'

'Yes.'

'I want to ask about the call for the last time. Don't worry. I won't make you listen to it again. But I wanted to understand what Rosie said to you about the call.'

Elaine Harper sighed and snatched a glance at Ben and Laura

again.

'She said they'd had a row and she'd called the police just to scare him, but I knew she was just saying that, to make me feel better.'

'You didn't trust what your own daughter said to you?'

'She was trying to protect me from the truth. No one wants to admit their husband is beating them, do they? And when I asked again, she told me, about Debbie.'

'Did Rosie tell you then, or later on, at any time, that Debbie threatened or injured her that evening?'

'No, but...'

'Without the explanation, please, of what you thought she meant. Did Rosie ever tell you that Debbie threatened or injured her that evening?'

'No.'

'Rosie actually told you the opposite, that the call was not genuine?'

'Yes, but...'

'Thank you, the yes was sufficient. When Rosie told you, a week later, about Debbie, you said she was cross with what you said in return. What did you say?'

'I told her I thought she should throw him out. But it seems that wasn't what she wanted to hear.' Mrs Harper dabbed at her eyes. 'Rosie could be quite headstrong. I suppose that's how she had done so well for herself.'

'Did you encourage your daughter to divorce her husband?'

'Of course I did. But divorces take time. I told her to kick him out there and then.'

'And she didn't appreciate that advice?'

'She said I didn't understand. I...me...with my Brian in the hospital. I shouldn't have to deal with all of that too.'

'And from then on, you didn't see as much of each other?'

'Brian died, within weeks of all this. His heart gave out. He adored Rosie and he couldn't bear to see her so distraught. We had the funeral and after that, Rosie was distant. But she was throwing herself into her work and she did kick him out soon after, even if she didn't like what I said at the time.'

'If I told you that Rosie confided in a colleague that you were vindictive and gloating and that was why she broke off contact with you, what would you say to that?'

Constance flinched at Judith's embellishment of Jason's words, began to compose a note for Judith, then scrunched it up into a ball and held it tightly inside her fist. Judith leaned forwards toward Mrs Harper.

'That's not true,' Mrs Harper began to cry again and she buried her head in her hands. Laidlaw scowled at Judith. 'It's often hard to get across what you mean, what you feel, in the heat of the moment,' Mrs Harper protested from underneath her hands. 'I just wanted what was best for my daughter. I can see how it probably sounds now to everyone, that I'm some kind of terrible person, prejudiced and nasty. This was my daughter, my baby, and she was so unhappy.'

The usher brought Mrs Harper another drink and, this time, she waved him away, before wiping her eyes.

'Cast your mind back twenty or so years to when Rosie told you that she and Debbie were getting married. How did you and your husband respond?'

'We gave them our blessing.'

'But you weren't totally happy?'

'It was more Brian, my late husband, than me. He said Danny

gave him a funny feeling, said he didn't trust him, thought he was false, fake. But we never let Rosie know that. We kept it to ourselves.'

'Isn't it true that your late husband disapproved of Danny because he grew up on a council estate?'

'No.'

'Was brought up by a single mother?'

'No.'

'Had a tattoo before they were fashionable, had a reputation for partying?'

'It wasn't like that. We didn't care where he came from or how he spoke. He was a footballer; we didn't expect him to be posh. Brian was always civil to Danny. They just didn't have much in common.'

'So neither you nor your husband approved of the marriage, but Rosie went ahead anyway. Did Rosie know you didn't approve?'

'We kept it to ourselves. We joined in all the celebrations. Now, of course, I wish I had listened more to Brian. I wish we had warned her.'

'Mrs Harper. I put it to you that you have absolutely no evidence that Debbie killed Rosie, do you?'

'I know Debbie was there. And I know Rosie was scared of Debbie. That's what I know.'

'Did she ever tell you she was scared of Debbie?'

'Not directly.'

'And when you told her to "kick Debbie out" she disagreed, you said?'

'Yes.'

'Because she was…headstrong?'

'Yes.'

'Then it doesn't sound like she was very scared of Debbie, if she chose, despite your maternal advice, to have Debbie stay, even if it was only for a few extra weeks.'

'She was scared of what he might say, what he might do, if she threw him out.'

'Rosie was scared about what other people might see or hear or think?'

'Of course she was.'

'Do you think that this fear you are talking about – assuming you are correct – might have been precisely that: Rosie was worried about what people might think, when news of her separation was made public, particularly given the circumstances, including her husband becoming a woman? And it was this she was scared about, rather than any fear that Debbie might harm her physically?'

'No.'

'But you accept that you never liked Debbie, neither did your late husband?'

'I do. I have to be honest.'

'And that when Rosie did confide in you, you fell out and didn't speak for some time.'

'It's true. If only she'd listened.'

'This, then, is your last opportunity to prove to everyone that you were right all along, isn't it?'

'No. It's not like that.'

'To show everyone, all your friends, whom you told frequently that Debbie wasn't good enough for your daughter. Lynn Harris, whom you befriended, was over the road, keeping an eye on things but, in reality, spying on the family, feeding gossip back to you. You told Mrs Harris that Danny had become Debbie, didn't you?'

'I did. But she'd have found out soon enough.'

'Even though Rosie had asked you and your late husband to keep it private?'

'Yes, but, I mean, it was all over the papers.'

'And you don't even have your husband now to confide in, so it's down to you, isn't it, to show everyone that you were right all along. Debbie was always bad news!'

'No!' Mrs Harper shrieked. 'It was never like that! If you had children, you would know how it feels when they make the wrong choices and you're powerless to help. She married a monster. I just wanted to protect her. How could he do that to her? To my baby. To make her so unhappy. He must have known when he married her what he was like. To trick her like that, for all those years. He's a fraud, a liar and a murderer!'

***

'Well that went well.' Judith sat quietly, pulling on a loose thread from her wig.

'I thought it was OK,' Constance tried to reassure her, her crumpled up note reminding Judith to be restrained, still rustling against the inside of her jacket pocket. 'Everyone knows she isn't a neutral witness. And she helped with the 999 call, by saying that Rosie insisted it wasn't genuine.'

'What were her last words? "A fraud, a liar and a murderer". That will make a great front page headline tomorrow morning. Take a look; perhaps it's trending already.'

'You had to do something to show she wasn't being fair.'

'You told me to go gently and I pushed her too far. And,

naturally, *if I had children of my own*, I would have understood, instead of being the cold-hearted bitch they'll portray me as when they play this back this evening for a million viewers. Is that one of the statistics they put up there for everyone to know, like those tables ahead of a big tennis match? But instead of height, weight, age, they substituted marital status and family and I got *widow* and *childless*. Is that how she knew to push that button?'

'It may not be too bad. You got in the class bit and it diverted attention from her saying Debbie was cold and Laidlaw didn't take the opportunity to ask her about that again. And I wasn't sure about the 999 call, but it was good for us, playing it again after you had taken Dawson through it. It really emphasised how Rosie never said she was hurt, that the call is nothing. You wanted Laidlaw to play it again, didn't you?'

'I thought if I said nothing then the judge might intervene and stop Laidlaw, to spare Mrs Harper's feelings. Once I forced her to choose between Laidlaw and me, it was more likely she would go with Laidlaw on this one. So now she owes us one. And you're right, after that session going through the wording on Monday, the impact of the call was diffused. But that doesn't change how monumentally I fucked things up right at the end. I was too brash, too insistent. Maybe I got excited by the cameras. I don't think I did. I tried business as usual. Oh God, they'll crucify me tonight, but I suppose I deserve it.'

'I thought Court TV was *complete garbage*?'

'How can I focus with that lens suspended above my head, sucking up my innermost thoughts and regurgitating them for moronic consumption?'

'You said Laidlaw was the drama queen.'

'I know what I said. I was trying to make the best of things and that was before bloody Andy Chambers and *body language* and *reconstructions* and *Q and A* and did you know someone even asked where I get my clothes from? It's impossible to exhale in there, without someone examining the composition of my breath.'

'Just ignore them, like you said.'

'You're the one who told me to play to the cameras, that public opinion mattered. Which is it to be?'

Constance leaned back in her chair. She didn't want to admit that she might have been wrong, that the impact of Court TV was profound and not necessarily positive. And Judith facing a crisis in confidence was the last thing Debbie needed.

'There's a partner at work who specialises in media law,' she said. 'I'll ask him if they're overstepping the rules.'

'You do that,' Judith said, taking a drink of water. 'Though, if they are, I'm not sure there's anything we'll be able to do about it.

33

'TONIGHT WE HAVE A packed show. Ooh it was a big day today, wasn't it just? Day three, middle of the week. What excitement!' Katrina opened the Wednesday night programme, beaming broadly. 'Later on, we're going to be talking about sportsmen and women, who have committed murders and other offences, with expert true crime historian Freddie King, author of *Shocking Sports Crimes*. And asking the question whether there is anything about competitive sports which might lead to crime. After that, our linked feature is an interview with three mothers who lost their daughters to crime, at the hands of their spouses.

'But before that, today in court. Andy, let's talk, first of all, about Caroline Fleming, Rosie Harper's friend, who Judge Nolan reprimanded in pretty severe terms. Did she really call her a liar, in front of millions of people?'

'You could say that. It's all a question of credibility,' Andy replied, hoping to bide his time, to ease into the topic, via some more general explanation about how lawyers selected witnesses in the first place. After all, and as Clare had reminded him when he crawled into bed in the early hours and had asked 'how was I?', hoping for praise, he was supposed to be providing explanation: how it all worked, what considerations were appropriate. He mustn't allow Katrina to hijack his part of the show.

If the answer's yes, just say yes, the voice in his ear hissed. Andy stared at Katrina. Had she heard the voice too? Her expression was unaffected. 'But, yes,' he said. 'That is essentially what Judge Nolan said.'

'In your professional opinion, as a lawyer, is that fair?' Katrina asked.

'There is a rule that witnesses mustn't be paid for giving evidence. It tends to taint their views.'

'That I completely understand. You wouldn't want to say, *Caroline, I'll pay you a hundred pounds…or sixteen thousand pounds*, in this case, *if you give me a false alibi*. But this is different, isn't it?'

'The difficulty is where to draw the line.'

'If the line is not to be paid to give evidence, then Caroline Fleming never crossed it, did she? She accepts she was paid for an interview, but that interview was due to be published after she gave her evidence. And the jury wouldn't know anything about it, anyway.'

'That's not the point. When witnesses talk to the press, the concern is that they'll exaggerate, enhance, embroider the truth, to make their story more marketable.'

'If the public want to hear the story, though, aren't we muzzling free speech, if we silence those people?'

'She can speak after the verdict…'

'But if this is different material from the things she talked about in court? The interview, I understand, went much further, touching on every aspect of Rosie and Debbie's relationship. Doesn't the public have the right to know those kind of things; you know "the truth, the whole truth and nothing but the truth"?'

'You're assuming Caroline Fleming was a truthful witness...'

'Are you saying she wasn't?'

'No. I can't go so far as...'

'You're saying, then, that the judge got things wrong...'

'Well, I...' *Just say yes*, the voice in Andy's ear was there again. He had intended to add a caveat, but the voice wanted him to answer the question. 'It's certainly possible,' he conceded.

'...leaving Caroline Fleming branded a liar,' Katrina protested. 'You know she gave an interview immediately after court. We can show it; here we are.'

The screen switched to a distraught Caroline Fleming being held together by family members as she sobbed into the camera and declared she would never be a witness again.

'I thought the purpose of justice was to be precisely that; fair and just. How can scaring witnesses off be the right way forward?' Katrina said.

Andy was thinking to himself that no one was paying any attention to what Caroline had actually said, or to Judith's expert dissection of her testimony, which he had hoped to major on today. Instead, he stared at the camera and said, 'You're right. It isn't.'

***

Constance was watching from home with a heavy heart. Not only was *Court TV BTS* proving considerably more opinionated and partisan than she had ever believed possible, the press and social media were taking every word up and amplifying it. Yesterday, all the attention had been on the profiler: 'Eminent psychiatrist says Debbie Mallard must be guilty', 'Has to be someone close to Rosie says psychiatrist to the stars' and 'Rosie Harper's assailant was jealous of her achievements.'

Today, quite apart from the bizarre support for Caroline Fleming, which was rising even before the after-show came on air, the Elaine Harper session had similarly set hares running. On Twitter, the 'fraud, liar, murderer' soundbite had been rapidly disseminated, but then lost momentum. It was too easy, served by Judith to the public on a plate. Twitter needed something more radical and it arrived with the condemnation of Elaine Harper for being a distant mother, for failing to intervene in her daughter's abusive relationship; some went so far as to lay the blame for Rosie's murder at her own mother's door. Although there was one unexpected positive line of tweets to lift her spirits, which she squirrelled away to give to Judith later on.

***

Back on TV, Katrina had taken a call from a viewer.

'David. You're calling in from Wimbledon. I understand you have a question for Andy about the jury. Is that right?'

'I know someone on the jury; that's what I want to ask about.'

Andy found his hand rising up, defensively, to shield his face. 'Don't say their name. You mustn't say their name,' he said.

'I know that, mate,' the caller said. 'Take it easy.'

Andy could see Phil gesticulating through the glass, making cut-throat gestures, but the voice was in Andy's ear again, overruling Phil. *We're going to run with this one*, it said. *Be alert.*

'Ask us your question, then. Go ahead,' Katrina said.

'This guy I know, the one on the jury. He said they're all watching your show. I just wondered how you felt about that.'

***

Constance wanted to share her fears with Judith, full and frank disclosure, to curse Andy Chambers for his betrayal of their profession, to warn Judith that she had to factor in how things would play out on TV when she planned her moves in court, to tell her about this new whistleblower revelation and debate its potential impact. But how to do that without making Judith more paranoid about every exchange?

'Hello there,' Judith said, picking up Constance's call. 'Are you ringing to ask if Laidlaw moonlights as Court TV's programmer? Is there anything we can do? What did your colleague say about it all?'

'I wasn't sure you'd be watching,' Constance said. 'Pretty bad, I know. He said that they were walking a tightrope, but not clearly out of line, but that was yesterday.'

Judith tapped her fingers against the back of her phone. 'Leave it, Connie. Let it go. At least for tonight,' she said.

'That isn't why I rang, though,' Constance lied. 'If it's any consolation, Twitter is full of love for you tonight,' she said, suddenly inspired to share with Judith the positive feedback she had just viewed.

'Twitter? Isn't this all too dull for Twitter? It's hardly *Love Island.*'

'I'm telling you, they're loving you. It's for what you said in court today, about using Debbie's name.'

'Using Debbie's name?'

'When Elaine Harper asked if she could call her "Danny" and you objected. It's everywhere. Memes and videos, mostly giving you huge support, recognising how important it is to be called by your own name.'

The silence on the line was not unwelcome to Constance. This was a much better way to motivate Judith than complaints and warnings.

'I got something right then,' Judith said. 'Hmph. And has the suddenly supportive Twitter posted any more polls recently?'

'It's shifting, slowly. Down to 60% guilty.'

'That is a shift. Maybe I should annihilate a few more Elaine Harpers, metaphorically of course, on live TV?'

'Noooo,' Constance shrieked – then, more mildly – 'thank you. Anyway, isn't it Ben tomorrow?'

'Oh yes. Poor Ben. It's such a shame Laidlaw wanted him. I wonder how he'll sleep tonight.'

***

Constance sat with the television on mute, playing with her food. A pep talk for Judith was only one battle won. She picked up her phone and sent a message to Greg.

Do you have time for a quick chat? she wrote.

***

'Hey there.' Greg called Constance five minutes after she had switched off her light.

'Oh hi. Thanks for calling back.'

'Did I wake you? I thought you and Judith would be burning the midnight oil.'

'It's 1am.'

'OK, the 1am oil. Should we speak tomorrow? Your message sounded urgent.'

'Oh, no…now's good. I don't think you can help though.'

'Try me? I'm usually good at those impossible, no-one-can-help tasks.'

Constance smiled and pushed her pillow up against the wall, resting back against it.

'I just thought you might be able to say something to your friend, the Court TV boss.'

'Ah, *friend* might be elevating the relationship a little. What kind of message were you hoping I could pass on for you?'

'You must know. The show is a farce. Andy Chambers saying that the judge was wrong to criticise Caroline Fleming, all these so-called experts analysing how we speak and how we move and true crime analogies. It's turning the trial into…mass entertainment.'

'Ooh, that's not the message I should deliver, if you want him to abandon his plans. I mean, who would've thought that law, real law, not the stuff that comes from LA, but law beamed to us from a crumbling old building with starchy judges, could be so sexy?'

'This isn't funny. He's making us look ridiculous.'

'I don't think so.'

'He is. Self promoters, whistleblowing jurors, lawyers who are just jealous of Judith 'cos she beat them fair and square! And it's sparked all this stuff on social media.'

'Social media was always going to have a field day with a case like this one. I don't see how you can blame that on Court TV.'

'But it's a consequence of so many more people watching.'

'Which, if I remember rightly, was the aim of the pilot. You need to take a step back and consider what you are really worrying about.'

'I've just told you.'

'Court TV is just doing what it said it would do; filming the trial and providing commentary on it, to educate the public.'

'It's not education, it's distortion!'

'Look, I understand that such close scrutiny of what you're doing is difficult, especially when you're not used to it, but you knew the case was likely to be filmed when you took it on. And it's always hard being first. In a few months, the novelty will probably have worn off.'

'That doesn't help us now…or Debbie.'

'If you feel the media are overstepping the rules of fair coverage and you can't defend Debbie, then I would say it's the newspapers who are more at fault here.'

'But they're only doing it to outdo the TV station.'

'If you say so, but no one cares *why* they are doing it. Look, I'm just giving you my opinion, from one step removed. I may be wrong, of course.'

'You won't say anything to him, then?'

Greg sighed. 'I think when you've slept on this, you'll realise I'm right. And maybe you and Judith need to just embrace the experience.'

'Embrace the experience?'

'The other players will be milking this for all they can; profile-raising, promotion, endorsements, speaking engagements. You could decide to join them. Most people would die to have such a large audience.'

'I can't believe you just said that.'

'I'm just pointing out your options.'

'I'm going to sleep.'

'Don't ignore what I've said because you're angry… At least then you'd have some benefit from all this discomfort. It isn't going to go away, but some limited exploitation could make it a little more palatable.'

Constance was silent, as her anger rose up inside her.

'Or if you don't like that idea, make sure you continue your brilliant performance. Make the public endorse every aspect of what you and Judith do. Then the DPP will love you too, even though you're on the other side. Do both, they're not mutually exclusive.'

'You said you wanted to help, but I'm sorry I bothered you or thought you would understand,' Constance said. 'Good night.'

She ended the call, turned off her light and lay down in bed, pulling the covers up tight under her neck.

34

THE CROWD OUTSIDE COURT had swollen from the previous day and spanned the full length of the road, from Newgate Street at the top to Ludgate Hill at the bottom. This time, a number of police officers were in attendance, talking calmly to the protesters, but clearly on hand in case things became more heated. The domestic violence group was still there in force, but it was dwarfed in size by the supporters of trans rights, who were chanting 'Deb-bie, Deb-bie, my name is Deb-bie' over and over again, occasionally alternating with 'Trans Rights are Human Rights'.

Nicki was on her way to the trial again. She knew there was a risk she would encounter journalists, but thought it unlikely they would recognise her out of context. In any event, the pull of the courtroom was too strong. She wanted to be there, where the action was unfolding and she was damned if a few questions from some ignorant police officer some weeks back, or the enquiries from Debbie Mallard's rather more curious defence solicitor, would prevent her from coming. Not only was she a member of the public, she had met Rosie, so she was perfectly entitled to attend.

She picked her way through the crowd and swept, panther-like, along the hallowed corridors and into the courtroom, just before proceedings were about to start. After a moment's hesitation, she headed for the last remaining seat, on the front row. She nodded to her neighbours on either side and then locked eyes with Ellis Harper. He froze at the sight of her, before rising stiffly to his feet and hurrying out.

***

Ben was calm and collected as he was sworn in, and resolute as he scanned the faces in the public gallery. But the moment he took in his father, seated in the dock, his lower lip trembled and he shot Constance a desperate look. Constance leaned forward to warn Judith, but Judith had seen it too.

'Your honour, the witness is clearly troubled. Could we take a short break, please, to allow him to compose himself,' Judith said.

Judge Nolan had been busy with her papers and hadn't noticed, but she nodded her agreement, before leaving court, stumbling up the shallow step to the exit.

'Probably looking forward to a double shot espresso, to see her through the morning session,' Judith muttered.

'She does look awful, doesn't she? Did you see the cartoon in the *Times*?'

'You mean the Red Queen with the axe?'

'Yes. I wasn't sure we'd even be here today, after that call last night about the jurors.'

'Oh that. They've decided to ignore it.'

'What?'

'I know. There was some big conference call early this morning. They dragged Bridget out of bed for it. All the most senior people. They decided it was bad, but stopping the trial would be worse. They're working on things for the next televised trial, like putting the jurors up in a hotel without TV or Wifi, but it's too late for us.'

'Do you really think they're all watching it – Court TV – like the man said?'

'Who knows? I'd probably be tempted. Wouldn't you?'

***

With Ellis' departure, Ben was left sitting alone in the corridor, awaiting Laidlaw or someone from his team. Constance peered at him, around the door and he beckoned her over.

'I shouldn't be seen talking to you,' she said, as she approached. 'You're a prosecution witness.'

'I'm sorry,' Ben mumbled. 'I didn't want to be on my own.'

'I can understand you feeling nervous, but it will be over very quickly, I promise.'

'I was OK, till I got up there and saw Dad. And then I started thinking that he's only here, dealing with all this, because of me.'

'This isn't your fault,' Constance said. 'You need to believe that.'

'Does he have to be there, listening?'

'I can't talk to you about…'

'You think I'm going to say something bad about him and I don't want him to hear it. It's not that at all.'

'No.'

'I just know he misses her too, Mum. He misses her the way we do, Laura and me and Uncle Ellis. And he can't even cry for her. And if I go in there and I start talking about her, about Mum, his wife, in front of all those people. Little things. Personal things. Things you keep in a family. It's not right. I don't want to do it.'

'I can understand that...'

'I never did. I said I would, if you thought it would help Dad. But I've been watching and I see what he asks, the other lawyer. And she does it too, Judith.'

'Look, I'll ask Judith to speak to Mr Laidlaw, see what we can do to have you released. But if we push too hard, they'll suspect it's because you have something bad to say. It may be better for your dad, for you to just give your evidence now, even though you don't want to.'

'What if he asks me where Mum went the night before she died?' Ben said, the words falling quickly from his mouth.

'Where did she go?' Constance looked around her to check they were alone as she was speaking.

'I don't know. But she got all dressed up; hair, makeup, new clothes, loads of perfume.'

'Was that unusual?'

'Yeah. I would have teased her that she had a date, but we weren't talking. I was planning to stay with a friend but, well I had a bit to drink and I didn't feel so good, so I came home instead. She got back really late. Should I have told you before? I didn't want Dad to know.'

'No, it's no problem,' Constance lied. 'And if Mr Laidlaw asks you, you must tell him the truth.'

***

'Jeremy? Could we have a word, in private please? Judith approached Laidlaw, at the back of the court, away from the microphones.

'What can I do for you?' Laidlaw was smiling openly, arms crossed, chest puffed out, like a friendly bouncer.

'Ben Mallard, your next witness. He's your witness, of course, but...concern has been raised with my solicitor regarding the impact this will have on him, testifying out there in front of the cameras, effectively, against his father. Is there any chance you might consider not calling him? His evidence is of limited value; it's only about the emergency call, isn't it? He's probably of more use to the defence, if the truth be told.'

Laidlaw thought for a moment. 'When I prepare for a trial, it might surprise you to know that I weigh up carefully who is absolutely necessary as a witness. I don't want to waste anyone's time and I certainly don't want to traumatise a sixteen-year-old boy unnecessarily. I have kids of my own.'

'You still want him then. I understand.'

'Why ask if you already knew the answer? I would have been with you and permitted him to talk behind a screen without any difficulty, but we all know that that wasn't going to be allowed. Insufficiently transparent for this new age of popular justice.' Laidlaw paused and looked across at the witness box.

'Look, there is something, just between you and me. Ben has some health issues; we're worried this might...exacerbate them.'

'Then you should have made that clear when we had the preliminary hearing, and you know I would have been accommodating. It's too late now.'

'Will you at least take instructions?' Judith asked.

'Take instructions? You don't think that my word is the final word? I heard you were going soft in your old age, but I didn't believe it.'

'Can you, for a moment, refrain from point-scoring and take what I am asking you at face value? There is no agenda. He's just sixteen, he's lost his mother and he's fragile. And if I should have handled things differently, then that's my mistake, but don't punish him for it.'

'All right. I will talk to my team and we'll take the football coach next, although we'll need a few minutes to find him and get him in here. I'm fairly sure we'll still want Ben afterwards, but I'll keep things to the minimum. That's the best I can do for your *concerned solicitor*, and more than I would usually concede.'

***

Judith had taken advantage of the short break to brave the crowds and rush to a nearby pharmacy for paracetamol. She rarely suffered from headaches, but today her skull felt like it was going to explode. Then again, she didn't normally navigate a trial on zero sleep, constant anxiety about how she looked, her body language and how she presented the evidence to ensure minimum offence. And now, on top of that, she felt that she should have taken more steps to protect Ben, rather than leave him exposed in this way. As she swallowed two tablets with a swig of water and ran from the shop, she bumped straight into Ellis, who was checking his phone in the doorway.

'Oh. Hello again! You're getting some fresh air too?' she said.

'I'd prefer a whisky. Maybe I'll have one, once Ben's finished.' Ellis marched next to Judith, as she hurried across the road. 'Listen, I know it's not really my business, but did you have to go in so hard on Elaine?'

Judith walked even faster. 'You're right,' she said. 'It isn't your business.'

'OK. I probably deserved that. But Ben is definitely my business.'

'And we're not calling him as a witness. But I couldn't stop the prosecution.'

Ellis stopped walking and he rolled his shoulders back with a deep sigh. 'I'm sorry,' he said. 'I didn't mean to take things out on you. It's just I've been with them both, Ben and Laura, almost constantly, for the last few weeks. I'm not complaining. I would do it again in a heartbeat. It's just it's painful to see, that's all.'

'I understand.' Judith said. 'It will be over soon. I need to get back.'

'Sure,' Ellis called after her, as he stopped to take a call. 'I'll make sure I'm there in time for Ben, don't worry.'

Judith waved one hand above her head as she was swallowed up once more by the protesting crowds outside the court.

***

'Mr Isleworth, you worked with Danny Mallard between 2011 and 2017, when he managed West Ham football club?' Laidlaw had been waiting for Judith outside the court, tapping his foot against the door. She had straightened her wig and gown and marched straight past him and into court. What was the expression? *Never apologise, never explain.* That pithy mantra summed up how she felt in that moment, as the pills kicked in and her migraine began to subside.

'That's right,' Mr Isleworth replied.

'You were the head coach?'

'I was.'

'Was Danny a good manager?'

'On balance, I'd say yes.'

'That suggests you are weighing up some good points and some bad?'

'There's always room for improvement. He had good ideas, was very hands on, but a bit inflexible. You know, if something didn't quite work out, he would say that the lads had to change, to do what he wanted.'

'Rather than what?'

'Rather than beginning with what you've got, you know, looking at the team, at their strengths and then playing to those strengths.'

'I see.'

Judith thought Laidlaw probably didn't. She couldn't see him having much insight into how the beautiful game was played. He would play something much cleaner and without any contact, most probably tennis...or badminton.

'Was Danny popular with the lads?' Now he was trying the vernacular, but it didn't suit him.

'It depends. Some of them really liked Danny; they respected his work ethic, but he certainly clashed with two or three players, and we had to let them go.'

'When you worked with the defendant, as you say, she was Danny, a male colleague?'

'Yes.'

'When did you first become aware that she wanted to become a woman?'

Judith waved a hand in Laidlaw's direction, as she half-rose.

'Much as this trip down memory lane must be fascinating

for those at home seeking to know more and more about my client's *personal affairs*, it appears to have no bearing on these proceedings,' she said.

'I will be getting to the point shortly, your honour. I accept this is background, but it is necessary background, in order to provide context for what will come next. From those five years working closely with the defendant, would you say that Debbie is a kind individual?'

Judith was on her feet before Laidlaw had finished his sentence. 'Your honour?'

'Ms Burton, I'd like to see where Mr Laidlaw is going with this, so I will give him a little latitude, as long as it's quick.'

'No, not kind,' Ken Isleworth said.

'So how would you describe the defendant?'

'It's difficult to say in a few words.'

'I can help you out with a few adjectives if you like. Was the defendant funny?'

'Not really.'

'Warm?'

'No.'

'Relaxed?'

'No.'

'Was she the kind of person who would flatter you, make you feel good about something?'

'No.'

'In summary, she was unkind, serious, cold, anxious and brutally honest?'

Now Judith understood. Laidlaw was going for the soundbite, tomorrow's headline, something for the press to sink their teeth into; *the real face of Debbie Mallard*. But he had not bargained for

Ken Isleworth as an adversary.

'You're twisting my words,' Ken said. 'If you were all those things you just said: *warm, kind*, the lads would walk all over you. You have to be tough and you have to be straight-talking. But what's wrong with that? Your job isn't to stand up in a court room and wave your arms around, it's to motivate the team to succeed, outside, in all weathers and even when things are going spectacularly wrong. OK, Danny was always a bit on the cool side, but nobody's perfect.'

'If you say so. When did the defendant tell you that she was becoming a woman?'

Ken ran his hand across his face.

'About two years ago, maybe a bit less than that. I'd noticed things, I hadn't said anything, but in a way that made it worse.'

'What kind of things?'

'She had something done to her hair, grew it longer, dyed it blond, had it cut different. And...' Ken swallowed but soldiered on, 'I noticed she'd started to develop breasts.'

Judith leaped up. 'Your honour, this is intolerable. This witness has nothing of any relevance whatsoever to say. Instead my client is being subjected to this inappropriate...strip-search on live TV, purely to titillate viewers!'

'Ms Burton, watch how you conduct yourself!' Judge Nolan had raised herself out of her chair. Judith remained standing, opened her mouth, then closed it again and sat down. While her words might have been over the top, there was no need to reprimand her in quite such an overbearing way.

'Mr Laidlaw, I don't want any more questions regarding personal details of the defendant's transitioning process, unless they are absolutely necessary,' Judge Nolan barked.

Laidlaw smiled with his eyes only and inclined his head ever so slightly towards the judge, by way of acknowledgement. At least he, too, was unhappy with his treatment.

'Did you speak to the defendant about what you saw?' Laidlaw continued.

'It was awkward. I didn't want to pry. But eventually, I made up a reason for us to have a coffee together and she told me.'

'The defendant told you then, around two years ago, that she was going to transition, to become a woman.'

'She asked me what I thought.'

'And what did you say?'

'I said that she had to do it, if she felt it was right. I mean, she must have thought really hard about it. And I thought it was brave; there, that's a word I would use to describe her, "brave". I was a bit shocked, if I'm honest.'

'You were shocked?'

'Even with the things I mentioned,' Ken gave a brief sidelong glance towards Judge Nolan, 'like her hair, I didn't imagine *that*. I mean, as I said, she had a wife and two children. And she was Danny Mallard. You can't get more of a macho hero than that. Lots of little boys all wanting to be like Danny.'

'Did you ask if Rosie was being supportive?'

'Not like that, but I probably said, "what does Rosie think?" – that kind of thing.'

'What did she say?'

'She didn't really answer the question, just deflected it, so I suppose that meant *no*. And I was right 'cos they got divorced, didn't they?'

'Just stick to the facts, Mr Isleworth. Did the defendant talk to you about leaving Rosie, moving out?'

'It just came up one day that she'd moved out. I'm not sure when.'

'Did Debbie like her position as manager of West Ham?'

'She loved it.'

'Why did she leave?'

'She fell out with the boss.'

'George Scopos, the owner?'

'Yes.'

'They had an argument?'

'That's what I heard.'

'Punches were thrown?'

'I don't know about that.'

'That's what the papers said at the time.'

'I don't always believe what's in the papers.'

'I can read you one of the headlines. "Mallard sacked after fist fight with boss". Or there's "Hammers lose hero coach after punch-up". Do either of those jog your memory?'

'I saw the headlines.'

'So she left her managerial position?'

'Pretty much straightaway.'

'The defendant didn't get another job coaching a premier league side, did she?'

'No.'

'How did she feel about that?'

'Not very good, I imagine. But that's football, isn't it? One minute you're up with the gods, the next you're down with the dogs.'

***

Judith tapped her pen against her pursed lips. She had little to ask this witness but, given his clear allegiance to Debbie, despite Laidlaw's relentless pressure, she wanted to glean something positive from him, if possible. He had said Debbie was brave; perhaps she could capitalise on that, make it her own takeaway point from the session. And the public had liked the bit about Debbie's name yesterday; that was probably why the crowd outside was mostly supportive today. She could try and push things even further, get them more on-side, get them to understand Debbie's struggle. What had David Benson said? 'Equality, Accessibility, Transparency'. Well she would focus on equality for now, which ought to start the influencers' juices flowing.

'Mr Isleworth, did many people know that Danny was intending to change gender?'

'At the beginning, I doubt it. She tried to keep it quiet.'

'The things you talked about, noticing changes in Debbie's appearance, was that before or after she left West Ham?'

'Now I think about it, it was probably only the hair before. We met up a few times afterwards, for a drink. She liked to hear news, how the lads were getting on, all the things we were planning. I think the stuff I noticed was probably then.'

'Do you think it would have been possible for Debbie to stay on as manager, after her transition?'

'She fell out with the boss, so...'

'If they hadn't fallen out?'

'No, no way, I mean, we only have, what six, seven black managers in the whole of the football league. A woman? No chance. And a woman who used to be a man? She wouldn't make it through the front door.'

'What do you mean, *a woman who used to be a man*? Why is

that so bad?'

Ken stared at Judith, as if she had grown three heads.

'It's, well, I don't know what you'd call it – a betrayal, isn't it? I worked with Danny, I liked Danny. I know he didn't suddenly lose all his skills, all those things we admired him for, just because he wore his hair in a ponytail, but even I couldn't get my head around it. I mean, why, when you're a man and a successful man, why give all that up and choose to be a woman? I'm sorry, I'm just telling it how I see it. And you have to remember, young men, who we work with, they're interested in women because they find them attractive, they fancy them. So, to have someone who you thought was one of the lads, who you might talk to about all kind of lads' stuff – about women, then move over to the other side. It was worse than, say, moving from Spurs to Arsenal.'

This time a loud peal of laughter rang out through the court.

'He would have lost the trust of the players?'

'Look, it was complete career suicide.'

'And, just going back to the rumours about what happened with Mr Scopos, did you believe them?'

'I didn't believe Danny would've punched George. Maybe he was feeling under a lot of pressure, with everything going on in his personal life and I didn't see it, but that was what came down from on high, so I accepted it.'

'Thank you, that's all from me.'

Judith was pleased with Ken's comments on Debbie's prospects, post-transition. But she was a little concerned by the way Judge Nolan was staring at Ken and tapping her pen, interspersed with gazing up at the camera.

'Mr Isleworth, I have a question for you,' Judge Nolan said, holding up her hand to indicate that everything else must wait.

'Do you think that the defendant changed, in terms of her behaviour, when she transitioned?'

'That's not easy to answer. I think, maybe, in small ways. Nothing I can put my finger on, but it was almost as if she thought we would expect her to behave differently. Although maybe I saw her in a different way, because of how she looked.'

'Hm. Did the defendant talk to you about the transition process or about any medication she took?'

Laidlaw was on his feet in a flash. 'Your honour is most likely aware that this is an enormously important topic, which we have been unable to explore during this trial, as a result of the absence of a suitable expert. Given your honour's clear interest, which must reflect that of everyone here today and those watching at home, piqued by Mr Isleworth's eloquent testimony, I should like to renew the prosecution's request to allow Dr Melanie Alves to attend and educate everyone on this crucial area.'

'As your honour ruled at our preliminary hearing, general information about the transition process is wholly irrelevant to this trial. Nothing has changed to make it relevant or admissible, for that matter,' Judith replied.

'But things have changed, your honour,' Laidlaw persisted. 'This witness is talking about how Danny's personality changed, the uncharacteristic brawl with Mr Scopos. He must have been under tremendous pressure. You, yourself, want to be educated, to know the answers to a few simple, basic, uncontroversial questions. And this is a high-profile case. There are millions of viewers out there, who won't feel satisfied with the process unless this part of the puzzle is complete. The whole basis for us opening up the courts is to educate, to illuminate, to enlighten, not to stifle, suppress or muzzle. And we are well within our time estimate.'

'This is…'

Judge Nolan raised her hand and stopped Judith mid-sentence. Judith held her breath but she knew, instinctively, what was coming. The last twenty-four-hour media coverage had rendered it inevitable. Poor, browbeaten, dishevelled, unfairly maligned Judge Nolan was about to cave in to public pressure.

'Thank you, both. I think, now, that it would be useful to hear from Dr Alves on a few, short and narrow points of information only. Let me know how soon she can be here. Let's take a short break.'

***

Judith thumped down in her seat as Judge Nolan left the room and the public gallery began to empty. She stared into the void at the centre of the court room, where Laidlaw was talking animatedly. When he noticed Judith, he had the good grace to stiffen up and to exit, chattering to his team all the way.

35

'Do you think Ben is being entirely straight with us?' Constance asked Judith, as they headed back to court, after the short break.

'Why do you ask?' Judith said, still preoccupied by the recent exchange in court and the high price she had paid for a moment's poor judgement.

'Well…he never told me, at the beginning, that the argument with Rosie was about him, then he called me that Sunday – you remember, when we were in the café – to say it was "all his fault" and now, suddenly coming out with this stuff about Rosie going out the night before she died. I mean, it's pretty key evidence and he kept it to himself till now. Why?'

Judith stepped back into a doorway, forcing herself to listen to Constance.

'His mother has died and his father has been in prison ever since. Ellis says he had anxiety or depression or who knows what before, so he must be enormously distracted. Look, I don't know why he's feeding us things in dribs and drabs and there's no point trying to second-guess. We'll hear from him soon enough.'

'Maybe we made a mistake with him, that's all? Maybe he's tricked us into thinking he's this poor, defenceless thing, when he knows a lot more than he's letting on. He goes to acting classes after all.'

'And I thought you thought Debbie did it.'

'That's unfair. I've never said that. I just said I found her hard to read, to empathise with. I don't think she did it.'

'That's a relief. Listen, perhaps I have been a little too blinkered with Ben, too ready to be sympathetic and accepting. But we have to focus on Debbie and what we need to do to defend her, and not go running off to follow up every new lead. And, yes, before you say anything else, which would only be what I deserve, I know I've been side-tracked myself, but that will change, from this moment on. And so, if I can get Ben to say something in that box, right now, that is going to help Debbie, that's what I'm going to do. Anything else can wait till afterwards.'

Judith strode on ahead, leaving Constance in the corridor, alone with her thoughts.

Constance was about to follow, when she checked her watch. Judith could manage without her for a short while at least. She knew Judith was right about their priorities, but she sensed there were many gaping holes in their knowledge of Rosie Harper and that finding out where Rosie had gone, the night before she died, might allow her to fill at least some of them.

***

'Ben, I know this must be a difficult experience for you, so I will do my best to keep it as short as possible. Please do your best to answer my questions loudly and clearly and do ask if you don't understand anything. Is that clear?'

Ben was back in the witness box for the second time.

'Yes.'

'Were you and your mother close?' Laidlaw began, and Judith gripped the sides of her lectern.

Ben nodded.

'Can you speak up please?'

'Yes,' he said.

'You must miss her terribly?'

Judith had heard Constance's doubts about Ben's motivation, but she still wanted to leap up and punch Laidlaw on the nose for a question which could only be designed to upset him to the maximum degree. Instead, she bit the inside of her lip and stayed silent.

'I do...but it's worse, because I haven't had my dad around, either,' Ben said, allowing his eyes to flicker over to Debbie, who smiled at him. Judith cheered quietly inside her head. Laidlaw coughed into his hand and moved on.

'Were you in court when a recording was played of a 999 emergency call, made by your mother in February 2017?'

'Yes.' Ben's voice wavered, but he bolstered himself by sitting up straighter and the next answer came out stronger.

'Do you know why your mother called emergency services that night?'

'No. I was asleep. I heard a noise. I think it was just Mum moving around and it woke me up. Then I heard her go into the bathroom and I heard her talking. That's when I went to the door and asked if she was OK.'

'And what did she say?'

'She told me to go back to bed. She said she was fine. I kind of hovered outside the door, so then she came out and smiled at me and gave me a hug. Then I went back to bed.'

'Was she hurt?'

'No, but she had been crying.'

'And where was Debbie during all of this?'

'I don't remember seeing Dad at the time. I thought he was probably in bed asleep too. Once he's asleep, nothing wakes him.'

'Did you wake up later on, when the police came?'

'Yes. They asked Mum some questions, then Dad, then they left.'

'Do you remember what they asked?'

'Not really. I stayed upstairs and I was half asleep. It was just stuff like was Mum all right, had they had an argument, and she said she was fine and that she didn't mean to call them.'

'Did you speak to either of your parents afterwards, about the police visit?'

'I asked Mum the next day why the police came and she said it was a *mistake.*'

'A mistake?'

'That's what she said.'

'Anything else?'

'No.'

'Can we move now to 17th June, the day of your mother's murder. Where were you that afternoon?'

'I was at school. I'd finished my exams and we had to go in for a day, to talk about sixth form. Then I went back to a friend's house. When I got home, around 6, the police were there.'

'Did you see your mum in the morning?'

'No. She leaves early for work.'

'Do you have any idea what she was planning to do that day?'

327

'I know dad was coming over. I don't know what else she had planned.'

'Why was Debbie coming over?'

Ben took a deep breath.

'To talk to Mum.'

'Do you know what they were going to talk about?'

Ben struggled with his composure.

'It was like Gran…Elaine said. I had this idea that I could leave school and go to acting classes or maybe to a college that taught performing arts, like Mum did. Mum wouldn't listen, so I asked Dad… Debbie, to go and talk to her.'

'You had asked your father, to intervene with your mother, on your behalf?'

'Yes.'

'Do you think it likely your parents would have argued about your future?'

'I'm sure they would, but I don't believe Dad would have ever hurt Mum. I mean, there've been lots of things over the years that they disagreed about, like most people. I bet you and your wife have different views about things, sometimes, don't you?'

Laidlaw coughed again and took a moment to consult his instructing solicitor. Then he glanced at Judith. Then he sat down, mumbling, 'Thank you, Ben. I have no further questions.'

***

'I have just one thing to ask you, Ben. It's just really to explain an answer you gave Mr Laidlaw a moment ago.' Judith looked across at Debbie and then snatched a glance at Constance.

'You were the one who asked your father to come over and talk to your mother, about what you plan to do next year?' she said.

'Yes.'

'Was your father sympathetic to your request to take acting classes?'

'I'm not sure. Debbie said she needed to talk to Mum first, to find out what she was worried about, but she did at least listen to me.'

'Have you been feeling guilty that you were the one who asked your father to arrange the meeting?'

'I feel awful about it.' Ben's lip trembled but he held it together. Judith took a deep breath.

'Is that because you think your father might have hurt your mother after all?'

'No! Never!' Ben's voice rang out loud and clear. 'It's just that it's my fault she was there, at the house. If I hadn't asked her to go, she'd never have been there in the first place. She'd have been at home or training, and the police would have actually tried to find the real killer.'

As Judith sat down and Ben was released, she turned around again to Constance. She wanted Constance's acknowledgement that Ben had been good for them, for Debbie, that there was nothing in his session likely to provoke a public backlash. But Constance had still not returned and Judith had to be content with her own assessment of her performance, which was never going to be anything but partisan.

***

As the session ended, Judge Nolan called the lawyers to her room. She was drinking a large glass of orange juice; she didn't offer either of them a drink or a seat.

'Mr Laidlaw, Ms Burton. I'm wondering. Were either of you proposing to re-call Chief Inspector Dawson?'

Laidlaw and Judith exchanged sidelong glances, neither wanting to speak first. In the end, Judith broke the ice.

'I wasn't intending to,' she said.

'Neither was I, your honour,' Laidlaw added, clasping his hands behind his back, tipping his weight forwards onto the balls of his feet.

'I am very surprised by that decision,' Judge Nolan said.

'Is there something that you feel needs further clarification?' Laidlaw ventured, after a few seconds without any follow-on from the judge.

'It's all over the papers. This "conspiracy theory" about the glove.'

'Oh that! Yes. I have read that.'

'Ms Burton. I'm surprised you're not with me on this one; you were the one who planted the seed, when you drew attention to the crime scene photographs. Don't you want to know what the inspector has to say about all of this?'

'No, thank you, your honour.'

Judge Nolan watched each of them and no one spoke.

'Well I want him back in court tomorrow,' she said, 'and I want you to ask him again about the glove. And if neither of you is prepared to do that, then I will do it myself. The court cannot allow these rumours to persist. The glove is a key piece of evidence, perhaps the only tangible piece of evidence linking Debbie Mallard to the murder. We have to get to the bottom of whether it was there, when those two police officers entered via the front door.'

'Perhaps Chief Inspector Dawson won't know the answer.' Laidlaw ventured.

'We won't know until we ask him, will we? And Miss Burton, please stop playing to the cameras.'

'I'm sorry, your honour. I wasn't aware...'

'Yesterday, with Elaine Harper, you insisted on making a stand for your client's right to be called "Debbie", which is featuring in all the major newspapers and appears to have earned you a small but vociferous fan club.'

'Well, I...'

'Today, your colloquial language and overbearing manner, when you objected to Mr Laidlaw's line of questioning...'

'They were extremely personal questions, your honour.'

'Nevertheless, there was a reason for them. And you over-reacted, no doubt, in the hope that it would make headlines again. I'm not having it. You both need to stay focused on what's going on in the court room, not what others might say about it. I'm expecting Inspector Dawson back tomorrow then.'

* * *

'

Oh God!' Judith muttered, as she and Laidlaw walked side by side away from the judge's rooms.

'I dislike it as much as you do,' Laidlaw replied, biting at his bottom lip. 'The irony of it all. She calls you out for performing to the cameras, but this thing with Dawson, she's only doing it for the audience.'

'You were happy to accept it when it suited you?'

'How do you mean?'

'The expert on...hormones! It's the most preposterous thing

I've ever heard. And you know it. And you know you were lucky. If the media hadn't rounded on her last night, she would have stuck to the rules.'

'You would have done the same, if it was the other way around.'

'No, not on that one. It's a travesty. What are you trying to do? Single-handedly orchestrate a national transgender hate campaign?'

'I take grave exception to that comment. I'm trying to prosecute this case safely and effectively. You were the one who suggested that domestic violence victims called the police for no reason.'

Judith folded her arms. Laidlaw did the same.

'All right. I accept that probably wasn't my best moment,' she said.

Laidlaw shrugged. 'I don't think it's just the press coverage; the TV and papers. Someone must have leaned on Bridget this time,' he said, 'maybe someone senior in the police or the CPS, to give Dawson a chance to have his say.'

'Or the opposite. As she keeps reminding us, "the world is watching".'

Laidlaw laughed and Judith, reluctantly, joined him.

'You know him a little, Inspector Dawson?' Laidlaw said.

'Yes.'

'Do you think he planted the glove?'

'I don't know. My gut says absolutely not, he's a sound policeman without too much of an agenda, but we have an obligation to check it out. Do you know what happened this morning with Leo?'

'She bottled it.'

'She what?'

'He was expecting to be hauled over the coals after the Caroline Fleming debacle, told to rein the papers in, threatened with contempt of court, all of that. But, apparently, she went easy on him. Told him that it was his responsibility to advise his clients and that she expected him to do so sensibly. And that was it.'

'They scared her off then.'

'I always thought they made her a judge too early.'

Judith opened her mouth to respond, but then thought better of it.

'I…appreciate that you went out of your way to go gently with Ben Harper. Thank you for that,' she said.

'And you didn't with Mrs Harper. Thank you for that.'

Judith smiled again.

'Do you ever get the feeling you're too old for this business?' Laidlaw said.

'I'm the one they're calling a veteran,' Judith said. 'But, yes. I'm not sure transparent justice is all it's cracked up to be.'

***

Nicki sat on a swing in the park opposite the Birdcage pub. The rocking motion soothed her nerves, which had been jangling since her face-off in court with Ellis that morning. She opened her phone and spent some moments scrolling back through photographs, pausing at some, skipping over others. In between, from time to time, she would glance up and check on Ellis.

She could see him, seated inside, his back to her, chatting to the barman. It wasn't his clothes or his hair; she would have recognised him just from the way he was seated, his feet crossed neatly and drawn in tight against the stool, his elbows wide on the bar, his glass raised in silent salute to whatever liquid it contained. Part of her willed him to feel the intensity of her gaze, to turn around and see her there and come to her. But perhaps she wasn't ready after all. The things she had prepared to say, rehearsed over and over, now overtaken by events.

A blackbird alighted near the base of the swing and rooted around in the earth, its splayed feet catching in the few remaining tufts of grass. Slowly and carefully, so as not to disturb its labours, she lifted her headphones to her ears, pressed the play button on her phone and closed her eyes.

***

Constance had been busy. She had reviewed police files and interviews from the early days of the investigation and found, buried at the very end of a report, a reference to a taxi driver who had confirmed dropping Rosie home the night before she died, having picked her up at a restaurant in the West End. There was no accompanying statement, but Constance quickly tracked him down via Uber. Of course, they insisted that they could not give away his contact details but would pass on Constance's and they were sure he would call, if it was as important as she said.

Constance sat in a café checking her phone every 30 seconds until, after around ten minutes, she decided to take action. She quickly found three people bearing the same name as the driver on Facebook, narrowed it down to two possibles and messaged them directly. Two minutes later, her phone rang.

36

'Tonight we are going to focus on the role of the judge in a criminal trial; what they do, what experience they need to have. And we'll look, in particular, at the judge in our featured trial, Judge Bridget Nolan. What do we know about her background?' Katrina was on the sofa of the Court TV studio, a large photo of Judge Nolan projected on the wall behind her. 'Andy, tell us why we need a judge in a criminal trial, in the first place.'

***

Andy had seriously considered calling in sick today. The more he reflected on his performance so far, the more he worried about what was coming next. Clare had found him locked in the bathroom and, after a frank exchange, had convinced him to return. Seeing her before him, hands on hips, formidable as ever, he wondered if Clare might have been a better choice for the show than he was, but he suspected it might be noticed if he sent her in his place.

'I don't understand the problem,' Clare had said, standing over him as he sat hunched on the edge of the bath. 'You do this for a living. Why the sudden panic?'

'It's not the same,' Andy tried to explain. 'I thought it would be, but it just isn't. It's not like when I'm in court and I know exactly what I need to achieve. OK, I might try to be charming or make the odd, gentle quip to lighten the mood, depending on the circumstances, but otherwise I'm prepared and focused and there's one objective only; sending the murdering bastard to jail.'

'It's the same with the show, isn't it?'

'No. It really isn't. There's the general objective of any TV show, I suppose, which is to be entertaining, which isn't as easy as it sounds, especially when you can't see your audience and you don't even know its demographics. Then, there's the professed objective of this show, which is to educate the public about the law, and then there's the unspoken objective, which is to say scandalous, outrageous things, to make our own new headlines on top of the ones we're reporting on. But I have to do all of that without knowing what's coming next and without offending anyone.

'And, on top of that, they're doing a feature on the judge tonight and they'll want me to comment on how she's doing, to analyse and criticise, like they made me do the other day. And, quite apart from what they'll say in chambers, I might find myself arguing a case in front of her next week; well, not next week, but once this is over. I feel like I'm on a tightrope with no safety harness, and Katrina is shaking one end up and down with a big smile spread across her face.'

Clare had laughed and then, seeing his total bewilderment, had held him close.

'It's something new for you and it will take a bit of time for you to adjust, but I know you will manage,' she said, kissing the top of his head. 'Remember you're all on the same side and just let people see a bit more of you, the real you. Then they'll love you, just like we do.'

***

'Thanks Katrina. That is a very good question,' Andy, in the studio, trying very hard to be himself, replied. 'In civil trials, for example, when I want to sue you for selling me a TV set which doesn't work, the judge makes the decision. But, in criminal trials their role is a bit more like a referee – probably quite an apt analogy in this case. The judge listens to the evidence and tells the jury which bits are the most important, which less so, and which parts they must ignore.'

'Are they allowed to ask their own questions?'

'They are, especially if a point isn't clear, but they try to remain as *neutral* as possible, for obvious reasons.' Phew! He had used the word neutral and Katrina had now asked two open questions in a row, a record for her.

'If you've got two strong personalities before you, though, like Jeremy Laidlaw and Judith Burton, is it hard to keep the peace?'

'It shouldn't be. First of all, Jeremy and Judith know the rules too, and they shouldn't be overstepping the mark in the first place.'

'Assuming they do, like with the late calling of this new expert, where they were clearly unable to agree...'

'The judge must weigh up the pros and cons and decide, on balance, whether it's appropriate to allow this evidence in.'

'But this expert on transitioning, I got the impression, from the look on Judith's face – here we can watch the exchange…there you are…we didn't need our body-language expert for that one – she was pretty surprised at that decision.'

'Me too. But the judge is in charge…and that's how it should be.'

Katrina stopped and nodded at Andy. He had stuck to his guns, answered fully and fairly and she had exhausted that line of enquiry.

'Why does Jeremy Laidlaw want this expert?' Now she moved on.

'I don't know,' Andy said.

'Oh come on! You must have an idea.'

Come on Andy, the voice said in his ear. *You know why he wants her*. Andy stayed calm.

'He wants to have evidence before the court about Debbie Mallard's transition,' he said.

'Isn't that a gross invasion of her privacy?'

'You were the one who said the public should see *the whole truth*.'

Andy, remember whose side you're on, the voice chipped away in his ear. Perhaps that had been a touch argumentative, Andy conceded and reminded himself to rein it in.

'You think it's appropriate, then, for medical professionals to give away confidential details about their patients?' Katrina asked.

'Debbie Mallard was never Dr Alves' patient. Her evidence is completely irrelevant. She's just some random doctor the prosecution is wheeling in to make trouble.'

There he had said it, exactly what he thought and it ticked all the boxes; amusing, informative, irreverent.

'That's a fascinating take on the new evidence and I'm sure it's

going to spark a lot of questions from our viewers,' Katrina said
and Andy believed she meant it. 'Now we're going to talk about
Judge Nolan's background. Stay with us, Andy, as we'll have more
from you later.'

***

Constance had popped home to shower and change before
rushing off to Judith with her latest discovery. Then her phone
buzzed and she ran from the bathroom to catch it on its final ring.
She wondered if it was Greg wanting to apologise for last time
and to chat about Court TV. Instead, it was another, less familiar
voice, with some less than welcome news.

***

'We'll ask for an adjournment; we need to have some time to
digest all of this,' Judith responded, as Constance had anticipated,
when she called her.

'Are you sure we need it? We have Laura tomorrow and you
said Dawson might be back. Then we can work on it over the
weekend.'

'Maybe. But we need to talk to Debbie properly about all of
this, not just a snatched fifteen minutes before court. Can you
message the judge now and ask for a late start, say 11am, and
follow it up in person tomorrow morning? Explain we've only just
received this. And go and see Debbie first thing. If you have any
issues come and find me. Oh, the snake!'

'Who? What?'

'Laidlaw. He was being all pally with me this afternoon when

Judge Nolan insisted we call Charlie back. Trying to pretend we were on the same side. And all the time he knew this was coming. Ooh. Sometimes I am so gullible. Never trust a man with polished fingernails. That's one my mother told me and mothers are usually right on matters of the heart.'

***

Debbie appeared surprisingly sprightly the next morning, dressed in a lemon suit with a pastel scarf thrown loosely over her shoulders, and she almost smiled at Constance's approach.

'We may be starting a little late today,' Constance began. Debbie nodded. 'There's been a development.'

'Oh.' Now the near-smile wavered.

'And not a good one.'

'What is it?'

Constance sat down and rested her elbows on her knees. 'Did you know that Rosie kept diaries?' she said.

***

Upstairs, as Constance headed back from her encounter with Debbie, she spied Laura at the far side of one of the waiting areas, smartly dressed in black trousers, sitting very upright, staring at her feet. She was about to go forward, when Ellis approached from the other direction. Laura leaped up, ran to him and threw her arms around him, hugging him tightly, burying her face in his neck. Ellis coloured, looked around him and unwound Laura's arms, consoling her as he did so.

'I didn't know where you'd gone last night,' Laura said. 'I'm so pleased you're here now.'

'I just went for a walk and then home to sleep. I should've said. But I was always going to come today and support you. You'll be brilliant. Don't worry about anything,' Ellis said. 'You relax and it will be over, before you even blink.'

'I said I would do it, but I'm not sure now.'

'You'll be fine.'

Constance sighed quietly to herself and retraced her steps. She would wait a couple of minutes before approaching again. Maybe Laura wasn't such a tough nut after all.

37

LAURA STRODE INTO COURT at 11am to begin the defence case. Debbie treated her to a hint of a smile, before deliberately turning away. Judith clutched her pen tightly and turned over two pages of her notes and began.

'Laura, hello. I appreciate this is a very difficult time for you. Do ask for a break if you need one at any time.'

'Thank you,' Laura said.

'Tell us about your family circumstances while you were growing up.'

Laura shrugged. 'What do you want to know?' she said. 'We were a normal family.'

'Did you eat your meals together?'

'Sometimes.'

'Did you go on holidays together?'

'Yes.'

'Were your parents loving?'

'They looked after me and Ben. When they were busy, our

grandma helped out.'

'That's Debbie's mother?'

'Yes.'

'Did you see much of Rosie's mum? Members of the jury, by way of reminder, that's Mrs Elaine Harper, who gave evidence on Wednesday.'

'When I was little, we did. But not so much the last few years. She and Mum didn't get on very well. We saw her at Christmas and birthdays and she and Grandpa Brian would meet me or Ben sometimes without Mum, just for a pizza, that kind of thing.'

'Was that for as long as you remember? When your grandmother gave evidence, she suggested that it was only recently that she and your mum had a falling out, beginning around the time your father told everyone he wanted to transition.'

Laura looked over at her paternal grandmother. 'Maybe it was worse recently. I don't think they ever got on very well. They both have...had strong personalities.'

'How about *your* relationship with your mother?'

'Mum spent more time at work than at home, but I understood. She had a lot of responsibilities and a lot of fans.'

'And were they always friendly, these fans?'

'Not always. She had some trolls, people complaining about the show.'

'And how did she respond to that?'

'She usually tried to reply, at first. I think, because she was in the public eye, she kind of wanted to explain, if she could.'

'And then what?'

'If they accepted it, fine. If not, or it got nasty, then she did the usual things; blocked them.'

'Did you have a lot of security at home?'

'A burglar alarm and a small gate at the front, and a camera which didn't work anymore.'

'If someone knocked at the door, rang the bell, what was the procedure?'

'You mean, did we check who it was before we opened it? There was a spy hole in the door and we had a chain, but that wasn't Mum's style. She liked visitors.'

'Your honour, Rosie Harper's door-opening habits are completely irrelevant,' Laidlaw objected succinctly for once.

'The prosecution is insisting there was no forced entry to the property, drawing the inference that someone familiar killed Rosie. I am simply trying to elicit from this witness how easy it would have been for a third party, not known to Rosie, to gain access. And I think we have the answer. Do you know a friend of your mother's called Caroline Fleming?'

'The woman who was here the other day? No, I've never heard of her before…or seen her – before the court, that is.'

'You're twenty-one years old now. When did you move out from home?'

'Two years ago, nearly three now.'

'But you studied in London, so you could have lived at home, couldn't you?'

'I wanted to move out and Mum agreed. She thought it would be good for me to be more independent. It wasn't because I wanted to get away from them.'

'Did you know that your parents were unhappy together?'

'I don't think they were.'

'You don't think they were unhappy?'

'No.'

'But they got divorced?'

'Look. It wasn't like when other people get divorced. They weren't fighting. One day Dad just left. There was no big explosion.'

'Perhaps they hid it from you? You had already left home.'

'So ask Ben. But he'll tell you the same. Well, he already did. I'm not sure what it is you want me to say, why you even asked me here. I don't know anything about who killed Mum, except that I'm absolutely sure it wasn't my dad.'

***

'Hello Laura. I just have a few more questions for you,' Laidlaw checked his compendious notes before continuing. 'Do you love your father?'

'Of course, yes.'

'So, it's natural that you want to protect him?'

'I don't know what's *natural* but I wouldn't want him to go to prison for something he didn't do.'

'Did you love your mother?'

'Yes.'

'You sound less sure.'

'Your honour. Is this really necessary?' Judith bobbed up from her seat.

'I will allow a little more. Miss Mallard, can you answer the question, please.'

'I thought I already did. If I sounded less sure, that's because Mum and I didn't always get on, like I just said. But I still loved her.'

'You mentioned that your grandmother, Debbie's mother, helped out when you were younger. Why was that?'

'Dad was often away and Mum left early. Grandma would

come over, help with meals, sit while Ben did his homework.'

'I heard you play football, like your father?'

'I used to play, and no, not like Dad.'

'Did you watch your father play?'

'When I was young. I don't remember much now.'

'You must have met a few famous players?'

'Probably.'

'You said *used to*. Why did you stop playing?'

'I hurt my knee.'

'And you don't play any more?'

'No.'

'You wouldn't have wanted to play in the local team your father coaches? I suppose it would be difficult to have your father as your boss.'

'I've said, I hurt my knee and I don't play any more.'

'You did, yes. Sharing the love of football, that must have made you and your dad feel close.'

'I suppose so.'

'Where do you live? We don't need the address, just to be clear, the area you live in.'

'I live in Shoreditch.'

'Close to the family home?'

'Yes.'

'How often did you see your mother, after you left home?'

'About once a month.'

'Did you speak on the phone, in between visits?'

'No. That's just how we were. Neither of us was really into chat.'

'And your father?'

'I used to go over to his flat once a week, sometimes every two weeks, when Ben was visiting.'

'So, without making you take sides here, in these difficult circumstances, might it be right to say that you got on with your father – that's the defendant – better than with the deceased, your mother.'

'Maybe.'

'You and your mum didn't always see eye to eye.'

'I think that's fair, yes.'

'Thank you, Miss Mallard, you can go now.'

38

'Mr Laidlaw, Ms Burton. Will we be hearing from Inspector Dawson today, please?' Judge Nolan was brisk in her manner, after Laura's swift turnaround. Judith thought she looked awful; grey in the face, hair tied back, with a few limp strands escaping and her voice had lost its resonance, so apparent in the early stages of the trial. No doubt at least some of the attention she had received via Court TV, which had been followed by criticism of various levels of sophistication in the press and social media, had filtered its way down to her. And the early morning call she had received about the whistleblowing juror must have been pretty unwelcome too.

'Your honour, he is detained on a matter of utmost importance today, but he will attend on Monday, although I have been asked if we can keep the time flexible,' Laidlaw replied. 'But Dr Alves is here, our expert on the transition process.'

'That's good,' the judge attempted a smile, but her face couldn't quite make the right shapes.

Dr Melanie Alves was ushered into court, a young, kind-faced woman. Laidlaw, keen to get on, was on his feet, even before she had been sworn in.

'Dr Alves. Can you tell the court what you do?'

'I work with people who want to change from their birth gender.' Dr Alves' mellow tones matched her relaxed appearance.

'What kind of work?'

'To begin with, I talk to people about their gender dysphoria.'

'Gender dysphoria?'

'It's a…a state of unease that some people experience, feeling that there is a mismatch between their birth or biological sex and their real gender identity.'

'Is gender dysphoria a mental illness?'

'It's certainly a mental condition, and can be accompanied by impairment in other functions, like depression or anxiety, or sometimes even suicidal thoughts.'

'What do you do in your sessions?'

'Like I said, we talk, usually over many months. I try to understand how the patient is feeling, the level of discomfort they are experiencing, what they want to achieve, and then come up with a treatment plan. There are a whole range of possibilities. The individual might be happy to live as the opposite gender or they might want to change their physical characteristics too. I can prescribe the appropriate medication where relevant and refer them for surgery, if that's what they want. I also need to assess what support systems they have in place, as this can be a challenging time emotionally as well as physically. We offer counselling where needed, including for families.'

'What medication would an individual take, when transitioning from male to female?'

'Men transitioning to women take hormones but, if you can imagine, they are taking female hormones which are suppressing male hormones, so I certainly wouldn't expect this to make them more aggressive; quite the contrary, if that's what you're interested in.'

'But some women do have quite dramatic mood swings caused by hormone changes, don't they?'

Judge Nolan raised her pen and Laidlaw stopped to look at her, but then she lowered it again, any desire to challenge Laidlaw's question blunted by her fear of being lambasted again in the press.

'Yes. And, again, I don't want to underplay how debilitating that can be for some women, but it's certainly not led to any murders, as far as I am aware,' Dr Alves attempted a smile, 'although it is fair to say that PMT – that's pre-menstrual tension – has, in a few very limited cases, been put forward by women as mitigation for violent behaviour.'

'Is there any other medication you routinely prescribe?'

'Pre-op transgender women will sometimes take a drug called finasteride, to suppress the libido. Again, this reduces testosterone.'

Constance began hurriedly searching on her laptop as Judith sat quietly, hands resting in her lap.

'Are there any side effects of this drug?'

'A few. It can induce anxiety or depression or sometimes physical symptoms like breast enlargement. Of course, the latter is usually not a concern for a trans woman.'

Laidlaw nodded knowingly and looked across at Debbie. Judith was halfway through an eye roll when she remembered the cameras and blinked heavily instead.

'Am I right that anxiety and depression are prevalent in the trans community?' he asked.

'Transgender adults are prone to depression and, well I know what people think about statistics, but we are told that around fifty per cent experience some kind of suicidal thoughts at one time or another.'

'But not aggressive behaviour?' Judge Nolan had joined in now.

'Not that I have seen,' Dr Alves snatched a glance at Debbie. 'But, like I said, transitioning is a very difficult process. And I couldn't rule out a person responding in a violent way to certain situations, particularly if that was in their nature before.'

'Levels of violence in the transgender community are high, aren't they?' Laidlaw didn't want to let this point go until he had achieved his objective.

Dr Alves frowned. 'That's not quite right,' she said. 'Violence perpetrated against the transgender community, particularly against trans women and, in certain areas, trans women of colour, is very high.'

'But some transgender women are violent...'

'I've already answered that question...'

'And this is often a result of violence they have experienced themselves as children. It's a cycle. It's hard to escape.'

'That's a disgraceful lie!' Mrs Mallard, silent and calm throughout the proceedings, stood up, shouted out her condemnation, then sat down again.

Judge Nolan dropped her reading glasses and they slipped over the top of her desk and onto the lap of her court clerk, sitting below.

'Mr Laidlaw, please stick to the facts of this case,' she ordered, saying nothing to denounce the heckler.

'Is it right that transgender women are discriminated against in society?' Laidlaw was trying a different tack.

'That's not my area of expertise, Mr Laidlaw. I'm a doctor, although, of course, this is an area I read about widely, to educate myself, so that I can do my job better.'

'You must hear from your patients, the stories of their lives?'

'Yes. And you are right that some of my patients feel unfairly treated by other people – employers, colleagues, clients – but that's probably true of many people.'

'And this causes them to become resentful, I imagine?'

'It might. I tend to find – generalising hugely and, as you know, I have never met Debbie Mallard before and know little of her particular background or circumstances – that the act of transition itself can be very liberating for many of my patients. It's a final realisation of what they've desired for years. It rights the wrong they feel they were dealt by nature.'

'Were you in court when Ken Isleworth gave his evidence yesterday?'

'I wasn't, no, but I watched the proceedings from home.'

Laidlaw smiled conceitedly. 'You heard him say, then, that Debbie Mallard's transition from Danny was "career suicide"?'

'I did, and that's unfortunate. But I think Debbie would have probably known that, before she made her decision to transition.'

'Do you have patients who regret their actions, later on, because they find themselves ostracised or humiliated?'

'I deal with patients pre-op and wouldn't generally see a patient who had concerns, say, after gender reassignment surgery. What I would say, though, is that those patients are sad about how other people receive them, but they still don't regret their actions. They more often believe that they had no real choice but to transition.'

'Does that make them angry?'

'Yes…and sad, too. And, like I said, there are high levels

of depression and higher than normal suicide rates in that community as a result.'

Laidlaw, evidently satisfied, nodded and sat down. Judith was about to pass up her opportunity to question Dr Alves, given that she had objected so violently to her presence. That was what she ought to do, to keep up appearances. She shouldn't dignify Dr Alves' involvement by participating in it. And, most of the things Dr Alves had said had been fair and verging on useful.

Then Constance tugged at her gown and thrust a piece of paper into her hand. She read Constance's note once and then a second time. She looked across at Debbie, who was sitting with her head down. Then she stared across at the nearest camera. She took a sip of water.

'Dr Alves, just a couple of questions from me,' she said, shoving Constance's note deep into her pocket. 'I think, but do correct me if I am wrong, that what you were saying when you answered Judge Nolan's question, earlier, was really only that people who have an aggressive nature before they transition may well be aggressive afterwards; in other words, the change of gender itself has no impact on personality.'

'That's right. And, in fact, taking oestrogen, as trans women do, will reduce aggression in virtually every case.'

'And this drug you mentioned; finasteride. Is it a drug we should all fear? I mean, you talked about side effects?'

'All drugs have side effects. If you read the leaflet that accompanies your paracetamol, you'll find warnings about vomiting, stomach cramps, swelling of the abdomen. That doesn't stop us swallowing tens of thousands of tons of them every year.'

'And is finasteride routinely used to treat other, more common conditions?'

'It's used widely used to help men with an enlarged prostate.'

'I was thinking of something even more usual?'

'Ah.' Dr Alves laughed. 'Yes. It's used for male baldness – widely used – has been for the last twenty years or so.'

'And you are not aware of any side effects in those men, no tales of bald men rampaging around, committing violent offences and blaming it on this common drug.'

'No, it's perfectly safe.'

***

'Your next witness is the defendant, isn't it, Ms Burton?' Judge Nolan was unusually thoughtful after Dr Alves' departure.

'Yes.'

'I can't see the point in beginning the defendant's evidence today then. We'll break now and reconvene on Monday morning. Thank you.'

As Judge Nolan shuffled out, no doubt to end her difficult week with a large gin and tonic, Judith looked across at the public gallery. Mrs Mallard caught Judith's eye, gave her a shallow nod and then left the court room quietly.

***

'Why didn't you tell me that you and Rosie were involved?' The early finish at court had allowed Constance the opportunity to head over to Hanover Terrace and confront a defensive Jason Fenwick. She had been itching to tackle him all morning, ever since her conversation with the Uber driver, but didn't want to encounter him at the studio and she also hadn't wanted to leave

Judith alone with Dr Alves, if at all possible, given her concerns about Judith's state of mind. The delay, however, had only heightened her anger at being deceived by him.

'Involved?' he whispered, motioning to Constance to keep her voice down.

'I asked about your relationship with Rosie and you insisted you just worked together, whereas, in fact, you were romantically involved.'

'Who told you that?'

'She got all dressed up to meet you for dinner, the night before she died and you kept it secret?'

Constance couldn't believe her own boldness, fired by her outrage at having been misled, but it had the desired effect. Jason hung his head. Then he sidled over to the lounge door and checked it was closed.

'We weren't *romantically involved*, OK?' He returned to his favourite armchair. 'I swear on the lives of my children.' He cast a fleeting glance at the nearby family photo for corroboration.

'But you accept you were out with her that night?'

'I invited Rosie to dinner, to talk about her contract.'

'Her contract?'

'We'd been doing the show together for eight years. She'd asked for more money and she wanted more flexibility.'

'Why did she want more money?'

'Why does anyone want more money?'

'I asked you whether she had money troubles…'

'I don't know that she did but…I accept that she had, suddenly, got hooked on her pay and she was insistent she needed a rise. That's why I didn't tell you about our dinner. I didn't want that to be Rosie's legacy. How would it have looked if I had stood up in court and told everyone that £150K a year wasn't enough for her?'

'Were you paid more than Rosie?'

'Look, you know it's not just me. And I had always done what I could to press for her to get as much as possible.'

'As long as it didn't impact your salary?'

Jason shrugged. Constance almost smiled. Judith had predicted this from the outset.

'I did, effectively, give up salary. If I pushed for Rosie to get more, it meant less for me. There was only one pot.'

'But it suited you if she stayed, so you made the sacrifice?'

'We'd built up a great partnership together.'

'Where did you go that night?'

'We met up at a restaurant near here and had a meal. Then we went to a bar and stayed late.'

'And then?'

'Then I took her home.'

'You drove?'

'Taxi.'

'Did you go into the house with her?'

'She asked me to come to the door because she thought the house was empty. Then she saw Ben's things in the hallway, so I said goodnight.'

'Did you go inside?'

'No.'

'Did you tell the police any of this?'

'They never asked.'

'Did you hear from Rosie after that?'

'A couple of messages the next morning, thanking me for helping her think straight, that kind of thing.'

'Do you still have them?'

Jason's eyes flitted over to his laptop. 'I doubt it.'

'Where were you on the afternoon of 17th June?'

'I was here, with Rochelle, and then I was visiting St Columba's school until around 5pm, to give out end-of-year prizes. It's my old school. I was with numerous people all through the day.'

'You haven't made any public statement, about Rosie's death.'

'We did a tribute show the week after she died, but the producers asked me not to talk while the police investigation was ongoing. And if I say anything the papers will misquote me, and what's the point? It just deflects interest on to me, when people should be mourning Rosie.'

'Is that why you haven't been to the trial? It might have been a nice gesture.'

'Look, I really don't know anything at all about who might have killed Rosie. I wish I did. She was a bright, funny, remarkable woman and I miss her all the time. And maybe some people find it easy to go and sit through hours of people talking about how someone they were close to has met their end, maybe it's cathartic for them. That's not me.'

'I understand.' Constance rose to leave. Jason took one step towards her and waved at her to wait.

'There is something else.'

'Oh?'

'It's probably nothing. I didn't want to cause trouble, so I didn't mention it before.'

'Go on.'

'It's about Laura. I was reminded, when I saw she was giving evidence today.'

'Laura?'

'Rosie didn't talk about the kids much; we were too busy when we were on set. But that night we went out, she told me she was worried about someone Laura was seeing – an older man.'

'Do you know who it was?'

'No, and Rosie didn't either. But she was upset, said Laura had started to tell her and when she hinted that Rosie might disapprove, Rosie had flown off the handle. She said the timing was bad, Laura caught her at a bad time and then, when she tried to be more sympathetic, Laura clammed up. Said she was twenty-one and she would do as she liked.'

'I suppose Laura had left home.'

'Rosie thought he might be married.'

'Oh.'

'Rosie was really angry at herself for screwing up, when Laura had been going to tell her. I advised her to wait a week or two and then take Laura shopping, just casual, and see if it came out then.'

'Did Debbie know about Laura's boyfriend?'

'I doubt it, but you could ask her, although I suppose it's just another thing they might have clashed over. Rosie used to say how laid-back Debbie was about the kids. It drove her nuts, actually.'

'How do you mean?'

'That she, Rosie, always had to be the mean parent, the strict one. Do you think it's important, about Laura?'

'I don't know. It could be. I really wish you'd told us all this earlier.'

***

Constance called Judith as soon as she got home.

'What is it, Connie? I thought we decided we would take a night off, begin again tomorrow.'

'I know, but I have something to tell you, well two things, and they won't wait.'

'Go on then.'

'Rosie went out with Jason Fenwick, the night before she died.'

'Hm. I knew he was hiding something.'

'He says they just talked about their contracts, that she wanted more money and less hours. He wanted her to be reasonable, not push for too much.'

'I bet he did. You saw the ratings. Before Rosie joined the show they were dire. Mr Fenwick clearly knew how valuable a commodity Rosie was.'

'She sent him some messages in the morning, to thank him for his "advice", but he no longer has them.'

'Ah! And the afternoon?'

'School prize-giving. I've passed his alibi on to Dawson to check out, but it doesn't really add up, does it? Why would he hurt her, if he needed her so badly?'

'No, it doesn't. And I see Jason more as a *poison in the teapot* kind of guy, or a bite from an exotic snake, rather than battery with a blunt instrument.'

'It would spoil his peach jumper.'

They both laughed.

'What's the second thing you wanted to tell me?'

'Jason says Laura was seeing someone too.'

'So what?'

'He says Laura started to tell Rosie about it, but Rosie went in too heavily and Laura clammed up.'

'I still don't see the issue.'

'Rosie thought he was probably married. She might have found out and confronted him, whoever it was.'

'At her house on a Monday afternoon? Not likely, but more food for thought. It's more interesting, isn't it, that Jason has suddenly decided to be our best friend and informer. I wonder what prompted that? Although it makes Rosie's life even more complicated. In addition to all those enemies she made at work and her feud with Ben over his choice of career, she had fallen out with Laura over her love life, she might have been romantically involved with her co-host and she was not flavour of the month with the people holding the purse strings on her contract. Maybe they all did it; you know – *Murder on the Orient Express* style.'

***

Nicki left the police station at 7pm that evening. She hadn't said much, on the advice of her solicitor, but there hadn't been much to say, in any event. Still, she hadn't appreciated the direction of some of the conversation and she particularly hadn't enjoyed the way Inspector Dawson had looked at her – or rather, through her. And he wouldn't even tell them what it was all about. He just muttered about her attendance being *voluntary* for now and *not being at liberty* to say anything more. 'They're just trying to rattle your cage,' her solicitor had said, 'because of all the protests you've led recently. Don't worry. If they had anything on you, they'd have said.'

But Nicki couldn't help but feel uneasy. The first time she had been interviewed, shortly after Rosie's murder, Dawson had opened the door for her and called her Miss Smith. Those niceties were glaringly absent this time around. Instead, he had insisted on calling her 'Nicola', and staring hard at her scar while he asked his tedious questions; stuff about her background, where she'd been living and where her income came from. When she was leaving, what were the words he had used? 'Please stay local. We may need to ask you to assist again with our enquiries.'

She wondered how much he already knew and how much was just fishing around and whether she needed to change any of her plans as a result. But, if he did know something, why hadn't he asked her directly? Well, Nicki had prepared for this eventuality and the events of the trial had played right into her hands. She would send out the call to arms today, via carefully selected channels, and there was plenty of time to galvanise the particular troops she required, in sufficient numbers by Monday. It would require some money changing hands, but not enough to make her concerned and the situation definitely merited it.

She wasn't a nasty or vindictive person and she had sincerely hoped she might not have had to embark on this strategy. She almost felt sorry for Dawson; after all, he was just doing his job and he probably worked long hours for little pay and no perks. Who would be a police officer these days?

She consoled herself with the strongly held belief that she would have happily left him alone to ride out his current difficulties if only he had done the same, but needs must. He was the one who had forced her to put into action a scheme which would, hopefully, scupper all his best-laid plans.

39

'WHAT A WEEK IT HAS BEEN, the first week of the trial of Debbie "call me by my name" Mallard and the debut of the Court TV channel!' Katrina was resplendent in a demure petrol-blue trouser suit when the jumbo, extra-long Friday night edition of Court TV began that evening.

'And tonight we've got a special report on the pressures on young footballers. You might be surprised to hear that it's not all glitz and glamour, despite those massive salaries. But before we hear more about that, we have some breaking news.'

'We do...sad news. There's been a suspected arson at the offices of *TransPress*, a magazine serving the transgender community. The fire brigade attended around 3pm, but the latest is that the offices have burnt down to the ground. No one hurt in that one, but clearly the police are concerned it might have some connection to the Debbie Mallard trial and, more specifically, to the evidence Dr Alves gave today, which received mixed reviews.'

'And, more serious, this one; there has also been an attack on four men in drag at a club in Salford, around an hour ago. The assailants, who all wore masks, are reported to have shouted: "This is for Rosie" as they beat the men. All of the victims required hospital treatment. One is reported as seriously injured.'

Andy felt nauseous. It was no comfort to him that he had voiced the view that Dr Alves should not have been in court in the first place. This was all down to Court TV for giving the case so much coverage. That was the problem with accessibility; you couldn't pick and choose to whom you gave that access.

***

Constance called Greg. She had been contemplating calling him before the news broke, as she needed help with her latest lead. Now she wasn't sure what she was going to say to him, but she was angry and he seemed like a suitable person to blame. He answered on only the second ring.

'Hi there. How are you bearing up?'

'Have you seen it, what's happened, because of your Court TV friend?' she spluttered.

'What do you mean? What's happened?'

'The attacks, in Salford and at the newspaper office. Four people injured.'

'Oh that! I have seen it. You can't lay that at his door.'

'I can and I am. They've been stirring things up all week. The judge would never have allowed Dr Alves to speak if Andy Chambers hadn't rubbished her in the first place, saying she got it wrong with Caroline Fleming. And no one would have heard the stuff Dr Alves spouted, if it wasn't all recorded.'

'I agree that it's awful, what happened. But some people are just mindless thugs with horrible, backward views. You can't blame Court TV for that. I think some of its coverage has been excellent and balanced and, if you've been watching this evening, you'll know they've already slammed the attacks.'

Constance was silent. She felt a little better, now she had got things off her chest, but she wished Greg wouldn't be so reasonable about everything.

'Look, I can see why you're angry. I'm pretty angry too. But this really isn't the fault of the TV coverage. You must be exhausted with so much going on. Is there anything else I can help you with? You know you can trust me.'

'The police have, finally, given me access to Rosie Harper's laptop and I need help with something. I thought I could do it myself, but I'm not clever enough. Could you...'

'I can come over, if you like.'

'When were...'

'Now, if it's urgent. You tell me. Is it urgent?'

'It's super-urgent. I'd like you to come.'

***

Judith sat, in her apartment, papers strewn around the floor, a large glass of red wine in her hand and a smoked salmon salad balanced on her lap. She paused the TV, put down her dinner and its liquid accompaniment and went over to her laptop. First, she Googled the arson incident in Liverpool. There were a few photographs of the offices burning and the firemen in attendance. Then she moved on to the Salford story, but it was too recent for anything more than the barest details and a picture of the most seriously injured victim, in happier times.

She took her wine back into the kitchen and poured it down the sink. Then she returned to collect her plate of food and tipped it into the bin. Finally, she slumped down in her armchair, stared at the frozen TV screen, leaned her head back and closed her eyes.

***

Constance was playing football with Jermain and her mum in Haggerston Park, or at least she was trying to dribble the ball past Jermain, to shoot at goal, but he kept tackling her over and over. 'Come on,' her mum shouted, still enthusiastic, her breath hanging in the chilly air as Constance advanced one last time, her shins smarting from the battering her little brother had administered. She dribbled to the right and, as Jermain closed in, she dummied him by stepping over the ball.

This time, as he kicked out to the right, his toe hit thin air as she ducked left and struck the ball cleanly, so it soared towards the waiting goal. Only her mother to beat now, her mouth gaping, ready to celebrate, when she saw her mother's gloves; not goalie's gloves, but enormous, black, leather, motorbike gloves, expanding by the second and filling the goal, and her hope turned to despair.

And then, as the ball spun in the air, and the gloves became larger and larger, Constance heard a light tapping sound. She tried to make sense of the tapping. Was it someone knocking some impromptu rounders bases into the soft ground, or the woody Wisteria bumping against the gazebo? The tapping increased in volume and then Greg was standing over her, in her bedroom, speaking softly.

Constance sat up. She had fallen asleep on her bed, fully clothed, slumped across her laptop. Her curtains were open, but it was dark outside. Greg stepped back.

'Sorry to give you a shock. I did knock and I thought I heard you say to come in.'

'It's OK,' Constance swung her legs around to the floor. 'I probably did. I talk in my sleep…apparently.' Greg retreated again to the doorway. 'So much for my good intentions and giving you space to work. How long have I wasted?' she asked.

'You probably needed it.'

'I can sleep once this is all over. You wanted me?' Constance began to focus and remember why she had invited Greg over.

'I've found something,' he said.

'You've found out if the diaries are genuine?' It was all coming back to her now, as her dream slipped away.

'The diaries? Rosie certainly wrote them, or at least they were composed on her laptop. That took me about five minutes to solve.' Greg threw her a boyish grin. 'I'll get to that in a minute. No, I've found something much more interesting, although I haven't got into it yet. This, you have to see.'

He crossed the floor in one stride and pressed a few buttons on Rosie's laptop. He re-ordered her downloads, pressed another key and then a folder with a padlock symbol appeared on the screen. Constance squinted at the name. Greg blew it up to 200%. Constance read the name out loud.

'Rapunzel,' she said.'

40

CONSTANCE ARRIVED AT Judith's flat shortly after 11am on Saturday morning. She was carrying the September edition of *Esquire* magazine under her arm, which she waved under Judith's nose.

'Oh,' Judith said, as her eyes skimmed the front cover. 'That explains the cufflinks then.'

'And the signet ring and the gold watch…and the makeup.'

Constance reclaimed the magazine and directed Judith's attention away from the photograph of Jeremy Laidlaw decorating the front to the article about him on page 62. There, Laidlaw posed in a series of designer outfits, across a double-page spread, replete with expensive accessories, under a piece entitled 'Legal: the new cool?'

'Is he allowed to do this?' she asked.

'I'm not sure,' Judith said. 'Probably. There are all the rules about not devaluing the profession, but in this new climate, when we're being forced to break down barriers and be more user-friendly, I imagine he'll say this is positive publicity.'

'Do you think he got paid?'

'Maybe not for the interview, but for wearing all the jewellery, definitely. Think of the enormous potential market, with two million viewers a night.'

'I suppose all he's doing is being entrepreneurial, at the same time as doing his job. Greg said we should do the same.'

'Greg?'

Constance's heart skipped a beat. Now she was uncovered, there was no point going back. 'Yes. I saw him a few weeks back,' she said. 'We had dinner. He predicted a lot of what's happened, actually, suggested you and I should take advantage of the opportunities too.'

'Did he?'

'He asked after you. I think he was worried you were lonely.'

'Was he?' Judith's face was hard, but only for a moment. 'All of this is right up his street, I suppose,' she said, "manipulating the public".'

'That's a bit unfair. He was trying to help, to give us some advice.'

'He's good at advice, as I remember.' Judith closed the magazine and allowed it to drop to the table. 'Let's leave Laidlaw's antics and Greg's advice to another day, shall we? It has the potential to be an enormous distraction.'

Judith ran her fingers over Laidlaw's face and then threw it across the room, to land on top of a pile of papers. 'You saw the two incidents yesterday; the fire and the assaults?' She looked away from Constance as she spoke.

'Yes.'

'I can't help thinking…'

'No.' Constance said. 'Some people are just full of hate. It wasn't you.'

'I lost focus and went for the headline. That's the only reason Bridget allowed Dr Alves in.' Judith's voice cracked and she coughed to hide her discomfort.

'Bridget allowed Dr Alves in because of all the things they said about her in the media. You know that.'

'Well I certainly didn't help. Shall we talk about Monday? That's presumably why you came.' Judith said. 'Debbie's turn to face the music.'

'Are we definitely going to call her?'

'We have to. Laura did well, really well, but it's not enough. I'll keep things short, though, and clinical, I think – remind her again of the need to present herself properly; calm and reserved, like we discussed.'

'You think Laidlaw will push her.'

'I would. Top of the list must be those diaries and what Debbie's going to say about them. Shall we begin there?'

'Sure, that's my first bit of good news. I got access to Rosie's laptop and Greg came over last night and has given me some ideas of what you could ask.'

This time Judith said nothing, but her face registered her suspicion.

'There wasn't time to start searching around for anyone else,' Constance said.

'You're right. I'm sure if there's something useful there, Greg will find it. I'll get the coffee and I bought cannoli. How much more are they going to throw at us before this trial ends, I wonder?'

Constance walked over to the pile of magazines in the corner. While Judith was in the kitchen, she picked up the copy of *Esquire* and tucked it back inside her bag. There was one more thing she hadn't yet shared with Judith and she wondered how best to do it.

***

'Hi there. How's it going? I need to ask you about some new leads we're following.' Constance thought back to her early morning visit to Debbie, the way she had tried to sound matter-of-fact, when her reason for calling in was anything but.

'Isn't it a bit late for that?' Debbie had leaned her head back against the wall, her hair long over her shoulders.

'They're things we've been working on all along, really, but they're all becoming more relevant now. Do you know someone called Nicki Smith? She's leader of a number of green protest groups. She used to pester Rosie for help.'

'I've never heard of her.'

'Here's a photo, although she's been in court at least once. She has a distinctive scar on the left side of her face.' Constance had shown the image of Nicki, on her phone, to Debbie, but there had been no flicker of recognition.

'You think she might be involved in Rosie's murder?'

'It's possible. And do you know anything about someone Laura might be seeing?'

'You mean like a boyfriend?'

'Yes, but maybe someone a bit older.'

'I've never pried into the children's relationships. Laura once brought a boyfriend home in sixth form, but Rosie was too busy to talk to him for more than five minutes.'

'There's a suggestion that Laura tried to tell Rosie about a new friend and that Rosie was worried he might be married.'

'She never said anything to me. Why don't you ask Laura?'

'I may do that.' Constance had sighed. 'And now, the last one, and it's a bit of a strange one,' she had said. 'Does the name Rapunzel mean anything to you?'

'No.' Debbie's mouth had said the word, but her face had said something different.

***

Constance flicked through her downloads and readied the folder to open it for Judith.

Judith returned with two pastries, nestled in the centre of a small plate.

'What is it?' she said, sensing Constance's anxiety.

Constance's fingers hovered over her screen.

'It's something you need to see,' she said.

41

THE CROWDS OUTSIDE COURT on Monday morning filled the pavement, the road and the side streets on either side. The underground passageway, leading to the public entrance, was impassable. Mounted police stood at each end of Old Bailey, their horses' tails twitching. A group of Japanese tourists, their phones on long-reaching selfie sticks, hovered on the periphery, pointing and chattering.

The stalwarts of the transgender rights groups were back, now simply chanting 'Debbie, Debbie, Debbie,' but with many more swelling their ranks. The domestic violence lobby was nowhere to be seen. Either they had stayed at home or, fearing a backlash, they had defected to support Debbie, the new underdog and victim. Then, marching along Newgate Street with the backdrop of St Paul's Cathedral, so that the traffic was halted in its tracks, was a large deputation. And while the other campaigners had been predominantly female and vociferous but controlled, this group was male-dominated and edgy.

It was scheduled to be a hot day and some of the men were only in vests, revealing an array of tattoos. 'Stamp out police corruption' their banners read, and 'F**k the police' and 'It's a fit up' and a number of them were punching the air aggressively, with hands wearing one black motorbike glove.

For a split second, it looked as if they would continue marching and burst through the doors of the building, but then they halted and jostled for position, joining ranks with the incumbent demonstrators and satisfying themselves with more shouting and waving. After a few false starts, the chant became the uplifting 'Debbie, Debbie, Debbie' answered by the subversive 'Fuck the police'.

'Who on earth are this new lot?' Judith and Constance retreated to a vantage point looking down Old Bailey and watched the crowd converge on the court.

'I don't know. But at least they're on our side.'

'They're not really on our side, or Debbie's side, are they?' Judith said. 'They just happen to be against the side who are pursuing Debbie, for a variety of perceived injustices. I find it rather terrifying, if I'm honest. I mean, all this anger. No wonder there were those attacks. I'd like to bring the people who wanted transparent justice here right now and stand them in the middle of this mob. Then we'd see whether they still thought it was a good idea.'

***

Nicki stood back from the road, just opposite the court entrance in an office doorway, watching the arrivals and departures and the general progress of the protests. She exchanged a nod and a wink with one of the leaders of the new, hostile delegation. The power of being well-connected. That was something she had learned early on and used regularly to her advantage. Most things could be sorted out in your favour, if you had enough people on your side.

***

Debbie stepped up into the witness box, in one large stride. Her hair was scraped back in an exquisite half braid, neat at the scalp but fanning outwards around her chin. She was wearing pale pink, her favourite colour, with a phoenix brooch pinned to her lapel. Nicki was there again, this time on the second row and Constance was surprised to see Jason slip in at the back, shortly before proceedings began. A couple of people smiled at him, one insisted on shaking his hand, another tapped him companionably on the shoulder. Constance returned her attention to Debbie. The entire public gallery collectively held its breath.

'Hello Debbie. You know the process now, as you've been sitting in court all last week. I am going to ask you a few questions and then Mr Laidlaw will take over. I may have some further questions after that. Let's begin with how you and Rosie met.'

Debbie folded one hand on top of the other.

'I first saw Rosie in a bar on Upper Street,' she said, speaking slowly but clearly, as Judith had directed. 'She was out with some friends, including Caz Fleming – that much she said was true; not much else. I bought her a drink, we spent the evening together, in a group. That's how we met.'

'And after that?'

'It was a bit slow to start. I was just on the brink of making it at Arsenal, into the full squad, so I was training and there were matches and Rosie asked me to keep it quiet. She wasn't famous then herself, but she still didn't want to be all over the papers. And she said her parents wouldn't approve.'

'Why was that?'

'They weren't very keen on her wanting to be an actress; they thought she could have done better, should have studied. And if they knew about me, they would flip, she said, would insist she come back to live at home.'

'You kept things quiet?'

'We did, and then she landed the job with Channel Four. It was just a research role and low-key, but then it grew and she was financially independent, so when I proposed she said yes.'

'Were you happy when she took over as the face of *Breakfast Time*?'

''Course I was. She loved the work, she was brilliant and she wasn't just doing it for the fame…or the money. She wanted to shine a light on important issues too. I was caught up in my own career and I didn't often tell her how proud I was. I should have done that more.'

'And your children?'

'We were lucky enough to have two wonderful children. As they've told you, we weren't perfect parents, but we loved them and we did our best.'

'You have had a distinguished career as…'

Jeremy Laidlaw was on his feet.

'Your honour. I am just wondering whether this is a murder trial or an episode of *This is Your Life*,' Laidlaw oozed.

'Yes. Ms Burton, let's have a question please, of relevance to the case.'

'Of course. I was just getting there. Monday 17th June. You went to visit Rosie at home. Why?'

'We needed to talk about our son, Ben. And there was an issue with money, but not what you've been told. When I moved out, I agreed to pay Rosie to help towards expenses, especially as Rosie paid for all the other properties we owned. It wasn't very much. Rosie earns…earned far more than me for the last three years; more just the principle. I wanted to still provide for Ben, if I could.

'I set up a direct debit, but there was a problem and I kept receiving the money back. Rosie was cross. I'm not sure she believed I had ever set it up. She used to do all our banking before, and I had never done anything – no online banking, nothing. I said I would bring along all my details and I would set the direct debit up again, online, with her there, watching. Then she could make sure everything was done properly.'

'And what time did you arrive?'

'About 1 o'clock.'

'What were you wearing?'

'A pale blue track suit. It was a warm day. I don't remember wearing a coat. I think Mrs Harris must be mistaking that for another occasion. I do have a beige raincoat, but I wasn't wearing it that day.'

'And your gloves?'

'I should wear them. I know they absorb impact if you fall and they protect your hands but, like I say, it was hot. We don't always do what's good for us.'

'You've seen the glove which was shown to the court last week. Is it yours?'

'I expect so. I don't want to be difficult. It's just that I don't think I wore gloves that day. And I haven't found the other one. I might have left them there on a previous visit.'

'Still won't admit it's hers,' Laidlaw muttered, before clearing his throat. Judith ignored him and ploughed on.

'What did you and Rosie talk about?'

'We started off talking about her. She had been going through her post, her messages, and some of them upset her. I tried to reassure her.'

'And then?'

'We set up the direct debit together. She said she was grateful. It was probably the closest we had been, since I left. She asked if I was happy, which was nice of her. But when we started to talk about Ben, things became...heated. She...accused me of "leading him astray". I said that I didn't want to stamp on his dream, that acting was his passion, that she had to accept he may not want to go to university. I told her she should remember how she had felt about acting when she was 16, that she should be able to understand more, because of that.'

'And what did Rosie say?'

'She said I was selfish; I didn't know then that she'd spoken to her mother the night before. Now I can see where that came from, as Rosie was usually a fair person. She was tough, but fair. She started to cry, said I didn't realise how hard she was finding things; that, if I had ever loved her, I would make Ben take his A levels.'

'And what did you say to that?'

'I said I would talk to him, but I thought if he moved to a sixth-form college, he might have more time for acting, or maybe I could find out about a stage school. We agreed to discuss things again in a week or so.'

'And what time did you leave?'

'About 2pm.'

'Did you return?'

'No.'

'Did you see anyone else when you left?'

'No.'

'And did Rosie tell you what her plans were for the rest of the day?'

'She said she was going to go through her fan mail. She liked to try to answer letters herself, if she could. That's all I remember.'

'Was anything else bothering Rosie?'

'Just the usual stuff about work, people always saying what they didn't like.'

Debbie's eyes wandered over the faces of the jurors before returning her attention to Judith.

'I need to ask next about the 999 call from 2017. Do you remember that?'

'I didn't know about the call, but I remember the police came in the middle of the night,' Debbie said. 'They hauled me out of bed. I stood there in my pyjamas and they asked me lots of questions. Rosie said virtually nothing. Then they left.'

'You didn't know Rosie had called them?'

'Not before they came. We had a row. I went for a walk to cool off. When I got back, Rosie was in bed. I climbed in too and I was fast asleep when they arrived, hammering on the door.'

'What did Rosie say about calling the police?'

'She said it had been a knee-jerk reaction, that she didn't want to call anyone she knew, so she'd dialled 999. Then she'd realised it was a mistake.'

'A mistake?'

'I never asked her exactly what she meant, but no one was hurt, she was just wasting their time. And she knew it.'

'Turning to the events of the evening of 17th June, why did you run away?'

'I was just finishing my training, when Inspector Dawson and PC Thomas arrived. They introduced themselves. Then they told me Rosie was dead; murdered. I was in deep shock. I couldn't breathe. I wanted to be away, outside; anywhere but there. And then I wanted to be with my mother. So that's where I went. I never meant to "evade capture" or whatever the newspapers had as their headline.'

'Were you ever violent towards your wife?'

'Never.'

'Did you kill Rosie?'

'No. I never touched her. I know what they've been saying, that I'm a footballer, that I played rough sometimes. It's not the same. Football's a physical sport and I played it in that spirit. That's all. But I do regret that we argued that day. It all seems so unimportant now she's gone.'

'Thank you. No further questions.'

***

Jeremy Laidlaw hastily scribbled a few notes into the margin of his notebook, then smiled at Debbie, as he leaned back and ran his tongue around his lips.

'Why did you marry Rosie?' he began.

'I loved her. I wanted to spend the rest of my life with her.'

'Was there a particular catalyst, though, which prompted you suddenly to pop the question?'

'I don't think so. We went to Barcelona and it was very romantic

England had an international match there and I smuggled her in, quietly, to watch from a box.'

'So she wasn't pregnant then, when you proposed?'

Constance gasped and then covered her mouth. Debbie stared at her hands.

'Could you answer the question please, Ms Mallard?'

'That's not *why* we got married. It was the 1990s, not the 1950s, and we were working up to it anyway.'

'But she was…pregnant, when you proposed?'

'Yes.'

'And you organised the wedding within a month; so – no time for anyone to change their minds?'

'We didn't want to wait and we had to fit it around the football season.'

'Rosie was offered a BBC role some years before she took the *Breakfast Time* slot, wasn't she?'

'Yes.'

'Why didn't she take it?'

'I was away a lot and the kids were young?'

'It wasn't that you told her she had to stay at home, then? Now you'd *caught* her, you didn't want her disappearing off all the time?'

'No. It wasn't.'

'You said you married Rosie because you were in love. When did that change?'

'It didn't.'

'It didn't change?'

'No.'

'But you no longer had a…physical relationship with her, did you?'

'Not for the last couple of years.'

'So, it was selfish to expect her to want to stay with you?'

'You could say that.'

'How long have you been dressing up in women's clothes?'

Debbie's eyes flashed defiantly. 'You make it sound like a game,' she said.

'I'm sorry?'

'You make it sound like it's something I play at; like musical chairs. I don't "dress up" in women's clothes. I wear them.' Debbie's voice grew louder and Constance tried to catch her eye to calm her.

'All right. How long have you been *wearing* women's clothes?'

'In public – the last two years or so.'

'And in private?'

'I can't remember. A long time.'

'Did Rosie know?'

'At first, not. I would buy a few things online and then wait till she was away to put them on.'

'But eventually?'

'Yes. I couldn't help it. I suppose I was showing an interest in her clothes more and more and she realised it was...unusual.'

'How did she respond when you told her that you wanted to become a woman?'

'Not well.'

'Can you expand on that?'

'She screamed, she threw a plate at me. She told me to get out. So I went off for a walk. It was that night – the one when she called the police.'

'Why do you think she behaved like that?'

'She said she was shocked but, like I said, she knew before

that something was wrong. I think she'd been hoping that things would go back to how they were before. This meant that would never happen.'

'When did you know you wanted to become a woman?'

Debbie took a deep breath before replying.

'I've always known. I'm not sure I could always express it in that way, but, for as long as I can remember, I have felt uncomfortable in my body. But there was no way for me to do anything about it. No one I could tell. The world was a different place then.'

'So you tricked Rosie into living a lie?'

Constance thought Laidlaw must have planned his questions before this weekend's events, given they were delivered with significantly less confidence than usual. Even so, she thought him incredibly insensitive to pursue this line. But Debbie remained calm.

'You've been listening to her mother too. There was no trick. I loved Rosie. But I got to the stage where I realised that time was running out for me. We had done our bit as parents. I hoped Rosie could accept that I was still the same person underneath.'

'But she couldn't?'

'No.'

'You were very…disappointed in her, then?'

'I understood. I even tried to imagine how I would feel if it was the other way around, but I had hoped for something better, yes.'

'You mentioned setting up a direct debit from your bank account that afternoon, together with your wife. Can you tell us briefly about your banking arrangements?'

'We had a joint account when we were married, for outgoings and we moved to separate accounts after our divorce. That's partly why things were confused.'

'I see. I know you've given an explanation about making a mistake with your direct debit, which you rectified, you say, conveniently, the day Rosie died, but can you explain two large payments made by Rosie – one in April 2017 and the other in January 2018?'

'No. I can't.'

'Let's take a look then, shall we? I'll put them up on the screen. This is a statement from your joint account. If you cast your eye down to the entry for 6 April 2017, in fact there are two entries. There's money coming in and then immediately going out. Can you read the figures out for me please?'

'Yes. There's £25,000 coming in from our savings account and then being paid straight out to a 'ABC Happy Inc.'

'Yes. And I will just forward the statement to January 2018. What can you see this time?'

'Another £15,000. Same thing but this time going to 'Shelf 123 Ltd.'

'Can you tell us what these substantial payments were for?'

'No. I've already said. I can't.'

'This was a joint account. You must have received statements periodically?'

'Probably, but Rosie dealt with all our banking.'

'You are maintaining you know nothing about these payments or who the recipient is?'

'That's right.'

'How much does gender reassignment surgery cost?'

'What?' Debbie's question rang out across the courtroom.

'Gender reassignment surgery.' Laidlaw enunciated each word slowly.

'That depends.'

'What does it depend on?'

'On what surgery you have.'

'How much did your surgery cost?'

Judith stood up to object, careful to keep her voice even, after the judge's last reprimand. 'Your honour. We are, again, delving into personal and irrelevant material.'

'Mr Laidlaw, where are you going with all this?'

'Your honour, it is the prosecution case that Danny Mallard took these sums from the joint account he shared with Rosie Harper, in order to fund his surgery. And that this is part of the reason why they argued on the day she died.'

'Do *you* know where the money went?' Judith was crisp in her question, addressed to Laidlaw.

'I'm in the middle of cross-examining your witness. I won't be cross-examined by you,' Laidlaw snapped.

'If you're unable to show a chain of payment from the account to whoever conducted my client's surgery, then this is no more than rumour and supposition, and your line of questioning shouldn't be allowed.' Judith focused on Judge Nolan. 'Your honour, even if these payments were taken by Debbie, which she has already denied, Rosie Harper's salary was in the region of £12,000 per month. She was very well paid. These were not sums which would render her destitute!'

Judge Nolan stared at Debbie, who was sitting calmly, hands folded, waiting for direction as to what to do next. Then she stared at Laidlaw.

'Mr Laidlaw, have you investigated who or what are ABC Happy and the other company, the apparent recipients of this money?' Judge Nolan asked.

'We know that Debbie Mallard had surgery in April 2017 and

February 2018 and these payments coincide almost exactly in time. We also know that the operations she undertook cost in the region of these sums. What we don't have is 100% confirmation that the money was used to pay for the operations. But it cannot be a coincidence, your honour. You must see that.'

'I can't allow further questions on this issue without evidence that this money was used as you suggest. If you can get it before the end of the trial, I'll allow you to recall the defendant, failing which I'll direct the jury to ignore it. Continue please.'

The knot which had begun to tie itself around Judith's stomach began to slowly unwind. Judge Nolan appeared to have remembered her obligations.

'Going back to your managerial position at West Ham. Did you like the job?'

'Yes.'

'But you lost it in 2017?'

'Yes.'

'Why was that?'

'I disagreed with George, the owner, on some issues. We thought it best I leave.'

'Did that disagreement involve the use of physical violence?'

'No.'

'Why did the newspapers think it did?'

'It sold more papers than the truth.'

There was a laugh from the public gallery, which echoed long after Judge Nolan's frown silenced the culprit.

'George Scopos didn't deny it, though, when he was asked to comment.'

'No. But if I had hit him, why weren't the police called? Why didn't they arrest me?'

'Quite. Perhaps that's another question which requires an answer. But not today. All right, Let's move on. Were you jealous of Rosie?'

'Jealous? Never.'

'The fact that her career was going forwards in leaps, while you were training a fourth division women's side.'

'No.'

'Are you certain? It's often hard to be eclipsed by a partner or spouse.'

'I was happy for her. And I was happy too.'

'Really? You had to move out of the family home into a flat, you lost your job, there were these, you say, *untrue* and very uncomplimentary stories about you in the media. The bubble had burst. The hero became the villain and you were powerless to do anything about it. You expect us to believe you were happy?'

'I don't expect you to understand,' Debbie muttered.

'I'm sorry. I didn't hear what you said, Ms Mallard?'

Judith shook her head at Debbie. 'Nothing,' Debbie said.

'Thank you. I want to focus for one moment on the murder weapon, which we talked about last week but which has slipped into oblivion since then. Let's have photo 22 please. It shows the mantelpiece in Rosie's house. Thank you. If you take a look, you'll see that there are a number of other items there. Can you see that?'

'Yes.'

'If we zoom in, can you help by identifying what these items are?'

'I'll try. On the left, there's a big glass vase. We bought that together in Italy, on holiday. Rosie loved the way the colours were mixed together; said it reminded her of clouds on a sunny day.

Then, a postcard. Ben sent it to us from a school ski-ing trip. Rosie joked that it might be the only time we ever received post from one of our children, so she liked to keep it there to look at. Um, a pottery bird Rosie picked up at a craft fair and a school photo of Laura and Ben.'

'Where was the trophy kept?'

'What do you mean?'

'When you first gave evidence to the police, before your arrest, and you were shown the murder weapon, you said it was kept on the mantelpiece.'

'I think it was.'

'Look at those items, though. They're evenly spaced, aren't they?'

'If you say so.'

'Oh they are. And Dr Marcus' report made it clear that the shelf had been dusted, so it was impossible to tell where on the shelf the award had sat – before it was used to batter your wife to death, that is.'

'I don't understand what you're asking me,' Debbie continued.

'Your action, taking your time *after* killing Rosie, to shift everything back on the shelf, to move everything around, so that there was no gap. It totally deflates Ms Burton's argument that you didn't clean up after yourself so you can't be the murderer.'

Debbie frowned.

'No one would even know something was missing. In fact, the dustbin men were due early Friday morning, as they have been every fortnight since 2010, but there'd been a problem in the depot and they were late. That's the only reason we found the murder weapon and thwarted your plan to cover your tracks.'

'I didn't kill Rosie and I didn't spend time moving stuff around the room. We had tea, we spoke about Ben. I left Rosie alive.'

Laidlaw inclined his head to one side and the left corner of his mouth drooped. Constance joked, afterwards, that he reminded her of a sulky teenager. But Laidlaw had kept his best point till last.

'You know that only last week we located some diaries of your late wife, on her laptop,' he continued.

'I've been told.'

'In the light of what those diaries say, do you want to change any of the testimony you have just given?'

'No.' Debbie stuck her chin out obstinately.

'Your honour. This is exhibit 12. I will put the text of the first entry up on the screen, so everyone can follow it. Please could you read it out, as loud as you can.'

'February 16th 2017, evening.' Debbie began reading. 'Danny came back from work today. He was tired. I asked him how his day had been and he didn't answer. He came downstairs in his jeans, but he was wearing a pink, flowery scarf. I asked him to take it off, because Ben would be home soon. He swore at me and then pulled me towards him, wrapping it tightly around my neck. For a moment, I couldn't breathe. Then he let go and stormed out of the house. I think I will have a bruise. He scared me.'

Debbie swallowed noisily.

'Continue please,' Laidlaw said. Debbie looked up at Constance. Constance attempted a smile in return but her face was unwilling to move. It was inevitable that Laidlaw would seek to use the diaries to maximum effect – Judith would have done the same – but it was still painful to watch.

'May 5th 2017 after midnight,' Debbie read on. 'Ben was staying out with a friend. Danny came downstairs in a raincoat and said he was going out. He wouldn't tell me where. I asked what time he would be back, just so I wouldn't worry. He grabbed my wrist and I could smell my perfume on his skin. His coat opened and I saw he was wearing a short black dress underneath. I felt sick. He pushed me hard and I fell back against the sofa. He said not to wait up.'

'August 11th 2017. Danny wants me to call him Debbie. It's very difficult after all these years. It's difficult even when I find him sitting at my dressing table, combing out his long blond hair. He has also now started wearing a bra. When he couldn't find it this evening, he went berserk, smashed a wine glass, then made me clear it up. The cleaner had put it away with my underwear, by mistake. He accused me of hiding it. I locked myself in the bathroom until I heard him go out.'

'October 25th 2017, Debbie was wearing my flowery dress today. I asked him to take it off because I knew Ben was on his way home. At first, Debbie refused. Said that Ben wouldn't be at all fazed. That only an "uptight bitch" like me would be bothered.' Debbie coughed once. 'When I objected, she stripped naked in the living room and forced me to wear the dress over my clothes. As she pulled it over my head, I sustained bruises to my neck and abdomen.'

'January 13th 2018. Debbie was walking around the house, practising speaking in a high-pitched voice. I asked her if she could practise upstairs as I had an important letter to finish and she was distracting me. Debbie then stood behind me, singing in a falsetto voice, until I couldn't stand it any longer. When I said I would go upstairs instead, Debbie grabbed me and forced me to sit down and listen to her reciting a poem. Only when she had finished, did she leave the room. My ribs were bruised and I have another bruise on my arm.'

'March 22nd 2018. Debbie moved out today. We waited till Ben was at school. She took three cases, mostly filled with papers. I asked about her clothes. She told me I could burn them or give them away. She said she would be living as a woman from now on and would not wear any of her male clothes. I asked her to take them with her. She pushed me and I fell down the two bottom steps, knocking my wrist against the banister.'

'June 6th 2018. Debbie called me. She was abusive and threatened to come around and punch me. All this because I cancelled Ben's visit, as he needed to revise for an exam.'

Debbie completed reading out the extracts and raised her head slowly to meet Laidlaw's gaze. Her face was empty of emotion, but her fingers gripped the sides of the witness box.

'Ms Mallard. I put it to you that these diaries reflect what you were really like to live with; a short fuse, a violent temper and a heavy right hand.' Constance willed Debbie to remain calm.

'They're not true,' Debbie said.

'Not true? So your wife...what? Just sat down one day at her laptop, perhaps in the middle of replying to her "fan mail" as you described it and thought, hey, I'll write some completely false things about my husband, shall I? Is that what happened?'

'I don't know.'

'These are *diaries*. They record Rosie Harper's private thoughts about what you did to her.'

'No.'

'She couldn't bear to tell anyone else, not her mother, from whom she was estranged or her close friend, Caroline Fleming, who might have said *I told you so*. So she wrote it all down. That's what people do when it's too painful to tell. That's why people keep diaries.'

'No.'

'Rosie Harper was subjected to a sustained campaign of domestic abuse, both mental and physical.'

'No.'

'You got her pregnant so that she had no choice but to marry you. Either that or go back to her parents.'

'No.' Debbie's answers were beginning to increase in volume and vehemence.

'You prevented her from taking a lucrative position at the BBC for more than ten years, until she finally defied you.'

'No.'

'You insisted she cash in her savings, in order to pay for your expensive treatment.'

'No.'

'Even though your relationship was clearly at rock bottom, you tried to coerce her into staying with you, because you didn't want to give up your comfortable lifestyle. You might even have told her you loved her, but these were hollow, self-serving words.'

'No.'

'When she finally persuaded you to leave, you stopped providing any financial support for Ben and sought to turn the children against her.'

'No.'

'And on 17th June this year, when you visited her, you decided you had had enough. You argued about the money you had taken, she said that you couldn't see Ben anymore. You told her she couldn't stop you. At some stage, you spied the hefty trophy across the room – her award for *best newcomer*, the role which cemented her in the public's hearts and minds – and, as she returned to her correspondence, you came up behind her and struck her once on the back of the head.'

'No.'

'When she turned around at the pain and shock and held her hands up to you, imploring you to stop, you hit her twice more, the second time causing her skull to split in two. She fell to the ground. Then you left her writhing in agony, in her death throes, and ran to the kitchen, where you collected a tea towel and calmly wiped the trophy clean. You left your phone at the house and walked down five doors to casually deposit the weapon in a neighbour's bin. You returned, collected your phone and nonchalantly rode off into the sunset. Somewhere along the way – we will never know where; perhaps even in the home you once shared with Rosie – you stripped off your blood-stained clothes and put on new, clean ones. That's what happened isn't it?'

'No.'

'Isn't it?'

'No!'

Debbie banged her fist down on the edge of the box and stared, wide-eyed at Laidlaw. He smiled conceitedly, and promptly sat down. Constance bit her lip. Judith sat very still in front of her, before rising slowly to her feet.

***

'Your honour. I need to re-call Inspector Dawson to ask him about these diaries, please. I should like to do that *before* re-examination of my client. Inspector Dawson is already prepared to attend again, to clarify some other matters.' Judith spoke quietly, as Debbie stood, head down, her chest rising and falling.

'What does Inspector Dawson know about the diaries?'

'He worked to retrieve them from Rosie Harper's laptop, with the police IT experts. And, depending on Inspector Dawson's testimony and Mr Laidlaw's position, we may also need an IT expert to give evidence.'

'Mr Laidlaw?'

'I am as in the dark as you, your honour, as to what Ms Burton is hoping to achieve here.'

Judge Nolan allowed her gaze to take in the public gallery.

'Then, let's hope that Ms Burton is going to lead us all into the light. Is Inspector Dawson here?'

'I understand he'll be here very shortly.'

'All right. Let's reconvene in an hour.'

42

DEBBIE WAS WAITING FOR Constance downstairs, tapping one foot lightly on the floor, her face pale and drawn.

'You did really well just then, especially talking about the diaries. It must have been hard,' Constance managed, as she entered and sat down next to Debbie. Debbie took a bottle from her pocket, tipped out two large capsules and threw them to the back of her throat, swallowing loudly.

'I know I shouldn't have got angry,' she said. 'But it was such bullshit and I just lost it.'

'It's OK. You did better than you think, really.'

'Is that what Judith thinks?'

'Yes, absolutely.'

'What's happening next? Do I get my chance to explain?' she asked.

'Judith wants the jury to hear from Inspector Dawson, then you'll get your chance. It's important to tell things in the right order.'

'If you say so. I would have explained then, if someone had let me.'

'I need to ask you again about "Rapunzel".'

'Oh. That.'

'This might jog your memory.'

Constance placed her tablet on the desk, in front of Debbie. She scrolled through some screens and then she pressed 'play' on the video she had shared with Judith on Saturday.

At first the video was dark and grainy, but then it grew lighter and the background noise transformed into clapping and cheering, with a couple of cat calls. A tall, blond woman was centre-stage of some intimate venue, burgundy velvet curtain for a backdrop, her hair tied in two long plaits, which hung down her back. She was wearing only a black lace corset and stockings and seated on the knee of a smartly dressed man. As she rose to her feet, teetering in three inch stilettos, the man withdrew from the stage and the Amazonian beauty came forward into the spotlight. The crowd grew silent, the beam of light intensified. She drew herself up to her full height, her bosom over-spilling the tight bodice and then she began to sing.

There was no mistaking. It was Debbie.

Debbie watched all the way through, some light tremors in her fingers revealing her struggle to control her emotions. At the end, she sat very still with her head down.

'Someone sent this video to Rosie, back in 2017. Do you have any idea who it was?'

'No,' Debbie whispered.

'We're assuming that it was supposed to make her feel embarrassed, or worse; we're searching for data on who sent it and why. We may want to use it, as evidence, in the trial.'

'No! Can you imagine? No! I won't let you.'

'It might help you.'

'How? How could this possibly help me?'

'We think it may be connected to Rosie's murder.'

Debbie sat back and placed both hands over her face. After a while, she removed them and sat up straight.

'Did you see everything that happened over the weekend?' she asked, 'the attacks, those poor men, their faces all battered?'

'Yes.'

'And did you hear what they were shouting this morning, outside court, when I arrived?'

'Some of it, yes.'

'I don't want more people to get hurt because of me – because that's what will happen if you show that.'

'I don't think so.'

'I do. And, if I'm wrong and you're right, that some people – decent people – they might begin to be able to understand…I don't want to get out of here because people feel sorry for me,' Debbie said. 'I don't want it to be that those eleven people find me not guilty because they feel responsible for what happened in Salford or at that publishers, or because they listened to what Dr Alves said about the "tragic life of trans women". Do you understand that?'

'Yes.'

'I want to get out of here because the jury, the public, the people watching at home, believe that I, Debbie Mallard, never killed my wife. How is that video going to help with that?'

43

THE CONGREGATION OUTSIDE court could only properly be described as an angry mob. They had been present all through the morning and showed no signs of losing interest. The human rights supporters were now chanting 'No fair trial', 'No fair trial', and the anti-police brigade were shouting 'Down with the police', having been advised earlier that if they continued to use the word 'fuck' they would be arrested for outraging public decency. Some people were shouting both. More officers had been drafted in and there was now a chain of around a dozen at the doorway, holding people back.

Judith saw Dawson arrive and force his way through, with uniformed officers on either side. He had almost reached the door when a tall man, bare-chested in black shorts, leaned over the barricade and spat at him. The spittle landed on his cheek, but that seemed to be the catalyst for a number of others to follow suit, so that as he burst through the door into the sanctuary of the inside hallway, his jacket was coated with beads of saliva.

'Friendly bunch,' he said to Judith, grabbing a handkerchief to clean his face.

Judith stared over his shoulder, to where the crowds were gathered. 'I wanted you to know that it wasn't me who called you back here,' she said.

Dawson nodded. 'OK. Now I know.'

'But now you're here, I will need to ask you about Rosie's diaries.'

'Understood.'

'I'm sorry about the other stuff too; the glove caused all this, I think,' Judith continued. 'I might have played some small part in setting that hare running. There'll be some questions about that today also. Did Laidlaw tell you that?'

'The glove was at the scene when I arrived...end of. I saw it with my own eyes. That good enough?'

'For me, yes.'

Dawson grunted non-commitally.

'And I'm going to ask you about the money.'

'Money?'

'The two large payments out of Rosie Harper's bank account. Where they went.'

Dawson's eyes narrowed and he shook his head. 'It's irrelevant,' he said.

'Laidlaw thinks it's the motive for the murder – well, part of it.'

'He's wrong, so you don't need to ask me about the money.' Dawson looked away.

'What do you know that you're not telling?'

Dawson fixed Judith with a serious stare. 'Don't ask me about the money,' he said again, very slowly and deliberately. Then, he squeezed a smile and loped off towards the court.

***

'Is Chief Inspector Dawson here now?' Judge Nolan chirped, buoyed up perhaps by the prospect of a prime-time revelation that would resolve 'glove-gate' and restore her reputation.

'He is, yes,' Laidlaw replied, with considerably less enthusiasm.

'Good. Might we finish today then?'

'It would be safer to say tomorrow,' Judith said. 'It depends, in part, on whether Mr Laidlaw will agree the expert technological evidence, relating to the creation of Rosie Harper's diaries, which I will talk about with Inspector Dawson, and then on the time I need with my client to complete the point.'

'Mr Laidlaw?'

'I should like to reserve my position on the expert until after Inspector Dawson has given his evidence.'

'All right. Let's get on with Inspector Dawson then.'

***

Dawson stood tall on the witness stand, staring unblinking at the camera. His tie was off-centre and his top button open, but, otherwise, despite his rough welcome outside court, his attire was neater than on his last appearance.

'Chief Inspector Dawson. Thank you for making yourself available at such short notice. You know, I believe, that entries you found on Rosie Harper's laptop were put in evidence this morning. Can you tell the court how you found them?' Judith began, trying to keep her voice light, on the sixth day of the trial.

Dawson nodded politely, then smiled at the camera before speaking. Judith wondered if he'd had coaching since last week on how to engage his audience. He was certainly determined not to be cowed in any way by his reception, or the enquiry hanging over his head.

'Yes,' he said. 'Our IT squad has a long backlog. It isn't their fault; they're an excellent team, but the volume of data we're having to process causes long delays. I had thought that Miss Harper's laptop had been examined, but I discovered, only ten days ago that I was wrong. I instructed our team to prioritise it and, a few days ago, after difficulty with multiple passwords, we found the diaries and, of course, informed the defence straightaway.'

'Thank you. For your information, Mr Laidlaw took the court through the full transcript of the diary entries earlier. But I am interested in your overview of the diaries.'

'They describe occasions when the defendant had been violent or abusive towards Rosie Harper.'

'How often did these violent outbursts occur, according to the diary?'

'Approximately every three months.'

'Was there a pattern you could determine?'

'They seemed to be sparked off by Debbie doing something a bit unusual. Rosie would comment and then Debbie would become angry and hurt Rosie.'

'Do you happen to know the date of Rosie Harper's divorce from Debbie?'

'Yes. It was June 2018, the 24th I think.'

'You have an excellent memory. That's exactly right. And do you know on what grounds their divorce was granted?'

'No. I can guess though.'

Judith saw Laidlaw watching her intently, a puzzled look on his face. Then he conferred briefly with his solicitor.

'That won't be necessary. Your honour, if I may spend one moment putting this into context for the jury. We don't have "no fault" divorce yet in the UK. Unless you and your spouse or civil partner have lived apart for substantial periods of time, then you have only two grounds for divorce; adultery or unreasonable behaviour.

'Unreasonable behaviour is the most common ground, used by 51% of all women divorcing. In order to be granted a divorce on this basis, the applicant must provide *specific details* of events, happening over a period of, say two years, describing what happened and the impact on them both physically and mentally. Most divorce practitioners, therefore, advise clients seeking a divorce on this ground, to keep a diary chronicling these events, to support their divorce petition.'

'Your honour, I object. I just about held my tongue at Ms Burton explaining the rudiments of divorce law to the court, but there is no basis for her to opine on what "most divorce practitioners" advise. I suppose, at a pinch, we could hear her *personal experiences*, but that would be purely anecdotal and of limited value accordingly.'

Judith reached for her glass of water and promptly knocked it over. It rolled on its side and the water spilled over her notebook, narrowly missing her laptop, before running along the bench towards Laidlaw, at an alarming rate. He jumped up and removed his notes from the fast-flowing stream and his solicitor leaped forward with some paper towels, to mop up the mess. Judge Nolan was surprisingly patient, while the lawyers cleared up and Laidlaw even poured Judith a new glass of water, which she sipped, before placing it at the far end of the bench.

'Ms Burton, the jury now understands sufficiently what you

were saying,' Judge Nolan said, 'and I would encourage them to channel any questions to me in the break if they do not, and, Mr Laidlaw, it is not appropriate for you to make reference to Counsel's personal experiences, even by way of analogy, as you well know.'

'My point is almost complete now, thank you,' Judith continued. 'Just remind the court, please, of the date of the first entry in Miss Harper's diary?' Judith was back in the saddle.

'16 February 2017.'

'And the last?'

'6 June 2018.'

'So the first entry is dated two weeks after police attended her house at night, and we now know that coincided with Debbie telling Rosie of her intention to transition.'

'If that's what she said.'

'And the last entry is dated three weeks short of the date their divorce was granted, Debbie having moved out in March 2018, a year after the first diary entry.'

'Yes.'

'Did you find any diaries of any kind, either on Rosie's laptop, or among her belongings, other than these?'

'No.'

'Tell me, have you had diary evidence in any other cases you've handled?'

'A few times.'

'What did those diaries look like?'

'Usually they're handwritten.'

'And kept where?'

'Somewhere they would be difficult to find.'

'Because they contain private thoughts?'

'Yes.'

'And, in your experience, those diaries you have seen before, are they just what the name suggests, a daily slice of the life of the writer, sprinkled with comment, reflection, opinion – that kind of thing?'

'Yes, I suppose so.'

'Was Miss Harper's diary written daily?'

'I've said it wasn't.'

'Weekly?'

'No.'

'Were there any entries talking about her work or going to the theatre, cinema, birthday outings?'

'No.'

'Shopping, a book she had read, worries about the children?'

'No.'

'There were just these entries recording *unreasonable behaviour* by Debbie?'

'I object again to Counsel making misleading statements. She is leading evidence that this diary was linked in some way to Rosie Harper's divorce,' Laidlaw interrupted.

'That is precisely what I am doing. Thank you. I wasn't sure if I was getting my point across.'

'Stop!' Judge Nolan bellowed and all eyes turned towards her. The camera man lifted one of his earphones. Twice the cameras had been extinguished. Was she going to make it a hat-trick? Judge Nolan coughed, stared out at the public but, when she eventually spoke, it was more measured.

'Ms Burton, do you have evidence that Miss Harper's diary entries are linked in some way to her divorce?'

'I do, yes. This is the IT expert evidence to which I referred a few minutes ago. It shows that a number of these entries were made *many months after* the date they purport to describe, and that they were made *on the same day*, casting considerable doubt on their veracity.'

'You are saying that Rosie Harper fabricated these diary entries, writing them later on, inventing the content and the dates, in order to aid a smooth divorce?'

'I am. And the IT evidence will support that. Of course, if my learned friend were to agree that evidence, then we could dispense with the need for yet another expert.'

'I understand. Can *this* witness assist any more with the diaries?'

'No, your honour.'

'Then I suggest we move on and remain focused.'

Judith fingered her notepad. She wasn't relishing the next line of questioning.

'There is one other matter on which the court would be grateful for your further assistance,' she began.

Dawson nodded.

'Since you first gave your evidence, last week, you will be aware that there has been a suggestion made, in the media, that the black, leather motorbike glove – exhibit two – which you testified was found at the scene of Rosie Harper's murder, was, instead, planted by you or by one of your officers, after the event, in order to secure a conviction.

'Dr Marcus, forensic pathologist, who gave evidence after you, did draw our attention to a photograph, which appeared to show the glove in the foreground, but that photograph was taken the evening after Rosie Harper died, and also after her body had been removed from the house. Are you able to provide us with any further help in relation to this item, please?'

Dawson looked from Judith to Laidlaw to Debbie and then back to Judith.

'No, I'm not.'

'Surely Inspector Dawson, there is something you can say, to reassure us that the glove was where you said it was from the outset?' Judge Nolan intervened.

'Your honour. I have been instructed by police lawyers that I am not to answer any questions in relation to the glove, even here in court, because the issue of the glove is now the subject of an internal police enquiry. What I can say, is that I stand behind everything I said previously, when giving evidence in this trial, as to what I saw and when.'

44

'DEBBIE MALLARD IN THE witness box.' Katrina Sadiq boomed out her introduction, accompanied by a thunderous backing track. 'Tonight we'll be going over her evidence.'

Then the camera panned out to show Katrina and Chris sitting side by side.

'She was asked some very personal questions, wasn't she?' Chris turned to Katrina.

'She was and she dealt with them all pretty well, until just before the end, when things became a bit heated. More of that shortly.'

'And we'll be talking about diaries. Apparently, sixty-one per cent of us keep them. But why?'

'And finally, do we trust our police? A hugely important question, brought back into the news by Chief Inspector Dawson giving evidence again today. An enormous crowd was waiting for him and they showed their displeasure in the most vocal and physical way.'

Behind their heads, a picture flashed up on the screen. A

photographer had captured the moment the first man had spat at Dawson, the spittle caught in mid-air, on course for a direct hit with Dawson's cheek. But it was the hatred in the eyes of the protesters that drew the attention and had led to a number of hard-hitting headlines throughout the day.

'It's looking increasingly likely that he will be suspended pending the enquiry into his handling of the Rosie Harper murder,' Chris added with a solemn grimace. 'We're expecting a statement from the Metropolitan police later today.'

Andy slipped in next to them, as the camera focused on Katrina.

'Welcome, Andy. Let's start with Chief Inspector Dawson, then. Why couldn't he answer questions about the glove?'

'It's like he said. There is an enquiry, so he really can't,' Andy said. There, that was clear and concise.

'It's rather like taking the fifth, then?' Chris joined in this time.

Andy frowned.

'I'm sorry?' he said.

'"The fifth", the fifth amendment. It's what they do in America, you know, you don't have to answer questions if it might incriminate you.'

'It's not quite the same. He will have been instructed by the Commissioner for the Metropolitan Police not to talk about it. It's not really his choice.'

'Are there any reasons why ordinary people, not members of the police, can refuse to give evidence in UK courts, then?' Katrina was leaning forward, a concerned expression spread across her face. Andy had to admit, privately, that that was a pretty insightful follow-up question.

'Not generally,' he said. 'There are very limited occasions where you can't be compelled to give evidence against your spouse. Otherwise, if you are summoned to court, you have to give evidence.'

'Or what?'

'Or you go to jail for contempt of court.'

'That's not very fair, is it? I'm sure our viewers will have lots to say about that.'

'I think it's totally fair,' Andy was beginning to assert himself now. 'The wheels would fall off our justice system if people could just refuse to give evidence on things they know about and there were no consequences.'

'What about Rosie's diaries?' Chris asked, neatly moving things on.

'Judith Burton pretty much established they had been invented, in order to help her divorce,' Andy was comfortable with the change of topic. He suddenly noticed the absence of the voice in his ear. That must mean he was fulfilling his brief, even without prompting.

'Should she be allowed to say those kinds of things about Rosie Harper, though, now she's dead and can't defend herself?'

'If it's the truth, why not?'

'Well, thinking back to earlier in the week, the judge told Jeremy Laidlaw that he mustn't put words into people's mouths, especially if they were dead.'

Katrina joined in. 'I remember those words, vividly.'

'Now, for whatever reason, she's allowing Inspector Dawson to do just that,' Chris said.

'Yes, I mean the metadata could easily have been changed on the diary entries, to make it look like they were all written at the same time. We only have Judith Burton's word on that. And you explained for us the devices she used on the 999 call.'

Andy took a deep breath and squeezed a brief, but warm, smile at both Katrina and Chris. We're all on the same side, he told himself.

'Judith is a barrister, like me,' he said. 'We are bound by our professional obligations to act with the utmost integrity. When Judith told the court that she had sought help from an expert, who'd confirmed evidence some of the diary entries weren't genuine, that will have been the absolute truth. It was always open to Mr Laidlaw to bring his own expert evidence to the contrary. The fact that he didn't bother tells its own story. And the diaries were important evidence. It was right and proper that Judith was allowed to test their authenticity.'

'I'm sure you're right,' Katrina said. Andy now knew her well enough to suspect this was the precursor to a really tricky question, but, tonight, he felt he could handle anything.

'Earlier in the week,' she continued, 'we talked about whether it was ever acceptable to bully a witness, particularly in the light of the Caroline Fleming debacle. Wasn't Jeremy Laidlaw's exchange with Debbie Mallard precisely that, especially towards the end?'

'It may have appeared harsh, but he was just doing his job,' Andy said. 'Sometimes, if a witness is hiding something and you apply pressure, the truth is forced out.'

'Apply pressure!' Katrina's eyes were wide, bottomless pools. 'That sounds rather like the end justifying the means,' she said.

'Which it sometimes does.'

'If we take that to its logical conclusion, we may as well torture confessions from our defendants and save the cost of the trial.' Katrina gave a half laugh, as she exchanged a knowing glance with Chris.

They both looked across at Andy expectantly. Andy waited for the voice in his ear to tell him which way to jump, but it was silent. He thought of Clare, at home watching, or perhaps busy with the kids, with the programme on record to watch later, and of his colleagues (or at least his pupil) viewing this from their local wine bar.

'I think that we risk being overly sensitive, speaking from this sanitised environment, when the reality is that seventy per cent of those prosecuted for murder are found guilty,' he said. 'The lawyers' job is to expose those individuals, to reveal their crimes, so that they can be punished and they won't go on to kill or harm anyone else. That's an enormous responsibility on our lawyers and we have to give them the tools to operate.'

Katrina opened her mouth to speak, but Andy kept on going.

'In other countries, it's acceptable to apply physical or mental pressure on suspects to find the truth,' he said. 'Some people would say that we should do the same here. That the best way to obtain a confession from someone who has beaten an old man to death with a brick to steal his pension, or knifed a shopkeeper for cigarettes, or kicked his pregnant girlfriend in the stomach till she lost her unborn child, is to respond in the only language they understand; that of violence.'

'Surely, you're not advocating...'

'Lawyers in this country, in England and Wales – to be fair in all of the United Kingdom – we have rules of procedure and rules of evidence, and quite rightly so. But that means that sometimes victims have to face their attackers in court and relive the horror of their experiences, or key evidence is disallowed, because of a technicality.

'When you view Jeremy Laidlaw's questions to Debbie Mallard

in that context; seeking to expose a potentially vicious criminal while complying with the rules imposed on him by a civilised society and trying to protect potential witnesses from harm at the same time, I think everyone at home will appreciate that his behaviour was totally appropriate. Digging around, pressing the defendant verbally to focus on the matter in hand and not avoid the issues, is really not oppressive when viewed against the background of a brutal murder.'

*** *

Constance had spent the afternoon industriously. First, she had taken the tracker from Debbie's phone and re-traced her steps from the day of Rosie's murder. Now she knew where Debbie had gone after leaving Rosie's house and before her training session.

Then, she had moved on to Nicki's emails to Rosie. They were long and rambling and rather disjointed, not like the words selected by the articulate person who had held her own – and more – during their interview. She had a sudden thought and spent a few minutes searching around the internet. Then she laughed aloud. She wasn't quite there, but the pieces of the puzzle were sliding into place.

***

Andy went straight to the bathroom at the end of his session, where he doused his face with water. He couldn't be certain (the usual debrief would come later this evening) but he felt, instinctively, that he had done well tonight, even if he'd ended up defending Jeremy Laidlaw. He had even begun, for a few brief seconds, to relax, which must be a good sign.

Not only was he proud of himself, he was relieved, too. He had never sent his draft contract with Court TV to Clare or the promised employment lawyer, knowing from his own reading of it that it contained some fairly draconian provisions and that he really wanted to sign up without making waves.

Andy walked back towards the studio and stood for a moment, looking through the glass at Phil, who was, in turn, watching Katrina and Chris in the studio. Then he wandered around the studio and stared out of the window at the London street below. Turning around, he noticed the closed door with the 'no entry' sign again, and this time, once more, it was slightly ajar.

He approached with some trepidation, then pushed it open and stepped inside. A man wearing headphones, with an integral microphone, was seated at a desk, with his back to Andy. He was watching the show through a small window, which corresponded to the dark window Andy had viewed from the other side. He was making notes on an iPad. Andy came closer and waited.

After a few seconds only, the man's back straightened and he turned slowly around.

'Hello,' he said. 'You found me then?'

Andy was silent. He wanted the man to speak some more.

'You were excellent tonight,' the man said. 'Quite a match for our presenters. That's why I didn't need....'

'Who are...'

'Apologies. My name's Gregory Winter. I'm a friend of Graham's,' the man said, holding out his hand for Andy to shake. 'I've been standing in for him the last few days.'

'Why are you hiding away?' Andy asked.

'I have my own reasons for wanting to keep my involvement

quiet – nothing *illegal*, before you become concerned. And sitting in here is perfect, without any distractions, I can focus really clearly on all of you.'

And Andy laughed aloud and with relief. The man's voice perfectly matched the one he'd been hearing in his head this last week.

45

CONSTANCE AND JUDITH SAT opposite each other in Caffè Nero on Cheapside the following morning. Constance had treated herself to a pot of yoghurt, Judith was on her second espresso.

'Poor Charlie.' Judith pushed aside a copy of *Metro* with an image of protesters surrounding Dawson adorning the front page. 'The Police Commissioner is bound to suspend him now,' she said. 'She doesn't really have any choice, but it's not right.'

'Would you still say that, if he did plant the glove?' Constance replied.

'Of course not.'

'You think the glove was on the floor all the time, then; just left behind?'

'Charlie said it was there when he came in and I believe him. Anything else, I haven't a clue. What do the Twitter polls say today, then?'

'40:60.'

'Only 40% think Debbie is guilty?'

'Yep. Well done you!'

'I'm not sure I'm so deserving of praise. Presumably, a lot of people still think Debbie killed Rosie, even after all we've done.'

'But look how far we've come.'

'Yes. God, when the diaries came out, I thought we'd had it. But there was something so manufactured about them, even Laidlaw was forced to accept that.'

'Rosie must have been desperate to write them.'

'Why are you always so charitable? She told lies, and pretty nasty ones, to get an easy ride through the system, and it's only thanks to…well, thanks to your persistence and Greg's skill, that she hasn't dragged Debbie down with her.'

'You didn't ask Dawson about the money?'

'No.'

'Why not?'

'He told me not to.'

'And you listened to him? You never do that.'

'I know. I saw him before we went in, after the mob roughed him up. He said it was totally irrelevant and he asked me, in the strongest possible terms, not to take things further.'

'What does that mean?'

'They must still be investigating and suspect some kind of fraud. Maybe that's why it took so long to extract information from Rosie's laptop.'

'You know there's a gap in the timing I haven't mentioned before,' Constance asked.

'Why do I get this tingling at the back of my neck when you say that?'

'Debbie went somewhere when she left Rosie's. She didn't go straight home. I asked her about it and she got pretty upset.

I wondered if it was…you know, Mr X, her new lover. She demanded that I didn't check it out.'

'So you did?'

'Naturally.'

'And?'

'It's a doctor's surgery.'

'Perhaps her new flame works there.'

'No. She's been seeing a neurologist there, for some months. A neurologist is…'

'I know what a neurologist is! She's ill, Debbie? Maybe we can use it.'

'I told you she was adamant not. That was before her whole speech to me this morning about winning on her own merit.'

'What?'

'She's seen all the stuff over the weekend. Who could miss it? And then I showed her the Rapunzel video, like we agreed. She doesn't want to win because she's trans. She wants to win because she's innocent.'

'Oh God!' Judith said. 'Talk about fussy!'

Constance opened her mouth wide.

'I was joking,' Judith said, seeing the look of incredulity on Constance's face. 'I am not totally devoid of empathy. I want that too and I'm hoping that's precisely what we'll get, which is no more than Debbie deserves. But forgive me for wishing that the sooner we finish and get the verdict, the better, before any more skeletons emerge.'

'There's something else.'

'Oh.'

'I've finally had the chance to look properly at Nicki's emails to Rosie.'

'And?'

'That's the thing. They're mostly copied, cut and pasted, from other articles. I checked with this app. That's why they don't read fluently.'

'What does that mean, then?'

'I'm not sure. Maybe it just means she was lazy or she isn't great with words; well, not written words.'

Judith checked her watch. 'What time did Greg say?' she asked.

Constance acknowledged the change of subject with a frown. Judith had never been very interested in Nicki.

'Now, he said now. He'll be here, just be patient,' she said.

And right on cue, Greg walked through the door and settled himself at their table.

'What have you got for us?' Judith asked.

'I haven't found the person who sent Rosie the video, yet.'

'What have you been doing then?'

'I worked all through Friday night on the diaries,' he said. 'Then I had to get the Rapunzel folder unlocked. Today, I've traced the email account to a coffee shop on Baker Street and I've been there just now. There's free use of the internet and an unknown person sent the video from there to Rosie Harper's personal email address on 1 April 2017. It must have been a nice April Fool surprise for Rosie. And before you ask, there is no way of telling who sent that email or the two follow-ups.'

'Follow-ups?'

'Asking for money, telling her where to send it.'

'Blackmail. Damn!' Judith stood up and walked a few paces away from them before returning. 'How stupid I never thought of that. At least that means it's unlikely to be Ben.'

'Should we tell Dawson?' Constance ventured.

Judith smiled. 'This time Dawson was one step ahead of us,' Judith said. 'That's why he told me not to ask him about the money leaving Rosie's account. But he can't have known about the video, can he? Had anyone else accessed that folder?'

'Not as far as I could see. It took me hours to open it and, I'd like to say, years of experience. I doubt the police had the time to devote to it – or the requisite skill.'

'But what do we do with it?' Constance asked. 'What does it mean?'

'And if we want to use it to shift suspicion away from Debbie on to whoever sent the video, we'll have to show it. And we can't do that.' Judith was pacing again.

'Why not?' Greg was serious now.

'Why not? Because all our efforts, weeks of work, have been to cultivate an image for Debbie of a quiet, demure, plain-speaking, loving, devoted spouse. That will all be thwarted by two minutes forty-two seconds of nonsense. If we show the video, no one will listen to the blackmail bit. They'll focus on what Debbie was doing at Madame Jojo's and how she looks. Hardly the shrinking violet.'

'Then you'll say it's totally irrelevant. That the blackmail is the key to it all.'

'Is it? You don't even know who sent it. Instead, Laidlaw will rub his hands with glee; Christmas coming early and all that. He'll ask whose knee she's sitting on. Debbie will have to confess her lover and then he'll say this was all about her lover and that she lied about being in love with Rosie and that if she lied about that, she lied about everything.'

'And Debbie has forbidden us to use it,' Constance added.

Greg motioned to both of them to listen. 'It's unlikely I can find where the emails came from – or not quickly enough to be of any use – but I have thought of a possible way of tracing who the blackmailer might be.'

'You have?'

'I'll need to do some research and make a few calls. I'll get onto it now. What should I do if I find out?'

'Go straight to Dawson, if he hasn't been booted out of the force by now. He'll listen. I know he will.'

'All right. But I don't think you should be so worried about showing the video, even if I don't find out who sent it. In fact, I really think you need to get Debbie to talk about it in the witness box, today.'

'Why on earth would we do that? You heard Connie. It's the last thing she's going to want to do,' Judith replied.

'I understand Debbie might not like it, but since when was that a consideration for you? This is how I see it. You've done brilliantly so far in picking holes in the prosecution case, and, inadvertently, in raising the profile of the whole issue of discrimination against trans women, but that's not the end of the story. The public hasn't connected with Debbie personally, yet.'

'Connected?'

'Hear me out. I've been watching all the social media platforms very closely. People are still not sure how much they like Debbie or trust her, even with all the anti-police stuff. And Laidlaw has made a good job of making her look selfish and mean. They adored Danny, and why did they adore him?'

'He helped his country win a huge international football title?'

'All right, but more than that, he performed when it was needed and he carried people along with him. There was an emotional connection. This is an opportunity for Debbie to steal the limelight, literally. To wear her heart on her sleeve, and they'll love it.'

'Why?'

'The public loves vulnerability. This "performance" has it in buckets. I doubt it will be the main reason she's acquitted – that will be down to all your hard work, raising a reasonable doubt and all that – but, if that happens, and I believe it will, she wants to have a life afterwards, not be hiding her face away. I mean, look at OJ! The lawyers got him off, but everyone thought he did it, even his friends. And within a few years he was back inside. And I can tell you, without giving away any confidences, that *Court TV BTS* will major on this video this evening.'

Judith picked up her coffee cup and then put it down again.

'Connie. You're more in touch with what's going on than I am. What do you think?'

Constance reclaimed the laptop from Greg and replayed the first part of the video.

'I think Greg's right,' she said. 'You know, if I think back, I never really believed Debbie was innocent, until the day they wouldn't let her wear her makeup.'

'What?'

'The prison guard took her makeup away one morning last week. Just for a moment, when she told me about it, I saw how that made her feel. Then she covered it up. But in that moment – that's when I believed in her. And the public don't care about cold, clinical evidence; gloves and trophies and money going in and out of bank accounts. They don't like people who are detached and distant and reined in, like Debbie has been, like we've encouraged her to be. They want people to be real and raw and to expose their souls. Then they will judge them as human beings.'

Judith shifted her weight from one foot to the other and then she laughed out loud.

'What's so funny?'

'I'm thinking back to David Benson's intro to all of this; his grand transparency scheme, allowing the public to "judge cases on the evidence". That's what he said. The irony is that you're perfectly right. The evidence only takes things so far. All right. Let's try. I can't see how we'll get Debbie to volunteer anything about this video, though,' Judith said.

'You'll find a way,' Greg said, grinning widely. 'You always do.'

46

DEBBIE CLIMBED THE STEPS to the witness box for the second and last time, shortly after 10am.

'Just get Ben out of there,' Debbie had requested, when she agreed, through gritted teeth, to do as she was asked. 'I can bear it, I think, but not for Ben to see it. Not up on that screen on the wall and in everyone's homes. And not for him to hear me talk about such personal things.'

And Constance had obliged, calling Ben en route to court, insisting that now would be a good time to meet up with her instead. It took a lot of persuasion, but he finally agreed to stay away from court that morning, with Laura following suit, on one condition; he wanted Constance to accompany him on a visit back to Rosie's house. He was enthused by the idea that they could plan a homecoming, of sorts, for Debbie, after the verdict was delivered. For once, Constance ditched her usual cautious response and went along with his eagerness.

***

In court, Judith rose to her feet and forced what she hoped was a reassuring smile at Debbie, conscious that she was alone again, Constance having disappeared off to attend to Ben. She could see Laidlaw out of the corner of her eye, grinning from ear to ear, both hands resting on his lectern, poised to rise for his closing speech. He was Gregory Peck in *To Kill a Mockingbird*, he was Tom Cruise in *A Few Good Men*, he was Matthew McConaughey in *A Time To Kill*. In contrast, her throat was like sandpaper. She reached cautiously for her glass of water, willing her hands to behave this time, and took a long draught.

'Your honour, I was planning, as you know, to finish with a short re-examination of my client this morning.' She took a deep breath. She snatched a glance at the empty bench behind her. She looked out into the public gallery. She stared, for a moment, into the camera and felt surprisingly calm. Then she returned to Debbie.

'We heard from Inspector Dawson yesterday about Rosie's diaries. Before this trial, did you know that Rosie made those entries?'

'Yes…and no,' Debbie said, her face pinched, her eyes mournful. The three spaces where Ben, Laura and Ellis had been sitting were now filled by unfamiliar bodies and Nicki was also absent. Only Debbie's mother remained, steadfast.

'Can you explain what you mean?' Judith said.

'I knew she had written something, but I never imagined it was like that.'

'Did you know it was something negative about you?'

'Yes.' Debbie lowered her head.

'And the entries, you read them out to this court, were they a true account of what happened?'

'No.'

'None of them?'

'None of them.'

'Why did you allow Rosie to write such terrible things about you, if they were all untrue?'

Debbie kept her eyes fixed on her mother, as she spoke. Mrs Mallard was as still as a statue, but her face was fixed with a soft and welcoming expression.

'We did a deal,' Debbie continued.

'You and Rosie?'

'Mm.'

'What did you offer?'

'That she could do what she needed to get a quick divorce. She sent me the papers to sign. I knew about the diary entries, but I never read what she wrote. I didn't really care. It did the trick.'

'Did you have to do anything else?'

'Yes.' Debbie blinked twice and her lip trembled. 'I had to agree to give up the West Ham position and not to coach another premiership side.'

'The newspapers said you were sacked?'

'I agreed with George, the owner, that's what we would say. He was kind and he understood it was easier that way. There was never any fight.'

'And why did Rosie insist you stopped coaching?'

'She knew people would find out about me, but she thought if I "disappeared" from public view, it would be easier.'

'And you were prepared to do all that?'

'Yes.'

'Because you loved her?'

'Yes, and because there was something else I really needed.'

'What was that?'

'My gender recognition certificate. I couldn't get it without Rosie's agreement.'

'What?'

Now Debbie had everyone's attention and she allowed her gaze to expand to take in the public gallery. 'That's how it works,' she explained, 'until the government changes the rules, and it's not top of their list at the moment.'

'You are saying that you allowed your former wife to fabricate these diaries, you gave up a lucrative job you loved, all so that you could receive papers that make you legally a woman?' Judge Nolan intervened.

'It was the only way for me. You have to have your spouse's consent, or you can't legally change gender. Well, not straightaway. Without consent you have to get a divorce.'

'But Rosie wanted a divorce, you said?'

'And I didn't. But I also didn't want to be made to wait, like you said, maybe *another* two years to go through the divorce before I got my certificate. I wasn't going to do all this and still have everyone telling me that I was still a man. So I agreed to everything she wanted.'

Two reporters raced out of court. A number of others sat on the edges of their seats. Tears began to stream down Mrs Mallard's face. Judith could quit now, while she was marginally ahead, or she could go for broke. She chewed the edge of her finger and stared at Debbie. Debbie nodded twice to her. There was no going back.

'Recently, I became aware of a video featuring my client, which

425

was filmed without her knowledge or consent in February 2017 and sent to Rosie Harper on 1 April 2017,' Judith said.

'A video?' Judge Nolan was engaged now.

'Yes.'

'And what does this video show?'

'It features Debbie, and it was followed by requests to Rosie Harper for money; £25,000 in the first instance, followed a year or so later with a request for £15,000. I think the best thing would be for me to show the video. I am assuming my learned friend has no objections.'

Laidlaw leaped up to object, his mouth already agape, but Judge Nolan waved at him to sit down.

'I'm sorry Mr Laidlaw. I don't think there is anything you can possibly say, which is going to prevent me from allowing Ms Burton to show us this video. You brought up the payments, so you may as well save your strength.'

The lights were dimmed once more and Debbie appeared on the screen, on stage, fussing with her long blond plaits. The close-up camera shot revealed her heavily-lined lids, her false eyelashes, her tight corset. Music started to play and she raised a microphone to her red lips. Then she frowned and took two steps sideways, fidgeting with her hair. The music stopped. The audience waited. The music began a second time. Then Debbie took a deep breath, closed her eyes and began to sing, in a rich tenor voice.

As she sang, the rowdy audience grew quieter and quieter, hanging on her every word, the poignant lyrics pulling at their heart strings, even those who were fairly inebriated by that stage of the evening. She finished to rapturous applause and took three bows before backing away and disappearing behind the plush curtains.

Debbie, in court, appeared considerably less at ease. Her face was crimson, she stared at the floor and her hands were tightly clasped together.

'Back in February 2017, when that video was taken, was it usual for you to go out *wearing* women's clothes?'

'No,' Debbie whispered.

'Why was that?'

'I was too scared.'

'What were you scared of?'

'I was scared of being recognised...of being found out. I was still "Danny" to the world, a heterosexual, macho man, a role model for young, male footballers, like Ken said.'

'So why that night?'

'It was the first Saturday night, after I told Rosie I wanted to transition. It had been a very hard week. I had questioned whether it was the right thing to do, because I caused her so much pain. She was so disappointed in me that I almost caved in. I almost gave it all up. But I had worked so hard to get to that moment. All my forty years of my brain telling me I was a girl, but my body showing everyone else something different.'

'Why didn't you give up?'

'Rosie said such awful things to me. The kind of things her mother, Elaine, told you: that I had tricked her into marriage, that I was selfish and that it was too much for her to bear. And in some ways, that made me more determined. Maybe if she had hugged me and said she understood, that she had guessed before, that she would always love me, the person underneath, the same person I've always been, then I would have decided it was not worth losing her. I can't say for sure. But I suddenly knew that there was no turning back. Not if I wanted to stop living the lie I had lived for so many years – my whole life really.'

'What about the clothes you are wearing in the video?' Judith spoke softly, coaxing Debbie on.

'The clothes? Ha! And the wig. When I was a little girl, I dreamed of having long blond hair, hair I could brush and style and touch, like the girls in my class. Every time my mother took me to the barber, I would cry myself to sleep. And the corset and the rest? I look at them now and think they look nasty and cheap. I feel ashamed that you, all of you, are seeing me like that, when I have worked so hard to…promote a different image of who Debbie Mallard is. I didn't have to be quite so…flashy, but somehow, at the time, it felt right. I was making a statement. I was saying "here I am". But I never expected such a large audience.'

'And the song you sang?'

'The song is 'I See The Light'. It's from *Tangled*. I took the kids to see the film when they were little and I loved it – probably more than they did. It's the Disney version of Rapunzel and it's the song she sings when she finally escapes from the tower. It's about realising all the things you've been missing all your life, until that moment. And never wanting to go back in that tower again.

'David, a friend of mine, and he really is just a friend and he's very kind. He knew I could sing. He thought it would be a good thing for me to do. And it felt…liberating. It really did. The memory of that performance, how people responded, it helped me get through those first few months on my own. But watching it here and now, I want the ground to open up and swallow me.'

Jeremy Laidlaw stood up and looked quizzically in Judith's direction. He appeared to be lost for words, but it was only short-lived. 'Your honour, I can't see that any of this morning's testimony is remotely relevant to this trial. I request…

Then the doors at the back of the court crashed open and Dawson rushed forwards, with Greg following closely behind.

***

Constance and Ben were walking along East Road with Belle in tow. Their progress was hampered by the dog's desire to linger over old haunts; a series of clearly familiar lampposts, gates, even manhole covers proved almost irresistible to her as they approached her old stomping ground. Eventually Ben prevailed, and they found themselves outside Rosie's house. The piles of flowers had been cleared away some weeks ago, but someone had placed a single, red rose on the top step. Ben rushed forward and picked it up, his fingers closing tightly around its stem.

'Dad always bought her roses on her birthday,' he said.

'That's nice.'

He peered in through the front window. Then he turned around and looked across the road at Lynn Harris' house.

'You don't have to do this,' Constance said.

'I have to come back sometime. Now feels all right. I think it will make me feel close to Mum again. Uncle Ellis keeps saying we should sell the house. I don't want to. If we move somewhere else, we'll lose her. Anyway, it was our deal to come here, wasn't it?'

Ben unlocked the door and they went inside. The living room was tidy, the rug shifted towards the back door, to cover the place where Rosie's body had lain. There was a slight hint of cleaning products in the air and post had been collected and laid out on the table.

'Looks like your uncle's been looking after the place,' Constance said.

Ben touched the letters, picking up one addressed to Rosie and returning it to the pile. He crossed the room and sat down on the sofa. Belle jumped up and curled up beside him, thrusting her face into his chest. It felt strange standing in the room Constance had examined minutely from hundreds of angles via a series of photographs. She found herself trying to work out how the pictures matched the real thing.

'Did Laura say she would be here soon?' she asked.

'Five minutes, she said, but it won't be. She's always late. Drove Mum mad.'

'I bet.' Constance reached one hand out and stroked Belle's head. Five minutes was enough to clear up a few points with Ben, if he was feeling cooperative. 'You know when you told us, me and Judith, that you felt guilty about something. Was it just about the argument your parents had, or was there something more?' she began.

Constance watched Ben carefully. He stroked Belle's coat and pulled her closer.

'I told you she saw someone the night before she died,' he said.

'Yes.' Constance waited. Ben took a deep breath.

'It was Jason. I should've said. I saw him from the window, in a taxi.'

'I know.'

'You know?'

'I found out he and your mum went out and I've talked to him about it, so don't worry.'

'I'm so pleased you know and it's OK.'

Constance had a sudden thought. 'Did Jason ask you not to tell anyone he was with Rosie that night?' she said.

'No. He never asked. It's just that he was so kind. He came over, the night…the night mum died. He hugged me, told me he'd look after me, said that he knew I wanted to act, that he'd put me in touch with some contacts of his. He even offered to look after Belle.'

'He looked after Belle?'

'I asked him. I couldn't take her to Laura's flat. First he said he would, then he said his wife wouldn't let him, then he said he would again, but by then Laura had arranged for her to go to a friend. I just…I didn't want him to get into trouble, I suppose, because he was being so kind. But if you knew already, I feel better.'

Constance's phone vibrated in her pocket, at the same moment as she heard a key in the lock and Ellis entered with a bag of shopping. She rejected the call. Something Ben said had jarred, but the call, and Ellis' arrival, had distracted her and she couldn't now recall what it was.

'Oh!' Ellis leaped back. 'You gave me a shock. You should have said you were coming. The place is probably an awful mess.'

Belle jumped at Ellis' voice and she began to bark loudly. Ben grabbed her lead and pulled her to him, whispering to her to calm down. She continued to bark, leaped off the sofa and almost pulled Ben off too, before he hauled himself to his feet.

'She doesn't seem to like me today,' Ellis joked, still holding his bags.

'She's just nervous, as it's her first time back here. And she's not great with men, generally. Hey, girl. It's Uncle Ellis, shush now,' Ben cooed.

But Belle barked even louder, interspersed with a nasal whining.

'I'll take her outside, just for a minute. Get her to calm down. Laura's not here yet anyway. Call me in when she arrives.'

Ben unlocked the back door to the garden, stepped through and closed it behind him.

'Laura is expected, is she?' Ellis asked, striding through the hallway and skipping down the steps to the basement kitchen.

'I asked her to come over, yes.' Constance followed him down, her phone buzzing again. She ignored it a second time.

'Why the welcoming committee?' he asked, unpacking some bread and milk and a couple of tins.

'Ben wants to plan for when Debbie comes home.'

'Debbie coming home!' Ellis didn't try to hide the sneer in his voice. 'Those diaries must have put paid to her chances, don't you think?'

'Not necessarily,' Constance said. 'Debbie explained why Rosie wrote them.'

'You're still feeding us that line? You're not in court, now. You can say what you really think.'

Ellis threw his plastic bags into a cupboard. Belle was still barking loudly in the garden.

'Ben, try to get her to be quiet,' he shouted up the stairs.

'You didn't want to be in court today, hear the rest of Debbie's evidence?'

'I've heard enough, thanks. I went mostly for Ben and when he said he wasn't going in today, it was welcome news.'

Ellis turned towards Constance and she could see a sheen of sweat spread across his forehead.

'Cup of tea?' he asked, grabbing the kettle and filling it through its spout. Then the doorbell rang.

***

'I'll go,' Constance said, and she climbed the stairs to open the door.

'Sorry I'm late,' Laura loped in, in her laconic fashion. 'I forgot my key. I didn't want to come, if I'm honest. I didn't want to disappoint Ben though. He's got some crazy idea of having a party here, he said. Is that right?' Isn't that a bit inappropriate, or is it just me? She closed the door behind her and stood, arms folded on the door mat.

'Where's Ellis?' she asked.

'In the kitchen,' Constance said.

'Why's Ben in the garden?' Laura crossed the room and waved at Ben through the window, before turning back to stand on the spot where Rosie's body had lain. She looked down, raised one hand to her mouth, stepped off the mat, then crouched down and touched the floor with her fingertips.

'Oh,' she said.

'Laura, can I ask you something?'

Laura stood up and folded her arms tightly across her body. 'Ask away,' she said, her voice quivering.

'It's about something you talked to your mum about. Something a bit sensitive…'

Ben flung open the back door and ran in, shutting an excited Belle out in the yard. In his hand, he held a very dusty black, leather motorbike glove.

'Look,' he said, waving it out in front of him. 'It's Dad's missing glove. It was here all the time.'

Constance ran forward. 'Where did you find it?'

'Belle found it. Well, she went straight to it, dug it up from underneath the fence. She must have buried it, in the first place. Will it help Dad, do you think?'

'That depends whose DNA is on it, I suppose. I know one person it will definitely help though.'

'But it's been under the ground?'

'You can't get rid of DNA that easily,' Constance said. 'Whoever handled the glove last, their DNA will still be there. I read a report on it recently. We'd better find something to put it in. I'll call Inspector Dawson right now.'

Constance was disturbed by a light rap on the front window. She spun around to see a woman's face pressed up against the pane. At first her features were distorted. Then, as she pulled back, Constance could see who it was. She opened the door and Nicki tumbled in, her chest heaving up and down. Seeing her audience, she stopped short, her eyes wide with surprise.

'Did you want me?' Constance asked.

'No…I…I thought… It doesn't matter. It can wait.' She might have left, if Ellis hadn't called to her from the top of the stairs.

'Hello Nicki,' he said. 'Looking for me?'

Nicki stood with her back to the door, her eyes flicking across Ellis' face.

'You two know each other?' Laura challenged.

'We used to,' Nicki said, 'before Ellis' tastes moved to even younger women.'

Ellis took a step into the room.

'Ellis. Who is this? I don't understand,' Laura said, her face crumpling.

'It's no one important. Just an old acquaintance of mine.'

And then the pieces fell into place for Constance.

'This is the older man you told your mother about, isn't it?'

Constance asked Laura, gently. 'But you didn't tell her his name.'

Ben stared from his sister to his uncle and then back again.

'What? You're not serious. You and Ellis?' Ben said. 'How could you do that? He's our uncle.'

'He's only mum's *stepbrother*,' Laura snapped.

'Did you tell Mum? Laura, did you tell Mum?' Ben was backing away, still gripping the glove in his hand.

'I told her I was seeing someone older than me. She got all pissed off, so I didn't tell her the rest.'

'But *you* did, didn't you, Ellis?' Constance drew the two youngsters behind her. 'So, what happened? You had an argument about it, Rosie got angry, so you hit her.'

Ellis laughed. 'You have a wonderful imagination,' he said. 'But you've got it completely wrong. I don't hurt women.' Then he turned to Nicki. 'Look what you've done. They all think I'm some kind of monster. Why are you here?' he said.

'I wanted to see you,' she said. 'You ignored my calls, my messages. I just wanted to talk.'

Laura had backed away from Ellis and was standing shoulder to shoulder with Ben.

'Haven't you done enough damage to this family?' Ellis said. 'You want to know who she is? She's the one who made Rosie's life miserable, not me. She paid you, twice; forty thousand pounds. That should have been enough. But you had to have more.'

'I only did it because you were ignoring me. I just wanted you to get in touch.'

'Ellis? Who is she?' Laura asked.

'He never told you about me? I'm the one he followed to Hong Kong, the one he promised to love forever, and I was stupid enough to believe him. But it was just a smokescreen. He was only interested in what I could do for him.' Nicki pointed to her cheek. 'I got this because of him.'

'No!' Laura shouted. 'Ellis loves me! You love me, don't you? We're going to get married.'

'Dad told Mum you were a wanker,' Ben said, 'and I thought he was being unfair. Turns out he was right all along.'

'Whoa!' Ellis held his arms up in the air for quiet. 'This is all getting quite out of hand. Nicki, this isn't the time or the place. Go home and we'll talk another time. I promise I'll call you, this afternoon. Laura, I do love you and we can work through this. I'm sorry you never got to tell your mum about us. I know she would have understood and been happy for us. And Ben, I'm disappointed in you. I know you love your dad and I know he and I don't see eye to eye all the time, but I love you and Laura and I loved my big sister, the TV star, and I would never, ever hurt her.'

Everyone was silent for a moment, digesting Ellis' words. Constance was wondering if she really had got things wrong again.

'You knew about the blackmail, though?' she said.

Ellis shrugged. 'Only after Rosie had paid up the second time. She told me about it, when we met up some months back. There didn't seem any point telling her I suspected Nicki – not once it was all done – but I told Rosie to let me know if it happened again. I said I would sort it out for her. Then Rosie called me up, the day she died, told me she'd had another request for money, asked me what she should do. I said I'd come over. I didn't want to tell her about Nicki over the phone. It was going to be pretty hard to explain that my crazy, jealous ex was blackmailing her to get back at me. But I didn't get here in time.'

Ellis sat down and lowered his head, and a tear streaked his cheek.

'I had a call from a client, wanted some new rugs, and I had to source them from China. It took me hours. By the time I was finished, it was already on the news. Rosie was dead.'

Nicki laughed quietly to herself. 'Very good,' she said. 'Recreate yourself as a loving brother and uncle; a protector. You told me about Debbie's transition, about how sensitive your sister was and you knew I would use it. You were just happy if it kept me off your back.'

'You are a very sad person,' Ellis said. 'And I feel sorry for you, but I haven't done anything wrong.'

Nicki frowned, then she reached a hand up to her cheek. Then she sighed. 'I don't know why I've waited so long for you,' she said. She turned to go. She placed one hand against the door and then spun around again and spoke to Laura. 'He'll use you and then he'll leave you,' she said. 'But then, what's new?'

She exited the house, leaving the door open behind her. As she descended the steps, a police car approached at high speed, pulling up right outside. Its occupants leaped out and ran towards her. Nicki looked at them, spoke to them briefly and then climbed into the police car with them. As the car pulled away, she gave a last lingering look through the window.

***

Constance called Judith.

'What's going on?' she asked.

'Dawson's stopped the trial,' Judith said. 'He says Greg found out who blackmailed Rosie. He wants to pause things while they investigate further. Bridget's thinking about it. No doubt she's phoning a friend to decide what to do. I called you, but you didn't pick up. Where are you?'

'At Rosie's. Listen, it was Nicki Smith who blackmailed Rosie, but she didn't kill her.'

'Nicki Smith? OK, if you say so. But then who did kill Rosie?'

Constance looked around the room and her eyes alighted on Ben and the glove, then on Belle, then on Laura, who was staring at Ellis and steadfastly refusing his advances.

'I think I know,' she said. 'Meet me at Regents Park underground station. See if you can persuade Dawson to come along too.'

47

JASON WAS SEATED ON his favourite chair when Rochelle ushered Constance, Judith and Chief Inspector Dawson in.

'Hello,' he said. 'To what do I owe this pleasure?' But he wasn't smiling.

Judith led the way and the two women sat down on the sofa. Dawson remained standing, by the window.

'The trial's been stopped,' Constance said.

'I heard on the news,' he replied.

'We know it was you,' Judith said.

Jason's eyes flitted across to the door, checking it was closed; closed doors, secrets kept secret, but not for much longer. He didn't reply.

'Rosie confided in you about the blackmail, didn't she? The Rapunzel recording. She wasn't going to tell Debbie or her kids. She told you instead, her "second husband".'

'Yes,' Jason said.

'Why don't you tell us how it happened, from your perspective?'

Jason gave a deep sigh and looked up at his portrait again before speaking. Constance and Judith exchanged glances. Constance switched her phone to 'record' and placed it on the table in front of her.

'Rosie came to me in 2017 and showed me the Rapunzel video. She was distraught. Said this was betrayal, a second time, by Debbie. Debbie had promised to go quietly, leave West Ham, not talk to the press and Rosie had agreed to a quickie divorce. Rosie'd managed to get through all of that, without it impacting her negatively. We'd managed it remarkably well. Then, like I say, this video suddenly appeared.'

'Did you know who it was from?'

'We had some IT people, trusted people, check it out, but it came from some internet café, untraceable. I had a few ideas, but the money the blackmailer wanted was well within Rosie's budget and we could spend that much on experts trying to find out. I was surprised it was so little, actually. I advised her to pay.'

'Did she?'

'She did. She worried it would get out anyway. But it didn't. It seemed well and truly buried and we went back to normal.'

'Then another demand came?'

'A few months later. This time Rosie didn't want to pay. She'd got over the initial shock, she was prepared to let it go public, said she wasn't going to spend the rest of her life with the shadow of Debbie hanging over her, said she despised blackmailers, that it was such a cowardly crime, preying on people's insecurities and fears. She wanted to go to the police. I told her that if she did, there would be a trial of the blackmailer and the video would be shown.'

'Maybe.'

'I said I thought it would be very damaging for her...'

'For your show, you mean?'

'Yes. It wasn't the video itself. You'll appreciate that it has a certain...charm about it. I just knew what it would lead to – much more interest in Debbie and her...lifestyle. That was the last thing Rosie needed – for Debbie to be back in vogue. I knew it would cause us real problems with the show. The producers would have to pretend it was fine, but they'd hate it.'

'What did you do?'

'I paid. Rosie kept refusing, so I paid and then I told her. She fussed for a while and then she accepted it was in her best interests – insisted on reimbursing me.'

'So why did you kill her?' Judith's blunt question shocked Constance, but Jason hardly blinked.

'This is ridiculous,' he said, looking across at Dawson, whose gaze remained fixed on a spot above Jason's head.

'Really? You never told us you went out with her the night before she died...'

'I explained that.'

'You tried to put us off the scent with stuff about Laura and Nicki Smith...'

'I was trying to help with your enquiries.'

'You lied about the day of the murder. Inspector Dawson checked with St Columba's school. You slipped away early afternoon, claiming you had a cold. And you said you were so upset to hear the news of Rosie's death that you were confined to your room. Instead, Ben tells me you were over at Rosie's house, offering him the prospect of future work.'

'So, I kept quiet about a few things. That doesn't mean...'

The door opened and Rochelle stepped inside. She stood there, staring at Jason, her eyes hard, her mouth quivering with tension. Jason's face turned pale, then it began to crumple, then his own lips began to shake.

'All right,' he said. 'Rosie and I went out that night, like I said. She invited me. She told me she was leaving the show. She'd been offered a Sat night chat show of her own – the first woman. She said she would get her evenings back; she was so excited. I tried to talk her out of it. She didn't realise how difficult the producers could be. I knew they'd promise things and not deliver. They'd never give her editorial control like they said. I'd always shielded her from it, with the breakfast show. I'd done all the negotiating, kept the show on the road. By the end of the evening, she was having doubts, I could tell. I dropped her home and she agreed not to sign up to the new job without talking to me again.'

'And that happened the next day?'

'We did the show in the morning. It was a really great one, you've seen it repeated so many times, since her death. Fabulous feedback, big viewing figures. Rosie went home without saying anything else, but there were always people around. Then she called me at lunchtime, said she'd listened to me, but she still wanted to take the new job. I begged her to wait, at least until I could come and speak to her again, and she agreed.'

'You didn't believe any of that, did you?'

'Why shouldn't I? Rosie relied on me. She knew I was much more experienced where these things were concerned.'

'You'd got it wrong about the blackmail, though, hadn't you?'

'No...I...'

'Paying up didn't stop it. Maybe you should have listened to Rosie for once. Sounds more to me like she wanted to get rid of you that evening and the best way was to pretend she agreed with you.'

Jason frowned and then his voice collapsed.

'No,' he said. 'I had persuaded her.'

'Next day she felt the same. The show had had its day. Even with Rosie, the figures were falling. She could see that; you couldn't. She was being kind to you, but she always intended to take the Saturday night show. Who wouldn't?'

'You went over there, didn't you? To Rosie's.' Constance stepped in.

'I was at the prize-giving, like I told you, but I got bored, feigned a cold. I headed over to Rosie's house. When I arrived, she was angry. Danny had just been over and they'd argued about stuff, so she was already wound up and she said she was behind with her mail. She asked me to leave. I told her she had to stay with the show. This time she laughed. She said I had held her back, all these years. Me! I created her! There would have been no Rosie Harper without me!'

'You told her that?'

'I did. I reminded her that I got her her first role, that I'd pressed for her pay to be increased, at risk to my own, that I'd saved her when Danny left her. I was the one she cried to, every night for at least a week, and I managed it, kept it low key. Do you know, at one stage she even talked about having him on the show, can you imagine? That…freak! With his Rapunzel hair and his puffed-out chest. Said it would be hard for her, but she thought it would make great TV and that maybe she owed him something, after all. I advised her against all of that. And I even paid off her blackmailer.'

'Let me guess. She didn't see it the same way?'

'Ingratitude. She said I had been wrong about everything, that she never should have listened to me. That she appreciated the *Blue Peter* role, but that was it, and she'd paid me back ten times over by staying so long.'

'So you killed her?' Judith said, for the third time.

'I want a lawyer,' Jason looked at Dawson.

Dawson blinked heavily. 'Sure,' he said.

Rochelle let out a sob and covered her mouth with her hands.

'Wasn't that a bit of an over-reaction?' Judith said.

Jason turned his attention to Judith again.

'Rosie wasn't easy to work with, did you know that? Everyone thought she was this sunny, easy-going person. She was opinionated and stubborn and she overvalued her own contribution,' Jason said.

'You were in good company, then.'

'I am a professional, with forty years in the business. I was a child star. I've been living and breathing TV from my first spoken word. She would never have got anywhere without me. I have contacts everywhere.'

'You threatened her, didn't you?' This time it was Constance who spoke.

'*Threatened* is too strong. I explained to her that, if she didn't stay with the show, I would tell her new producers about Rapunzel and the blackmail.'

'Which was your idea in the first place.'

'So what? Can you imagine what the papers would say if it came out that she had paid off a blackmailer? And why? Because of that pathetic video.'

'That's why you did it, isn't it? That's why you advised her to pay up in 2017 – not to help her, to make sure she was forever in your debt.'

'She didn't like what you said, I imagine?' Judith took control again.

'She pushed me, quite hard, lay her hands on me. I fell back onto the sofa.' Jason waited for Rochelle's response. She was sobbing quietly into her hands.

'Then she laughed,' Jason said. 'Said I looked ridiculous. Said I was ridiculous. Said she hated everything about me; my clothes, my hair, my speaking voice. She said she hated the way I said "good morning" on the show, the way I introduced the guests, the way I crossed my legs, the way I laughed. She said she'd always hated me, that she'd felt sorry for me at first, but then it became hate. She said she bitterly regretted choosing me over Danny, that she had been wrong, that she felt he had real integrity, him, her, "Rapunzel". That I was the false, fake, phoney.'

'You just wanted to stop her talking?'

'I did. I wanted her to stop all that vile stuff coming out of her mouth. Then I saw it glinting there, on the mantelpiece – the trophy. I remember when she won it. We were all there. Of course, we already knew she had won, but we had to act surprised. Her first big award, the first of many. I picked it up. She turned towards the back of the house. The dog was in the garden, scratching at the door. She stood up to let the dog in and I hit her. It made this popping sound, like when you crack an egg on the side of a bowl. It felt like that too, a fragile exterior giving way to allow the liquid interior to flow out. She turned and raised her hands, but she was still smiling, like it was all one big joke, like I was the joke. So, I lifted the trophy high above my head and I brought it down on Rosie Harper's ingratitude-filled skull, with all my might.'

Constance moaned and then coughed to cover it. Judith gave

a sigh and switched off the recording. Rochelle crumpled to her knees. Dawson surveyed the scene before him. He hoped Jason would come quietly now, given the presence of all these women. His back wouldn't handle a fight.

48

'So Nicki Smith and Ellis Harper knew each other?' Judith, Constance and Dawson sat in an airless room at Hackney police station. In one interview room was Ellis, sitting with a lawyer, in a second, Nicki, on her own.

'They met in around 2013, when she was still Nicki Sampson. Moved in together. She had tried to turn her life around, after some convictions when she was young. She got a job with Huawei, out in Hong Kong. Pretty amazing, given her background. He decided to follow her.' Dawson answered Judith's question.

'And then what?'

'They lived together. He started an interior design business and began working on the homes of wealthy people. He made a big point of promoting Western design. But he wasn't hugely successful. She was the main earner.'

'Then what?'

'A car crash. She was driving, no seat belt. She had to stop work for rehab. Word is that Ellis ran away back to the UK, leaving

Nicki behind in the hospital.'

'And she was pretty cross with him for ditching her?'

'Maybe. If we believe what she said to you at Rosie's house. Whatever happened, she was still in love with him, but he had moved on, to Laura. Nicki pulled herself together, stopped moping and Nicki Smith was born, new name, new identity, sadly old tricks. She sets herself up as a kind of campaigner for hire, shows up at events and brings a crowd with her. She's suddenly in demand.'

'Was her interest genuine?'

'I doubt it. With the increase in celebrity attention for all these causes, it gave her access to lots of wealthy people. Once she became more well known, she would offer her time, usually free of charge, to help organise demonstrations and publicity. But, at the same time, she was looking for opportunities to blackmail them – badly kept secrets she could exploit.'

'And one of them was Rosie?'

'She targeted Rosie in 2017, not long after her return from Hong Kong. She knew about Debbie from Ellis and she sensed, rightly, that Rosie was touchy about Debbie's transition. She didn't ask for much money, though, not relative to Rosie's earnings.'

'It wasn't about the money,' Constance said. 'It was a way of getting Ellis to notice her again.'

'Pretty extreme way, then.'

'Did she take the video?'

'Yes, she followed Debbie around for a while. The performance was a gift.'

'All her complaining about the third runway was a front, then?'

'Yes and no. It fitted her agenda, but she was also setting things up, trying to get Rosie's personal email. Then she sent Rosie the video of Debbie, with the nickname *Rapunzel*, and asked for money.'

'And, as we now know, Jason persuaded Rosie to pay up?'

'Debbie said Rosie wasn't interested in conventional security, said the danger was all online. Now we know why she said that. How much do you think Nicki stole?' Constance asked.

'Hundreds of thousands. That's why she could be so generous with her time.'

'And that's why you didn't want me to ask you about the money leaving Rosie's account, when you were in court?' Judith added.

'Yes, but I couldn't believe you would do as you were told, for once. We knew about the payments out of Rosie's account, but we didn't know what they were and we hadn't found the Rapunzel folder.

'My team did some digging on Ellis, her stepbrother; school dropout. We couldn't be sure where he had gone when he left the UK, but you helped with that Judith, with the design stuff.'

'Design stuff?' Constance asked.

'I suggested to Uncle Ellis that I might like some interior design tips,' Judith said. 'He couldn't resist sending me his favourite projects. It was quite touching how proud he was of his work, but he'd labelled them by address, which I passed on to Charlie...'

'The Hong Kong police, with typical efficiency, made some enquiries, and showed Nicki's photo around too. He'd taken her to more than one of his clients' homes. She had a good eye for colour, they said.'

'How did you know Nicki sent the video? Greg said he couldn't trace the emails.'

'No, but the camera she used gave her away. Mr Winter rang us early Tuesday to tell us about the emails and the video. Then, well, you know, he came over here a couple of hours later. Said he could see that the video had been filmed on a phone with a special zoom lens, only been made for the Chinese market, by one or two manufacturers, something about "lens flare". I didn't listen too much, but he was pretty certain.'

'And one of those manufacturers was Huawei.'

'It was. Changed her name, kept her phone. Funny what people get attached to. It was lucky I was here, actually. I had been told to clear out by the end of the day and I wasn't minded to hang around.'

'Then you knew?'

'Well, it still required some working out, connecting the pieces, as you like to say.'

'I saw the Huawei packing crates in her office,' Constance said. 'I never thought it was important. I even had photos of them.'

'So that's Nicki, Rapunzel and the money,' Judith said.

'I liked her,' Constance said, 'when I met her. I liked Nicki. Is that bad?'

'Did you?' Judith stared at her.

'She seemed genuine. I admired that she was working class but was doing something important with her life. Then, when I found out she'd copied everything she wrote to Rosie from someone else, I was disappointed in her. And then, when she appeared at Rosie's and declared her love for Ellis, I just felt sorry for her.'

'Don't,' Dawson said. 'Blackmail is just plain nasty – preying on people's fears.'

'What about the money she stole? Is it all gone?' Constance asked.

'We haven't found it yet. But that's strictly off the record.'

'And you can't ask her victims, I suppose.'

'Why not?'

'Because most of them still want their secrets kept.' Dawson smiled at Judith again.

'Why did you suspect Jason?' Dawson said.

Judith and Constance were both silent.

'I think it was the painting,' Judith said, and they both laughed.

'What painting?'

'I was joking. Connie, you got there first, I think. You tell.'

'I should have realised earlier, but it was only when we were at Rosie's house that Ben told me Jason had been over the night after the murder to console him. I couldn't think of any reason on earth why he should lie about that.'

'You did brilliantly getting his confession,' Dawson said.

'Rochelle helped, didn't she? I'm not sure he would have cracked without her watching him.'

'Do you think she knew?' he asked.

Constance shrugged. 'Even with Rochelle, I still thought he was never going to get there. He would've taken hours, if Judith hadn't kept hurrying him along.'

'It had been a long ten days. I just wanted a drink.'

'So it was all because Rosie wanted to leave the show?'

'And because she didn't appreciate him,' Constance said, shivering at the memory. 'He was jealous of her.'

Judith stood up and slapped her hand down on her thigh. 'So that pretender criminal-profiling woman was right all along. Ha! On day one. We didn't need a trial after all. And I called her a charlatan.'

'You admit it, then, that Court TV got it right first time. We could team up with her for our next case. Save a lot of tax payers' money.'

'A lucky guess, that's all. There is one very important player in this whole puzzle whom we have yet to acknowledge, though,' Judith said, tapping Constance on the arm.

'Who's that?'

'I never thought I would say it, but let's hear it for Belle the dog, digging up the second glove!' Judith laughed at her own joke. 'She's saved your bacon this time, hasn't she, Charlie?'

'Yep. Although being framed by man's best friend, is probably a fairly unusual conclusion for internal affairs to draw.' He laughed aloud and Constance and Judith followed suit.

***

'Somehow, with all these loose ends to tie up, we seem to have missed our celebratory drink,' Judith said, as they left Hackney police station and walked towards the glass high-rise of the City of London.

'Where would you like to go?'

'Ooh somewhere low-key and dark, I think. Now I'm a celebrity, I have to keep a low profile. Don't want to find myself on the front cover of *The Sun*, with my underwear on show, do I?'

'I know somewhere perfect,' Constance laughed, 'but I'll only accompany you on one condition.'

'No, I refuse to work with the psychologist on our next case.'

'Not that. I think you should call Greg,' she said.

'What?'

'If only to say thank you. Just call him, OK. I think he'd really like that.'

***

'Tonight, we report on the shock ending to Debbie Mallard's trial. For those of you who have just tuned in, Debbie Mallard is innocent and has already been released.' Katrina was wearing a white blouse with a bow at the neck and navy trousers, considerably more demure than usual.

'And Rosie Harper's co-presenter of eight years, Jason Fenwick, is in custody,' Chris added. 'More on that later.'

'That's right, and on the show tonight we have Jeremy Laidlaw, prosecution counsel, to talk about the trial, and Lynn Harris, her neighbour, to tell us all about the Rosie she knew and loved.' Laidlaw sat to Karina's left and Lynn to her right. Each was beaming at the camera.

Andy was in the studio with Graham next to him. He had checked, but the secret room was open tonight, with no one inside. Andy wondered if he should say something to Graham about Greg, that he'd been a good choice of substitute, but he didn't want to sound like he was sucking up and, if Graham had wanted their views on Greg, he would certainly have asked.

Andy had given Katrina his usual list of possible topics for the show, and this time she had focused on one of them, nodded thoughtfully and said she wanted to use it. Andy's face had flushed with a mixture of pride and relief. He had a feeling the next three months would be fun after all.

***

Constance sat on her sofa in her pyjamas, with her knees tucked up to her chin. She had texted Judith when she got in: *For once, I can't wait to watch Court TV tonight, to see Debbie's face! You?* but received no reply.

Then Constance's phone beeped, but it wasn't Judith. It was Greg. *Meeting Judith for dinner on Saturday to celebrate your win. Will you join us?* his message read. Constance glanced at it, before turning her phone to mute. She would decline, politely of course, leave the two love birds alone to kiss and make up, but not tonight.

***

On Court TV, Katrina was speaking again.

'But we should take things one step at a time. The first big event, early this morning, before the sensational adjournment, was the sharing of a video which has melted hearts across the globe. This is Debbie Mallard, in character, as Disney's Rapunzel, singing the moving words which Rapunzel sings when she is finally released from her prison to join her beloved prince. So here it is, the song from the film *Tangled*. This is "I See The Light".'

'And it's the most downloaded song so far, this year,' Chris added.

When Debbie had finished singing and taken her bows, the video panned out to the Court TV hosts.

'That's so beautiful,' Katrina said, blinking back a tear.

'Yes, it is,' said Chris, wiping both his eyes.

49

CONSTANCE AND JUDITH SAT in Rosie Harper's house. The front window and back door were thrown open and the autumn sun streamed in. Debbie sat opposite them in a flowery dress, with matching hairband.

'You moved back in here?' Judith began.

'Ben was so keen. I couldn't disappoint him,' Debbie shrugged. 'And I always hated my flat. This gives us a bit of time with Rosie around us, I think.'

'How have you been?' Constance asked.

'I should be ecstatic, I know; *victory snatched from the jaws of defeat* and all that.' Debbie fiddled with the beads on her necklace. 'But I miss Rosie. I know she wasn't perfect, but who is? And I go back through that day, what we said to each other, how I behaved. I told her she was being selfish, that she should think more of what was best for Ben, when I had been the selfish one. If I could turn back the clock…'

'It's always the way,' Judith said. 'We always want one more day, hour, minute with people we love.'

Constance stared one moment too long at Judith.

'Will you go back to coaching?' she asked.

Debbie rubbed her hands together. 'The girls still want me, they said, so I'll be back there, once things have settled down.'

'But I heard you had a special visitor?' Constance said.

'John Bane, the England captain. He came to see me yesterday. He said I shouldn't rule out returning to the premiership, said he would back me if I was interested... I don't think I will.'

'You're quite a celebrity now,' Judith said. 'You could probably do photoshoots for the rest of your life.'

'And I saw the interview you gave to the *Mail*. It was good, positive stuff,' Constance said. 'Very novel, beginning with some football in the local park. The photos were fabulous.'

'It's good to play while I still can,' Debbie said.

'Why didn't you tell us about your neurological problem?' Judith asked.

Debbie looked at both women. 'I've had symptoms for a couple of years, but I try to ignore them. They aren't sure what it is. Sometimes my hands shake. They think it might be the beginning of Parkinson's. I told you I was taking paracetamol, but it was some tablets prescribed to help.'

'If it's Parkinson's...'

'It will affect my movement, yes. But football has been my life for twenty-five years; I can't just stop.'

'But you don't have to hide now.'

'Rosie's death and all the press coverage has given me back my freedom. It's all out there; nothing to hide any more. Truly *transparent*. Someone's even started a Twitter account called "When Danny met Debbie" and it has two million followers.

None of that would have been possible without the cameras.'

'Hm,' Judith grunted.

'Will you take John Bane up on his offer, then?' Constance asked. 'He is the England captain after all.'

'You mean, maybe I can become the UK's first wheelchair-bound, female, transgender Premier League coach? I'm not sure we've come that far.'

'Why not?' Constance said. 'You should embrace the experience,' thinking of Greg as she spoke.

'How's Belle?' Judith asked.

'I've been making a big fuss of her. Jason must have found my gloves lying around and it was the perfect opportunity for him to frame me, but he hadn't counted on Belle burying one of them. I would never have suspected him, you know, not in a million years. I didn't like the guy much from the odd occasion we met; not that I really knew him. I kept my distance, him the same, but I thought he genuinely cared about Rosie, about her career and wellbeing. I thought he was a decent human being. I could never see him being violent either. He always seemed so…fragile, you know, like a paper bag blowing in the wind.'

'He pulled the wool over our eyes too,' Judith said. 'For a while,' she added hastily.

'Will there be another trial?'

'No. With his full confession on tape, his lawyer advised him to plead guilty. He'll be sentenced soon. He'll get a minimum of fifteen years, but the prosecution will argue for more, say it was premeditated, that he abused a position of trust – anything to get the sentence increased,' Constance said.

'And how's Ben?' Judith asked.

'He's gone back to school. He missed the first couple of weeks, but they've helped him out. He's going to keep his acting going too.'

'And Laura?'

'Laura is having a hard time.'

'Poor Laura.'

'She feels very...deceived.'

'By Ellis.'

'By the world. He's still pretending he cares about her. Can you believe it?'

'Maybe he does? He did look after her and Ben for all those weeks, before your trial.'

'He's all false. It's all an act. He never really accepted Rosie's achievements. He thought he should have had what she had, despite having only a fraction of her talent. Whatever he says about loving her, he didn't. He resented her. Maybe it wasn't his fault. Their parents put Rosie on a pedestal and Ellis couldn't even get to the bottom step. That's why he kept asking for handouts, and Rosie agreed, because she could afford it, and she felt guilty for her success.

'But, taking Laura – he knew that would hurt her. And you know what? The more Rosie would have objected, the more it would have pushed Laura towards him. And he knew that too. I know he didn't hurt Rosie physically, but he was a cruel and selfish bastard and Laura was a convenient target. I should have seen what was going on.'

'She wasn't living at home. She kept it secret. How could you know?'

'I was focusing so hard on "reinventing" me, and on feeling sorry for myself too. I forgot that maybe other people needed me.'

'This wasn't your fault,' Judith said. 'You need to tell yourself that over and over, till you really believe it.'

'I drove Rosie away. After twenty years of trust. She couldn't even bear to tell me about the blackmail. She went to him instead – Jason.'

'She probably wanted to protect you.'

Debbie walked over to the window, placed her hand on the glass and looked out, just like the morning at Denmow prison. A cloud outside moved across the sun and the room was suddenly dark.

'I knew it was recorded,' Debbie said, suddenly.

'What?'

'My performance, my Rapunzel act. I looked out into the audience, part way through and I could see this young girl with her phone in her hand, pointing it at me. She didn't keep it secret. I thought about it afterwards, that night, lying in bed with Rosie next to me. I know what I said to you about being embarrassed, horribly embarrassed, and it was all true, but part of me was waiting for that moment, to see that film played back sometime. I wanted Rosie to see it and to understand.'

'Jason said…'

'I'm sure Rosie understood,' Judith cut across Constance and Constance closed her mouth tight.

'Can I ask a question?' Constance began, Judith frowning at her to rein her in.

'As long as I don't have to answer it.'

'I just wondered why Laura stopped playing football. Was it really her knee?'

'Poor Rosie. Her kids were all messed up; her daughter wanted to be a professional footballer and her son wanted to be on the stage. She would have been OK if it had been the other way

around. She blamed me, of course, said I had "poisoned genes".
She didn't mean it. Words were the only thing she could fight me
with, in the end. But Laura heard us arguing about it and, after
that, her knee injury was suddenly too bad for her to play again.
I think she felt that if she gave in to Rosie, went off and had a
sensible career, then Ben had more chance of getting his dream.'

'How's Laura's knee now?'

'I haven't asked recently, but she joined us, me and the *Mail*
reporter, when we had the knock-around in the park. I'm hoping
she'll have another go, but no pressure from me. Now I have a
question for you.' Debbie stared at Judith.

'Oh.'

'Where did you get the vegetarian stuff from?'

'You mean about Rosie? It was in an article I read; *Grazia* I
think.'

'She told people she was vegetarian because that was what they
wanted to hear, but she had lapses, lots of them. She liked Italian
food too much – one dish especially.'

'I think I can guess what that might have been,' Judith replied.

Debbie smiled for the first time and then moved towards the
door.

'He called me, you know?' She paused with her head tipped
to the side and her chin raised, the same pose she had held at the
end of her Rapunzel performance.

'Who?' Constance asked.

'You mean Mr X, don't you?' Judith said.

'Yes. Mr X. Eddie. That's his name. Said he was sorry. Said he
had watched all the trial and always voted for me in the polls.
Asked if we could meet up.'

'What did you say?'

'I told him to piss off, that's what!' Debbie roared with laughter and Judith and Constance followed suit.

'Goodbye,' Debbie said, once she had stopped laughing, extending a hand to each of them in turn. Constance looked out through the front window and thought she saw the curtain opposite twitching. 'I do appreciate what you did,' Debbie said. 'I think what I appreciate most is that you both believed in me, when I wasn't even sure if I did.'

Constance and Judith both nodded and smiled, as it was easier than more words, and Constance leaned forward and hugged Debbie tight.

Then they chorused 'goodbye', in unison, as they exited the house and headed off, shoulder to shoulder, along the road.

THE END

ACKNOWLEDGEMENTS

This time around I seem to have an inordinate number of people to thank for helping me write my fourth Burton & Lamb story: *The Rapunzel Act*. I think (I hope) this reflects its evolution and many layers, rather than my having forgotten anyone the previous three times.

I have dedicated this book to my three wonderful boys: Noah, Nathan and Aron, who are a constant source of joy and pride, as I watch them grow and flourish. Importantly, without them, I would not have known what a *nutmeg* was or a *golden goal* and Debbie Mallard's back story might well have been quite different.

Particular thanks also go to Isabella Segal, for sharing her inspirational story with me with such clarity and honesty, and for all her support in the writing of this book. I am also grateful to All About Trans with its professed aim of seeking to 'positively change how the media understands and portrays trans people' for providing a wealth of information on its website, focusing on how to treat people in the trans community with respect.

Thank you (again) to Dr Stuart J Hamilton, Home Office Registered Forensic Pathologist, for input on the forensic medicine content; our conversations are always so colourful and informative – I hate to think what anyone listening in might think.

I must also thank Professor Paul Thaler, whose two wonderful and illuminating books, *The Watchful Eye: American Justice in the Age of the Television Trial* and *The Spectacle: Media and the Making of the OJ Simpson Story,* provided much food for thought when this story was beginning to take shape, and whose encouraging words and support were most welcome.

Thanks also to Pulitzer Prize-winning journalist, Henry Allen, for allowing me to use his quote at the beginning of the story and for making me laugh a lot, in our recent correspondence. And to Verso Books for giving permission to use the quote from the late Jean Baudrillard.

And to my dear friend, Pen Vogler (aka @PenfromPenguin), for, once more, being a wonderful sounding board and providing a thoughtful, constructive and kind critique.

My thanks, as always, go to all the team at Lightning Books: to Dan Hiscocks for his continued support and belief in my abilities, to Scott Pack for his incredible editing skills and guidance, to Amber Choudhary at Midas PR for her superb marketing skills and Simon Edge for his novel and highly creative publicity drives, to Hugh Brune for his enthusiastic sales campaign, to Nell Wood for the fabulous cover design and to Clio Mitchell for meticulous copyediting and typesetting.

I must, of course, also acknowledge the enormous contribution of my parents, Jacqie and the late Sidney Fineberg, both inspirational teachers, who encouraged me and my sisters to spend all our waking hours reading.

Finally, a gigantic thank you goes to everyone who has reviewed this story or *The Cinderella Plan, The Aladdin Trial* or my first novel, *The Pinocchio Brief*, for taking the time to read my books and share their views in a variety of ways, including in radio broadcasts, space in some of our most prestigious national publications, hosting me on their blogs and websites and taking the time to post online reviews. Their support has provided me with the confidence to continue writing, and without their backing I would not have been able to reach such a wide audience; I am forever indebted.

ABOUT THE AUTHOR

Yorkshire-bred, Abi Silver is a lawyer by profession. She lives in Hertfordshire with her husband and three sons. Her first courtroom thriller featuring the legal duo Judith Burton and Constance Lamb, *The Pinocchio Brief*, was published by Lightning Books in 2017 and was shortlisted for the Waverton Good Read Award. Her follow-up, *The Aladdin Trial*, featuring the same legal team, was published in 2018, with *The Cinderella Plan* following in 2019.